Blood & Bones: Rook

Blood Fury MC®
Book 7

Jeanne St. James

Photographer: Christopher John at CJC Photography
Cover Artist: Golden Czermak at FuriousFotog
Cover Model: Mitch Mathes
Editor: Proofreading by the Page
Beta readers: Andi Babcock, Sharon Abrams & Alexandra Swab, Author Whitley Cox
Blood Fury MC Logo: Jennifer Edwards

**Sign up for Jeanne's newsletter: https://www. authorjeannestjames.com/
Join her FB readers' group for the inside scoop: https://www.facebook.com/groups/JeannesReviewCrew/**

Sign up for my newsletter for insider information, author news, and new releases: https://www.authorjeannestjames.com/

Blood Fury MC Series

Blood & Bones: Trip (Book 1)
<u>Blood & Bones: Sig (Book 2)</u>
Blood & Bones: Judge (Book 3)
Blood & Bones: Deacon (Book 4)
Blood & Bones: Cage (Book 5)
Blood & Bones: Shade (Book 6)
Blood & Bones: Rook (Book 7)
Blood & Bones: Rev (Book 8)
Crash: A Dirty Angels MC/Blood Fury MC Crossover (Book 8.5)
Blood & Bones: Ozzy (Book 9)
Blood & Bones: Dodge (Book 10)
Blood & Bones: Whip (Book 11)
Blood & Bones: Easy (Book 12)

Character List

To avoid spoilers this list only includes the characters mentioned in the previous books

BFMC Members:

Trip Davis – *President* – Son of Buck Davis, half-brother to Sig, mother is Tammy, Runs Buck You Recovery

Sig Stevens – *Vice President* – Son of Buck Davis, mother is Silvia, three years younger than Trip, helps run Buck You Recovery

Judge (Judd Scott) – *Sgt at Arms* - Father (Ox) was an Original, owns Justice Bail Bonds

Deacon Edwards – *Treasurer* – Judge's cousin, Skip Tracer/Bounty Hunter at Justice Bail Bonds

Cage (Chris Dietrich) – *Road Captain* – Dutch's youngest son, mechanic at Dutch's Garage

Ozzy (Thomas Oswald) – *Secretary* – *Original* – manages club-owned The Grove Inn.

Rook (Randy Dietrich) – Dutch's oldest son, mechanic at Dutch's Garage

Dutch (David Dietrich) – *Original* – Owns Dutch's Garage, sons: Cage & Rook

Dodge – Manager at Crazy Pete's Bar, did time with Rook in jail

Whip – Mechanic at Dutch's Garage (formerly known as the prospect Sparky)

Rev (Mickey Rivers) – Mechanic at Dutch's Garage (formerly known as the prospect Mouse)

Shade (Julian Bennett) – works at Tioga Pet Crematorium (formerly known as the prospect Shady)

Easy – works at Tioga Pet Crematorium

Tater Tot – *Prospect* – Works at Crazy Pete's Bar

Possum – *Prospect* – Works at Crazy Pete's Bar

Ol' Ladies:

Stella – *Trip's ol' lady* - Crazy Pete's daughter, owns Crazy Pete's Bar

Autumn (Red) – *Sig's ol' lady* – Accountant for the club's businesses

Cassidy (Cassie) – *Judge's ol' lady* – Manages Tioga Pet Crematorium

Reese – *Deacon's ol' lady* – Civil law attorney

Jemma – *Cage's ol' lady* – Hospice nurse, Judge's younger sister

Chelle (Rachelle) – *Shade's ol' lady* – Elementary school librarian

Former Originals:

Buck Davis – *President* – Deceased, Trip's father

Razor Stevens – *VP* – Deceased, Sig's father

Ox – *Sgt at Arms* – Deceased, Judge & Jemma's father

Crazy Pete – *Treasurer* – Deceased, Stella's father

Tin Man (Tinny) – Deceased

Others:

Tessa – Trip's younger sister, Cage and Jemma's house mouse
Reilly – Reese's sister, works at Dutch's Garage
Henry (Ry) – Judge's son
Daisy – Cassie's daughter
Syn Stevens – Sig's sister
Saylor – Rev's sister, Judge and Cassie's house mouse
Dyna – Cage's daughter
Josie (Josephine) – Chelle's younger daughter
Maddie (Madison) – Chelle's older daughter
Jude – 12 yro rescued by Shade
Silvia Stevens – Sig's mother, Razor's former ol' lady
Tammy Davis – Trip's mother, Buck's former ol' lady
Bebe Dietrich – Cage & Rook's mother, Dutch's former ol' lady
Clyde Davis – Buck's father, Trip & Sig's grandfather, deceased
Lizzy/Billie/Angel/Amber/Crystal/Brandy – Sweet butts
Max Bryson – *Chief of Police* – Manning Grove PD, Bryson brother
Marc Bryson – *Corporal* – Manning Grove PD, Bryson brother
Matt Bryson – *Officer* – Manning Grove PD, Bryson brother
Adam Bryson – *Officer* – Manning Grove PD, Bryson's cousin, Teddy's husband
Leah Bryson – *Officer* – Manning Grove PD, Marc's wife
Jet Bryson – *Officer* – Manning Grove PD, Adam's sister
Tommy Dunn – *Officer* – Manning Grove PD
Teddy Sullivan – Owner Manes on Main, Adam Bryson's husband
Amanda Bryson – Max's wife, owner Boneyard Bakery
Carly Bryson – Matt's wife, OB/GYN doctor

Levi Bryson – Adopted son of Matt & Carly Bryson (birth mother: Autumn)

Prologue

When life kicks you in the balls and drops you to your knees...

RANDY SAT behind the wheel of the 1974 Pontiac LeMans and stared through the windshield. The neighborhood was sketchy as shit.

While he didn't expect a gated, luxury community, the shit-hole house surprised him.

He'd found the Baltimore address along with her name in scratchy handwriting on the back of a torn envelope buried deep in his father's dresser drawer. Under a loaded .40 caliber handgun with the serial number ground off and a full box of ammo.

Randy wondered why those three things were kept in the same spot. Was Dutch planning on coming down here for a final reunion? Did he hate the woman that much?

He wouldn't be surprised if his father did.

They weren't allowed to speak her name in their house. Not since the day she walked out.

That was three years ago. When he was twelve and his brother Chris was eight.

Three damn years.

Randy wondered if Dutch knew where she was all that damn time and never told them. Knowing his asshole father, he probably fucking did.

From where Randy had parked the piece of shit Pontiac at the curb, he twisted his head and studied the duplex through the passenger-side window. He had no doubt which one Bebe lived in.

The one with the rebel flag covering the front window.

Randy's lips flattened. *Figures.*

One-by-one, he peeled his fingers off the steering wheel and gritted his teeth. He needed to get the hell out of the vehicle and go up to the door. He didn't drive all this way for nothing.

He didn't risk stealing the LeMans only for shits and giggles.

He was here now. He was doing this.

He was here to find out why.

Why a mother would just up and leave her sons. Never see them again. Never talk to them again.

Forget they ever existed.

He pulled a deep breath in through his nose, held it and blew it out his mouth.

Fuck this.

The driver's door creaked loudly as he forced it open. He had to slam it shut twice to get it to latch closed.

"Piece of fuckin' shit," he muttered, giving the door a good kick. He should've stolen a Corvette or something. However, this vehicle had been easy to pinch and he could start it with a screwdriver. It was why he picked it.

Plus, it wasn't flashy. Like a Corvette.

His goal was to get from Manning Grove to Baltimore and back without getting caught.

By his father or the pigs.

He rounded the front of the Pontiac sedan, dodged the garbage bags piled at the curb, strode over the cracked concrete sidewalk and up the porch steps. The storm door that used to hang on her side of the duplex now leaned against the siding. The screen was busted out like someone had punched it and the wood frame was splintered.

He hesitated for the few seconds it took him to take another deep breath before using the side of his fist to beat on the wood door with the peeling paint and no window or peephole. She would have no clue who was standing on the other side.

She would either answer it or she wouldn't.

"Who the fuck is it?" came from the bowels of the house.

If he answered that question, she might not open the door. Instead, he pounded again. This time harder and louder.

"God-fuckin-damnit! Keep your fuckin' pants on!"

A lock clicked and the door abruptly swung open with an ear-piercing creak.

And there she was. The woman who had pushed him out of her snatch a little over fifteen years ago.

His upper lip curled as he took her in.

Her dark blonde stringy hair had three inches of solid gray roots. She wore frayed Daisy Dukes that showed way too much skin for her age or body size. Her cottage-cheese thighs squeezing out of the bottom of the denim shorts reminded him of a popped zit.

She had on a threadbare T-shirt that told people to "Get Fucked." The neckline had been cut out and sliced down the chest to show off her tits. Ones not contained by any bra.

As she stared at him, she squinted one dull blue eye when the smoke from the Pall Mall swirled into it.

She looked like hell. Way worse than what he remembered.

When both eyes narrowed on him, she yanked the cigarette from her mouth. Probably so it wouldn't tumble from her lips when they gaped open at the sight of him on her front porch.

"Which one are you?"

What a cunt.

Her gaze roamed from the top of his head down to his toes, then back up before she answered her own question. "Randy."

Ding, ding, ding. You won the "Mom of the Year" award for recognizin' your first-born son.

"Got tall," she muttered.

"Yeah, no longer twelve."

"What you doin' here?"

Great to see you, too, Mom. He jerked up one shoulder. "Just in the neighborhood."

She peeked her head out the door and peered around. "Yeah? You know someone 'round here?"

Holy shitballs. "Yeah, I used to. Gonna let me in?"

It would be nice to at least get the chance to drain his snake since he only stopped once to piss in the woods during the four-hour drive.

She took another long drag on her Pall Mall, blew it out the door over his head and stepped back. She jerked her head toward the darker interior.

He guessed that was as good of an invite as he'd get.

She closed the door behind him, turned and raked her gaze over him again. "Kinda look like your father."

"You mean Dutch?"

Hopefully she wasn't going to surprise him by naming someone else instead.

When she ignored his question, he glanced around the tiny living room. He thought she left for bigger and better things. Looking around her place, it was clear she'd missed that mark. By a mile.

More like a hundred miles.

The house she gave up in Manning Grove might not be some big, fancy mansion, but it was a hell of a lot better than this rat trap.

The place was filthy. Worse, it stunk.

Overflowing ashtrays were scattered around the room. Empty beer cans littered every table. The couch had bare patches on the ass-indented cushions and what fabric remained was stained.

He had no idea what color the carpet should be.

He didn't care, either.

Thank fuck she hadn't taken him and Chris with her. He'd deal with Dutch being a dick any day over this hell hole.

After seeing what he saw, he decided he'd rather pee in the woods once he left Baltimore. He might catch crabs by using her bathroom.

"How the fuck d'you get here?" She yanked a corner of the rebel flag away from the window. The cigarette hanging from between two fingers came close to touching the dirty fabric that covered the equally dirty window. He didn't warn her since it would be for the best if this place burned to the ground.

"Your asshole father ain't here, is he?" She peered out, and jerked her chin up at the LeMans. "Whose car is that?"

"Mine."

She let the flag drop and turned on him. "You ain't old enough to own a car." Her brow furrowed and she used a cracked, dirty fingernail to scratch the corner of her mouth, then took another long drag on her cigarette. The ash hanging off the end had to now be an inch long. "You even old enough to drive?"

"You don't know?"

She didn't answer, which was his answer. She didn't even know how old her sons were anymore. Or didn't care. Most likely never did.

She'd forgotten about them both the second she walked out their front door with her shit packed in garbage bags.

The ash finally fell off the end of the Pall Mall and landed at Bebe's slipper-covered feet. Of course, she paid it no mind.

His mother should've stuffed herself into one of those black garbage bags because she was absolute trash, too. She hadn't been like this when she was with Dutch. She hadn't been mother of the year material then, either, but from what Randy remembered, Dutch always rode her ass about taking care of the house and his sons. He would also get on her about her appearance. Randy didn't think she listened to his dad, but the way she had spiraled down since leaving proved he was wrong.

Dutch and Bebe would get into some nasty fights. Both Randy and his brother had learned some really good curse words that way. It wasn't the only thing they learned during their spats. Their parents would fight, sometimes even come to blows, then fuck through their anger. Didn't matter where they were at the time.

Kitchen, living room, bedroom... Even on the front porch one night when she locked Dutch out of the house, accusing him of banging some other woman.

He made her come out of the house and get on her knees to sniff his dick to prove he hadn't, then Dutch bent her right over the porch railing. It had been rough, loud and angry for both of them. It had been like two snarling tom cats fighting.

He and Chris, who were nine and five at the time, watched from the front window while the neighbors watched from theirs.

When Dutch was done fucking her, he forced her to her knees and made her suck his dick clean. Then he locked *her* ass out of the house for being a bitch.

Someone had called the damn pigs and both of them ended up spending the night in jail to dry out and for a shit-load of minor charges. One of the women from the club had come over to stay with them that night. She slept in their parents' bed with one of Dutch's club brothers and they made a racket, too. Lots of squeaky springs, headboard slamming and screams of "fuck me harder!"

"So, why you here, boy?"

He mentally shook away that memory. "Why does Dad have your address?"

She only stared at him with those dull, empty blue eyes.

He came here for fucking answers and he was going to get fucking answers. "Why does Dutch have your fuckin' address since you left us all behind? Why would he need your fuckin' address?" He was trying not to shout but, by the end, he was shouting.

That made Bebe scowl at him.

Too fucking bad.

"That ain't your business, boy."

"Don't call me boy."

"You're my boy, I can call you what I want."

"You gave up that right the second you walked out on us."

She took one last drag on her cigarette and ground it out in a mountain of butts in the nearest overflowing ashtray.

"Dutch told you I walked out on you?" She glanced around, spotted an open pack of Pall Malls, slid another one out of the pack and tucked it between her lips.

"He didn't have to tell us. We watched it, remember? You had me carry the garbage bags out to your fuckin' car."

"Shouldn't be cursin'."

"A little too late to try parentin', *Bebe*."

She frowned as she tried to light the cigarette with a Bic. When she couldn't, she shook the almost empty disposable lighter as if that would magically fill it. "Still your mother, still older than you. I can knock you into next week if I want."

She could try. Randy doubted she'd succeed.

"Want the truth?" she asked. After a few more flicks of the Bic, a half-assed flame stayed lit long enough for her to light her smoke.

"What I came here for."

"Thought you knew someone in the neighborhood."

Randy planted his hands on his hips, dropped his head and shook it. No wonder Dutch was always yelling at him for doing stupid shit. He got his lack of smarts from his birth receptacle.

"Your father forced me to leave."

Randy's head snapped up. "No, he didn't."

"The fuck he didn't."

His thumping heart was so loud he had to yell over it to hear himself. "You asked if I wanted the truth. I want the fuckin' truth!"

"That's the truth, boy."

He frowned. "I don't get it."

"Ain't for you to get."

"I'm your fuckin' son. I should know why you left."

"I left because he paid me to."

Randy's pounding heart seized and his ears began to ring. "You're lyin'. Why would he do that?"

"'Cause we fuckin' hated each other. 'Cause he forced me to have you two rug rats. 'Cause I didn't wanna be tied down to you brats. 'Cause I didn't wanna suck his cheating dick anymore. That's why."

He thought she left because she'd had enough of the club after all the shit that went down. The fighting, the killing, the—

"And 'cause I got knocked up by Tinny."

She did what?

He knew they weren't faithful to each other. From the moment he could remember and understand it. He saw them both doing shit with other people. At the warehouse, at the house, in the garage. In their bed.

But...

Randy glanced around the living room again for some signs of a young kid. "I got another brother?"

Bebe shook her head and plugged the cigarette between her lips again. "Fuck no."

"A sister?" When she turned away, he asked, "What d'you do with him?" Or her. His half-brother or sister. Did she keep the new one after dumping the old ones?

"Used some of the scratch Dutch gave me to suck that leech outta me soon's I could."

Randy blinked as he watched his mother pick up open beer cans around the room and shake them. It took her a few tries, but she finally found one that sloshed and she chugged the remainder down.

She kept her back to him when she admitted, "Woulda done that with you two if he woulda let me."

Randy was having a hard time breathing. It wasn't from the stink in the house or the heavy cloud of cigarette smoke, but the fact the woman standing in front of him was supposed to be his mother. She'd never been one. Not once that he could remember. So anything she said shouldn't surprise him.

It still did.

He never should've come here.

She was a piece of shit Dutch scraped off his boot for good reason.

Dutch might not be perfect but at least he wanted his sons. He took care of them. Randy just wished he would've picked a better cum dumpster to grow his sperm in. Not the cunt on the hunt for another can with a backwash of beer.

"You want the truth? Here's the hard truth, kid. He pays me to stay away."

Pays? As in currently pays? No fucking way. "You're lyin'."

"Boy, I ain't lyin'. Ask him. He's stupid enough to think I'd want visitation or custody of you and... and the other one." She laughed. "I never did but pretended to and every time I threaten to hire a lawyer, he sends me more fuckin' dough."

"You're blackmailin' him?"

Bebe shrugged. "I see it as compensation for giving the bastard the two boys he wanted. And ruining my tight pussy when your big heads stretched it. The other one ripped me damn near in half."

"The sons you never wanted."

"You know what kids are?"

"Blood," Randy muttered. At least that was what they should be.

"Parasites who suck your blood. Suck the fuckin' life right outta you. And after I gave him the sons he demanded, he still stuck his dick in our whore of a house mouse."

"You fucked Tin Man!" he screamed, the heat from his fury burning his cheeks.

She most likely fucked a ton of other bikers. Whether from the Blood Fury MC or other clubs. She had no right to judge Dutch for fucking around when she had done the same damn thing.

"Now you know why I left."

"You woulda stayed if he hadn't paid you off?"

Bebe shrugged and flicked the growing ash of her Pall Mall near an ashtray but totally missed. "Why not? Had a roof over my head, food in my belly and plenty of dick to choose from."

Not one of those things she listed included her own flesh and blood.

Randy pressed his lips together and nodded. More to himself than her. Yeah, she didn't leave because she was scared of the shit going down with the Fury, she left because she was a greedy, selfish cunt. And the only way Dutch could get her to leave him was to pay her to do so.

She did that willingly and without a fight.

Bebe got what she wanted.

Dutch got what he wanted.

And two kids got confused. As well as lied to.

"You got any cash, boy? I'm outta beer."

He lifted his head and stared at the woman who used to be his mother.

He dug into the front pocket of his jeans, pulled out a quarter and flipped it at her.

Bebe watched as it fell to the floor at her slippered feet. "Think that's funny?"

"You hear me laughin'?"

Yeah, maybe it was good he came. Got the truth. He could now put the woman out of his head and never think about her again. Maybe tell Chris she was dead.

Because that was what she was. Dead to him. Dead to his younger brother.

"Better take that fuckin' quarter, 'cause that's the last cent you're gonna get from a Dietrich. Tellin' Dutch to never give you a fuckin' dime again. Gonna tell him your threats are empty. Also gonna tell him to shoot you right between the fuckin' eyes if you ever show the fuck up in Manning Grove again. You hear me, you worthless slit?"

Her mouth got tight and her fingers curled into a fist like she was thinking about belting him one. "You don't speak to your mother like that."

His eyebrows shot up. "Wouldn't, if I had one."

He was done.

With her.

With this shithole.

With all of it.

He spun on his boot, jogged out the door, down the porch steps and didn't stop moving until he was in the LeMans and headed north out of Maryland.

He didn't stop until he was forced to.

By the red and blue flashing lights behind him.

He had no choice but to pull over since the Pontiac piece-of-shit would never outrun the souped-up Crown Vics the state pigs drove. Maybe he should've taken the back roads all the way home instead of the interstate.

Too late now.

He slammed his palm against the steering wheel and muttered a curse under his breath as the uniformed pig approached the back of the LeMans with one hand already resting on the butt of his gun.

Randy didn't have to roll down the window since it was already open. The LeMans didn't have air conditioning and, being late afternoon in the middle of August, it was ball-sweating hot outside.

"How you doing, sir?" the pig oinked.

Sir. Randy's tight jaw shifted.

"Need your license, registration and insurance. Assuming you have all that even though the registration plate seems to be missing."

Randy stared straight ahead, waiting. His fury from his *used-to-be* mother still bubbling like lava in his gut. Now he had to deal with a pig of a different kind.

"Must have lost the key, too, since I see you've made your own with a screwdriver. Do I even need to run the VIN to see if it's stolen?"

"Do whatever gets you off."

The pig leaned closer to the window, tilting his head just slightly. "Sorry, I think I missed that."

Randy turned his head slowly and stared straight up at the pig who wore one of those stupid-ass hats on his head with the black strap across his double-chin. Dumb fucks didn't even know how to wear a hat right.

This time Randy repeated it slowly, loudly and in very clear English. "Said do whatever the fuck gets you off."

"Huh. Guess my ears don't need cleaned. I heard you right the first time."

"Yeah, you ain't deaf, just dumb."

The Trooper slid his sunglasses down his nose far enough to peer over them. "How old are you, kid?"

"Eighteen," he lied.

"Must have a glandular problem, then."

Randy grabbed his crotch. "Had no problem fuckin' your mom's hairy snatch. She even begged me for more."

"Why don't you step out of the car."

"Are you askin'?"

"Did I make it sound like I was?"

"Did your sister tell you I throat-fucked her 'til she gagged and swallowed my hot, salty cum?"

A hand reached into the driver's side window so quickly,

Randy didn't have time to dodge it. Fingers snatched the collar of his T-shirt, while the pig's other hand grabbed his neck, and he was yanked bodily through the window. He landed hard on the searing hot berm of the road.

After registering the pain, his first thought was that vehicles were driving at a high rate of speed not that many feet from his exposed melon.

As he tried to get up, a boot on his back shoved him back down.

"I was wrong. I do think I need my ears cleaned because I couldn't have possibly heard what I did."

Randy spit a little bit of blood out onto the blacktop in front of him. "Nah. You heard me right. Fucked your mom, fucked your sister, then I blew my load up your daughter's tight ass. It was sloppy seconds, though, you musta gave her the first load."

The boot on his back turned to a knee and the pig's crushing weight made it hard to breathe.

Randy heard a clicking sound before feeling the press of a metal rod to the back of his neck. One of those expandable metal sticks that five-o carried. The one they loved to beat innocent people with. *Fuckers.*

"Good thing you're eighteen. Otherwise, you'd end up in juvie for grand theft, instead. They'll like fresh meat like you in prison. Tight hole. Sweet, young mouth. Just enough hair around your asshole so Bubba can pretend it's a virgin pussy. Hope you like big, black dick."

"Know your wife loves it," were the last words he recalled saying.

He didn't remember anything after that.

Not for a long time.

Chapter One

Rook followed the same well-beaten path through the woods they'd followed a few times before. One they knew was free of booby traps. Or at least it had been the last two times he and Easy hoofed it up the mountain and searched for Shade.

They'd hit the edge of the main clearing, then the two of them would branch off and begin their search for their missing brother.

Rook hoped like fuck he didn't stumble over the man's body in the dark. That would freak him the fuck out.

He would've skipped going up Hillbilly Hill tonight because he was horny as all fuck and would've rather gotten laid instead of trudging through fucking woods filled with a dangerous and crazy cult, but fuck no...

Instead of sweating over some wet snatch, he was sweating as he tromped over wet leaves and uneven terrain in boots definitely not made for hiking. They were made for riding his sled. Or kicking in someone's teeth. Or stomping on someone's fingers because they needed to be broken and the asshole needed a lesson.

Yeah, not made for flitting through the fucking woods like a forest fairy.

But Shade was not only their club brother, he'd gotten really close with Easy, who was now more like his blood brother.

And, of fucking course, that was what family did. Had each other's backs.

Or at least real family did.

Not sperm donors and cum dumpsters. Those didn't count as real family.

He muffled his frustrated sigh.

They were as quiet as possible whenever they came up here to search. The plan was if they crossed any Shirleys old enough to grow hair on their balls, they'd take them out if the opportunity was right, but right now, their main goal was to find Shade.

The man had been on the Clan Plan by himself and already gotten beat to fuck by one of the inbred hillbillies and had to take two weeks off to recover. However, the moment Shade was allowed back on his feet, he ghosted.

Judge had pinged the tracking app on Shade's cell phone several times, but the thing had been turned off. Or destroyed.

It was too weird the man just upped and disappeared without a fucking trace.

Judge and Trip didn't want to give up looking for their brother until they either found him, dead or alive, or they at least heard from him.

From what Shade last told the prez and sergeant at arms, only about eight Shirley males remained breathing. Well, now seven since Easy took out one on their last trip up.

Maybe since they were running out of Shirley males, they trapped Shade and was using him for breeding like they'd done with Autumn. It was a desperate way to bring in fresh blood since the Shirley bloodline was so damn incestuous that their family tree looked like a twig.

Rook cringed at the thought of having to fuck Shirley snatch. He'd rather have his nuts cut off.

He could lose his fucking nuts if he didn't pay attention and triggered one of their booby traps.

He hated this fucking mountain and hated the Guardians of fucking Freedom, the stupid name of the Shirleys' so-called sovereign stupid-ass nation.

Rook bit back a snort.

A cult. That was what they were, no more, no less. The Shirleys reminded him of the followers of Jim Jones or David Koresh. Or a hillbilly militia.

From the info Judge passed on to him and Easy once Shade went missing, the younger brother thought they might start bringing in more males from other locations, like the Ohio clan, and then take on the Fury.

War.

That was what Shade had thought. That the uncle-brothers were preparing for war.

The hair on the back of Rook's neck spiked at the possibility. The Fury had been destroyed once, they would not let it happen again. If the hillbilly goat fuckers wanted war, then the Fury would give them one.

Only, Trip wanted to avoid that shit at all costs. Not only because their brothers were creating families with women and children, but because it would cause issues for the MC with law enforcement. Most likely of the federal, state and local kind. Or all of the above.

No one in his brotherhood wanted to be in their sights.

No one in his brotherhood wanted to do any more time in the joint, either. Rook especially. Been there, done that, though he didn't have the prison tats to prove it. But he did come away with some valuable and invaluable lessons and experiences. Some he never wanted to learn or try again.

About fifteen minutes prior, he'd gotten a text from Easy saying he was heading in a different direction back to the Honda.

Rook had to assume Easy hadn't found shit, either, and that wasn't good. They still had no fucking clue what happened to Shade. On their first trip up, they tried to check a lot of the buildings. Now they were checking the surrounding woods. But they were only staying for short stretches of time when they went up. The longer they stayed on the mountain, the higher the chances they'd get caught, injured or killed.

One missing Fury member was already one too many.

He slipped in some mud and leaves, barely catching himself before almost landing on his ass.

He hated this fucking mountain.

He finally saw the spot where he'd parked the Honda sedan he'd borrowed from the garage without Dutch knowing.

Easy was already there waiting on him. Rook almost didn't notice him at first leaning against the car since E was wearing all black, just like Rook.

"Nothin'?" he asked when he got within hearing range.

Easy shook his head. "Woulda texted you if I found somethin'."

"Maybe they buried him." That possibility churned Rook's gut.

E winced. "Been lookin' for that, too. No fresh graves." He sounded hopeful.

"Fuck," Rook muttered and dragged both hands down his face. "If he don't show up soon..."

"Need to know either way, brother."

"Yeah," Rook answered on a sigh. "Gonna kill him if he's alive."

"Kinda defeats the point of us lookin' for him, don't it?" Easy's normally easy laugh sounded a bit strained. "Anyway, found a new stash of weapons, though, and also stumbled across a little shack where they're makin' ammo. Thinkin' as soon as they have enough, they're comin' for us."

"We should steal the weapons but leave the ammo. Don't trust their reloaded casings."

"Agreed," Easy said. "'Specially if they're doin' it the same half-assed way they're makin' meth." He grinned when he added, "And babies."

"Besides the weapons, they're gonna need a bigger army." Seven men could still do a lot of damage. There were only thirteen patched Fury members, plus two prospects, right now. Even so, that meant the Fury was double the size of the Guardians of Incest. But he'd like to have a better advantage than that. Better weapons, reliable ammo, more bodies. More brains. The element of surprise would help, too.

"Besides the army they're already breedin'?" E asked.

"They got a shitload of spawn but most are too young yet." At least the ones he'd seen.

"Not all of 'em. They probably can hold a gun before they're off their momma's tit. Definitely long before they're old enough to breed."

"They breed their bitches pretty fuckin' young," Rook reminded him.

"Yeah. Saw a young one tonight. In one of the isolated cabins higher up. Couldn't be more than... fuck, maybe thirteen. Fourteen at the most. Her fuckin' belly was about to burst open with another Shirley spawn."

"Christ," Rook muttered. "As soon as they bleed, they breed."

"Yeah. Should feel bad for her, but really fuckin' don't."

"They don't know any different." That still was no excuse.

"Don't mean it's right."

"Yeah," Rook agreed, "it ain't right. Shit's gotta stop."

"We can only do so much without us drawin' heat. Takin' out those motherfuckin' bastards is one thing. Women and children is another."

That was for fucking sure. No one on the exec committee wanted to make that call. But all the male Shirleys? They were on their hit list. Every fucking single one of them. For not only doing what they did to Autumn, Sig's "Red," but for kidnapping Rook's niece Dyna.

Can't take a man's baby girl, his flesh and blood, and expect to keep breathing.

The club gave the Shirleys a warning not to fuck with the Fury after they rescued Autumn, but they were too fucking stupid to listen. They caused what was currently happening to their clan by not taking that warning seriously, by knocking out Jemma and stealing Dyna.

Once they did that, it was on like Donkey fucking Kong.

"Let's get the fuck out of here before..." Headlights came over the rise in the road. "Before that." Rook groaned. "Fuck."

"How much you wanna bet it's five-o?"

"Of course it fuckin' is, who the fuck else would be drivin' down Copperhead Road at this hour? God-fuckin-damnit."

"Just play it cool. Story is we were on our way back to the

farm from a party and pulled over to piss. Hell, maybe it's just a local."

"Yeah, right." The local residents stayed away from this part of the mountain. For good reason.

But of course it was a local. A local pig. *Fuck.*

The black-and-white pulled off the road behind them and the spotlight was pointed straight at the rear of the Honda where he and Easy still stood.

They should've just got into the fucking car and left. Talked on their way back to the farm. But Rook hadn't wanted to leave until he checked with Easy to make sure he didn't come across anything suspicious first. Just in case they needed to go back up and check it out.

Now look at what was happening because of that delay. They were being blinded by that fucking spotlight, like two bucks standing in front of an oncoming eighteen-wheeler.

Rook raised his arm to shield his eyes to keep the light from searing his corneas. *Asshole.* Whoever it was.

He knew them all. He'd dealt with them all.

He was forced to make nice with them all.

Why? Because they all had their personal cars and the PD's cruisers repaired and serviced at Dutch's Garage. Rook had personally turned a wrench and changed the oil on every single vehicle any of those pigs and their family sat in.

Dutch made good money off their business. Because of that, Rook bit his tongue whenever one of them came in.

Were the local pigs any better than the countless screws he'd had to deal with in County or in the state pen? Yeah. But that didn't mean he wanted to take them on a fucking picnic or send them a fucking Christmas card.

They still carried cuffs, a taser and a gun.

Due to being an ex-con, Rook wasn't allowed to carry any weapons to protect himself. As for the cuffs...

Well...

Because of the spotlight, the body walking in their direction was nothing but a silhouette. He knew which one it was simply by her shape alone.

Only two females wore badges and duty belts for the Manning Grove Police Department. Two related to Chief Max Bryson. His sister-in-law Leah, who was married to Max's brother Marc, another badge-carrying Bryson. And Max's cousin Jet Bryson.

Like the Shirleys, the Brysons liked to keep it in the family, too, when it came to the police department.

"What are you boys up to?"

Yep, he was fucking right, those hips and thighs belonged to none other than Officer Bridget "Jet" Bryson. Rook hadn't dealt with her too much yet since she was the newest member of the force, but he'd seen her around town and at the garage plenty of times with and without her uniform.

But not naked. Though, he'd imagined it a few times, especially when her hair was down, her jeans were hugging her ass and she wasn't wearing a Kevlar vest which turned her tits into a shapeless ramp.

Rook cocked an eyebrow and glanced around. "Who you talkin' to?"

"You."

"I ain't a boy." Rook whacked Easy's chest hard with the flat of his palm. "Easy certainly ain't no boy, either. Are you, E?"

Easy grabbed his junk and shook it. "Fuck no, can prove I'm no boy."

Jet sighed and moved to where they could finally see her without being blinded. "Okay, *gentlemen*, what are you up to?"

Rook pursed his lips and purposely raked his gaze from

the top of her long dark hair pulled tightly to the top of her head to the tips of her boots. Too bad that uniform made her look more like a man than a woman. "You seem easily confused, darlin'. No gentlemen here, either."

"Okay, *assholes...*" She smiled. "Is that better?"

That smile didn't quite reach her crystal blue eyes. It was too dark to see the color right now, but he knew what they were. The same as the rest of the Brysons. They all looked similar. Dark, practically black, hair with light blue eyes that could pierce you.

Especially this one's. She had a tendency to stare right through him, like she could see all his secrets. Whenever she dropped off one of the PD's cruisers—or even her personal vehicle—for maintenance or repair, he always caught her looking at him with those eyes slightly narrowed. Like she was waiting for him to fuck up so she could book his next vacation behind steel bars.

Easy grinned. "That's about right."

What was about right? Oh yeah, that they were assholes.

Jet rolled her eyes and shook her head. "Want to tell me what you were doing in these woods after dark?"

"Havin' a picnic," Rook answered.

"I'm not thinking that's true."

Rook slammed a palm over his heart. "You wound me, darlin', by not believin' me."

"Not *darling*. Officer will do. And I don't see your picnic basket."

"We already put it in the trunk."

"Do you want to show me?" Jet asked.

"You have a warrant?" Rook returned. "Or probable cause to stop and question us?"

"I got the PC. Want me to explain it?"

"Nope."

"I kind of find it suspicious that you two would be parked here in the middle of the night. You know, two in the morning is not the best time to have a picnic."

Rook shrugged. "Unless you're havin' one with Yogi Bear."

Jet tilted her head. "You still watch cartoons, Rook?"

"Sure. Don't you?"

"We were headin' home," Easy explained, "and I had to piss."

"You're not that far from the farm."

"I got a big dick but a small bladder," Easy said. "It's a problem. Not the big dick part, the small bladder part."

"Are you sure it isn't a prostate problem? You should get that checked," Jet answered with a straight face.

"Don't know. You wanna check it for me?" Easy turned around and planted both hands on the rear fender of the Honda, bending over and pushing his ass out. "Just be gentle."

"Is that how you made friends last time you were in jail?" Jet asked him.

"Why d'you think we call him Easy, darlin'?"

"Officer," Jet corrected him.

"Why d'you think we call him Easy, officer darlin'?"

She sighed and jerked up her duty belt. Rook preferred to see her hips without that bulky thing. Especially since that belt held a whole bunch of shit that could make his life miserable.

"I don't want to catch you here again," she ordered before turning on her boot heel and walking away.

"It's a free country, ain't it?" he asked Easy.

Easy answered, "Last I checked."

"Hear that, officer darlin'? It's a free country. We wanna have a romantic picnic together in the woods at two a.m., we're damn well gonna have one," he yelled at her retreating back.

Rook leaned back against the cage, crossed his arms over his chest and watched her climb into her cruiser. A few seconds later the spotlight went out. *Thank fuck.*

His brother whacked his arm. "Bet she's hot as fuck in bed. All bossy and shit. Black leather corset, whip, cuffs. Fuck yeah. That makes me hard thinkin' about it." Easy adjusted himself. "Wouldn't mind havin' a taste of that."

Unfortunately, Easy wasn't the only one.

THE FUCKER WASN'T DEAD. He wasn't injured. It turns out Shade ghosted his brothers and his woman Chelle for two weeks without a word. Said he had shit that needed to be handled and then returned with a kid in tow. A fucking kid.

Not a little snot monkey. A twelve-year-old. Then tried to say the boy was his. Rook wasn't sure anyone believed that bullshit.

But if Jude needed a place to belong, they'd give him one. That was just the way real family should be. Family wasn't always blood. In fact, sometimes it was better if they weren't.

He had no idea who or where Jude's mother was, but Rook only hoped she wasn't anything like Bebe.

Now that Shade had a woman and a kid, along with Chelle's two girls, to be responsible for, Judge wasn't sure Shade should continue going up the mountain to deal with the Shirleys. Mostly because he didn't want to risk leaving Shade's new family "fatherless."

Most of the Fury members had survived shitty childhoods. It was one common bond between them. Most of them were also determined to do things differently with the next generation.

Whether that happened or not remained to be seen.

But keeping Shade off the mountain meant Easy and Rook needed to continue to do their part. Their focus turned to the rest of the male Shirleys, by grabbing one whenever it was possible, or at least doing recon. Basically, trying to keep ahead of whatever war they might be planning.

Tonight, he was alone. Now that it wasn't a rescue mission for Shade, they figured it was easier to spy on the clan, or make a Shirley magically disappear, by going solo.

The Shirley men seemed to be staying in small groups now. Safety in numbers, Rook guessed. And all of them had some sort of high-powered rifle slung over their backs, big knives on their hips, as well as thigh holsters with some pretty large caliber handguns. Small cannons, more like it.

Yeah, they'd had enough with their fellow uncle-brothers and brother-cousins disappearing. They were protecting the few who remained.

Shade had been right, though. They'd soon have to shut down the Clan Plan for the winter. The cover was getting thin and once snow hit the mountain, anyone going up there would stand out like a flashing beacon and make an easy target.

Rook would prefer not to get shot at. About as much as he preferred not to get dragged back to jail for breaking his current parole.

Which he did about every fucking day. Especially since he was trespassing right now and had not only a loaded Beretta tucked into the back of his waistband, but a ten-inch knife on his belt. He also had a joint tucked in his wallet. But he'd left that back in the Honda where he'd parked it in their hiding spot. The same spot where they'd found the crematorium's van the night Shade got his head bashed in by an aluminum baseball bat.

Shade had built a good hidey-hole for the van, so they kept using it. Problem was, they'd been lazy and hadn't used it the last time when Jet Bryson came across them. They weren't making that mistake again. Because of that fuck-up she was sure to keep an eye on the area and had probably spread the word around their pig pen.

Five-o might be on high alert for any questionable activity on Copperhead Road.

For some reason, they didn't fuck with the Shirleys, but they didn't want anyone else fucking with them, either. Rook guessed they didn't want anyone poking at the sleeping bear.

He ducked behind a bush that wasn't so bushy any longer. But the night was dark since the moon was in hiding due to the cloud cover, so he doubted he'd be spotted.

Fuck, he hoped he wouldn't be spotted. No matter what, he wasn't moving. He was staying right where he was so he could watch what the fuck was happening in the main clearing tonight.

It wasn't what he expected. Normally, if the women were working late, they were either making meth or reloads, or both. The men usually took care of the moonshine stills and assembling long guns out of parts they got from wherever the fuck they got them.

Buying rifle parts on the black market and putting them together to make semi-automatic or even fully-automatic weapons probably made them untraceable. Bonus, no ID and background check required like normal citizens trying to legally purchase a firearm. The Guardians of Freedumb didn't believe they should have any kind of government identification, that it violated their freedoms.

What-fuckin-ever.

Whenever those inbred goat fuckers got tossed in the slammer, they were given something to identify them, whether they liked it or not. A mug shot, a set of prints in the system and an inmate number. It was easier to stay off the government radar if you didn't get caught.

Not one of the snot monkeys spawned from Shirley loins were born in a hospital, had a birth certificate or a social security number. Not one.

So, yeah, no Shirley existed until they got caught doing something dumb.

Or dangerous.

Like making and selling meth. Making and selling moonshine.

Or fucking girls younger than the legal age of consent.

However, Manning Grove PD tended to turn a blind eye as long as the Shirleys didn't bring their fuckery to town. What a bunch of goddamn hypocrites.

If Rook knocked up a fourteen-year-old, where'd he end up? In the joint.

If he made and sold moonshine? In the slammer.

If he made and sold meth? Behind bars.

If he drove a vehicle without a license, registration or insurance?

For fuck's sake... With a cracked-open skull and a lack of memory along an interstate before spending a couple of years in juvie.

Once he got out, his father taught him a lesson the Dietrich way about stealing cars and getting caught. That lesson was almost as bad as the lesson the State Trooper taught him along Interstate 83 late one afternoon. Not quite, since Rook hadn't woken up in a hospital when Dutch was through with him.

But one lesson his father did teach him was, when you make a fucking mistake you'd better learn from it.

Rook did.

Though, he made a few more mistakes before he got good with stealing vehicles.

However, his last bid in County had nothing to do with stealing a cage. Nothing at all.

But when he got sprung the last time, he was too old and too big for his old man to teach him a lesson about getting caught.

Dutch was too old, too. Not to mention, too fat and too focused on chasing tail to worry about what his oldest son had done. He no longer gave a fuck when Rook ended up in jail. In fact, now he expected it.

He wouldn't even visit. Not once.

Didn't matter. Why the fuck did he need family when he was doing a bid? He'd made plenty of "friends" inside.

Like Dodge.

And some others he'd been trying to convince to come to Manning Grove, clean up their act and join the Fury.

Unfortunately, their club was still light in numbers. Especially if they might go to war with the Shirleys, since it looked like they were increasing their numbers, too. Shade was right about them bringing more bodies into their clan, but wrong about who.

It wasn't men climbing out of the piece-of-shit sixteen-passenger van with the dark-tinted windows. No men at all except for the driver. From what Rook understood about these ass-backward backwoods bumpkins, the women weren't allowed to drive. They weren't even allowed to *learn* to drive. That kept them hobbled to Hillbilly Hill.

Rook wasn't sure he'd call the former occupants of the van women. None of them seemed fully cooked. Maybe mid-to late-teens. Young, fresh, but old enough to ovulate. The clan must be bringing in new blood so the new babies wouldn't be so cross-eyed and confused.

But only seven men remained, if their count was correct. Seven.

They already had almost thirty women in the compound. Not including some of the teen girls. Adding eight more women would keep those seven studs busy as fuck. Unless some of the teen boys were going to take a "wife" or two.

But still... Seven men weren't enough. Maybe more men would arrive next.

Fuck.

The arrival of the van was causing too much activity, so tonight would not be a good night to try to snag a Shirley. But what *was* happening would be of interest to Trip, Sig and Judge.

Rook watched long enough to make sure all of the new women who'd arrived didn't seem to be restrained or forced, like Red had been.

Surprising—or maybe it shouldn't be so surprising—they all seemed to want to be there and were dressed in a similar way with homemade dresses, long hair pulled up, knee-high socks and sneakers. They worked their way around the clearing introducing themselves to the other women and children who had gathered like it was Manning Grove's Christmas parade.

He wondered if the women got to pick their "baby daddy" or if the man was chosen for them. The one they'd end up "marrying." Though, Rook doubted any of them were legally married. Wife was just an empty title to them.

Just like mother had only been an empty title for Bebe. Should mean something but didn't.

Not that he was ever getting fucking married. He'd lasted

thirty-four years so far without a ball and chain. The only ring he might consider wearing was a cock ring. But right now he didn't need one of those, either. He had no problem getting and keeping his dick hard.

No problem at all.

A bonfire was lit and the crowd began to gather around it. Mason jars, most likely full of moonshine, were being passed around. Children were playing in the dirt. The teenagers— probably all related—were flirting with each other in small groups. And the seven men took turns talking to the newest females of the clan.

Kind of like speed dating but redneck-style with a whole bunch of missing teeth.

Those men probably couldn't care less about intelligence and conversation but more about the width of their hips and their sturdiness for pushing out snot monkeys.

He had no doubt that if he checked back in six months or so, all eight of them would be knocked up. He wouldn't doubt if a couple weren't knocked up in the next week. Their belief was the more children they had, the closer they were to God.

However, if there was a God, he was probably frowning down upon the Shirley clan. But then Rook had never been a religious man and didn't know what the fuck was in the Bible, so maybe their god condoned everything the Shirleys did.

Since they were all settled in for the night—and the only ones wandering away from the group might be the teens looking to do a little diddling—no reason remained for Rook to stay. His bed was waiting for him and he planned on staring at the back of his eyelids soon.

Unless some sweet butts were hanging around when he got back. He wouldn't mind at least one good blowjob before hitting the sheets. Crystal was great at deep-throating. Maybe once he got back to the Honda, he'd text her and see where she was or who she was with. Even if she already took a load from one of his brothers, she could still use her mouth.

He must have tripped a dozen fucking times making his way back down the narrow path. Even though he knew the way by now, not having any moonlight made it more treacherous. He also didn't trust the Shirleys to not discover their path and add a few booby traps along the way. If they were smart...

Yeah, never mind.

That was one benefit his brothers had over the Shirleys, a few of them actually had some brain power. It also helped none of them were inbred. The Originals had done some fucked up shit back in the day, but having babies with their own blood wasn't one of them.

Thank fuck.

It was bad enough Bebe was his birth mother. If she had been his aunt, too...

He stumbled over a hidden root and smothered a curse when he tweaked his ankle. He was almost to the bottom but sound carried at night and he didn't want to risk catching the clan's attention. The women and children looked innocent enough but they were far from it. Any of them would fill Rook's ass with buckshot or attempt a homerun using his noggin as a baseball, if given half the chance.

He straightened, tested his ankle and winced. It wasn't bad but enough to piss him off. He walked more carefully through the dark, relying on his limited night vision to find the spot where he'd hid the Honda.

Only, it was no longer hidden.

Fucking motherfucker.

Chapter Two

A DARK FIGURE waited for him at the uncovered Honda with hands planted on her hips.

He paused on the path and glanced over his shoulder back the way he'd come. Was it better to die by the Shirleys or deal with Jet?

That was debatable.

He growled, sucked in a breath and kept moving forward.

One armed woman versus a whole bunch of armed hillbillies. He might be stupid, but he wasn't Shirley stupid. And after he was done dealing with Officer Bryson, he could still get back to the bunkhouse in time for that head job. If he was dead, he couldn't.

That right there made the decision much easier.

"Hi," she chirped, pretending to be much happier to see him than she was.

"Fuck you." No point in him trying to pretend. If she didn't like seeing him here, the feeling was mutual.

"Most people usually answer a greeting with a similar

greeting. Unless you're not happy to see that person. That makes me think you're not happy to see me, Rook."

"You ain't wrong." He walked right past where she stood at the rear of the Honda, dug out the key fob from deep within his front pocket and hit the unlock button.

"Well, that hurts my feelings."

Somehow, he needed to rid himself of the Beretta from the waistband of his cargo pants before she saw it and hauled his ass in. It was bad enough he couldn't hide the Buck knife. Hard to miss that on his hip.

Technically, he violated his parole right in plain sight. He could end up wearing steel bracelets whether she saw the gun or not.

Fuck.

"Doubt that," he muttered, trying his best to keep his back turned from her. His shirt was covering the Beretta but that didn't mean it wasn't printing. And her being a pig and all meant she'd recognize the shape.

His preference was to not get shot, tased or cuffed tonight, if at all possible. No, his goal was only that damn blowjob.

"That I have feelings? Or that you hurt them?" she asked.

Jesus Christ. What was she blathering on about? Oh yeah, hurt feelings. "Both."

"Well, if I didn't have feelings I wouldn't be so pissed at you right now for going up that damn mountain when I told you to stay off it the last time I caught you here."

Rook's eyebrows shot up and his head tilted. "You told me what?" *For fuck's sake,* she was a bossy little thing. He wondered if she'd been like that before she ever wore a uniform.

Probably. It was most likely in the Bryson blood. And their blue blood was thick as tar.

"You heard me. And I thought you heard me last time. I meant what I said."

Did she now? He was done with her games. He needed to come down a woman's throat and then get some shuteye. He did not need this shit from her. He was tired, his ankle now ached and it might even be swelling in his boot. It didn't help his mood that he was only seconds away from being arrested. But dumbass that he was, he still couldn't stop what he said next. Something with her bossiness pushed his fucking buttons and not in a good way. Not like it had Easy. Rook didn't want to submit to her, if anything he wanted her to submit to him.

He wanted to force her to her knees and come down *her* throat, not Crystal's. Then he wanted to strip that goddamn duty belt off her hips, yank those ugly-ass uniform pants down her thighs, bend her over the trunk of the Honda and fuck her until she was screaming his name and begging him to fuck her harder so loudly the Shirleys would hear it all the way up the mountain.

And wanting all of that pissed him the fuck off, too.

Because he would never, ever fuck a woman who wore a badge.

Never.

A woman who would take away his freedom in a second if she could. That was her job. Stripping people like him of their freedoms.

Fuck her.

"Don't know who the fuck you *think* you are," he began, "but let me tell you who the fuck you ain't. You ain't my momma, you ain't my sister and you certainly ain't my fuckin' woman."

"Would you listen to any of those three?"

"Fuck no."

Her chin rose only enough that he noticed it. "Let me tell you who I am, then."

He planted his hands on his hips, lifting his own chin. "Know who you are, Jet. Just don't give a fuck."

"You will if I take you in."

An armed woman allowed to carry a Glock in her holster versus an armed man not allowed to have a Beretta stuffed down his pants. She had a huge set of fucking balls. Personally, he preferred his women without them.

"You ain't takin' me anywhere." He wondered if her balls would be so big if she knew about his gun. Ever since he walked up to the Honda and she saw the knife on his hip, she had watched his hands carefully. They probably wouldn't be having this conversation at all if she knew about the .40 at his back.

"That sounded like a challenge," she said.

Unlike her, he wouldn't hesitate or have second thoughts about killing someone. If she killed someone, even in the line of duty, she would likely take a while to recover. Taking someone's life would affect her way more than it ever would him.

He did what he had to do to protect himself every time he was locked up. He did what he had to do to protect his club, his family and himself. If that meant someone had to die, then they had to die.

She might hesitate, think twice first. He wouldn't.

"If that's what you heard."

"That's what I heard." She tilted her head. "I know you're on parole. I also know what for. I've seen your extensive sheet, Rook—"

"Why? What fuckin' reason would you have to check my record?"

"Why wouldn't I? I'm a cop wondering why you keep

coming back to this mountain mostly owned by redneck militia wannabes who have a mistaken notion they're some sovereign nation and don't have to follow any rules. Kind of like you..." She tipped her head toward his knife. "When I checked the conditions of your parole, I swore it said you couldn't possess any weapons."

"Don't remember my PO sayin' anythin' about knives," he lied.

"Then you weren't listening."

"Been accused of that before."

"Right. Like when I told you I didn't want to catch you back here again. Your issues with listening might be why you're single."

"Who said I'm single?" When she didn't respond, he grinned and took a step closer to her to remind her he was much bigger than her. And much more dangerous.

He stared down into her face even though it was dark and he couldn't see it perfectly. But by crowding her, he could still make his point. "Maybe you've been checkin' into me more than you wanna admit, darlin'. More than just my criminal past. That so?"

Maybe if he played with her a little, she'd get flustered enough to just leave him be. He hadn't broken any laws that she knew of besides the conditions of his parole with the knife. If he could get her to leave before she spotted the gun, everyone would walk away unscathed from this. Most of all him.

"Also seen you checkin' me out at the garage. Seen you starin'." He wet his lips with his tongue, then dragged his thumb over his bottom lip slowly and deliberately.

Her eyes narrowed on that motion. "I always keep an eye on sketchy subjects."

"That ain't it."

She took a breath and a step back. "I'd be a fool not to keep an eye on you, Rook. Especially right now with that gun at your back."

Fuck.

"I don't know what the hell you guys are doing up on that mountain, but you need to stay off it. The fact that you're heading up there with weapons..." She shook her head.

"Maybe I'm just visitin' a friend," he suggested.

"If that was so, why wouldn't you just drive up there?"

"Because maybe it's a secret thing between us. A forbidden thing." He shot her a knowing grin.

"You're in love with one of the Shirleys?" she practically squeaked.

"Who said anythin' about love?"

Jet wrinkled her nose. "You're having sex in the woods like two animals?"

"It's much more excitin' than it sounds." Which might be true if it didn't involve a Shirley.

"I'll take your word for it."

"Or I can show you, darlin'," he whispered, closing the space she had made when she stepped backward.

"You call me darling one more time and I'm shoving that darling up your ass."

"Wouldn't be the first time—"

Her eyebrows shot up her forehead.

"Wouldn't bet on it being the last, either. But I haven't called you *darling* once." He had emphasized the G. "*Darling*," again drawing out the G, "is used by uptight, rich motherfuckin' snobs, which," he drew a hand in the air from his head to his boots, "I ain't."

"No shit," she muttered.

"Called you *darlin'*. Since pigs are supposed to be so fuckin' detail-oriented, you shoulda picked up on that." He took another step forward until the tip of his boots bumped hers. "Now, *darlin'*—"

"Step back," she ordered.

"Never been a day I've taken orders from a woman. Not one fuckin' day. And today's not that day, either."

"Rook, I'm warning you, step the fuck back."

He dropped his head until his face was just above hers. She was panting softly. He bet, if he could see them, her eyes would be dilated.

He also bet her pulse was racing in her throat.

All of that could mean one of two things. She was interested in way more than his criminal past.

Or she was scared of him.

The second would surprise him since she didn't act scared of him at all, but if it was the first, he wanted to know why. Because he had seen the way she looked at him every time she'd been at the garage.

Maybe she just wanted to taste something she couldn't have.

That forbidden fruit.

Yeah, he might not know shit about the Bible but he knew Eve had eaten an apple she shouldn't have.

Maybe Rook was that apple. And Jet was Eve trying to resist that ultimate temptation.

That apple was enticing her to pick it. Bite it. Savor it.

Every time she'd shown up at the garage, while Rev and Whip fawned all over her and preened their cocky feathers in front of her, Rook had always kept his distance.

Yeah, she was hot. But what she wore, what she was, turned him cold.

He smiled.

She didn't. "Step. Back."

"Or what?" he whispered, lowering his mouth to barely inches above hers. "Whatchya gonna do, *darlin'*?"

The crackling sound made his blood instantly turn to ice before his body went stiff and he lost all control of it. He dropped like a crash test dummy to the dirt, unable to move, unable to think, since his heart, his muscles and his brain had seized.

He was fucking helpless right now but he only had to wait it out. The second she released the trigger on her taser, he'd be able to move again. That very fucking second.

He just had to wait.

Wait.

She didn't release the trigger until after using her boot to roll him onto his stomach. The second the voltage stopped coursing through his body, she had a hold of his right arm and yanked up behind his back with his thumb cranked all the way to his forearm. Unfortunately for him, his wrist didn't bend naturally like that.

He tried to suck in air as she drove a knee into his back with all her weight. She wasn't heavy, *thank fuck*, but it still hurt like hell.

As he tried to roll and dislodge her weight, she jerked his hand higher, almost to his neck. He heard the familiar clicking sound of metal teeth and a millisecond later the bite of the cuff as she slapped it on his right wrist. Then, his Beretta was gone.

"Fuckin' son of a bitch!" he shouted. The way she had his arm pulled up, if he struggled he'd risk popping it from his shoulder socket.

He knew this dance. All too well. Pain used as a tool to make him comply.

If he fought her, she'd add resisting arrest to any charges she might drum up on him. He only needed to wait it out.

See what game she was playing. Whether she was taking him in or teaching him a lesson.

He clenched his teeth when she ordered, "Give me your other hand. Or are you going to fight me on this?"

He took one breath. Then another. "Fuck you," he growled, but gave her what she wanted. The cold metal bracelet cinched tight on his left wrist, too. A second later the knife was removed from its sheath. Now he was hobbled on the ground with his face in the fucking dirt without a weapon.

Fucking motherfucker.

He should've shot her.

He could have dragged her body up the mountain and her family would blame the Shirleys for her death. Simple. Then, instead of the war between the clan and the club, it would be between the clan and the PD.

Because if those oinkers thought the Shirleys did something to one of their own? The Brysons would decimate that mountain and everyone on it. Maybe they'd do it legally, unlike the club, but it would be done and the club's hands would be washed free of that problem.

She wasn't even out of breath and zero shake could be heard in her voice when she said, "Now... I don't care if you've never taken orders from a woman before. But when a woman wearing a badge gives you one, you might want to listen next time."

He had learned a long time ago, once he was in custody, to keep his mouth shut, so he said nothing.

Let the uniformed assholes do all the talking and once representation was obtained, then communicate through the attorney. But not a fucking minute before. Because those fuckers could and *would* use everything he said against him.

Those Miranda rights were the only rights he had once he was detained.

"And you're right. I'm not your mommy, your sister or your woman. I'm also not your *darlin'*. I'm an officer with the Manning Grove PD. You seemed to have forgotten that and needed a little reminder."

He gritted his teeth when he realized she wasn't done.

"All I asked you to do was stay away from this area. You didn't. I asked you to step back. You didn't. So, I really don't give a fuck how you don't take orders from a woman because right now you no longer have a choice." She dropped her mouth close to his ear. "Here's the thing. You treat me with respect, and I'll do the same with you. Now, think carefully before you answer... Do I need to call for backup? Are you going to continue to be a dick?"

Fuck you! screamed through his head. He was trying to keep his cool but he was failing. He was beginning to spiral down to the place he always landed whenever he was taken into custody.

Every fucking time.

He needed to keep his shit together. With what she said, it sounded like she was only teaching him a lesson. If he fought or insulted her, that lesson would quickly turn into an arrest.

It wasn't only him he needed to worry about anymore. It was his club, along with pissing off Trip and Judge. Everyone would be ticked if he ended up doing time, not only for breaking parole, but for any new charges she could get to stick.

Resisting arrest. Possession of the weapons. Trespassing.

Tick, tick, tick. Each charge adding on to the time his parole officer would give him for violating parole. He'd be locked up for fucking months, if not a couple more years.

He also had a niece to help raise. A baby girl who now smiled and did "grabby hands" whenever she saw him. And cried when Rook didn't hold her.

Dyna might not be able to talk yet, but he *heard* her. And he, Cage and Jemma were determined to do everything in their power to give her a good life. Especially after Dyna's birth mother dumped the baby because she didn't want her. Just like Bebe dumped him and Cage. And Jemma's parents had been pieces of shit, too.

Between them, Dutch and the club, Dyna would never feel unwanted. Not for one fucking minute.

But he hated this shit. Being forced to comply. Not only by a pig, but a female one.

He blew out a breath and reluctantly announced, "Done bein' a dick."

"Sorry, what?"

She'd heard him. What a bitch. "Done bein' a dick!" he yelled.

"Are you sure?"

"Gonna let me go if I am?"

She didn't say anything for way too long. Eventually, the pressure from her knee disappeared, allowing him to breathe a little easier. "I have every right to take you in, Rook. You have broken almost every condition of your parole. And I'm sure you've broken the rest, too, just not in front of me."

None of that was a lie.

"But I'm interested in what the hell is happening here. Why you guys are stalking the Shirleys and what's also going on up there in their compound. I saw the van. I couldn't see who or what was inside, but I want to know. I'm assuming you do."

"Don't know shit."

"You might want to wait until I remove the cuffs before

lying to me." She sighed and when she unlocked the cuffs, he sighed, too. But his was one of relief. "Get up. Don't do anything stupid."

He planted his palms into the dirt and pushed himself to his knees.

"Were they too tight?" she asked, watching him rub his wrists once he was back on his feet.

"Yeah."

"Too bad."

He stared at her. Yeah, he did not like women like Jet. He preferred them to be soft, pliable and willing to please.

The woman before him was none of that.

She acted like a hard-ass and thought she was tough. She would never be pliable for any man. She'd be a fucking thorn in her man's side his whole fucking life. Making him miserable by fighting him at every turn and with every decision.

Fuck that, Rook wanted a woman who did what she was told.

If he ever claimed an ol' lady, he wanted one who, when he told her to drop to her knees, she'd do it. Not ask questions. Not argue.

Hell, maybe Jet was a dyke. Preferred pussy over dick.

Though, if that was true, it didn't make sense why he'd caught her staring at him at the garage like she had. Didn't matter who was talking to her at the time, she still kept her attention on him.

Could go back to that fantasy thing. The forbidden fruit. The fruit being him.

Though, not literally. He wasn't into men. Never had been, never would be.

"Am I free to go, *officer?*"

"In a minute."

"Got a fan-fuckin-tastic blowjob on my to-do list yet tonight. You're fuckin' that up."

"You giving it or getting it?"

"Only one person in that scenario is gettin' on their knees and it ain't me."

"Then maybe I'm doing the woman a favor by keeping you here since you're two-timing her by having sex with a Shirley in the woods."

The woman was sharp, he had to admit that. But, again, sharp like an irritating thorn. Who the fuck would want to tie themselves to that?

Some motherfucking fool, that was who. The pussy better be worth the problems that went along with it.

Didn't matter, that wasn't his problem. His problem was getting the fuck out of there before he did or said something stupid and ended up face-planted in the dirt again or cuffed and stuffed into the back of her cruiser, going on a joy ride.

Or surrounded by a shitload of Brysons, all with their service weapons pointed at his chest.

Yeah, he could do without any of that.

All he wanted to do was text Crystal and have her ready, willing and waiting in his room. "Got thirty seconds of that minute left before I get in the Honda and drive the fuck away."

Her eyebrows rose but when she put her taser back in its holster, he noticed she had his gun tucked into her duty belt. He had no idea where his knife was.

He had a feeling he wouldn't get either his Beretta or Buck knife back. *Fucking son of a bitch.*

"You have the mistaken assumption that you're in charge here."

"You're mistaken that I'm assumin' shit. Right now, you

got the advantage with a fucking taser, two handguns and my knife. All I got right now is my deadly good looks."

"You forgot to mention I have a badge, too."

"Don't give a fuck about the badge, Jet. That badge ain't a bulletproof shield."

"That sounds like a threat."

"Ain't a threat, it's truth. Wearin' a badge don't make you invincible." He sighed. "We done here?"

"Know you're anxious for that blowjob, but I have a couple of questions for you first. I want to know who was in that van."

"Don't know," he lied. If she wanted to know, she could find out for herself. He wasn't doing her damn job for her.

"Are you sure about that?"

"Would I lie?" he asked.

"Yes." She didn't even hesitate with that answer.

"Then maybe you shouldn't bother askin' me questions."

Her whole body went tight. He knew he was pushing her but he couldn't fucking help it. She annoyed the fuck out of him.

"I heard your club and the clan had an issue a while back. Something to do with Levi."

If she was only mentioning Levi and not Dyna, that meant the PD was probably clueless as to what happened with that second incident. The club would like to keep it that way.

"Didn't hear a question."

"What happened?"

"You ask your cousin?" Levi, the baby Autumn gave up... Where he came from, how he came about was nobody's business but Red and Sig's and the couple who adopted him, which happened to be her cousin and fellow pig, Matt Bryson, and his doctor wife. "Figured your family's tight."

"Matt's being tight-lipped about it."

"Then maybe that's your sign it ain't none of your business."

"Anything illegal going on up that mountain, as well as down here, is my business. And why you guys are trespassing is my business, as well."

He pressed his lips together.

"Not sure why Max didn't intervene if Levi's existence—"

He cut her off. "'Cause it ain't none of his fuckin' business, either, that's why."

"Levi's his nephew. He's also the chief of police in this town, if—"

"They happy?" He was done talking about this shit with her.

She looked at him in surprise. "Of course."

"Baby happy?"

Her brow furrowed at his question, but she answered anyway. "Levi's great."

"Then that's all that matters, Jet. That's it. Nothing else. Leave it the fuck alone."

"It's just—"

"Leave it the fuck alone. Don't open a can of worms you'll regret openin'. And trust me, you'll regret it."

She stared at him. Even in the dark he could see her wheels turning. She slowly turned her head to glance up through the woods toward the Shirley compound, even though she couldn't see it from where they stood. All she could see was a bunch of trees and darkness. And whatever thoughts were running through her mind.

But he didn't like the look on her face when she turned her attention back to him.

She wasn't going to leave it the fuck alone.

Fuck no.

Nobody wanted anyone to know Levi had Shirley blood. Everyone who knew where he came from, or how he was conceived, kept their mouths shut about it. For Levi's safety and also so the kid wouldn't be judged or bullied when he got older.

He'd become a fucking Bryson the second his adopted parents held him, which was the same second he was born. And nobody was going to fuck that up.

Especially Jet.

It would be stupid to piss off her own cousin, too, just to get to the truth she didn't need to know.

"Leave it alone, Jet," he growled. "Swear to fuck, you'll regret it if you don't."

"Again, a threat."

"Ain't a threat, it's a warnin'. And you'll regret it 'cause diggin' won't affect the Fury, but it'll affect you Brysons. It'll affect that baby boy." He shrugged. "But do what ya gotta do, Jet, if you wanna fuck all that up."

She didn't say anything for the longest time. She was long past the minute she wanted from him. It was time for him to get the fuck out of there.

"Is there anything else in the vehicle I need to know about?"

Christ. "No," he lied.

"If I let you go tonight, will I see you here again?"

"No," he lied once more. Though, he hoped that lie ended up being true. They'd have to work harder on hiding any vehicle he or Easy used to return to Copperhead Road.

"Then get out of here, but... Two strikes already, Rook. I catch you here one more time, you'll strike out."

"Can I have my shit back?"

She laughed. "Right. I'll hold onto them for now."

"'Til when?"

"Until you're no longer a convicted felon."

She was being a total fucking bitch again. She knew there was no way he'd ever not be a convicted felon. He'd have to be pardoned by the governor for some of the major crimes he'd committed, like agg assault on a pig or for stealing cars, for that to happen. Which never would. No, he'd have that ex-con label for the rest of his life. There was no scraping free of it.

"You not being allowed to own or even possess weapons is not only due to your current parole for the stupid shit you did on your last conviction, it's all the prior offenses, too."

"Basically, I'm fucked."

"Should've made better choices in life, Rook."

"Guess I shoulda," he muttered.

"Well, if you want them back you can get Cage or Dutch to pick up the gun and knife at the station. But just remember, you can't own or possess them."

"Guessin' you haven't checked out Dutch's sheet."

She shrugged. "Then your brother. His sheet doesn't have anything on it preventing him from claiming them."

His sheet might not, but his past did. Only, Cage hadn't gotten caught for some of his worst offenses.

Lucky fucker.

"Or send one of the other club members who doesn't have any felonies or misdemeanors on their record prohibiting them from owning or possessing a deadly weapon."

Not many of them existed. Most of them had a past that prohibited them from having weapons. Didn't mean they didn't, it only meant they had to be careful about it.

"You have a wonderful rest of your night, Rook. I'm sure we'll meet up again soon."

He hoped to fuck not unless it was at Dutch's Garage for vehicle maintenance.

"By the way, enjoy your blowjob. Hope it's everything you dreamed it would be." She snickered and headed back to her black-and-white.

Right. Now he wasn't in the fucking mood for a fucking blowjob. Not just from Crystal, but from anyone.

That might be a first.

Fucking pigs had to ruin everything.

Chapter Three

Rook stood at one end of the table since he wasn't allowed to fucking sit at it. No, a couple of years ago when Trip and Judge visited him during his last bid in Lycoming County Jail, they'd offered him a place to land but denied him a spot at this very table while his fucking younger brother got to be road captain.

Cage sat at that table tonight, along with Trip, Judge, Sig, Deacon and even Ozzy, the only Original who had a spot on the executive committee.

So, yeah, Rook wasn't good enough to sit at the table, but was good enough to do the club's dirty work.

His ass was still chapped from his encounter with Jet last night. And the lack of getting the blowjob he needed. Tonight, he'd skip the first and make sure to get the second since he needed to get his mind off the dark-haired pain-in-his-ass who ended up in his dreams last night.

He'd woken up with a raging hard-on and ended up jerking off in his bed, and then again in the shower, to rid himself of any thoughts of that badge-wearing bitch.

For fuck's sake, he wanted to make her submit to him.

He ground his teeth. That was all it was. He wanted to be the one to put her in her place.

He wanted it to be her on her knees tonight, swallowing his dick with her crystal blue eyes turned up toward him as she swallowed his hot load down her throat. He wanted strings of saliva clinging to her lips and her mascara to be smeared by her tears from how deep he fucked her face.

That was what he wanted.

Christ.

He adjusted himself.

"Brother, the talk about Shirley women gettin' you all worked up?" Cage asked, wearing a crooked grin.

Fuck, he'd gotten so caught up in that fantasy, he'd forgotten where he was for a moment

"Need a fuckin' minute?" Judge chuckled. "If so, take it outta this room. We don't wanna watch you jerkin' your gherkin."

"The talk of teenage Shirley girls shouldn't be gettin' anyone in this room worked up," Trip growled.

Ozzy, the club secretary, raised both palms, but wore a shit-eating grin. "Not me. I like my meat more thoroughly cooked."

"I like women who ain't cross-eyed and don't have an extra tit growin' outta their back," Cage announced.

"Damn, an extra tit would be kinda cool," Deacon laughed.

"You can't handle Reese's two titties as it is," Sig razzed him while cupping two invisible tits in front of his chest.

"Don't think so?" Deacon asked with a grin. "She got no complaints."

Trip slammed the gavel a couple of times on the table,

getting everyone's attention. "Jesus. Let's get back to business."

Thank fuck. He needed to forget Jet Bryson and get back to the business at hand. "So, yeah, van came up, eight girls got out. Seemed like a big deal for the clan. They were all gathered at the main clearing mixin' and minglin' like some kinda date night."

"You said all young." Trip ripped his baseball cap off his head and raked his fingers through his hair before slapping it back on.

"If any of them were eighteen, I'd be surprised," Rook told the committee.

"You see the plate?" Trip asked. "See what state it was from?"

"No, not the way it was parked. But knowin' them, it probably didn't have one."

"Even if it only came from Ohio, hard to travel that far without one," Cage mentioned.

Yeah, Rook learned that about nineteen years ago. A hard lesson about always putting a plate on a car before driving it, even if it's stolen. *Especially* if it's stolen. Rook wondered if his brother said what he said for a reason. A reminder of what happened when Rook was fifteen.

"Don't matter where the van fuckin' came from," Judge said.

"Maybe, maybe not," Trip murmured.

"Already know pockets of Guardians of Freedom exist elsewhere. Only thing we don't know is if those clans have bloodlines other than Shirley. There could be other inbred families. Same cult, different families," Deacon said.

"Could be," Trip agreed. "No men?"

Rook shook his head. "Just the driver. Bet he's headin' back to wherever he came from."

"His hillbilly haven," Sig muttered.

"So, women—or girls, more like it—all within breeding age, right?" Trip asked.

"Yep," Rook answered with a single nod. "Probably all over fourteen and the men who we haven't taken out yet were all over them, almost like speed dating. Seven men, eight new girls. One's either gettin' a bonus or they're passin' her on to one of the older teen boys."

"Christ," Judge barked. "Fuckin' sick motherfuckers." Jury, his American Bulldog, groaned with how hard Judge was rubbing her head. But the dog's eyes were closed and she didn't lift her head from Judge's lap, so she must like it rough.

Yeah, he wanted to give it to Jet rough.

Fuck!

She needed to stay the fuck out of his head. The motherfucking bitch tased him and took his ass down. He should want to shoot her with a bullet not with his cum.

"Yo!" Trip yelled at him. "You with us? Or you back fantasizin' about underage Shirley pussy?"

Rook shook himself mentally. "So, now what?"

"Need you and Easy to keep the Clan Plan goin'. Even if you don't grab a Shirley, keep an eye out. Report back with anythin' out of the ordinary. At least anythin' out of the ordinary for a Shirley. Need to know if vans start showin' up with men. Shirleys or not," Judge said. He yanked at his long beard. "Can't figure out why they'd bring in women before more men."

Rook should tell the committee about Jet nosing around. About her finding him and Easy. While he should, that might get everyone's panties in a bind. And Rook could handle one female on his own.

He and Easy would just need to be more careful from now on. Switch up the times they go up since both nights Jet caught them it was during the PD's midnight shift. Being low man on the totem pole at the PD, she might always be stuck on midnights. He and Easy could go up early morning while it was still dark enough.

Though, getting up that early would suck donkey dick. Especially if he had to work all day at the garage afterward. If he fucked up a repair, Dutch would crack him upside the head with a wrench.

Even so, no matter what hour he and Easy hit the mountain, with winter coming they were running out of time. They would soon need to stop going up there at all, even to nose around.

"Winter's comin'," Rook reminded them.

"What is this, Game of fuckin' Thrones?" Deacon asked.

"Means cover up there's becomin' scarce. Might have to table the Clan Plan 'til spring."

"Yeah. Don't need either of you getting' caught up there. Don't need to deal with another sitch like Shade," Judge said. "In the meantime, need to keep our women and children protected 'til we got a better handle on what those goat fuckers are plannin'."

"That's why I got potential prospects waitin' downstairs," Rook reminded the enforcer.

Trip smiled and sat back in his chair. The same spot at the table and the same exact damn chair the former prez, Trip's father Buck, sat in. Trip slid right into that role like he was born for it. Which he was.

But he wasn't the only son of an Original in that room. A few of them had Fury blood running through their veins. Trip needed to remember that. He wasn't the only one who could lead the Fury. It would only take a vote—

"We done talkin' about those inbred rednecks yet so we can check out the fresh meat?" Sig asked, also sitting back in his chair with an evil grin and rubbing his hands together.

"Appreciate you findin' them, Rook," Trip said. "But you bein' their sponsor makes you responsible for them, you know that, right?"

Rook nodded. "Yeah, know it. But like Dodge, these three had my back while inside."

"All durin' the same bid?" Judge asked, surprised. The man was always suspicious of bringing new blood into the club. The enforcer would eventually do background checks on them all. He liked to know who and what they were dealing with.

"No. None of them know each other."

"Any of them from other MCs?" Trip asked.

"Not that I know of." None of the three prospective members had colors tatted onto their backs. And he'd seen all three in the shower and shirtless plenty of times. Privacy did not exist while doing time. You got to know your cellblock mates better than your woman sometimes.

"Just convicts," Ozzy concluded.

"None of them did shit to women or children, right?" Judge asked with one eyebrow cocked.

"No. Just stupid shit... like the rest of us."

A murmur went around the table. Some of them did worse stupid shit than others.

"If these three stay after we talk to them, will have room for one more in the bunkroom since it holds six. It'll be awhile before Puss for Brains and Tater Snot move into their own rooms, if they make it at all," Trip said. "Fuck, was hopin' someone with Fury blood would roll in. So far, nothin'."

Sig shot a frown at his half-brother. "Who you think's out there?"

Trip shrugged, spinning the gavel's wood handle within his fingers. "Not sure. As much as the Originals fucked and with just as many different women, you'd think there'd be fuckin' enough Fury blood out there to make a town."

"If there is, some of those might've been made unwilling-ly," Judge reminded Trip, giving him a look.

Trip's lips pressed thin and he nodded. "Yeah. Who'd wanna join an MC where your underaged or fucked-up momma was forced to submit by an asshole biker. If anythin', they'd hate this club for that reason alone even though the current Fury had nothin' to do with it."

"There were more than us, weren't there?" Sig asked. "Had to be. Stella and Jemma weren't the only girls born to Originals, right?"

"Don't need females from Fury blood, need more males to fill the ranks. There's only thirteen of us, includin' Dutch." Trip dropped the gavel to the table and scratched the back of his neck. "Thirteen makes us light. Especially when we got a wannabe militia fuckin' with us."

"Got Ry," Cage suggested.

"No," Judge answered immediately. "My boy's gonna stay on the track he's currently on. He wants to change the direction of that track after he finishes his degree, that's on him. But 'til then, his ass is goin' to college."

"Ry's pretty damn straight, too. We need some who are a bit more crooked," Ozzy said. "Brothers who don't mind gettin' their hands dirty if needed."

"Want this club to stay straight," Trip reminded Ozzy.

"You want this club to *appear* straight," Ozzy corrected their prez. "Get it right. There's a fuckin' difference."

Trip's mouth pinched tight.

"No matter what's been happenin', we still ain't the Originals, Trip," Sig reminded his brother. "You ain't Buck. Judge ain't Ox. Shit's different. You got what you wanted."

"Didn't want us to be tied up in a bunch of bullshit with a clan of rednecks," the prez muttered.

Cage shifted in his chair. "If it hadn't been for Red—"

Sig slammed his hand down on the table, making everyone jump. "Shut your fuckin' mouth, asshole, or I'm gonna shut it for you. You wouldn't have left her ass on that mountain, either."

Rook glanced at his brother and saw Cage's nostrils had flared and his jaw had clenched.

Sig would defend Red to the death. Cage wasn't blaming Red, he was blaming the situation the Shirleys put Red in. However, you couldn't tell Sig that. He was always touchy when it came to his ol' lady. And the fucker had a nasty temper that didn't take much to make flare.

"All right!" Trip yelled. "Enough! It is what it is. Now we gotta deal with it and we'll deal with it. Just wanna get it done so we can continue on the path I envisioned. Fightin' a bunch of dumb fuck hillbillies ain't it. Wanna get it done soon. Don't want that shit hangin' over my weddin'."

"We'll get it done," Judge murmured. "Just gotta do it right."

"Yeah, we said that before Dyna was taken," Cage reminded their sergeant at arms.

"Again, it is what it is," Trip said louder. "Let's move on. Discussin' shit we can't change ain't doin' us any good. What we *can* change is our numbers, if we get the right men. Rook thinks he found some. Long as they pass our inspection. If anyone sittin' at this table gets a bad feelin' about any of them, speak up. Don't matter if they can hear you. In fact, better to put them on the spot to see how they react. So, throw whatever at them and see who's still standin' at the end."

"Where they at?" Sig asked Rook.

"Waitin' downstairs with Whip and Rev," Rook answered.

Trip glanced at Sig. "Text Rev and tell him to bring them up."

Sig nodded and sent a message on his phone. Not even a minute later, boots could be heard stomping heavily up the wood steps.

"Bring them in," Trip ordered Rook.

Rook went over, opened the door and gave a chin lift to the men. Each gave him an answering one as the three men filed through the open doorway. He closed the door once they entered, shutting Rev out.

Rook had them line up at the end of the table across from Trip, where he previously stood. As they did so, Jury broke free from Judge and trotted around the table to nudge each one in the nuts like she always did.

All three newcomers took being molested by a big bulldog better than Rook thought they would.

Good first test.

Justice, Jury's littermate, yawned and reluctantly got to his feet from where he'd been curled up under the table near Deacon. He lumbered his way much more slowly over to the men, his curved tail up like a rudder as he sniffed the men's boots.

Neither dog had wagged their tail, both reserving judgement on the new blood just like the brotherhood would.

The fucking dogs were smart.

He needed to get one. A pit bull or something. Something badass. They could use a dog at the garage instead of all the cats that lived in the boneyard behind the building.

Yeah, he should get a black pittie and name it Jet.

He smothered his grin.

Trip didn't even bother to stand when he started his spiel. "Don't give a fuck about your names. If you survive this first step, you'll be assigned a prospect name. You'll keep that for your first year. You survive that year, then you get to choose your road name when you get your patches. Not 'til then. Got a bunkhouse downstairs and it's required you live here. You ain't livin' with Mommy and Daddy, or your regular pussy or butt buddy. You live here." He jabbed his index finger into the table a couple of times. "One room has bunk beds, you all share that and a common shitter. You don't like that idea? Leave now. Ain't as bad as prison, but close. *If* you make it through your first year, you get your own room with your own shitter.

"Got a kitchen full of food. You make a meal, you clean up your fuckin' mess. A brother wants you to make him food and serve him in bed while you're naked with a rose 'tween your teeth? You do so. No backtalk. You also clean up that mess. Keep yourself clean. Keep your space clean. Keep your shitter clean. The bar downstairs in The Barn is fully stocked. Don't be dumb about it. Might be asked to do somethin' at any time, better be sober enough to do it.

"You'll get prospect cuts. When you wear those you represent the Blood Fury. Take pride in those cuts, but remember they can be stripped at any time. You're gonna be treated lower than," he pointed to the two bulldogs, who were both sitting near the three men, looking bored at Trip's speech, "their shit. Kinda like how the screws treated you in prison. You think you're gonna have a problem with that? Leave now.

"Listen carefully to what I'm about to say 'cause violatin' this next rule will get more than your colors stripped." Trip leaned forward and planted the knuckles of both fists onto the table. "What happens in this club, on this farm, in the bunkhouse or The Barn stays within this club. Don't think you can keep your fuckin' mouth shut?" Trip pointed toward the way they came in. "There's the fuckin' door." Trip sat back and crossed his arms over his chest. "Rook's your sponsor. That means if you fuck up, it won't just suck for you, it'll suck for him. So, don't fuck up or you'll have to deal with him first, then the rest of us after. You got questions? Ask him. Got an issue? Take it to him. He can't fix it, then he'll bring it to one of us. But make sure it's an issue he can fix, 'cause we really don't give a fuck about your issues.

"You gotta work. That's non-negotiable like everythin' else I just told you. That means your ass is up and outta the bunkhouse when your ass gotta be outta the bunkhouse. No lazy fuckers in this club. We work so we can fill our fuckin' bellies and drink 'til we're drunk. On the same note as fillin' shit, keep your dicks outta the sweet butts."

"Any female in this club is off limits," Judge cut in. "Hang-arounds are not. A hang-around wants to fuck you, have at it. Just wrap it tight. You don't treat any of the women in this club like shit. You touch them, mouth off to them, disrespect them in any fuckin' way, you're done."

Sig leaned forward and rapped a knuckle on the table. "And by done he means you are *done*."

Judge picked back up. "Remember these names: Reilly, Tessa and Saylor. Don't even look in their direction. Don't even whack off to fantasies of them. You do, I'll know and—"

"You're done," Sig finished in a growl.

Trip took the reins back. "You listen to the orders of any patched brother in this club. You listen to any of the ol' ladies. They tell you to do somethin', you do it. I don't care if it's lickin' the mud off their fuckin' shoes. They order you to do it, you drop to your knees and start tonguin' their muddy shoes. You got that?"

Two deep "yeahs" and one whispered one rose up from the line. Rook knew exactly who whispered his answer. He sighed.

"You ain't nothin' but a slave for the next year. Remember that," Judge said.

"Also, no hard drugs on this property. Wanna get stoned? Fine. You bring in anythin' harder than that? You're gone. I don't care if you see a patched brother snortin' an eight-ball off the naked tits of a sweet butt. You better say no if he offers. You can't stay off the hard shit?" Trip jabbed a finger toward the door again. "Get the fuck out now. You end up busted for somethin', anythin' other than somethin' we asked you to do? You're gone. That means keep your fuckin' nose clean unless one of us sittin' at this table orders you to do it."

"These terms can change at any time," Judge added.

Trip narrowed his dark eyes on the three men. "Since you assholes are all still standin' there, thinkin' you wanna stay? That right?"

"Yeah," again came in unison from the three men.

"Welcome to the suckiest year outside of prison in your fuckin' life, boys," Sig announced with a shit-eating grin.

"Now we get to pick your new names. You're probably gonna hate it but we don't give a fuck if you do."

"Oh, pick me! Pick me!" Ozzy yelled, raising his hand and bouncing in his seat like he was no older than Daisy, Cassie and Judge's six-year-old daughter. "I get to fuckin' name them this time!"

Trip and Sig exchanged glances. The VP shrugged, so Trip continued with, "All right, Ozzy here's gonna give you your prospect names. That's what'll go on your cuts for now. For the next year you go by those names and nothin' else. You got that?"

More "yeahs" but quieter this time. Rook glanced at his

prison buddies, seeing none of them looking too excited. But all of them had done time and doing a year as a prospect shouldn't mean dick to them.

They'd all make it if they wanted to.

Ozzy had left his seat and now stood in front of the three men with his hands on his hips, inspecting them from head to toe while sucking loudly on his teeth.

The secretary stepped in front of Charlie Black, a light-skinned Black man who would be the first Black Fury member in the club's history, *if* he made it. The Fury had always been made up of white men, but Rook figured good men were good men and loyalty was the most important thing, not the color of a man's skin.

Charlie was one of Rook's cellmates while doing a short stint in Cumberland County Prison. Besides Dodge, Charlie had been Rook's best and closest cellie. Rook had checked with Trip about Charlie not being snow white like the rest of the Fury members and the prez had no problem with it.

Thank fuck.

Charlie would be an asset to the Fury. He got along with most people, unless he was given a reason not to. If you fucked with Charlie, you wouldn't regret it because you'd most likely no longer be breathing. And if you were unlucky enough to still be breathing, you'd wish you weren't.

Charlie was six-foot-four and built like a brick house. He spent a lot of time honing his muscles every time he did a bid. Which was a lot. Rook warned him he'd need to do his best not to go back.

"This fucker's as big as a fuckin' castle. Your name's Castle."

Charlie stroked a hand over his short black goatee. Probably to hide a grin, since the name Castle didn't suck.

Ozzy moved to the man in the middle. Fitzgerald, the

only name Rook knew the man by, was just above average height and heavily tatted. Rook had been his cellblock mate at FCI Schuylkill a few years ago. Out of the three new prospects, he was the one Rook worried about sponsoring the most. He trusted the man, for the most part, but wasn't sure if Fitz would be able to stay out of prison. The man was institutionalized. He knew not much else other than life behind bars.

He was also the oldest of the three. At forty or so, he was already set in his ways. Good or bad. His beard sported a few grays and the wiry hairs along his jaw were split by a long scar from a knife fight. That knife fight was why Fitz ended up back in federal prison. He'd broken the terms of his parole, along with a man's hand, jaw and a few ribs.

"Got a teardrop tattoo. Only stupid fucks have to advertise that they've killed someone. You think that tat makes you look tough and scary, when it makes you look like a fuckin' pussy." Ozzy jerked his head backward. "You see anyone sittin' at that table with a fuckin' teardrop tattoo?"

Fitz's narrowed, dark eyes scanned the table. "No."

"Right. We don't advertise it, dumbass. It's like never zippin' your fucking jeans and always lettin' your junk hang out. No one needs to know what you're packin' down there 'cept the slit who's suckin' or fuckin' it. Keep that shit a mystery."

"Agree with that," Trip called out. "Thinkin' you need to remove it if you wanna prospect with us. Shit like that draws unwanted attention, 'specially with the pigs. You willin' to get it lasered off if the club pays for it?"

Fitz shrugged. "Yeah, sure. Ain't attached to it."

"You got any kinda Nazi shit inked on you? Any white supremacist bullshit?" Judge asked.

Charlie, now Castle, gave Fitz the side-eye.

Fitz didn't bother looking back at him. "No."

Judge nodded. But Rook had already known that answer. He wouldn't knowingly bring that shit into the club. He knew better than to invite anyone with that kind of mindset to become a prospect.

"You're ugly as fuck, too, besides bein' dumb, so... Gonna name you Scar."

"What the fuck, Oz!" Sig yelled, just about jumping out of his seat. "Prospect names are supposed to suck ass."

Ozzy grinned and shrugged. "This stupid ass will probably keep that as his road name because he's a dumb fuck. He'll think the name will scare people just like that stupid tattoo."

Rook rolled his lips under so he wouldn't snicker. Fitz, now Scar, was probably fighting the urge to pound Oz into the ground. Rook was glad the man kept his shit packed tight. The man could do a lot of damage in a fight, but he was no match for every Blood Fury member in that room. Not to mention, the ones waiting downstairs. A man has to be smart when he was outnumbered.

Ozzy finally stopped in front of the last man. Simon was the youngest out of the three. He'd been way out of his comfort zone while housed at Lycoming County Jail. Dodge and Rook had taken him under their wing, saved his virgin ass from being tapped and becoming a jailhouse bitch, then helped him nut up. The kid had been in way over his head while wearing orange and needed some guidance. Apparently, still did.

The club would give Si the home he needed and help him become the man he wanted to be. Or at least, that was Dodge and Rook's hope for him. Si had gone to jail for something minor. The problem was, once caught in the system, sometimes it was hard to break free of it. Rook thought of him as a kid, though he was far from it. Si might be twenty-two or twenty-three. Old enough to be a man.

"Namin' you Bones, kid, since you're nothin' but skin and bones. Better work on that. A fuckin' gust of wind would blow you over."

Sig dropped his head and shook it.

Trip snorted at Sig's disgust at the names Ozzy was picking. "Won't make that mistake again."

Ozzy turned toward the table, raising both hands with the palms up. "What's wrong with those names? They suck."

"Justice, bite that motherfucker's ass," Deacon yelled. Justice got up from where he'd been sitting, yawned and moseyed back over to his daddy, taking his good ol' damn time. Deacon patted him on the head. "Okay, shit in Ozzy's bed, then, yeah?"

Justice whined and plopped his head in Deacon's lap for ear scratches.

"They better all have sleds," Trip warned.

Cage and Rook were already working on that. Only Scar owned one and it needed some work since it spent a lot of time in storage, just like Scar.

Bones needed to learn to ride. Whip said he'd teach him and then help find him a cheap used Harley for now. Whip would be a good one to pair with Bones since they were closer in age and temperament since Whip was on the quieter side.

Castle used to own an Indian but lost it in a divorce. So, they were setting the man up with an old Softail Dutch had. Castle would owe Rook's old man, but he said he didn't mind working extra to pay for it.

The prospects would be working for the club, so it would take them a while to earn enough to clear any debt incurred for their sleds, but at least they'd have a rack to sleep in, heat to prevent blue balls, a roof over their heads, food in their gut and plenty of free booze. Plus, opportunity for plenty of pussy as long as it was the right pussy.

The wrong pussy might be the last mistake they made. As their sponsor, Rook would make it clear several more times who was off limits. Not just with names but by pointing them out.

"Motion to accept these three new dog turds," Sig said loudly.

"Second," Ozzy said as he went back to his seat.

"All in favor?" Trip asked.

Everyone at the table—except for Cage who couldn't vote as road captain—yelled out a loud *aye*.

Trip slammed the gavel on the table. "Now get the fuck outta here. We got real business to handle." He pointed his gavel at the three new prospects. "Don't fuck up."

Rook jerked his chin up at his brothers, all of them wearing smirks and probably thinking about how they're going to torture the new recruits. Rook shook his head and followed the newest Fury prospects out and down the stairs.

Chapter Four

Jet leaned against the entryway wall that separated the kitchen and the living room in her aunt and uncle's farmhouse. Her eyes bounced from one Bryson to the next as they crowded into the living room. While it was a big house, with the way the family was expanding, it was beginning to feel small.

Since Teddy and Adam got married last Christmas, and Jet moved to Manning Grove right after that in January, they all decided it was best to start combining family holidays. Like today.

Everyone's belly was full from the insane amount of food served at the early dinner.

She should be getting a few hours of sleep before her midnight shift but it was difficult to pull herself away from the people she loved on Thanksgiving.

But it wasn't family or the holiday that were on Jet's mind.

No, it was what was happening on that mountain and the

reason the Blood Fury MC was involved. It had been eating at her.

It shouldn't since it didn't bother any of her fellow officers, who had been working for the PD a lot longer than her. Or the off-duty cops sitting in the room before her, including the chief of police, her oldest cousin, Max. The man who hired her. The same man who could fire her.

It was kind of funny, Max wanted to diversify his force by hiring another woman. But really, by bringing in another Bryson, he didn't quite do that. While Leah and Jet now made up the only two women on the twelve "man" force, both of them were Brysons. Leah by marriage and Jet by blood.

That made six Brysons, including the chief, working for the Manning Grove PD. Six. But it bothered Jet that five Brysons, other than her, ignored the Guardians of Freedom and whatever they were up to. She wanted to know why.

When she first joined the department last January, she got the nickel tour by her platoon leader, Corporal Rivera, who said the same thing Max had. *Leave that mountain the hell alone.*

Which meant leave the Shirleys alone. *Unless* they came to town and made trouble.

No one was to go up that mountain unless they absolutely had to and if they did, either the state or county emergency response team was to be called in to assist. Max didn't want any of his officers going up that dirt lane without heavily-armed backup.

Clearly, that meant the Shirleys were bad news.

Maybe Max wanted to avoid the same as what happened in Waco, Texas, with David Koresh. He didn't want women and children getting caught up in a war between a cult and law enforcement and possibly paying the ultimate price.

Even though she'd been warned, she'd been doing drive-bys down Copperhead Road at least two times every night she worked, looking for Rook and the other biker named Easy.

Easy.

She shook her head. She wondered how Randy Dietrich earned the nickname Rook.

Didn't matter. What did matter was she hadn't seen either of them or any other Fury member on Copperhead Road. She also hadn't spotted any more vans heading up the Shirleys' mountain lane.

It didn't mean they weren't arriving during the daylight hours. It also didn't mean Rook and Easy weren't going up there in the light of day, either. And maybe even other Fury members, too.

But those bikers had to have a reason to be heading up to somewhere they didn't belong in the middle of the night.

Jet wanted to know why. She planned on finding out, too, one way or another.

Her aunt and uncle, along with Jet's parents, were settled in next to the fire as the babies were being cuddled, the younger children played games on the floor and the older children had their noses buried in electronics. The middle generation sat around talking, laughing and drinking. With three generations of Brysons, the living room was tightly packed and loud, like normal for one of their family gatherings.

She bit back a yawn. She'd only gotten about three hours of sleep before dragging herself from her warm, comfortable bed and into a hot shower, so she could be on time for the huge Thanksgiving spread.

Maybe she could catch a little shut-eye during her shift tonight if the radio stayed quiet. That was, after she took a ride down Copperhead Road to check for any suspicious activity. She wouldn't put it past the bikers, or the Shirleys, to be up to something, even on a holiday.

Her gaze circled her family again and landed on her boss. Max was holding Devlyn, the newest Bryson born earlier this year to Marc and Leah. The chief had a soft smile on his face as he bounced his niece gently.

At this point, her Uncle Ron's side of the family was done reproducing. There were now six grandchildren on their side, not including Max's wife Amanda's special needs brother Greg, who Ron and Mary Ann also considered their grandchild.

Now the pressure was on for Jet and her brother Adam to give their parents grandchildren, too. Hopefully, they weren't expecting six. Adam wanted at least one. Being gay, he and his husband Teddy would have to bring children into the world by adoption or using a surrogate.

And Jet?

She grimaced.

She had no desire to have children at this point. Even if she had a partner to have them with. Doing her time in the Marines, then joining another male-dominated career, law enforcement, the mothering instinct seemed to have been beaten out of her. Maybe for good reason.

But then, she had time yet. She only turned twenty-nine two months ago. A lot of people were having kids later in life nowadays. Like her cousins.

"Don't get any ideas," Adam murmured behind her.

She turned to face her brother. "On having kids?"

"Yes. Teddy and I are next."

"You have at it, brother. I'd rather be an auntie than a mommy."

"For now."

Jet lifted one shoulder sloppily and let it drop.

"You'll break Mom and Dad's heart if they don't get as many grandchildren as Ron and Mary Ann. They act like it's a competition. And if it is, they're already losing big time."

She bugged her eyes out at her older brother. "Then you and Teddy better get cracking. And by cracking, I mean cracking some surrogate eggs with your sperm. Because they better not rely on me to pop out five or six grandkids."

"Only one is the plan for us right now."

"You could line up six surrogates. Three for you, three for Teddy." She grinned and nudged him playfully. "Raising six babies at the same time would be a blast."

Adam looked at his husband across the room chatting animatedly with Amanda, the hairdresser's best friend. "Let's see how Teddy does with one first."

"He'll do fine."

"With one. Six... Probably not."

"Would you want six?" Jet asked in surprise since she'd only been joking.

Adam snorted. "Fuck no."

Jet laughed.

He also laughed softly when he said, "That's why Mom and Dad are relying on you."

She shoved him. "Eat shit, brother."

He patted his very flat stomach. "I don't think I can eat anything else after that meal, so I'll pass on your sweet offer, sis. By the way, good luck staying awake on your shift tonight after all the turkey and carbs."

"When do you work next?"

"I'll be there bright and early tomorrow morning to relieve you."

"Good. Don't be late," she teased.

"Like I'm ever late," he scoffed.

He never was. In fact, Adam arrived on station for his shift way too early. You can take the man out of the Marines, but not the Marines out of the man.

Or woman.

She was just as punctual. For most of the Brysons, arriving on time was considered being late.

"Speaking of work, I need to talk to Max."

Her brother frowned. "Today?"

"Why not?"

"Uh, because it's Thanksgiving, dumbass. He's in a good mood right now and I'd rather you not get him cranky."

"I won't get him cranky. Promise." She made sure he noticed her fingers crossed behind her back.

"Yeah, right." He sighed, then suddenly his whole demeanor changed, he almost went electric. "So... speaking of reproducing..." Adam grabbed her arm and dragged her into the kitchen.

She frowned. "What?"

He leaned close and whispered, "We're pregnant."

"What?" she yelled. That was the last news she expected.

Adam clamped a hand over her mouth. "Quiet!" He released her but gave her a warning look.

"Oh. My. God. Adam!" Not only was that exciting news for Adam and Teddy but that took some of the pressure off Jet to "find herself a good husband and settle down."

He scowled at her. "Don't make me regret telling you."

"You found a surrogate?"

"Yes. But we were keeping our search hush hush for good reason."

Jet didn't blame him. Being gay didn't relieve Adam of any of the same pressures to procreate that their parents put on Jet. In fact, now that Adam was married, those pressures had increased.

"Is she pregnant by you or Teddy?"

"Does it matter?"

"No!" She tried not to squeal. "Adam, I'm so happy for you both."

"This stays between us for now. It's early in the pregnancy yet and we don't want to get everyone excited only to have something go wrong."

"Nothing will go wrong. But you haven't even told Mom and Dad?"

"No."

"Do we get to meet her?"

"No!" Adam almost yelled and his blue eyes went wide. "I'm not subjecting her to this family."

Jet laughed. "She'd be adopted in no time."

"That's my worry. It would be like having a baby with a family member."

"Yeah." Jet wrinkled her nose. "But wait... Did you..."

"No!" Adam made a "yuck" face that made Jet snort. "We both," he jerked his fist back and forth, "into a cup and they," he swirled his finger around, "so we don't know..."

"Okay." Jet raised a hand to stop him, pretending to gag. "Thank you for that visual, brother. One I didn't need."

"Well, you asked."

"My mistake. How the hell is Teddy not bouncing all over the room, screaming the news at the top of his lungs, tossing confetti and doing pirouettes?"

"I threatened to divorce him if he did."

"No, you didn't."

Adam laughed. "Okay, truth? I threatened him with no sex."

Jet sighed. "More TMI."

"You asked."

"You could've made up a lie."

"I did and you didn't believe me."

She laughed. "True."

"Anyway, keep your mouth shut."

"Can *I* at least meet her?" Jet asked. She was dying to meet the woman willing to give the gift of a child to her brother and brother-in-law. She knew they had been struggling to find the right surrogate, not only one similar in looks to either Adam or Teddy but one who was willing to carry the baby of a gay couple.

"No."

"C'mon, Adam."

"No. You'll meet the baby when he or she gets here."

"Or they."

His brow wrinkled. "They?"

"Multiples are always possible with AI."

Adam groaned and actually turned a bit pale. "Shut your mouth. I better hear only one heartbeat when we go to the first ultrasound."

She grabbed her brother's shirt, went up on her tiptoes and pressed a kiss to his cheek. "Seriously, though, I'm really happy for you both. I know you've wanted this for a while. Teddy's going to make a good mommy."

Adam laughed. "He'll be a mess."

"That's what you love about him. That's what we all love about him. He's the rainbow glitter to your boring dull steel."

Her brother smiled and his normally piercing blue eyes went soft. "Yeah, he is. All right. Now I need to drink a shot to forget the possibility of having more than one baby."

"Just think, you could get Mom and Dad caught up to Ron and Mary Ann with just one pregnancy."

"Sometimes I hate you."

"Don't lie. You love me."

"Don't bet on it."

Jet grabbed his arm before he moved away. "Hey, do me a favor? Ask Max to come in here without making a big deal out of it."

He arched a dark eyebrow. "What do I get for that favor?"

"I'll stay quiet about your sextuplets."

Adam rolled his eyes. "You would anyway."

He was right. Growing up, they had always kept each other's secrets. Especially the one when Jet figured out Adam was gay long before he did. Then they both kept it from their parents until he was ready to come out. Unfortunately, that took a lot longer than Jet thought it would. Adam had been worried about their father's reaction, a Marine and cop himself.

He shouldn't have.

They were lucky they had such a loving, supportive family. Not everyone did. Being a cop herself, she saw that way too often. Neglected and abused kids. Forgotten family. Parents who kicked their children out because they weren't straight. Or because they dated out of their race or religion. Or whatever.

Sometimes parents were just looking for an excuse to shed themselves of their own children. It made no sense to Jet. Why have them if you're looking for the smallest excuse to cut them out of your life?

Max coming into the kitchen pulled Jet from her thoughts.

He no longer had the soft look on his face as when he was holding Devlyn. "You want to talk about work now? We couldn't do it at station?"

"You have me on midnights, Max. When are you ever at station at the same time as I am?"

His eyebrows shot up. "You could wait for me at the end of your shift."

Maybe. But most of the time she was dog-tired and needed to crawl into bed. She hated midnights. They tended to be boring. If there were enough people working, they usually rode two in a car at night. But lately, their shifts were light, so she'd been working by herself.

However, most of her fellow officers, including her brother and cousins, were only a call or text away from backing her up, even at three in the morning. Everyone on the force was required to live in the PD's coverage area for that reason. A quick response time could save a life.

"Something's been bothering me and I need to ask you about it."

Max sighed, planted his hands on the counter behind him and leaned back against it. "Shoot."

"Copperhead Road..."

Max's body transformed before her eyes. His jaw became rock hard, his blue eyes intense and every muscle in his body went solid. "Jet..."

"Max, it's bugging me. That mountain is a part of our jurisdiction. We're told to stay out of there, but they have to be up to no good. So, they get to break the law when the rest of the citizens don't?"

"Who says other citizens don't break the law and get away with it? We all do."

"Minor shit. Jaywalking, speeding, rolling through a stop sign, sure. But something bigger is going on up there."

"Says who? Have you gone up there after you've been told not to?"

Not yet. "No. I saw a van go up there full of people, I couldn't see who was in it."

"So, you've been nosy."

"I can't just look the other way if something's wrong."

"Vehicles come and go from that compound, Jet. The Shirleys even come into town to shop. But as long as they aren't stirring up trouble in town, they can rot up there for all I care."

"What if they *are* stirring up trouble?"

Max narrowed his ice blue eyes on her. "What trouble are you talking about?"

"Well, how the hell do you think Matt and Carly got Levi?"

Her older cousin blinked. "Because Autumn wasn't ready to be a mother and the father had skipped out on her."

"That's what they told you."

His spine snapped straight and he pushed himself off the counter. "Did my brother *and* employee lie to me?"

Jet pursed her lips. *Shit.*

"Are you saying Levi is tied to that clan somehow?" Max demanded.

"I... No." *Fuck.*

"You better not be lying to me, too." He shook his dark head. "Stay away from them, Jet. That's an order."

"They're breaking the law, Max." Though, other than them not having driver's licenses, vehicle registration and insurance, she had no proof of what was rumored and what was suspected. Yet.

"They break the law the second they're born. They don't exist on paper. They all live off the grid. They've been living like that for decades."

"What about the moonshine they're making? They might even be cooking meth."

He cocked an eyebrow at her. "Have you seen it firsthand?"

"No, I've been *ordered* to stay off the mountain. It

surprises me, Max, that you'd bury your head in the sand when it comes to the things they're doing up there."

"*Might* be doing. And at least I still have my head. I need you to keep yours, too. I don't want you going up there because I don't want you dead."

"You think I can't handle myself?"

"Did I say that?" His deep voice got louder and anger tinged his words. "I can't lose one fucking officer, Jet. Not one. And you're more than an officer, you're family."

"But I have a job to do."

"That *I* hired you for. But I have a job to do, too. Keeping my people breathing. I do not want to get into some gun fight with a bunch of armed rednecks. People will die. It'll end up being a nightmare for this town, which relies on tourists visiting to survive. We don't mess with the Guardians of Freedom, they don't mess with us."

"Basically, turn a blind eye."

His jaw shifted. "Don't make me regret hiring you, Jet. If you need a reminder, you're still on your probation. You're at will right now. Let's not forget that."

"What if it's more than moonshine?"

He jabbed a finger in her direction. "If I find out you went up there, I'm firing you. Take this as your only warning. Because I will not be the one to knock on your parents' door," he jabbed the finger toward the living room, "to give them my condolences. Do you understand me?"

Jet pinned her lips together and nodded.

"Now, why don't you go home and get some sleep before your shift."

That wasn't a suggestion but an order.

She opened her mouth but he stopped her with, "You're the youngest and the greenest officer on my force, Jet. When your chief tells you to do something, you do it."

"I thought today you were my cousin."

"I was until you brought up this shit. One thing you'll notice is when our family gets together, that's what we are, family. Nothing more. When we're at work, we're co-workers, not family. You need to learn to separate the two. It's why it works for us. Don't mess it up, Jet, by discussing work during family time. And let's keep family shit out of work time."

She nodded again. "Sorry."

But she really wasn't because now she knew exactly where the chief stood on the Shirley matter.

She would either have to sit on her hands and ignore whatever was going on up there and what the MC was doing on that mountain, or she'd have to find a valid reason for the PD to get involved without getting herself fired. If she did, that would suck and make it harder for her to get hired at another department. Especially if it was her own cousin firing her.

She loved her job and was lucky Max hired her since her former department had sucked. The male officers constantly disrespected her for being a woman doing a "man's job" and called her a lesbian, and worse, behind her back. Or maybe they didn't realize she heard them because they said it enough and didn't try to say it quietly.

A couple of the officers there had actually suggested that she prove to them that she wasn't gay by having sex with them. While she had told Max she was having difficulties with her former department, she hadn't dug deep into the details. If her cousins or brother, or even her father and uncle, both retired cops, had found out how she'd been treated, they would probably go have a word with those officers.

And she wasn't having that. She could handle it herself. Just like she could handle the job.

Just like she could handle a couple of bikers doing something they shouldn't.

However, they knew what was going on up there. So, if she couldn't go up there herself, they were her best bet to get the proof she needed so Max would take action.

Not that either would want to talk to her, but maybe she could convince them.

Or one, at least.

Maybe she'd have to pay that man a little visit and do some careful negotiating.

Chapter Five

Rook carefully carried the small dented metal bowl outside, trying not to spill the water on himself. Stepping out into the bright morning light, he squinted as he glanced around the front parking lot of Dutch's garage looking for the mini-monster.

A fierce yapping promptly commenced under one of the vehicles scheduled for repair parked in a spot along the side.

"Cool your jets, asshole, I'm bringin' you fuckin' water."

He went over to where the food bowl sat. He glanced down at it and toed it with his boot. Half-empty. Most likely because a raccoon or possum ate some during the night. But he guessed the large night rodents didn't like to eat Mexican.

Especially a nasty little shit with a big mouth.

The Chihuahua scurried from under the Chevy where it was hiding and lunged in Rook's direction before circling back to its hiding spot.

"Don't make me rethink givin' your puny ass food and water." And a fucking box with a blanket to keep the little shit's ass warm at night since it wouldn't let any of them catch him. Or her. It. Whatever.

When he'd shown up at work two days ago, the little asshole was running in circles in the middle of the front lot, doing what it did best. Barking. And it had been barking and showing its miniature alligator teeth ever since, too.

They were hoping it would find its way home. No such luck.

Or that its owner would come looking for it. No luck on that, either. The former owner was probably thanking their lucky fucking stars the little bastard was gone. Or they'd been the one to abandon it on the garage property. A drop and dash.

This was the third morning he'd arrived to find the fucker still here and still alive. If the coons and possums didn't want it as a snack, maybe an owl or hawk would. And a snack it would be since it might be only three pounds at most.

That first morning when he'd spotted it, he went inside and found his father. "Whose fuckin' dog is that?"

"That what it is?" Cage asked. "Thought it was a rat that taught itself to bark. Rats are pretty fuckin' smart, you know."

"That thing's uglier than a rat," Rev called out from where he stood under a lift. "Hell, it's uglier than Possum. And that prospect's butt ugly."

Rook snorted at that truth as Dutch shrugged. "Been out there all mornin'."

He sighed. "Assholes are droppin' off dogs now, too?" Kittens were always being dumped at their garage. Even a baby had been abandoned once on the property. That was how they found Dyna. Dropped off in a box like a litter of unwanted kittens. "Anyone try to catch it?"

Whip came out of the office and raised his hand, which sported a few Band-Aids. Five, at least.

Rook's brow lifted. "Christ, that little fucker do that to you?"

The young mechanic nodded. "Yeah, went to pick it up and it snapped at me like a fuckin' crocodilly."

A what? "Should we shoot it?" Rook asked his father.

"Don't you dare!" came a female yell from inside the office. "Nobody's shooting it!"

"Don't get your thong in a wad, Reilly," Rook yelled back to the shop secretary. "Christ." Reese's sister could incinerate a man alive without blinking, but when they talked about shooting a four-legged pest? That was a no-go for her.

Women.

"Didn't you say you wanted a pit bull?" With hands on his hips, Cage stood in the open doorway and jerked his head outside.

Over his brother's shoulder, Rook could see the little black and tan short-haired terror standing out in the middle of the lot. Even from where he stood, Rook could also see it shaking on three legs, one foot hovering in the air with its tail tucked and glued to its own belly.

"That don't look like no pit bull," Rook muttered, moving closer to Cage to stare out past him.

"Right. Those little ankle-biters are worse."

"It got tags?" Rook asked him.

"Go catch it and see," Rook's brother suggested with a grin.

"Someone needs to catch it. It might scare off customers."

Cage shrugged. "Any time someone walks through the lot, it runs away barkin' like it needs to bark just to propel it forward. Like when Tater walks and farts."

Rook side-eyed his brother. "Propel's a big word for you."

"No bigger than douchebag."

Rook narrowed his eyes on his younger brother. "Sounds

like you finally got the road name you deserve. Jemma call you that when she's ridin' your pencil dick?"

"No, she calls *you* that when she's ridin' my monster cock." Cage grabbed his crotch and shook it.

"At least she's thinkin' of me while fuckin' you."

"Yeah, she's really into gay porn. You know, when one man's churnin' butter in another man's ass. She figured you became an expert at that with all the time you did inside."

"It ain't gay when you're doin' the churnin'," Rook said.

"Guess your butt buddy told you that."

"He told me a lot of things."

Cage had whacked his arm, shook his head and walked away, throwing over his shoulder, "All whispered romantically into your ear in the dead of night."

Rook snorted at the memory from the other day, but that snort quickly disappeared as he now watched the Chihuahua eyeing him suspiciously when it took a few tentative steps toward him.

Maybe the fucker was hungry.

Rook toed the food bowl and yelled, "This shit's for you, you little rat bastard!"

The dog skirted away in a fresh frenzy of barking.

"Shut the fuck up. Don't you know you're not supposed to bite the hand that feeds you?"

He had tried to capture the dog that first day. And the second day. Rook wasn't so sure he was going to try it again today.

The dog was like a woman. Loved to be difficult. When you tried to give it a little loving, it snapped at you.

Rook stepped away from the bowls, squatted down and held out his hand. He waited there for a good ten minutes with the rat dog peeking out at him from under Rev's old

Bronco, occasionally letting out a single bark to remind Rook how ferocious it was.

Maybe he *should* get a pit bull. It would rid them of the four-legged problem they already had and maybe some of those stray cats out back, too.

He pursed his lips. His arm was getting tired by keeping it extended. Fuck that thing, he had work to do. He dropped his hand, stood up with a groan and gave the dog the finger. "Fuck you then, asshole."

He caught movement from the corner of his eye. It wasn't the ungrateful dog, fuck no, it was a Manning Grove PD cruiser pulling into the lot. He turned his single finger salute to the person driving the pig mobile. Then held it there until the vehicle pulled up next to him and the driver's side window rolled down.

"Well, hello to you, too. You need to learn how to greet people better, Rook."

"Way I do it has worked the last thirty-four years. Why should I change now?"

Jet's lips twitched. "You can put it away now."

"Depends on why you're here."

"Maybe I'm here to drop off this car for service."

Rook dropped his hand and shook his head. "Lies. I know it's not on the schedule."

"Maybe I only called Reilly a little while ago."

"More lies."

Jet smiled. And, *fuck*, when she did he had a hard time hating her. She took his insults like a pro and she had a stronger backbone than most men. She probably liked to be bossy in the bedroom, too.

He wasn't into that shit.

He was into the woman begging, not him. Jet would never be that type of woman. No. She'd suffer first before pleading for what she wanted. She'd break before she begged a man for anything.

Rook's eyes narrowed on her. He'd like to break her.

Make her walk naked across a room on her knees until she was at his feet, begging for his dick.

Christ. That thought just gave him a half-chub.

He shook himself mentally.

"You okay?" One of her sculpted dark eyebrows rose and she rolled her lips under.

No. He wasn't.

Jet was the last woman he should be having that fantasy about.

The very fucking last.

"Was okay 'til you showed up." At least that was somewhat true.

Her head turned as they heard a few yaps coming from behind Rook's sled. The little bastard was now peering at them through the rear wheel spokes of his '14 FXSB Breakout. If that dog lifted his leg on Rook's pride and joy, he *would* end up using the rat as target practice. Fuck Reilly.

"That your dog?"

Rook answered, "That ain't a dog."

She frowned at the creature. "Why is it running around loose?"

"'Cause it can."

"There are leash laws, Rook."

"It's on our property. Mind your own fuckin' business instead of harassin' us."

"I'm not harassing you. I just never saw it here before."

"Didn't know you were keepin' track of our pets, too."

Her lips pressed thin. "It's going to get hit by a car."

"Good."

"Good?" She turned wide blue eyes up to him. *Fuck!*

Those eyes. Peering up at him through those thick, dark lashes.

"Would serve that motherfucker right."

"Why's that?"

"'Cause it thinks it's a pit bull in a three-pound body," he answered.

"Chihuahuas are like that."

"That what it is? Thought it was a rat."

"You don't know? Thought it was your dog."

"It is."

"Mmm hmm. What's its name?"

"Jet."

She blinked up at him. Once she recovered, she muttered, "Funny."

"Ain't funny. The little fucker's name is Jet."

"Why did you name it Jet?"

"So when it pisses me the fuck off, I can dropkick it."

She tilted her head to the side and stared up at him. "You hate the dog that much."

"Nope, hate you that much."

"Well, the feeling's mutual."

"Then why you still talkin' to me?"

"Get in."

Say what? "You fuckin' kiddin' me?"

She jerked her head toward the passenger seat of her cruiser. "Get in, Rook."

"The only way I'm gettin' in that pig mobile is if I'm doin' it unwillingly by bein' cuffed and stuffed into the back."

"If that's your fantasy, I can make it happen."

"Got a lot of fantasies and none of them include you."

She sighed. "You want to talk here? We can talk here."

"Got nothin' to talk about, Jet. Unless you're droppin' off

this cruiser for service, like you lied about. Reilly's in the office, she'll take the keys and write up the work order."

"I'm not here about the car."

He hunched down to look directly into the driver's side window. When their gazes locked, he said slowly, "Then fuck off."

Her eyes narrowed just slightly but still held his. "Not going to do that."

"Yeah, you will."

"I think you're mistaken."

"Made plenty of mistakes in my fuckin' life and this ain't one of them."

"I could've taken you in that last time I caught you on the mountain, Rook. I gave you a break. Now I need you to give me one."

Huh. She wanted to use that night as a bargaining chip. Or blackmail. He should've known his freedom had strings attached.

He straightened, glanced behind him at the garage, then back at Jet. *Fuck.* He wasn't willingly getting into a cage that had its own cage. No fucking way.

"Would you rather me go pick up Easy and talk to him?" she asked.

"Would rather you fuck off."

"That's not going to happen, so choose. You or Easy."

Damn, this woman did not give up.

He pursed his lips and stared down at her as she stared back up at him. She slowly dropped her dark sunglasses from the top of her head back over her eyes, hiding them. "Get. In."

"Dutch will have a fuckin' fit if I just leave."

"Then go in and tell him you need to go on a test drive with me to listen to the noise I hear in the engine."

Christ. The woman was far from dumb.

His left eye began to twitch. "Don't like you givin' me orders." He rubbed at it.

"Don't care."

"You should."

"Why?"

"You don't wanna be my enemy, Jet."

"I think that ship has sailed. But actually? You don't want to be mine."

"You talk tough for someone with tits."

She smiled at the insult. "And you talk tough for someone with tiny nuts. Heard they're the size of almonds."

"Then you won't choke on them when they're both in your mouth."

She dropped her head and her chest rose and fell in slow motion. When she twisted her head and glanced back up at him, she was still grinning.

That pulled a reluctant smirk from him. He shouldn't like sparring with her this much, but she was a good opponent and held her own. As good as any of his club brothers. "Goddamn it, wait here," he muttered and went in to tell Dutch he was heading out on a test drive with Jet.

A few minutes later, with the rat bastard snapping at his heels, he climbed into the passenger seat and said, "Run that little asshole over on your way outta the lot."

"I'm not going to do that," she murmured, putting the black-and-white into Reverse and backing it around.

"Bet you don't take orders from any man."

After putting the vehicle into Drive, she turned her head to stare at him. She opened her sweet mouth for a fraction of a second, then snapped it shut. With a shake of her head, like he wasn't worth her time, she hit the accelerator and shot the Ford like a rocket out of the lot and onto Main Street. He was surprised to see her heading out of town instead of toward the pig pen.

"Where we goin'?"

"You worried?" she asked.

"Does it look like I'm worried? Told you this before, that badge don't make you invincible."

"Do you hate all cops or just me?"

"Really need to ask that?"

"I've seen you be civil with some of my fellow officers," she admitted.

"Yep."

"So, it's only me, then."

"Nope."

She sighed and kept driving, taking a back road out of town.

"Why am I in this cage, Jet?"

She shot him a quick glance before turning her attention back to the road. "I didn't put you in the cage. You're sitting in the passenger seat."

"Know what I mean."

"Why do you call cars cages?"

"'Cause that's what they are," he answered.

"Can't be as bad as the cages you spent a lot of time in."

"Gonna keep mentionin' my record?"

Her fingers tightened on the steering wheel. "No."

He stared at her fingers. Slender with short nails. Plain. No color on them like most women. Not a ring in sight, either.

He lifted his gaze from her hands to the side of her head. With her long, straight hair pulled up and back, he could see her ears. Double-pierced with simple gold balls. Nothing someone could easily grab and rip from her earlobes, like the big-ass hoops some of the sweet butts wore.

He let his gaze slide over her profile. The shape of her nose was kind of cute. The curves of her parted lips tempting.

"What are you doing?" came out of her on a ragged whisper.

"Eyein' up my enemy." His nostrils flared and he dragged his attention away from her.

"We don't have to be enemies, Rook."

"Yeah, we do."

"We could help each other out."

He didn't like that suggestion one bit. "That why I'm in this fuckin' pig mobile?" When she didn't answer, he said sharply, "What game are you playin', Jet?"

She still didn't answer, instead she turned the wheel she was gripping so hard that her knuckles had turned white. He glanced out of the windshield to see where she'd turned off.

Nowhere. That was where.

They were in the middle of fucking nowhere.

"Not likin' this, Jet. Not at all. Ain't gonna be accused of doin' somethin' to a pig when I didn't do shit. Ain't gonna be set up like that."

She put the shifter into Park and glanced at him. "Get out."

He glanced around. If she made him walk back to town from here, it was a hell of a walk. He was only wearing his coveralls over a pair of jeans and a long-sleeved thermal. His phone was back at the garage on his Snap-On tool box where he kept it while he worked. He should've fucking grabbed it.

Dumbass.

"You got somethin' to say, say it. Don't need to get out."

"Get out," she ordered again.

His heart now pounded in his throat. He was a little more worried than he should be. Jet might be a woman with a badge, but he'd taken down plenty of bigger motherfuckers than her. Ones who wouldn't blink twice before killing some-one. Jet would always think about it before doing it. That alone made her vulnerable.

She'd deny she would, but it was human nature before taking a life. Unless you had no soul. Or a damaged one.

He pushed out a breath. "Get in, get out. Just like a fuckin' woman. Can't make up her goddamn mind."

She pushed her sunglasses up to the top of her head and gave him an impatient look.

He sighed. "Gonna shoot me?"

"No."

"Gonna leave me here?"

"No."

"Why we here, Jet?"

"To talk."

He frowned, then shook his head. "Don't wanna talk to you."

"You made that clear, but this is important."

"To you. Not to me."

"How do you know it isn't important to you?" she asked. "You haven't heard what I have to say yet."

"Just fuckin' say it, then. You didn't need to bring me out here and I don't need to get out of this fuckin' vehicle for you to talk."

"Why are you so worried?"

"'Cause I don't trust you."

"What have I done to you that made you distrust me?"

"Uh... how 'bout tasin' my ass and then cuffin' me in the fuckin' dirt?"

She shrugged one dark blue uniform-covered shoulder. "You deserved that and also to be arrested. I didn't arrest you, Rook. You should be appreciative of that fact."

"*Riiiight*," he drew out. "So, you brought me out here for me to thank you for not arrestin' me."

"No."

"Christ. Then what the fuck for? Losin' my patience here." Her smile made him crankier than he already was. "Don't fuckin' smile."

Her smile widened.

He shook his head. "You're awful fuckin' brave bein' out here in the middle of nowhere alone with me."

"Why's that? Do you want to hurt me?"

His nostrils flared and he turned his head away from her to stare out the passenger-side window.

Right now, he didn't want to hurt her, but he did want to wipe that fucking smile off her face. Just not in the way he'd do it to any other cop. He wanted to do it like he would with a woman. Because beneath all that bullshit she was wearing, that was what she was. A fucking woman.

With those goddamn soul-piercing eyes and those fucking lips that would fit perfectly around his dick. And her tits might be shapeless right now under that bullet-proof vest but he knew what they looked like in a snug T-shirt. He also knew what her ass looked like in a pair of fucking jeans.

And he fucking hated that he'd noticed.

"If you have to think that hard, then I'm thinking you do want to hurt me. Tell me otherwise."

"Don't do anythin' to deserve it," was all he said in warning.

"Again, I only brought you out here to talk."

"We got nothin' to talk about."

"Yes, we do."

He turned his head and yelled, "Then fuckin' talk, Jet!"

Chapter Six

Jet blinked at his outburst, then stared at him. "Outside," she said again, way too calmly.

Yeah, now he understood why she wanted to get out of the cruiser to talk, because sitting that close to her was bugging the fuck out of him. He had a feeling it was bugging her, too.

He needed some distance, anyway.

He shoved the passenger-side door open and climbed out, a layer of brown fallen leaves crunching beneath his boots. The only good thing about this remote pull-off along the edge of the woods was that he doubted any of his brothers would be riding by. Because, *fuck him*, the last thing he needed was for any of them seeing him talking to a pig. Willingly, that was.

Even so... "Pop the hood!" he yelled over the roof of the vehicle as she started to unfold herself from the driver's seat.

"For what?"

"In case someone comes by and sees us here together.

Dutch and the guys think we're on a fuckin' test drive. Let's at least make it look like the cage has a fuckin' issue."

She wasn't the only one with good ideas.

Without another word, she popped the hood and he strode around to the front of the vehicle to prop it open. He wandered back to the passenger-side front fender, the side facing away from the road, leaned against it and folded his arms across his chest.

"Start talkin' or I'm gonna start walkin," he ordered over his shoulder.

His gaze automatically got stuck on her as she came around the cage and stopped in front of him with her arms crossed over her chest, too.

Her dark sunglasses once again covered her eyes.

"Take your sunglasses off," he ordered.

"Why?"

"Need to watch your eyes when you say whatever the fuck you're gonna say."

She licked her lips and he felt that right down to his fucking nuts. *Damn it.*

After sliding her sunglasses off her face, she tucked them into the collar of her uniform shirt. "Better?"

No, it would be better if she was naked.

He dropped his eyes to his boots for a second, trying his best to wipe any sexual thoughts of Jet Bryson out of his head.

He couldn't go there.

He could never go there.

Even to scratch a quick, but foolish, itch.

He had to remember that he was the fly, and she was the spider who'd built a sticky web. He was not getting caught up in that shit.

"I want to work with you."

He lifted his head. "You wanna do what?"

"I've been given orders by my chief not to go up that mountain."

"No shit. You actually listened to a man?"

She ignored that. "I want to know what's going on up there."

"You ain't gettin' that from me." He'd eat a dick cheese sandwich first.

She took a step closer to him. "You've been up there. I don't know why and I don't know how many times, but you've most likely seen what the Shirleys are up to."

"No good." That was a simple answer to a very complex situation. One that Jet didn't need to get her ass involved in.

She nodded. "Exactly. If they're involved in illegal activities, I want to know why the PD isn't involved."

"'Cause your cousin's smart, Jet. Most of his family's on the force. He don't want any of you dead. If you go up there, that's what you'll be."

She shrugged. "You aren't."

He pinned his lips together.

"Why are you going up there?"

He sucked on his teeth, keeping his expression blank.

"I'll make you a deal."

Oh fuck no. "Don't like dealin' with the devil."

The corners of her lips twitched. "You have that backwards."

"Maybe." He spat a couple of feet to the right of her. "It ain't safe dealin' with the devil, Jet."

"Dealt with him before."

Rook should find that comment surprising, but he didn't. Everyone he knew had dealt with the devil at some point in their life, or still was. Some survived, some didn't. It was the risk one took.

"You know who was in that van the other week. You tell me what you know, you tell me what you see when you do your little hikes up there, and—"

"And you'll leave us the fuck alone as long as we give you intel."

She tipped her head to the side in answer.

He shook his. "Fuck you."

"Then if I catch you up there again, I won't let you walk away like last time."

He took his time tipping his head from one side to the other, cracking his neck, then cracking his knuckles. "Gotta catch us first."

"You're something else, Rook."

He smirked. "You noticed."

"That wasn't a compliment."

"No?" He pushed himself off the car and when he did so, she automatically took a step back and her hand instinctively landed on the butt of her holstered gun. Her thumb didn't unsnap the strap but it rested there. Ready.

He ignored her wide stance and leaned toward her, tipping his face down to hers since she was about a half foot shorter than him. "Here's the thing, darlin'. You ain't gonna like the reason we go up there. And we do have a reason. While I actually don't give a flyin' fuck about whether a Shirley lives or dies, they're more dangerous than you think and shouldn't be allowed to do some of the shit they do."

"Like the moonshine?"

"Moonshine ain't nothin'."

Her eyes lit up. "What else are they doing?"

"Pretty fuckin' sure I didn't agree to work with you."

"Then I'll go up there myself."

"No, you won't."

Her spine snapped straight and those blue eyes turned to ice.

But he wasn't done telling her how it was and how it would be. "I find you up there, I'm goin' right to Max."

"No, you won't."

"Try me. If you don't know it yet, you made a fuckin' mistake by tellin' me your chief don't want your ass up there. Already figured that, but you just confirmed it. I see you take one step up that mountain, gonna be givin' Max a call. Doubt you wanna be fired."

Her delicate nostrils flared and her icy eyes turned into blue diamonds, hard and sharp. "Why are you such a dick?"

One side of his mouth pulled up. "'Cause I can be."

"Let me get this straight, you'll work with my cousin by snitching on me, but you won't work with me."

"That's right. Because you're a problem and Max will solve that problem for me. I won't have to get my hands dirty to get you out of my fuckin' business." He followed that with a smart-ass grin.

"Why are the Shirleys your business?"

That flattened his grin out. "If I give you that, Jet, you gonna take me back to work and stop with this bullshit?"

"Sure."

That was a lie if he ever heard one. But he'd give her a crumb to see if she'd hold herself to a bargain. Because if she broke this deal, she'd break them all. He was not going back inside, especially for the shit he was doing up on Hillbilly Hill. If he did, he'd never see the light of day again unless it was through a razor-wire topped fence.

"'Cause they touched what was ours."

"Levi's birth mother?"

He ignored that question. It wasn't only Autumn they fucked with, but Dyna, too. And as much as Red was family now, Dyna was blood. Not just Fury blood but Dietrich blood.

Those fuckers had also shot at Trip. They'd shot Dodge and injured Ozzy and Shade, too.

If that wasn't enough, they knocked up young girls.

Rook couldn't give a shit about the meth and moonshine. Or even their weapons, as long as they weren't pointed at anyone in the Fury.

He looked at the female in front of him. She would, though.

He wondered out of everything the Guardians of Freedom were involved with what would bother her the most. Not that it mattered. He wasn't working with her and she'd be stupid to go up there by herself. She'd also be stupid to risk her career.

He'd heard the rumor she'd done a stint in the Marines, so she should know how to take orders. She should also know what happens if she defies them.

Cops as well as prison guards considered themselves paramilitary organizations, which meant they had a chain of command. Max Bryson was at the top of hers, cousin or not.

Rook considered that important bit of information.

Maybe they *could* make some sort of deal. But would she really risk her career to cover for a criminal like him?

He should test that theory. Because if they made a deal, she'd go down along with him if he got caught. Having her on his side could be some kind of insurance.

She didn't have to know all the details. He could feed her as much or as little as he wanted since she wouldn't know any different. She'd have to trust him for any info received. Which would be a big mistake on her part.

That could work in his favor. As a bonus, getting her

involved would be a good way—once the Shirley men were all gone—to deal with the women and children.

Nobody wanted to talk about that. Nobody wanted to make the decision about what to do with them. But in the end, they couldn't leave those brood bitches up there raising more Shirley spawn to only fuck with the club years down the road.

That meant, if they're going to solve the Shirley problem, it needed to be solved for good. The club learned their lesson the hard way with only giving the clan a warning. They didn't listen to it, which led his brotherhood to now doing something much stronger than a warning.

Destroying those inbred motherfuckers.

But, yeah, it was risky for them all, even though the Shirleys would never go crying to the PD. They hated all government organizations and they hated pigs even more than Rook did.

So yeah, maybe he should work with her, but leave Easy out of it. This way Rook would control the situation. Because if he didn't, she might try to.

And that could get ugly.

For both of them.

"We do this, you'd have to be satisfied with anythin' I give you." Once he realized what he said, he smirked.

If she picked up on the sexual innuendo, she ignored it. "If you agree, you can't feed me lies."

He reached out to grab her chin and tilted her face up at the same time he dropped his. "Darlin', there are always gonna be lies between us. You don't show your hand to the enemy."

He didn't miss the fact her fingers curled tighter around the butt of her gun and her thumb once again settled on the snap.

For a second, he imagined those same fingers curled around his dick.

But only for a second, though.

And that was a second too long.

Because she *was* the enemy. As long as she wore a badge, she always would be.

He couldn't forget that. Not even for the brief second he allowed himself that fantasy.

"Get your hand off me." Her warning was low, slow and spoken distinctly.

He slowly raised an eyebrow. "Or?"

"Or I'll shoot you. And not with my taser."

He stared into her blue eyes for one heartbeat, then a second one before releasing her chin. He waited a few more before he stepped back.

He did not miss the pulse leaping in her throat. Or the dilation in those eyes.

Or the way her breathing had changed.

He didn't miss it because he felt all of that himself.

She would be a problem.

Not only if he didn't work with her, but if he did.

And not because of her, but because of him.

Because, *for fuck's sake*, he was having a hard time ignoring the woman beneath the uniform.

Rook thought back to all the times she kept her gaze glued to him when he was in her sight at the garage. He was also curious about her reaction when he'd held her chin.

"You won't shoot me," he said softly.

"Try me."

Her two words weren't a challenge but much more than that. He could see it in her face and he wondered if she knew what those big eyes of hers were revealing.

She really wanted him to try her.

She really wanted him to touch her.

Maybe he should give her what she wanted. Just not the way she wanted it.

In two long strides, his hand was curled around her long neck, like a trap snapping shut on its victim. A soft gasp escaped her as he swung her around and shoved her against the cruiser where he pinned her with his hips.

Starting at the base of her neck, he slowly slid his hand up her throat, keeping his grip firm, until it hit her jaw and forced her head to tip up and her delicate throat to be stretched tight.

He stared down directly into her eyes and her throat rolled under the press of his palm.

Crushable.

He could take her life instantly.

She should be scared.

Very fucking scared.

Those blue eyes held no fear.

No. They now held the challenge her words hadn't. A dare.

Tempting him.

Alarming him.

A slow breath slipped softly from between her lips. "Decide what you're going to do. Kill me or kiss me."

He wanted to do both.

Through flared nostrils, he sucked in much-needed oxygen to prevent himself from doing either since he didn't know which one would be worse.

He felt the slow roll of her throat again.

"You should be fightin' me," he murmured. Tasing him. Shooting him. Trying to break free. At least showing some resistance.

"Maybe I don't want to." Her husky words swirled

through him, got swept up in his veins and landed heavily in his dick.

No, no fear at all.

"You shouldn't want this," he growled, his fingers tightening on her throat.

"But I do," she answered, her voice now strained from the pressure of his grip.

"I hate you, Jet," he whispered.

"I hate you, too," she whispered back.

He dipped his head and dragged his lips across hers. Not a kiss, but a reminder.

That he could easily steal her breath. Suck her soul from deep within her and keep it for his very own.

Keep her for himself.

Jesus fucking Christ. What the fuck was wrong with him?

He abruptly released her at the same time he stepped back. Creating space between them. Giving them both room to breathe, and a much-needed opportunity to clear his thoughts.

He also needed to see her clearly. Who she was. What she wore. What she was currently leaning against.

A glaring reminder of what she was.

What family she belonged to.

He abruptly spun on his boot heel and began to walk.

"Where are you going?" she called from behind him.

He didn't answer her.

He *couldn't* answer her.

He needed to get the fuck away from her.

Away from that remote spot on a quiet country road.

Away from the temptation whose name was Jet Bryson.

Because a few feet wasn't far enough. Miles weren't far enough. A fucking ocean between them might not be far enough.

For fuck's sake.

"I can drive you back," she shouted.

No. She couldn't.

He didn't want anything to do with her. He didn't want to be near her.

Behind him, he heard the cruiser's hood drop into place, the door slam shut and the Ford's Police Interceptor engine roar to life. The tires chirped as she rushed to pull out onto the road.

He kept his eyes straight ahead and walked faster, lengthening his stride. He was tempted to run, but he didn't run from anything.

Not even his own weaknesses.

Within seconds, she pulled up next to him with the passenger-side window rolled down. "Rook, get in. I'll take you back."

He continued to ignore her.

"We're miles from town."

He didn't give a fuck.

"Rook!"

He stopped dead in his tracks and so did the vehicle. He twisted his head to look at her. "Fuck off, *Officer Bryson.*"

"Rook..."

"Fuck. Off."

He was done.

With her. With this "talk." With the whole situation. And definitely with his fucked-up thoughts about Jet Bryson.

He began to walk again along the edge of the desolate road in the direction of town. He didn't care how far he was from the garage, the walk would do his stupid ass some good.

He heard the crunch of the tires on the asphalt as the vehicle rolled up next to him again. "I'll tell Cage to come get you."

When he didn't answer her, the window powered back up and the black-and-white shot past him.

A few seconds later, it disappeared over a rise in the road ahead.

If she wasn't a fucking pig...

If her last name wasn't Bryson...

He would have taken her alongside the road. Then worked hard on getting her in his bed.

But because she was, he would work harder to keep her out.

He'd made a lot of mistakes in his life and he'd make a lot more.

One thing was for sure, he'd make damn sure Jet Bryson wouldn't be one of them.

Chapter Seven

What happened on the side of the road two days ago bugged the shit out of her.

Not because Rook hadn't agreed to work with her—okay, that might be a small part of it—but because of her reaction to him.

Jet had no idea why she was drawn to such a freaking asshole.

Not just a freaking asshole, a rude and crude one, who wouldn't know manners if they bit him in the ass.

Her unacceptable reaction was a damn mystery.

She'd dealt with alpha males and their egos practically her whole adult life. While in the Marines, during the police academy and then at her first police department after she graduated.

The male egos at Manning Grove PD could also get a little annoying. From both her own family and the unrelated male officers, too.

So, why then was her ass currently planted on a barstool in Crazy Pete's?

If it wasn't so late, she'd text her mother right that second to ask her if they dropped her on her head when she was a baby. That would be the only plausible explanation.

Stella had dropped off her Jack and Coke and wandered away. It wasn't like the club president's ol' lady was going to hang out and chat with her. Neither would Dodge, the bar manager.

Or the two young guys who wore prospect cuts as they worked.

In the past, the couple of times she'd come into this bar to have a drink with her cousins, a "no colors" sign had hung outside the front door. But that had been when Pete was still alive and the Fury wasn't.

She noticed that sign was no longer displayed and even Dodge wore his colors while he worked the bar and tables. None of the patrons seemed to blink an eye because of it. Maybe because it was now well-known in town the Fury owned the bar.

On the surface, the MC seemed to be staying in their lane. Jet knew that was complete bullshit and they were swerving over the lines like a drunk driver with a .10 blood alcohol level.

Max had also warned her, after she was hired, to leave the club alone unless they crossed those lines. He had a good relationship with Dutch, one of the Originals, Cage used his classic Impala convertible to haul the chief's ass in the annual Christmas parade every year and Dutch's Garage held the service contract for the PD's fleet.

The women from the club were also her brother-in-law Teddy's clients at his salon, Manes on Main.

So, the PD and the club were intertwined more in the Grove than they normally would be in any other town or city.

Especially since Autumn, the club VP's ol' lady, allowed Matt and Carly to adopt her baby, Levi. That alone was probably the biggest and most important connection of all.

So, yes, her oldest cousin had warned her not to fuck with the MC to simply mess with them. They didn't need to be "run out of town" or "shut down" as long as they kept their shit clean.

Everyone knew shit was never clean. It was dirty, messy and stunk.

Most likely like the Fury at its very core.

She clutched her drink as she spun her stool around to face the interior of the bar. While a mirror lined the wall behind where the liquor bottles were shelved, it didn't give her a good enough view of the rest of the bar.

Being a cop, she'd learned to never have her back to the door, so you wouldn't be taken unaware. But in this particular establishment she wanted to keep her eye on not only the door, but the bar's occupants.

Or one in particular.

As the jukebox blared Mötley Crüe's *Home Sweet Home,* the man who'd caught her attention had his arms wrapped around a curvy brunette as they shuffled around the floor. They weren't the only couple dancing but the only one Jet was interested in.

The woman was stuck to Rook like a fly on sticky trap paper and Jet had no idea where her hands were because her arms were completely hidden under his cut. Jet knew exactly where Rook's hands were. They weren't hidden at all.

One was under her snug shirt with his fingers spread wide over the bare skin of her mid-back, the fingers of his other hand were tucked into the waistband at the back of her brown leather skirt, probably skimming the upper curves of the woman's generous ass. She had no idea how big the woman's breasts were because they were drilled into Rook's chest.

Jet didn't know who was doing the grinding. Him. Her. Or if it was mutual rocking against each other. Certainly not in time with the music, unless they had a different song playing in their heads.

The second Rook had spotted her sitting at the bar, his eyes had narrowed and locked on her.

She lifted her Jack and Coke in greeting, then drained half of it, but didn't look away. Nor did he. If anything, the intensity of the couple's grinding increased.

He only dropped his eyes from Jet when his dance partner giggled and glanced up at him with a huge, probably drunken, smile.

He grinned back down at her until her hand appeared from under his cut and brushed over his short hair and down his beard before disappearing again. The second the brunette planted her cheek back on his chest, his eyes found Jet once more and his grin disintegrated.

With his gaze glued to Jet's, he leaned over a little more, pressed his mouth to the woman's ear and said something that made her hold onto him even tighter and her closed eyes open.

"You should be fightin' me."

"Maybe I don't want to."

"You shouldn't want this."

"But I do."

A shiver slipped down her spine at that memory. Of what he said. Of how he said it. And the low timbre of his voice when he said it.

In actuality, Rook scared her.

Not because she was afraid of him hurting her, but

because of how her body reacted to him. She feared the man could turn her to putty within his fingers.

A man who was a freaking ex-con.

Not just a convicted felon, but one with aggravated assault on a police officer not one, not two, but *three* times on his record.

She had read the incident report of what happened when he was fifteen, the first time he'd been charged with that particular offense. Though, not the first time he'd been arrested as a juvenile.

A felon at freaking fifteen.

When the slow song ended, Rook peeled the brunette off him, whispered more words into her ear and closely followed her to the end of the bar nearest the rear of Pete's. His eyes were no longer on Jet but on the brunette's ass as she led the way.

Jet downed the remainder of her drink and stared at the now empty floor space in front of the low stage since apparently no one wanted to dance to AC/DC's *Highway to Hell*.

"Get you another?" came the deep, rumbly voice behind her. She twisted around to face the bar and the thirty-something, dark-haired, dark-bearded man who wore an equally dark knit beanie on his head, even as he worked.

The man was smoking hot.

If Dodge wasn't a club member, she'd look at him in a different light. Quite possibly the light from the lamp on her nightstand as he laid in her bed. However, he belonged to the MC and also had a criminal record almost as extensive as Rook's.

Some of his offenses were petty, some of them not so much.

Either way, he wasn't for her.

Just like Rook wasn't.

"You like working here?" she asked, wondering if, being a part of the club, he had no choice or if he did it because he enjoyed it.

"Love it," he answered in a grumble.

Dodge knew who she was, even out of uniform, so she didn't blame him for not being chatty with her the same as he would be with other customers.

But he was pretty to look at. "Why?"

"Lots of pussy." He wiped the bar down in front of her with a rag even though she hadn't left a mess. "And my place is right upstairs so it's convenient."

She could imagine he had no problem convincing any woman to follow him up those steps. None of them probably had to be three-sheets to the wind, either.

The man oozed bad boy. If he hadn't been wearing his cut, with his rich voice, she would guess he belonged to a band. Just like Stella.

With their tattoos, their looks and the way they dressed, she could see the two of them hitting the road and stages across the country. But most likely the man with the curious dark brown eyes set on her couldn't leave the state. At least for a while yet.

The truth was, even when someone was freed from prison, they really weren't free. Dodge was most likely limited to whatever the conditions of his probation were.

Just like the man standing at the end of the bar, his eyes now turned her way again. *Their* way. He was watching the exchange between her and Dodge carefully.

Similar to how she had watched the exchange between Rook and his "dance partner."

"Want another one or not?"

Jet ignored the impatience in the bar manager's question. She didn't care if her presence annoyed him. "Sure."

With a single nod, Dodge swiped her empty glass from in front of her and went to make her another drink.

She dug into her front pocket of her jeans and pulled out a wrinkled twenty and attempted to smooth it out on her thigh. She didn't need to look up to know who, in that time, had sidled up next to her. She did, anyhow, once she placed the twenty on the bar.

With a twist of her head, their eyes met and held.

She waited.

He waited.

And while they waited, her blood began to heat up and race through her veins.

"Why the fuck you here?"

That was enough to douse the fire roaring in her center and bring her back to reality. "Unfortunately, your greetings haven't improved one bit, Rook. Hopefully, the one you used on the woman currently giving me the stink eye was a little more polished."

"Not here to impress her. Or you."

"Then you've achieved your goal. With me, at least. Maybe that one there likes a Cro-Magnon man. Or at least she did until you walked away from her to go talk to another woman. Maybe you should knuckle-drag your way back over to her before she decides you're not worth the wait."

"Always worth the wait, darlin'."

She rolled her eyes, making sure he didn't miss it. "Doubt that."

"Could prove it but I don't fuck pigs."

Jet jerked her head toward the woman now talking to Dodge with her eyes still on the two of them. Somebody was acting possessively. "Is she more your type?"

"Does she have a snatch?"

Good grief, he wasn't even at the Cro-Magnon level. He just lowered himself to a Neanderthal. "Is that all you need?"

"That's all I need tonight," he answered before taking a long draw on the draft beer in his hand.

"Simple requirements for a simple man," she said on a sigh.

"Pretty much. You're the one tryin' to make my life more complicated."

"I took you walking away from me as your answer to my deal. So, you're the one making it more complicated by standing here talking to me."

"Ain't talkin' to you, Jet. Just wanna know why the fuck you're here."

"I'm only here for a drink. I didn't realize you were moonlighting here as a bouncer. I thought being a wrench monkey would pay better."

"Don't gotta be a bouncer to tell you this ain't a pig bar."

"I didn't see a sign outside preventing me from being a patron. If you didn't know, my family sometimes drinks here."

"Wouldn't care that you're here if you didn't have a fuckin' agenda."

"An agenda," she repeated softly.

He only tipped his head.

"I had no clue you were here, Rook," she lied.

He leaned in close and whispered. "Bullshit, darlin'."

She shrugged and drew an innocent expression over her face. "Think what you'd like."

Not a second later, Dodge dropped off her second Jack and Coke. Dodge's dark eyes sliced from her to Rook and back before he was smart and got out of Dodge.

She stared at her drink for a moment, wondering why she even agreed to a second one. She wasn't a big drinker. She didn't smoke. She tried to run in the afternoon after she woke up and before her midnight shift. Keeping in shape and her body clean of toxins was only habit.

When you had to stand next to men who didn't think you were good enough to do their job—who thought you weren't as strong or as tough as them—you tended to keep yourself in the best shape you could to prove them wrong.

Rook probably smoked much more than tobacco, most likely drank too much, too, and he certainly didn't roll out of bed early in the morning to go for a jog. Even so, he still looked pretty damn good.

"Dodge is trying to move in on your girl down there," she warned him.

Rook didn't even bother to glance over his shoulder to see if what she said was true. "Then we'll share her."

She raised one eyebrow. "You two are that close?"

"Hard not to be when you share a cell. Those long nights can get lonely."

Her attention left Dodge and the woman to land back on the man standing just inches from her. "That's how you met?" She hadn't compared their criminal records to see if they both did time in the same facility.

"Finish your fuckin' drink and go, Jet."

"And if I don't?"

He spun on his boot and strode back to where the brunette sat.

She guessed that conversation was officially over but she didn't get the answer of what would happen if she didn't leave.

The answer unfolded before her.

Dodge's smile was anything but innocent when Rook wrapped an arm around the woman's hips, leaned in and said something into her ear.

She reached out and slowly raked her long nails down the arm Dodge had propped on the bar as he leaned against it like a kickstand. When Rook straightened, he gave his former cellmate a chin lift and helped the woman rise to her feet.

Without removing his arm from her hips, Rook guided her around the end of the bar and through the swinging door that led to what Jet could only guess was either the kitchen or a storage room.

Jet's gaze followed Dodge's path as the bartender approached the heavyset prospect, had a few quiet words with him, then disappeared the same way Rook and the woman did.

Jet stared at that gray door as it swung back and forth a few times before finally coming to a rest. Then she stared at it some more, waiting to see if one of the men came back out.

An invisible hand squeezed her throat when neither did.

Jet ignored her full Jack and Coke, grabbed her coat and did her best not to sprint out of Crazy Pete's.

Rook's actions shouldn't affect her like this.

They shouldn't.

But, *damn it*, they did.

Rook worked his way through the dark, his mind on Crazy Pete's last night instead of where it needed to be, on where he was headed.

He needed to concentrate on what he was currently doing. Not *who* he wanted to do. He needed to scrape Jet Bryson out of his fucking brain. Even if it was with a rusty spoon.

He was fucking pissed at himself. He had planned on fucking that woman—he didn't even know her damn name—

last night, but once he got her up into Dodge's apartment, he no longer had any desire to.

Instead, he sat in a chair and watched Dodge fuck her.

But most of the time he was lost in his own damn head. Everything Dodge was doing to that chick, Rook was picturing doing the exact same thing to Jet.

Jet on her hands and knees, with him behind her, fisting her long, almost black hair so tightly that her neck couldn't arch back any farther, the cries and pleas coming out of her mouth, encouraging him to fuck her harder, to smack her ass, to pull her hair.

To make her submit.

By the time Dodge was done with the woman, Rook's hard-on was raging to the point of pain. But he still turned down the offer she gave him to fuck her once Dodge was done and headed back downstairs to finish his shift. She'd been disappointed and annoyed, but Rook didn't give a fuck.

But he *did* give a fuck about the reason he couldn't take what she so freely offered.

That Bryson bitch.

He hated her before. Now he hated her even more.

She fucked up his night and his plans on getting laid. All by simply showing up at Crazy Pete's and putting her nose where it didn't belong.

If Jet thought he'd ever work with her, she was goddamn wrong. He didn't want to be anywhere near her. Not while she wore a badge, a uniform and that tool belt of torture.

Fuck. Her.

He knew the path he took through the woods like the back of his hand now. The one he and Easy had worn down with all the times they'd climbed that mountain. First searching for Shade, then taking over the Clan Plan after he was found. Or, actually, after he returned home.

Rook had been tempted to head up Hillbilly Hill last night after he left the naked woman in Dodge's bed, still whining about not getting the threesome she hoped for.

When he'd slipped out the rear door of Pete's, he was relieved to find the stool Jet had been sitting on empty. He was even more relieved to not find her waiting out back for him by his sled.

That could've been bad. Really fucking bad.

Especially in the mood he'd been in.

He figured a trip up the mountain to bag himself a Shirley might relieve some of the frustration that had been building. To the point he was ready to fucking blow.

And if he did, it might get ugly.

Concentrate, asshole.

His warning came too late when the tip of his boot caught on something under the carpet of leaves and, before he could catch his balance, he keeled over and face-planted in the dirt with a grunt and an abrupt loss of air.

He searched for his breath, waiting for his lungs to refill, before pushing himself back up to his knees. "Fucking stupid ass. Always doing stupid shit. Got stupid ideas. Fucking up everything."

He allowed himself a few seconds more to berate himself. Then he got over it, like he always did. Wallowing in his bad luck or a shitty situation had never helped.

He pushed to his feet, wiped his muddy hands on his black cargo pants and stared up the dark path.

He should just head back down. He was too fucking distracted tonight. He could easily fuck up, which could end up being his final fuck-up.

Would anyone even care if he was gone?

Yeah, maybe someone might care. Maybe.

He hadn't been a good enough son for his mother.

For years, he had disappointed his father.

He and his brother were always on uneasy terms.

The only one who accepted him completely was Cage's daughter Dyna. That was because she was too young to know better. The baby held no expectations for her uncle. At least not yet. That day would come, though. It always did.

He skirted the main clan compound and took the left fork in the path to head higher up the mountain. Shade had told him about a cabin that was more remote and the male Shirley living in it was on the younger side. He'd be easy to over-power, especially if he didn't know what hit him.

That was the preferred way for Rook to hunt. He preferred not to be seen at all. Go up, do what he had to do and get out in one piece.

The problem was, the Shirleys had been staying in groups so it had been hard to single them out lately.

But this late at night, he was hoping most of the men had either gone to bed or to breed their brood bitches before getting some shut-eye. All except for the one or two on guard at the first clearing where their clan leader lived.

Since Sig took out Vernon Sr., his oldest son, Vernon Jr., had stepped into his boots. He'd taken his father's wives as his own and continued Senior's legacy of building their sovereign nation of inbred goat-fucking rednecks.

Rook wondered if Junior's own mother was now one of his wives.

He swallowed the rising bile and continued climbing higher through the woods. They really needed to stop for the season and begin again in spring. Cover was now sparse and the darkness of night wasn't enough, especially when the moon was out, like it was tonight. He'd talk to Trip and Judge about suspending the Clan Plan for now.

But not tonight.

No, tonight he needed this.

Then he'd find another way to work out his anger and frustration.

Billie was always an option... Whatever Rook could dish out, the sweet butt took willingly and returned the favor many times over. Sometimes he couldn't even walk after she was done. But at least both of them parted with a smile. The best part was she wasn't a clinger, a problem when it came to some of the others.

One thing was for sure, one dose of Billie's medicine lasted Rook a while.

But Jet Bryson would probably fuck that up, too. Just remembering his hand squeezing her delicate neck while her eyes held no fear... When they should've. Remembering her encouraging him to kill her or kiss her... When he wanted to do both....

It instantly got his dick hard.

The problem was, once he started kissing her, *really* fucking kissing her, he wouldn't be able to stop. Not until he took everything he wanted from her and gave her whatever she foolishly wanted in return. The raw want and need she'd been unable to hide on her face.

Or maybe didn't want to hide.

She apparently didn't give a fuck that he knew.

He'd also watched her closely when he was dancing with the brunette last night. Her reaction was the reason he took the woman up to Dodge's apartment while Jet watched. Originally, he had no plans to share her with his club brother and former cellie, until he realized he wouldn't be able to follow through with the intentions he had whispered into her ear.

Unfortunately, while he whispered those words into one woman's ear, he had imagined he was whispering them into another's. The dark-haired woman sitting on a stool at the other end of the bar.

He came to a dead stop and ground the heels of his palms into his eyes. *Stop it, you stupid motherfucker.*

He needed an exorcism.

Or a lobotomy.

He growled, dropped his hands and continued, picking his way more carefully on the dark, treacherous path that became narrower the further he went. A path originally created by whatever four-legged creatures lived within those woods.

His heart leapt into his throat and then dropped out of his chest as his foot hit something he couldn't see. Panic swept through him as his boot got caught and whatever snagged it tightened. Before he could pull his foot free, he was launched helplessly into the air like a drunk on a trampoline. He bounced a few times as the tree branch above him creaked loudly, then his body came to a rest hanging upside down by one leg like a side of fucking beef.

What the fuck!

He'd been snared.

Fucking *snared* like a damn animal.

And now he hung vulnerable in a fucking tree.

The thick tree branch above him creaked dangerously again and he hoped to fuck it didn't snap from his weight and crash to the ground, taking him along for the ride.

He'd be dead. Or wish he was.

He grabbed for his cell phone as it began to slide from his unsnapped cargo pocket. As he tried to catch it, it slipped through his fingers and he helplessly watched it drop onto the dirt below him with a dull thump. Of course, out of fucking reach.

He stretched his arm toward the ground as far as he could

and tried to reach it, anyway. The gap between his fingertips and his electronic lifeline had to be at least three feet.

"What the fuck!" he growled, trying to stem his rising panic. Blood rushed into his head, his whole chest now thumped with each heartbeat, his vision was narrowing and his ears rung so loudly, he almost couldn't hear his own thoughts.

He could very well die tonight if he didn't figure a way out of this.

Dumbass he was, he never set up the voice commands on his phone. If he had, then maybe he could've called one of his brothers for help. *Goddamn it!*

He needed to calm his spiraling thoughts and figure out a damn solution to this latest fuck-up.

If the Shirleys found him, they wouldn't hesitate to slice his fucking throat or plug a bullet between his eyes. No different than what the Fury had been doing to their clan these past couple of months.

He tried to kick his boot free from the snare, but it only tightened even more around his ankle. His attempt at wiggling his foot free of his boot got him nowhere, either. With a groan, he tried to fold his body up enough to reach the loop and loosen it.

Fuck, he needed to start working out or something. He couldn't even pull his own weight up to where he needed it.

His reach was just short. He groaned as he curled himself up again, stretching his arm and fingers as far as they could. With another groan, his body flopped back down like a fish dangling off a fisherman's line. He took a few breaths, gathered his strength and tried again.

He got a hold of his cargo pants below his knee and shimmied his pant leg up, uncovering the Buck knife he had strapped to his ankle. He needed to stay calm and take his time, so the knife didn't fall out of the sheath, just like his fucking phone, and land out of reach.

Because then he really would be fucking fucked.

If he could get a grip on his Buck knife, he could cut himself free. The snare wasn't wire but seemed to be made of paracord or something similar he could saw through. Whatever it was was strong enough to hold his weight. Only, once he cut himself free, the drop to the ground would hurt big time. Especially if he landed on his fucking head. But it was better than being caught helpless and swinging in the breeze for any Shirley to come along and find him.

He walked his fingers slowly, pulling the fabric of his pants higher up his leg until the knife was almost exposed.

Steady, keep it fuckin' steady.

The hem of his pant leg caught on the hilt of the blade. He grimaced as he tried to work it free without the knife dropping out.

Slow.

Slow.

Slow.

He released a sigh when it unhooked and the knife was finally accessible.

Christ, he'd been hanging upside down long enough that his head felt like it was going to pop off or just explode.

"Fuck!" he shouted before he could stifle it as he watched the knife slide free and tumble to the forest floor. Just like his fucking phone.

Now both his phone and his knife laid there, mocking him. Just out of fucking reach.

This was all Jet's fault. If she hadn't caught him last time with a knife on his hip, he wouldn't have felt the need to hide it on his calf. If he'd still had it on his fucking hip, he'd be cutting his own ass free right now.

But, of fucking course, she had to fuck this up for him, too.

He took a couple of deep breaths trying not to let his hatred for that woman distract him from his current dilemma.

He'd survived his childhood.

He'd survived his time in concrete boxes.

But, *fuck him*, if this was how he was going to die.

In the goddamn woods on Hillbilly Hill.

Chapter Eight

If he died like this, he was going to haunt that fucking bitch for the rest of her fucking miserable life. And if her life wasn't already miserable, that would be his first goal as a ghost.

Rook closed his eyes and ground out a "fuck" that would sear the hair off most men's balls.

He needed to think. To form a plan. To somehow get his foot free.

He refused to die like this. Not here. Not now. Not by a Shirley hand.

The last time he'd taken this part of the path, either the trap hadn't been there, or he had somehow miraculously missed it.

He was guessing the first one. He also guessed he or Easy were the target, not Bambi. He doubted the Shirleys trapped any animals, they just used their shotguns or semi-auto rifles to blast whatever they wanted to kill.

He opened his eyes. "Okay, now what, dumbass?"

If he could hook his one free leg around the snared one,

then curl his body up enough to use his pants as leverage to pull himself higher, he *might* be able to eventually reach the noose encircling his boot. Somehow, he'd need to pull himself up higher than his foot, grab the paracord and relieve some of his own weight from that snare to loosen it.

Fucking easy.

Right.

He was really kicking his own ass for not working out more in the small gym Trip had set up in one of the sheds. If he got off the mountain alive tonight, he'd make sure to start using it more. Maybe start drinking and smoking less, too.

Yep.

As he began to pull himself up his own body, he paused and held his breath to listen more carefully.

Footsteps.

Not one set. A few.

He reached for the Beretta he kept at the small of his back. His fingers found nothing.

Nothing.

Fucking. Nothing.

The gun must have been thrown out of his pants when he got whipped into the air. He had no fucking idea where it landed.

Fuck!

He was dead. Totally fucking dead.

He couldn't even protect himself.

Right now, he was as helpless as Dyna.

He began to swing, the tree limb's creaking getting louder as he tried to get his body weight up high enough to grab the bottom of his boot. If he could, he might be able to hold himself up there long enough to unlace his boot and slip his foot free.

But he was running out of time.

"Jesus fuckin' Christ," he muttered under his breath.

Maybe whoever was walking nearby wasn't there to check the trap. Maybe they were headed down to the main compound to some incestuous fuckfest and would skirt the area where he hung like a curing side of beef.

He twisted at his waist and glanced in the direction he heard the trampling of undergrowth. A single light bobbed through the woods, the beam bouncing off one tree, then another, as it got closer.

Fuck!

Whoever belonged to those feet were heading his way. They were on his direct path.

He lifted one arm to shield his eyes when the blinding flashlight beam hit him directly in his face, making it impossible to see who held it or who else was with the person leading the group. Or to know how many Shirleys just found his defenseless ass.

"We got one of those motherfuckers!" a woman crowed.

"Told you this snare trap would work!" another woman exclaimed loudly.

"Now what're we gonna do with 'im?" another woman asked.

"I got a suggestion," Rook said with a grimace. "You could cut me down and let me go."

One of the women cackled.

"Bet he's one of 'em that's been takin' out our menfolk."

Another one said, "Let's just gut him like a deer right here."

"Yeah, watch him bleed out like they did to Vern Sr."

"Cut his dick off and shove it in his mouth, too."

Rook cringed. He hadn't seen the actual deed Sig had done to the former clan leader, but he'd heard about it. At the time, he was glad he hadn't witnessed the actual act because shit like that would give him nightmares.

He especially didn't want it done to him, either. Particularly while he was still breathing. Being fed his own severed dick was not on his bucket list.

"Go get Vern, Jr."

"No. Not yet. Got a better idea. After that, V.J. can have his ass and do with 'im what he wants. But first, he's mine."

Rook didn't like the sound of that.

"What d'ya mean, Sally?"

Yeah, Sally, what the fuck do you mean?

"What d'you think I'm gonna do? One of these fuckers took my Jimmy from me, leavin' me with no man. Leavin' me with no poppa for my kids. This one needs to pay for that."

"That's what we're gonna kill 'im for."

"That's too easy. I got plans for him first. Gonna use him to make up for what he done tooken from me."

What the fuck did she mean? And what the fuck was *tooken?*

"You gonna share him? He and his kin done took my Tomlin from me, too."

"And mine," the third one said.

"There's only seven of our menfolk left right now, not includin' our boys. We could use the fresh blood."

Rook wasn't liking the turn of this conversation. Maybe he'd rather die on Hillbilly Hill. And quickly.

"Vern Jr. and the rest of the men ain't gonna like it, Sally."

That's it, woman, you tell Sally what a bad fuckin' idea it is.

"They don't gotta know if everyone keeps their trap shut!" Sally barked. "They ain't gonna know if the baby's one of theirs or this one's. They talk about bringin' in new blood.

From Ohio. Kansas. Even Alabammy. But we don't know how long that's gonna take. What do we do 'til then? Share the seven of them? There's too many of us and too few of them. An' two of 'em are my own damn sons."

A murmur ran through the women.

Someone needed to convince Sally this was a really bad idea. "Uh... Ladies..."

"Shut up," one of them barked at him.

"But..."

"Shut up, you. You got no right to say shit. Not after what your clan has done to ours."

"Ain't a clan," Rook said weakly.

"Shut up!"

Getting them pissed off when he hung there helplessly wasn't going to help him. He needed to be convincing, so they'd cut him down. Though, he really doubted they'd just let him walk away. But if he could get to his feet, he might be able to overpower the three of them.

He assumed it was only three since only three spoke. That was confirmed when they stepped closer, surrounding him. One of them poked at his gut.

Another grabbed his nose and held it shut so he'd open his mouth. Probably to look at his damn teeth.

He struck the hand away and his body began to swing like a flopping fish again.

One woman stopped his movement with two hands on his ass. And then she squeezed it like she was checking to see if the bread was fresh.

For fuck's sake! "Just slice my fuckin' throat and let me bleed out," he said, on the verge of begging.

"Didn't I tell you to shut the fuck up? Gimme somethin' to shut him up with, Pammy," what sounded like the leader of the trio demanded. "Don't need all his caterwaulin' bringin' the men up here wonderin' what's goin' on... Let's tie up his hands, too, so he don't knock one of us silly."

Oh, fuck no.

If they gagged him and tied his hands up, he was done. Completely fucking done. He'd have no way to get out of his situation.

None.

One woman grabbed his arm but before another could grab the other one, he swung at them both. His body spun on the rope uncontrollably and the tree branch creaked even louder, then cracked.

Good. Let it fall and kill him. If that was his only escape from this nightmare of being shared by three Shirley women, he'd welcome death.

In the end, once they handed him over to their leader, he'd be dead anyway. Most likely even tortured and not just by Shirley snatch.

He kept swinging his arms and kicking with his free leg until the handle of the Maglite smacked his arm like a hammer, then collided with his temple.

That made him see a few stars.

"Don't knock his ass out! We need him conscious."

No. No, they didn't.

He swung helplessly at them again, hoping they'd knock his ass out.

Two of the women grabbed his arms, overpowering him enough to tie his wrists together while the third Shirley shoved a rag or something gross into his mouth. Before he could spit out whatever it was, another strip of cloth held it fast.

Done.

Toast.

Finished.

Fucked.

He closed his eyes, wishing himself elsewhere. Anywhere but there.

He ignored them poking at him again.

"He's got good bones."

"Looks purty strong."

"Purty face, too."

"You got smarts?" one of them asked him, leaning in close and putting her face right in front of his to the point he could smell her rotten breath.

No, he wasn't smart. He was a dumb motherfucker for getting his ass caught. So goddamn dumb.

He had no idea how the fuck he was going to get out of this situation. They could keep him at their mercy for maybe a day before any of his brothers came looking for him. Those women could do a lot of damage in a day.

A lot of fucking damage.

He was not going to be a stud to make a bunch of Shirley spawn.

Christ, he hoped his swimmers were all belly-up and useless if they tried.

And if his brothers didn't rescue him before the women were finished with him, then Vern Jr. and his uncle-brothers would finish him off.

The flashlight beam landed on his phone. And his knife. He still had no idea where his Beretta was. Probably launched deep into the woods.

"Won't be needin' this," one of them said, moving his phone to a rock and using the Maglite to smash the shit out of it, each strike almost bringing a tear to his eye.

Destroying his cell phone made his damn location app useless, the one Judge had insisted he and Easy download so they could be located if shit went sideways.

Like now.

"Lookie here." The one named Sally picked up his Buck knife. "Gonna keep that for myself." She flung a hand up in the air. "Lower 'im enough that we can tie his ankles together."

Rook heard a rustling behind him and the paracord jerked abruptly, making his heart leap into his throat. Some female grunting ensued and he was slowly lowered inch by inch until they could reach his ankles. More cord was used to tie them together.

Once he was secured, the next command came. "Now cut 'im down."

Oh shit.

He dropped with an *oof* in the dirt. Even though he'd tucked his chin so he didn't land on his noggin, it still hurt, especially since his temple had yet to stop throbbing from one of them clobbering him.

"Grab his feet. Pammy, grab one shoulder, I'll grab the other."

"Where we takin' him, Sal?"

"Right to my bed."

His opinion on that ended up being muffled behind the dirty cloth in his mouth.

The three Shirley women hauled his ass like a pig heading to the spit during one of the club's parties. One got a hold of his legs, the other two his shoulders and they made their way through the dark woods.

He wished they would trip and crack their skulls open, or their men would come along and see what they were planning and put a quick end to it.

But, fuck no, they made it to his final destination without any of that happening, and he was not happy to see the small one-story cabin that looked like it leaned to the right. Or was that just him leaning to the right?

That journey with them carrying his weight had all three women winded. But one managed to get the door open without dropping him and they carried him into the dark cabin.

The three women set him on the bed and while two of them tied his wrists and ankles to the crudely welded steel headboard and footboard, the other one moved around the cabin lighting old-fashioned oil lanterns giving the cabin a really fucking romantic glow.

Christ.

He tested his restraints but none had any give. That meant they knew how to tie someone down without them escaping. Maybe they'd done this before.

He knew they'd kept Autumn tied up for a while. So, maybe they were pros at fucking people against their will.

He bucked his hips in frustration and screamed behind his gag. If he had a chance to break free, he'd kill all three of those prairie dress wearing bitches.

All three looked related. Even the way they wore their hair was the same. They wore knee socks and combat-style boots and the only thing different about them was the pattern of their homemade dresses. That was it.

Fucking cult.

And there was no way his sperm was going to make more members of that fucking cult.

The three women stood at the side of the bed, staring down at him. Thirsty as all fuck.

Fuck!

As long as his body didn't cooperate, he'd be safe, right?

They couldn't do shit with him, if they couldn't get his dick hard.

What if they had another method? Like Viagra.

Holy shit, would they force-feed him a pill that would give him an erection? Would that work? Would he just turn into an unwilling pole for them to ride?

"I'm gettin' him first," Sally, who seemed to be the oldest, said.

Great.

He knew plenty of men in prison who got hard when they were raped. It wasn't because they wanted it or enjoyed it. It was a natural response they couldn't control.

But that was when one asshole was fucking another.

He wasn't sure about women raping men. What if they stuck something up his ass? Would that work?

He squeezed his eyes shut and jerked at his restraints again.

He'd survived all his time inside without getting raped. All that fucking time. He'd fought off men larger and stronger than him.

And, usually, he formed alliances with others to prevent it. Like Dodge.

Like the three new prospects he was sponsoring.

All of them had each other's back. Whether from being jumped, fucked or killed.

And now, three goddamn women...

Women!

"Open his pants and get him ready for me."

"Who's gettin' him next?"

"I don't care," Sally announced. "But it's gonna take more than once. You know that. We'll hide him here 'til we get what we want from him. 'Til we're in our fertile time."

"Thinkin' I'm there now, so maybe I should go first," the youngest woman said, grinning down at him while she stroked his arm. Just her touch made his skin quiver.

"Pammy, you can get him next. When he's still fresh and got plenty of seed."

For fuck's sake, he could wake the fuck up any time now. He'd had some fucked up nightmares before, but this might take the fucking cake.

Wake the fuck up, asshole!

"Well, how d'you know I ain't in my baby makin' time?" the other one asked. The one that almost looked like a twin to Pammy. Probably a sister-cousin.

"You keepin' track, Tammy?" Sally asked her.

"Are you?" Tammy asked back in a smart tone.

"Get his pants down enough to get his dick out," Sally answered, annoyed.

He didn't even bother to fight the whimper as Tammy and Pammy jerked him around like he was a piece of meat. Yanking off his belt, ripping down his cargo pants, then shoving down his boxer briefs until he felt the air whispering across his dick.

Which was soft, *thank fuck.*

It needed to stay that way.

This was the first time in his life he actually wished for a dick dysfunction.

"He needs to get hard."

"No shit, Sally," Pammy told her sister-aunt, or whatever the fuck she was.

"Get 'im hard."

Rook squeezed his eyes shut as one of them wrapped a hand around his limp dick and began to jerk it.

Don't get hard.

Don't get hard.

Don't get fuckin' hard.

He had to think of something else. Anything else. Like the day his mother left.

Like the day he showed up on her doorstep in Baltimore.

Like the first time he got pulled over and got his ass beat to fuck by a pig.

It was working...

"Suck 'im or somethin'," seeped into his brain.

If there was a God, the higher power needed to kill him now.

Now.

Right now.

For fuck's sake, God, right the fuck now.

A lightning strike.

A flood.

Locusts.

Anything.

"I'm gettin' on. Maybe that'll help."

Rook ignored the sound of fabric sliding over skin. He ignored the rock and roll of the lumpy mattress when a knee dug into it as she began to mount up.

But there was one thing he couldn't ignore...

The smell wafting up from under her dress might be the miracle he needed.

Maybe there was a God.

Who just ensured his dick might never get hard again.

Chapter Nine

Jet slipped around the corner of the cabin after the three women carried Rook inside.

The stupid ass was tied up and being carried like a rolled carpet.

That was not what she had expected to find when she had followed the path that led from where she found his Honda. Of course left in a new location than the last time she caught Rook coming down the mountain.

He thought he was being sneaky, parking it elsewhere. But her headlights had caught on the car's rear reflectors through the dead brush he'd covered it with, giving it away.

Tonight she had worked the rare three-to-eleven shift instead of her normal midnight, and her gut had told her to take a slow ride down Copperhead Road on her way home. Not as a police officer on official business, but as a "concerned citizen."

Her instinct was dead on.

Especially since she hadn't caught him out there in the last few days. Because she still did a drive-by every night she worked. She was not letting what could be happening up at the Shirley compound go. Not yet.

Max might be pissed if he found out, but if she discovered something worth investigating, he'd have to see it differently.

Or, at least, she hoped so.

She couldn't imagine he'd turn a blind eye to any egregious offenses the Guardians of Freedom were up to, especially something like trafficking women, which was her suspicion when she had spotted that van the other week.

If she had proof, then Max or no Max, she was getting the feds involved. She could not sit idly by and allow women to be bought and sold under the PD's nose.

That was everything she told herself as she followed the worn, dark path up the mountain.

When she came across the remainder of what suspiciously looked like a trap—cut paracord hanging from a tree—her heart began to beat even harder than it had been already.

Had Rook come this way?

She heard faint rustling and footsteps ahead, so she quickened her pace, doing her best not to trip over any hidden roots or rocks, her hand automatically reaching for the gun on her hip.

Nothing.

Of course her gun wasn't there. She was in civvies. She paused only long enough to pull her personal weapon, a compact .38, from her ankle holster, then hurried up the trail. She had to rely on the bright moon and her night vision to find her way. A flashlight would help, but, if she had one, it would also make her an easy target.

The Shirley Clan hated cops. It would be bad enough if they found her trespassing, but if they discovered she was law enforcement?

They wouldn't even think twice to make sure she took her last breath.

Maybe Rook hadn't even come this direction. Maybe he was somewhere else and she was only following some Shirleys moving through the woods in the dead of night.

Since she'd already come this far, she might as well take a peek around. Take a good look at where this particular path led.

Maybe it would be a goldmine for her. The info she needed.

Or maybe it would be nothing and only a waste of time. Time she had plenty of since her life only consisted of work and occasionally her family.

Other than that, she had no freaking life.

Whoever was moving ahead of her, was shuffling their feet and moving slowly.

The grunts and groans of women finally hit her ears.

What the hell was that? What were they doing?

She didn't want to come upon them accidentally, so she took her time and picked her footsteps carefully because if she fell, they would hear it. Then they'd most likely come and investigate the noise.

She slowed her breathing and kept an eye out. Occasionally she'd catch some movement in the shadows way ahead. A flash of something. Light-colored fabric. Maybe a dress.

More shuffling and the murmur of women bitching. More than one, for sure.

She hesitated, ducking behind a tree to let them get farther ahead. Once they hit a clearing, Jet could stick to cover and see why they were tromping through the woods this late at night.

Thirty seconds later, she began to move again. Until she saw it. A very small clearing, if it could even be called that.

Some of the high, dead weeds around a tiny cabin were trampled enough to make her think the cabin wasn't abandoned.

But she didn't give a shit about the weeds or the lack of property maintenance.

What she gave a shit about... She blinked to make sure she was seeing right.

Blood drained from her face and her pulse began to rush. No wonder the women were lumbering along and making all kinds of noises. They had been burdened with the weight of one Blood Fury member by the name of Rook.

Holy shit.

They had captured Rook and tied him up, maybe even gagged him, but it was hard to see the details clearly with the darkness and distance. Even so, she couldn't imagine he wouldn't be complaining loudly about what they were doing if he didn't have anything preventing him from speaking.

One of the women had opened the door to the dark cabin and they hauled Rook's tied-up ass inside.

Jet jerked when the door slammed shut, abruptly bringing her back to the present.

Holy fuck, they took that stupid ass as a captive. Were they going to kill him?

And if they were, why didn't they just do it where they caught him? Why bring him back to this shitty little cabin further up the mountain?

Unless they were going to torture him first? Did he have info they wanted to get from him? Like the reason the MC members kept coming up their mountain?

She wanted to know that, too.

The two windows at the front of the cabin were now glowing and flickering as if they were using candles instead of electricity for light.

Blowing out a breath and trying to gather her thoughts

on what she should do, she crouched down and moved as low as possible over the beaten-down vegetation, with her gun ready in both hands, the barrel pointed toward the ground.

When she made it to the cabin without being detected, she pinned herself to the side and finally took a deep breath after holding it for so long. She repositioned her gun since her palms were beginning to sweat and her trigger finger had become twitchy.

Her cell phone was in her jacket pocket. Maybe she should call for backup.

What was she thinking? She couldn't call anyone. Not even her brother. Adam would be just as pissed as Max if he knew she had gone up the mountain alone. *Damn it.* She'd risk her job if anyone found out.

She needed to figure out how to get Rook out of there by herself.

Or, *hell*, maybe she should just leave him there.

He deserved it. It would serve him right for being such a dick.

No, she couldn't.

Could she?

No.

For shit's sake, she couldn't leave him. They'd kill him. She couldn't let that happen to him. To anyone.

Protect and serve. That was what she vowed to do. The oath she took when she was sworn in as a police officer.

Protect and serve, even a dumbass like Rook, was what she needed to do.

Even so, she couldn't just walk in and start shooting. She also couldn't simply walk in and demand they free the biker.

No, they'd just capture her, too. After they laughed, most likely. Then they'd both be in a pickle. The Shirley women wouldn't give a shit she was a police officer. Instead, that fact would work against her.

Just like it had with Rook.

She hunkered down near the window to the left of the crude wooden door and slowly rose to peek through the dirty glass.

They now had Rook tied to a bed and they were touching him. Like *touching* him.

In a way he would not enjoy.

In fact, in a way he would hate and object to if he could. He was not there because he wanted to be, he was there because he was forced to be. And the women were forcing their attentions on him.

Now she could see his mouth was gagged and his eyes squeezed shut.

She needed to do something and needed to do whatever it was quickly. Especially since his pants were pushed down and one of the women was shucking her own underwear and pulling them from under her long dress.

Holy shit.

Holy shit.

Think, Jet.

She needed a way to distract them. To pull them away from their victim.

In horror, Jet watched the woman climb onto the bed and straddle Rook's thighs. With the two other women encouraging her.

What the hell?

Oh fuck, please stay limp. Don't let her—them—do this to you.

If she shot off her gun, that could attract more Shirleys and they'd both be screwed. What could she do?

Fire!

She needed to set a fire. Just large enough to pull their attention from Rook. Maybe get them out of the cabin all together to investigate the smoke.

Once they were out and dealing with the fire, she could go in and free him.

And, more importantly, not get caught. She couldn't help him if she got caught.

They'd both be fucked. Him quite literally.

She rounded the cabin to the rear, where she noticed not one damn window. She couldn't monitor what was going on inside. Maybe that was better and she could just concentrate on figuring out how to start a fire.

She moved along the back of the crude structure. If it didn't have electricity, it didn't have heat except for a fireplace or wood stove. She kept moving until she saw it. A pile of split wood, some stacked, some just scattered along the ground. And an axe sticking out of the tree stump used as the base to split that wood.

She could use the axe for her plan, plus the wood. Plus, the dried brush and overgrown weeds around the cabin.

This could work. She only needed to stay focused and not think about what was happening to Rook in that cabin.

She could save him, if she did this right.

He better fucking appreciate her efforts.

She shook herself mentally. *Concentrate.*

She yanked the axe from the stump and began to unpeel the duct tape, which was flammable, wrapped around the handle. Once she had enough, she crumpled it loosely into a ball.

What else?

She collected some dried dead leaves and some very thin twigs. Then it hit her.

She had a tube of Chapstick in the pocket of her denim jacket.

She remembered the survival hack that Chapstick was flammable. She pulled the tube out, placed it on the stump and used the back of the axe blade to crack it open.

She quickly smeared the waxy material onto the duct tape and more on the kindling. Her heart was now pounding in her throat and her ears. She needed to stay as calm and focused as possible. She needed to also remain aware of her surroundings.

She didn't need to be ambushed by any Shirleys or her efforts would be for nothing.

Once she had a small pile of flammable shit to start the initial fire, she dug into the inside pocket of her jacket.

Since her discharge from the Marines, she'd always carried a Leatherman Multitool with her. On-duty in her patrol bag and off-duty on her person. She even kept a spare one in her glovebox. Just in case...

Thank fuck she did.

Being up in northern Pennsylvania she always carried the multitool specifically made for camping. Too many desolate and wooded areas existed, like the one she was currently standing in.

Being a Marine, and now a cop, she had always wanted to be prepared for any emergency. Her father had drilled that into her since she was very young. Her father had also been the one to suggest carrying a multitool and bought her first one as a birthday present when she was twelve, a present she didn't appreciate at the time.

Thank you, Dad.

She would thank him in person the next time she visited. She might not be able to tell him why, but she'd do it anyway.

She flipped the multitool open to find the one she

needed. The ferrocerium rod. She never in her wildest dreams thought she'd ever use that particular tool. Never.

Best. Investment. Ever.

She held the blade of the axe near her pile, and used the striking rod on the sharp edge.

She cringed and glanced up to check her surroundings. The noise the rod made against metal in the dead of night was deafening. But she had no other choice, unless she charged inside the cabin, swinging the axe like a crazy woman.

That would be option B if option A failed.

She'd rather sneak in and sneak out without those women being the wiser. If her plan held, her distraction would give them a head start down the mountain before they even realized Rook was gone.

She kept striking the rod against the blade's edge, willing it to light the small pile. A few sparks flew, giving her hope, but they died out as soon as they landed.

She didn't give up, quickly striking the blade over and over, causing multiple sprays of sparks. Some of them landing on her and some landing on her little pile of lip balm-covered dry leaves and balled-up duct tape.

"C'mon," she muttered under her breath, her fingers trembling. She glanced up every few seconds, worried they'd discover her.

Her breath arrested as a spark finally ignited her little pile causing the tiniest flame. Dropping to her knees, she cupped the makeshift kindling within her hands and blew on it gently. Too hard and it would put out the weak flame. Too soft and it would simply burn out.

As soon as the flame began to grow, along with her hope, she placed it back on the ground and, still blowing softly, began to build the fire by adding a few more dry leaves and nearby twigs.

Once she was sure the fire was established, she grabbed a burning twig and, keeping low and close to the side of the cabin, began to light the batches of dry, dead weeds surrounding the cabin.

Thank fuck they didn't give a shit about mowing or weed whacking. The dry overgrowth was perfect to start a roaring fire. *Once* it caught.

She sent out another thank you into the universe when it did and quickly began to spread and smolder. Exactly what she wanted. Lots and lots of smoke.

She waited only long enough to make sure the fire was going strong, then waved her hands to push some of the smoke toward the cabin, doing her best to not inhale it and cough, giving her away, but hoping it would permeate the logs and seep inside.

With a nervous last glance at the spreading fire, she ducked once again around the rear of the cabin where she wouldn't be spotted if the women rushed out.

Keeping an ear open for any signs of them exiting the structure, she rounded the other side of the cabin nearest the window she had peered into previously. The window closest to their escape path.

With her body pinned tightly to the side, she waited, attempting to slow her harsh breathing, and listened.

Rising slightly, she could just see inside. The oldest of the three was still straddling Rook, his eyes remained pinned shut and it seemed as though the two other women were trying to help Rook rise to the whole fucked-up occasion.

It was probably one time the man was relieved he couldn't get it up.

Good for him, not so good for the women's intentions.

Jet had no idea why they'd want to do what they were doing, but the reason didn't matter. What mattered was getting the man out of there before they succeeded.

A little bit of relief swept through her when she heard, "You smell smoke?"

"Like from the meat smoker?" another one asked.

"No, Tammy, not from the damn meat smoker. Like from a damn fire."

"That's usually where smoke comes from," Tammy responded.

"Like somethin' burnin' that shouldn't be." The woman whose back was to Jet and was straddling Rook had stopped whatever she was doing. Jet couldn't tell exactly what it was because the long dress she wore covered the both of them. Jet certainly didn't want to analyze what she was doing or attempting, either.

Not right now.

The woman on Rook tipped her face up and sniffed loudly. "I smell smoke. Pammy's right."

"From your fireplace, Sally?"

"Haven't needed a fire in the fireplace yet this week."

"Where's the smoke comin' from, then?"

"My guess?" Sally asked. "From outside."

Holy crap, how long were they going to discuss it before they investigated?

Jet's relief of them smelling smoke quickly turned to impatience.

Adam was right. The Shirleys weren't the sharpest tools in the shed.

"Smoker ain't goin', neither?" Pammy or Tammy asked.

"Nope. Haven't smoked anything in a coupla weeks."

"Maybe we'd better check it out."

Yes, maybe they'd better. And soon. From where Jet

stood, the smell of smoke was strong, which meant the fire was growing even bigger. The only good thing about that would be it would take them longer to put it out, hopefully giving Jet more time to rescue Rook.

"Go out and check," Sally ordered one of the other women.

Jet ducked around the corner of the cabin as she heard the front door open and a rush of feet heading away from her before a rush of feet returned with an accompanied panicked yell, "Fire! The woods are on fire! The cabin's startin' to burn!"

"What the hell?" Sally asked.

Jet couldn't see shit as she didn't want to risk looking in the window since it was on the same side as the only door in the cabin.

"You got water up here?"

"No."

"How the hell are we gonna put it out?"

"Call the men!"

"Whole damn mountain might be burnt down afore they get here. We gotta get the fire out now."

"Got shovels? Might have to shovel dirt on it."

"Fire might be too big for that."

"We gotta try. Pammy, you run down and get some of the men. Tammy, you help me try to smother the fire. Go now. Run, Pammy!"

Jet held her breath as she listened to the scrambling women. When she peered around the cabin she saw one woman running down the dirt lane, not taking the path she and Rook would need to take.

Thank fuck!

She counted another thirty seconds off in her head, then peeked around again, saw no one, and rushed into the open front door of the cabin. She kept her gun in her right hand and her multitool in the other.

"Holy shit," she whispered as she now saw Rook clearly on the bed. "Holy shit. Holy fucking shit."

She rushed to the bed, using the small knife on her multitool, carefully cut the cloth tied around his face first, then quickly sawed through the paracord tying his wrists and hands. As she did so, she risked glancing down at him, even though she needed to focus on not accidentally slicing his skin since the cord was so tight it was digging into his skin.

His brown eyes were now open and staring up at her. Even though he was trying to hide it, his panic was clear.

"Need to get the fuck outta here." His voice was raw and rough like it hurt for him to speak. Had he been screaming the whole time while she had worked on the fire?

He jackknifed up as soon as she had both arms free and she immediately moved to his ankles. As she sawed at those restraints, he yanked his underwear and pants back up over his hips, securing them.

As soon as both ankles were free, he rolled off the bed, grabbed her arm and yanked her behind him as he began to surge toward the door she had closed behind her. He flung it open, rushed outside, dragging her along with him, toward the path in the woods, not hesitating one second.

Like he was running from the devil.

He probably was.

She had so many questions and so many thoughts, but she didn't let any of them escape. Time for that was later. Right now, they both needed to get the hell off that mountain in one piece while they could.

Jet only glanced over her shoulder once to see the glow of the spreading fire before they ducked into the woods.

After that, she only looked forward toward escape as both

of them raced down the narrow dirt and dark trail, hoping neither of them fell and broke anything.

They made it down the mountain in record time, broke free of the woods, sprinted across Copperhead Road and down the berm to the hiding spot where she'd parked her SUV behind the Honda.

Even though she was a runner, she was almost wheezing as hard as Rook, mostly because of her adrenaline and the effort it took to run down the dark, rough terrain.

From now on, she would find places to run cross-country. Hiking paths, nature trails, whatever. Not that she ever wanted this kind of adventure again.

When they got to the vehicles, Jet spun around, leaned her ass against her Toyota and bent over at the waist, planting her hands above her knees and trying to catch her breath and her racing thoughts.

Rook immediately opened the trunk of the old Honda, pulled out his cut, and shrugged it on before collapsing against the car. He dug inside his cut and when his trembling hand reappeared, he was holding something thin and white.

Even in the dark, she could see it was a damn joint.

He flicked a lighter with his other hand, taking a long hit of the pot and holding it in his lungs as long as he could before blowing it out and panting again from the previous exertion.

"Do you think it's smart to do that in front of me?"

"You think I give a goddamn fuck right now?" he growled, still out of breath.

No, she supposed he didn't. "We need to get out of here."

"Fuckin' go, then. Nobody's tellin' you to stay." He turned his head to look up the mountain they'd just left behind. "Busy fightin' that fire, anyway."

Did he actually sound a little impressed by her efforts?

That couldn't be right. "But probably not for long. They might come looking for you."

He took another long drag off his joint, this time blowing out the smoke slower and more calmly. "You got a gun."

Her eyebrows pinged her hairline. "I'm not going to shoot them."

"I will." He held out his hand, like she was just going to hand over her .38 to a felon to kill people on her watch.

Uh huh, sure. That would turn tonight's nightmare into a colossal cluster-fuck. "They need to be arrested and charged for sexual assault, Rook."

It didn't matter if he didn't actually penetrate that woman or not. What they'd done to him was clearly assault. Not to mention, kidnapping. At minimum. She could stack on other charges, as well.

"No."

His answer didn't surprise her. "They can't get away with what they did and also what they... tried to do."

She grimaced as she remembered how he looked tied to the bed, his pants and underwear pulled down with his crotch completely exposed. She had kept her eyes averted from that area as best as she could to not make it worse for him.

"They get charged, so would I. Was trespassin'. Break a law, break my parole. I go back behind bars."

Shit. But they couldn't just ignore what happened. "Well, I can't bring the charges. I was never on this mountain, so you would have to do it. You'd have to file a report. They can't get away with what they did to you."

He pushed himself off the Honda and pinched out the end of the joint. With stiff, jerky movements he tucked the remainder inside his cut and turned to face her. "No, Jet," he growled. "Never fuckin' speak of tonight again. You fuckin' hear me? Never. I ain't tellin' anyone, you ain't, either. You do, you'll regret it."

She stared at him, again not surprised at his words, but still... "Is that a threat?"

"Take it for whatever you think it is." He turned abruptly and in two long strides was at the driver's door, yanking it open. He didn't look at her when he muttered, "I need to shower in goddamn bleach."

He shrugged back out of his cut and tossed it into the car onto the passenger seat. Without another word, or even a damn thank you, he got in, slammed the door shut and drove off like his ass was on fire.

That was one way to avoid talking to her any further about what occurred up there. If he ignored her, she'd go away, right? Simply forget everything that just happened.

Thank you or not, he now owed her for saving his ass.

And she planned on collecting.

THE TIRES of the Honda squealed as he gunned it as fast as he could into the garage lot.

His heart was still hammering, but at least the pot had stopped the shake of his hands.

He was still pissed.

Pissed at himself for fucking up.

Pissed at those bitches for overpowering him. Pissed at himself for letting them.

Pissed that he couldn't free himself.

Pissed that Jet had to be the one to fucking rescue him.

First time in his fucking life where a pig did something decent for him. Probably the last time, too.

She wanted him to walk into a fucking pig pen and make a damn report!

Right. He'd get right the fuck on that. Because that was what he wanted to share with others. The fact he'd been over-powered, restrained to a fucking bed and he'd had three hill-billy cunts trying to...

Trying to...

Use him as a breeding tool.

Use his seed to produce more of those fucked-in-the-head motherfuckers.

He parked the Honda in its spot, shoved the shifter into Park, shut the engine off and, once the cage was quiet, he dropped his forehead to the steering wheel.

Thank fuck for Jet.

Thank fuck.

Thank fucking fuck.

He'd spent all his years inside without getting raped. And, *Christ to fuck*, it almost happened by three inbred Shirley bitches.

He blew out a breath, lifted his head and blew out another less shaky one.

He had no fucking cell phone. His gun was gone. So was his knife.

He didn't even have his fucking dignity after what Jet saw. He would rather his brothers had found him in that situation than her.

Any-fucking-body but her.

"God-fuckin-damnit!" His shout filled the interior of the Honda.

He heard a muffled barking in response.

Fucking stupid motherfucking dog.

Why hadn't anything eaten that little piece of shit yet? Why hadn't it run out into the road and gotten flattened? He would just stop putting out food and water for the fucker. It would have to leave or die.

Something.

He growled and shoved open the driver's door, unfolding himself from the sedan.

It was once again using his sled as a barrier between them.

"You piss on my sled, I'll skin you a-fuckin-live, asshole!"

He ignored the incessant yapping as he strode across the lot to return the Honda keys to the office. If Reilly found them missing in the morning, she'd relentlessly ride his ass about it. And he was really not in the mood to deal with her ass.

He dug into his front pocket to grab his key ring...

Nothing.

Fuck.

He dug in his other pocket. Nope.

He'd lost his fucking keys up on the mountain somewhere.

This just was the bitter fucking icing on the rotten cake.

He slammed the shop door with his palm, then spun around.

For fuck's sake, that meant he lost his sled keys.

And the keys to the bunkhouse and his room.

He tipped his head back, closed his eyes and screamed to the sky. "Fuck you, you inbred hillbilly redneck goat-fucking motherfuckers!"

He spun around as the barking got louder and he lunged at the little four-legged shithead, sending the rat dog running away in a fit of more barking with its tail tucked.

"You stupid fuck!"

He squeezed his eyes shut, slammed his back against the

garage bay door and slid down it until his ass hit the cold concrete.

He dug his elbows into his bent knees and dropped his head into his hands, roughly raking his fingers through his hair. Then he just breathed.

Breathe.

He was still alive. Those cunts didn't get what they wanted from him.

And Jet saved his ass.

From both of those things. Because eventually he wouldn't have been able to not respond to their touching him whether he wanted to or not.

He had to dig deep and relive some awful fucking memories to fight his body's natural reaction to the stimulation. Eventually, they would have mentally worn him down enough he could no longer fight his body's response. Even with as much as his mind was screaming no.

Once they were done using him, stealing his seed, he would've been killed, if not tortured.

So, yeah, Jet saved his goddamn ass.

Her being nosy and all up in his business had fucking saved him.

He should thank her, but he wasn't sure if he could face her. Not until that memory of her expression, as she hovered over him while cutting him free, was forgotten. Unfortunately, it might never be forgotten because it had been seared into his brain.

She'd probably seen worse while doing her job...

He lifted his head when his ankle became warm and wet. The fucking asshole had his leg lifted and was pissing on him. Marking him like a fire hydrant.

The perfect fucking ending to a perfectly fucked-up day.

He should dropkick the motherfucker across the lot.

But what did it matter? Did anything fucking matter anymore?

He dropped his head back into his hands and groaned. When the quiet of the night swallowed him, he realized the dog was no longer yapping.

No, he was suspiciously quiet.

Maybe the fucker was shitting on his boot. Or humping his Harley.

Leaving his head down, he only lifted his eyes so he could sneak a look to see what torture the little bastard had planned for him next.

He was surprised to see the black and tan Chihuahua standing in between his spread boots, one front foot up in the air and his tail still tucked, shaking like a damn leaf in a hurricane.

He should be scared. He was lucky Rook didn't have his damn gun.

"Asshole," Rook whispered.

The dog jerked and only did a little "woof" instead of its constant barking.

Keeping his head tucked, Rook slid his right hand down his leg from his knee to his shin. The dog watched it suspiciously, still trembling.

"You bite me, you're dead, asshole." He left his hand on his shin and waited.

Within minutes, a little cold, wet nose touched one of his fingers.

Then poked another finger.

Rook held his breath, waiting for the mini-monster to take a big chomp out of his flesh.

A tongue, not teeth, flashed quickly and touched the back of his hand.

Had the asshole licked him?

Was he trying to make peace? Or was the little fucker feeling sorry for Rook because he recognized the fact that Rook's life sucked more than a homeless rat. "Trust me, from one asshole to another, tonight my life sucks way more than yours."

He stared at rat dog and rat dog stared back at him, still quivering, but not as badly.

Then the little tongue hit his skin again.

And again.

The tiniest licks had turned into a peace offering.

Rook slowly peeled his hand off his shin and let the dog sniff his palm. Then he stretched out his fingers and used one to scratch under the tiny chin.

The dog tilted his head and Rook swore he heard a groan when he added a couple more fingers to scratch the fucker behind the ears.

Rook automatically jerked his hand back when the dog lunged.

Not to bite him. Fuck no. But to jump into his lap.

As the dog wedged himself more comfortably in the V between Rook's gut and thigh, then practically burrowed himself under his cut, Rook shook his head. "Guess us assholes gotta stick together, huh?"

The dog curled up and tucked his nose under its own tail and released a little groan.

"Sucks I can't name you Jet now."

Chapter Ten

JET PRESSED her eye to the peephole to see who the hell was pounding on her door at midnight on her night off.

Anyone related to her and any of her coworkers would know she'd be trying to catch up on sleep. They would call or text, not do the equivalent of a "knock and announce" on her damn door.

There had better be a gas leak, a fire, a herd of rabid jackalopes terrorizing the town or... *something*.

The pounding continued as she saw the last person she expected filling up the peephole. "Holy shit," she whispered.

The very last person.

Why the hell was he here?

Well, Jet, guess you'll get your answer if you open the door and ask him. Duh. She grimaced and glanced down at herself. *Shit.*

She was wearing a pair of dark blue men's boxers and a white wife-beater-type tank. No bra, no underwear, no—

The pounding continued.

Shit, shit, shit. "Hold on, I need to get dressed," she yelled through the door.

When the pounding didn't cease, she yelled, "You'll wake up my landlord!"

And worse, get her evicted. *Asshole!*

"Open the fuckin' door."

She gritted her teeth at the growly demand, flipped open the deadbolt and flung open the door. "What?" she asked, making sure her annoyance was crystal fucking clear. She blocked the doorway with her body, one hand on the door frame and one on the door itself.

He didn't even ask to come in. He just plowed right through her, knocking her out of the way.

"Hey, come on in!" she muttered, flinging an arm out and turning to face him. Crossing her arms over her unrestrained breasts, she at least tried to cover her nipples which were doing their very traitorous best to poke a hole through the thin cotton. *Damn it.* "Once again, your greeting skills are lacking, Rook. You really need to take an etiquette class."

He took his sweet ol' time raking his gaze from her quickly finger-combed hair, down her sleep-deprived face, over her chest, then her belly and hips before his eyes took a *looong* lazy stroll down her bare legs, finally landing at her feet.

She held her breath and her heart began to thump wildly when he leaned closer, his brown eyes now even darker as they raised to hers. His arm brushed against her shoulder, causing her flesh to pebble, when he flung the door shut behind her with a bang.

She wouldn't be surprised if old man Danson had an eviction notice tacked to her door in the morning. Her landlord was not only ancient, he was cranky, too. He liked peace and quiet. And his privacy.

So did Jet. However, she wasn't getting any of those three things at the moment.

She stared at the reason. "I didn't invite you in." She made sure her annoyance was even thicker in her tone.

"You opened the door."

"Yes, well, I open the door for the UPS man, too. Doesn't mean he's welcome inside my apartment." Her eyebrows pinned together. "And, anyway, how the hell do you know where I live?"

That fact was a bit disturbing. But a risk when working in a small town where practically everyone knew everyone. It didn't take much to find out the latest gossip or news. And, of course, everyone knew the Brysons. To get info on any of them, all you had to do was ask.

Hell, the whole town probably knew every time Amanda or Leah was pregnant even before their own husbands. The second either of them bought a pregnancy test at the Olde Town Pharmacy, or even Target, her cousins-in-law swore the town's call tree was activated.

But Rook had also lived his whole life in this town. At least, when he wasn't doing time. Between being born in Manning Grove and working with his father at the busiest garage in town, she was damn sure he knew everyone, too.

"You ain't hard to find," he answered, now only standing about three feet away from her.

She tightened her arms across her chest. "Why are you here, Rook? Are you here to call me a pig? To tell me how much you hate me? To issue another threat to keep my mouth shut about what happened two nights ago? What? What could you possibly have to say to me at almost midnight? And why would you feel the need to come to my residence to say it?"

He leaned closer again, this time she noticed the slight

flare in his nostrils and his pupils widening, that was after they took in the compressed curves of her breasts again. Slowly.

He actually added a little lick of his lips.

He might as well have flicked her clit with the tip of his tongue.

Holy shit, she needed to get him out of her apartment.

Like now.

She dropped her arms and blindly reached for the doorknob behind her. "If you're not going to answer me, then you can just haul your ass right back out of here."

"No."

Her eyebrows launched into orbit. "No?"

"No."

"Which of my multitude of questions was that the answer for?"

"Don't know since I wasn't payin' attention to your damn questions."

She sighed.

"Hard to listen when you're standin' there like that."

Should she ask? She probably shouldn't. *Fuck it.* "Like what?"

He let his gaze rake down her body again. When he did it this time, his lips were pursed and he did it... so... much... slower.

Holy shit.

If he wouldn't notice, her toes would be curling right now. Instead, she pressed every single toe flat to the floor and held them there against their will.

She'd dealt with plenty of assholes like him. In her job, in the Marines, even in high school.

She should *not* be attracted to one of them.

A felon asshole biker, she reminded herself.

A *cop-hating* felon asshole biker.

Her breath caught and her heart skipped a beat when he took the two steps to bring them practically face to face.

She *hated* that he was taller than her. That she had to look up. It was a power move on his part. An attempt to intimidate her.

Well, *fuck him*, she wasn't afraid of him.

Still... When his eyes followed the roll of her throat as she tried to swallow...

Heat burst from her center and rushed outward to every cell of her body. And then the flicker at her center got stronger.

Cop-hating felon asshole biker!

His eyes narrowed. So did hers.

His lips parted. So did hers.

His chin rose slightly. So did hers.

She tried to suck in air, but her chest was tight and her nipples screamed for his touch.

Why, why, *why* did he have to be the one to make her feel this way?

Every damn time she'd see him at the garage, she couldn't pull her eyes from him. Worse, like a horny teenager, she secretly hoped she'd catch his attention, too.

Why? Why him?

What the hell did he have that her traitorous body needed? Wanted? Ached for?

Nothing!

He's a cop-hating felon asshole biker, Jet!

But, *lord*, she wanted to lick every damn inch of that cop-hating felon asshole biker's body.

She wanted his dark blond, spiky hair to tickle the skin along her inner thighs.

She wanted to taste the salty tang of precum beaded on the tip of his cock.

Her head snapped back at her runaway thoughts. *She* had snapped. A complete mental break.

Where were the men in white coats? Would they be pounding on her door next?

"Why are you in my apartment?" Those whispered words had to be forced from her seized throat.

"'Cause you let me in," he whispered back.

Oh good lord, his voice. It should be like nails on a chalkboard, not the background music to panty-soaking porn.

"You forced your way in."

"You opened the door."

Where was her damn common sense? Her street smarts? Her instinct for survival? "We covered that already. And if you kept pounding on the door like a damn gorilla you might've woken up my landlord. I'm not ready to lose my security deposit yet."

Not because of a cop-hating felon asshole biker.

She was going to make an appointment with a therapist in the morning. Because there was no other reason every inch of her body was throbbing in tune with her heartbeat unless she was one hundred percent certifiably crazy.

"Darlin'." The low rumble of that word rolled slowly through her, picking up speed and crashing into her center like a rogue wave against a sea wall.

She dug her fingernails into her rationality and clung for dear life.

Hold fast, Jet! Hold fast!

"Why are you here?" *Gah! Why did that come out so breathless?*

"Got somethin' to tell you."

She failed to swallow the boulder wedged solidly in her

throat. "Then say it and leave." Planting her palms on his chest, she shoved but he didn't budge. No, *he* was that invincible sea wall. "You need to back up. Stop crowding me."

"You scared?"

He would love it if she was.

She forced out a dry laugh. "Of you? Hell. No." *Of my reaction to you? Hell yes.*

"Maybe you should be."

Her pussy vibrated from his purr as if he'd said it with his lips directly against the swollen, damp flesh.

"I did a lot of self-defense in the police academy," she warned him.

"I was in prison."

That statement should be like a cooler full of ice dumped over her head, bringing her to her senses. It did nothing but fan the flames. "Is that your way of telling me you fight dirty?" Her voice cracked on the last word.

"Had to."

"And now?"

Her breath caught as he bumped her chest with his, forcing her back a step. She gained her balance and pressed her hands to his chest again, leaving them there this time, trying to keep some distance. Maintain some breathing room. A safe space.

He bumped her again, then pressed on until her back was to the door and his chest was pinned to her breasts, sandwiching her hands between them.

"Can still fight dirty if you want me to. Want me to fight dirty, darlin'?" His words whispered over her parted lips.

Hell yes, she did.

No.

No.

No!

"I always like a challenge," she whispered back. In truth, her challenge should be to resist him.

But, *shit*, it was so hard. Especially when he planted both of his palms on the door behind her, one on each side of her head, effectively boxing her in. Imprisoning her with his arms.

The energy snapped and crackled in the air between them.

It made it difficult to breathe. To think. To remember why he was so, so bad for her. Why she shouldn't be attracted to him.

Her fingers curled into the soft cotton of his long-sleeved T-shirt under the open leather cut. She expected to feel the shock of electricity beneath her fingertips. But she didn't. Instead, she felt the man. Solid. Warm. Dangerous. His chest rose and fell steadily beneath her palms.

Tipping his head down, he stared at her breasts.

Peaked and aching. Swelling.

Screaming for him.

"You scared?" he whispered again.

"No."

Without warning, his hand seized the front of her throat, like that day outside of her cruiser. A hand that could easily cause damage. End her life.

His fingers tightened and his thumb, calloused from years of being a mechanic, slowly traced the line of her racing pulse. "Now?"

Up... Down...

Up...

Down...

"No," she whispered, making sure her answer sounded confident.

"Should be. You're alone in your apartment with a man

who hates you. A man who's got his hand on your throat. You think you can overpower me 'cause of your trainin', but you're mistaken, darlin'. You can't. Your life is caged by rules. In the military. In your job. In society. In prison, to survive you can't be knee-capped by those same rules or you will die. Or become someone's bitch. Fightin' dirty ain't a choice, it's a fuckin' way of life."

She inhaled every single one of those powerful words whispered over her lips.

Holy shit. She was disintegrating from the inside out. As a trickle of arousal slipped from her, she was afraid it would escape her loose boxers and slide down her inner thigh where he could see it.

Undeniable evidence of how much she wanted him in that moment.

Cop-hating. Felon. Asshole. Biker.

Cop-hating, felon, ass—

"Kiss me," she moaned, unable to stop herself.

He jerked violently at that demand. Like he expected her to fight, not encourage him to continue.

Quite possibly, not fighting was her way to win. To be victorious.

Simply do the opposite of what he expected.

He pressed his mouth to her ear and growled, "Only kiss people I don't hate."

His words, his breath, stirred her hair, stirred something inside her she'd never experienced before. Not with anyone. Not like this.

Searing want. Unbridled need. Powerful desire.

A fire roared deep within her belly.

Her attraction to him had to be the allure of wanting something she shouldn't have.

The forbidden.

The tempting bite of an apple you couldn't resist even when you know it would destroy humanity.

The soul-deep aching need only he could extinguish.

She unlocked her fingers from his shirt and slid her hand between them, down to where he was hot, heavy and hard.

For her.

"Do you normally react like this over someone you hate?" Every thought took effort. Every word had to be forced.

"Only one."

"Why is that one different than the rest?"

"About to find out."

He crushed his lips to hers, like an army rushing a battle-field. Overwhelming and powerful, in a battle to win. A strategic move to crush the enemy.

He tasted like pot and beer. Morning-after mistakes. Irrefutable regrets.

And bad, bad decisions.

A groan surged up from her chest and he stole it from her as he swept his tongue through her mouth, taking every inch as if it belonged to him. As if he had won the skirmish and she was the prize.

Continuing his siege on her mouth, his hips tilted, driving his denim-covered erection against her palm. Her pussy clenched uncontrollably when she wondered what it would feel like for him to take her completely. Right where they stood. Against the door.

It wouldn't take much to shuck her boxers. Only seconds to be totally naked and succumb to his actions.

She bit back her urge to beg him to do just that.

She should be fighting him. Beating him off.

Taking him down. Kicking him the hell out of her apartment.

Not allowing him unfettered access to her mouth.

Not cupping him where he was hot and full.

Not gripping his shirt and keeping him close.

But she didn't want to let go. Not of his shirt, not of his balls, not of his mouth.

She wanted more.

She wanted everything.

To hell with the consequences.

But still...

She ripped her mouth away, to draw in oxygen, to try to think more clearly. To keep her desire for this man she shouldn't want anything to do with from drowning her. To remind him that he didn't kiss people he hated. "You hate me, remember?"

Their cheeks were glued together as they both panted, his cock throbbing hotly under her fingers as she stroked him. Wishing the denim didn't separate them. Wishing they were skin to skin.

Wishing she could hold his hot flesh in her palm while thumbing the tip to gather the silky precum...

Bring it to her lips.

"Haven't forgotten."

Her throat convulsed. "Then why are you doing it?"

"'Cause I can't fuckin' resist."

Holy shit, she almost came simply from his tormented confession. Those simple words that weren't so simple.

No, they could cause a whole lot of complications.

This could cause a whole heap of problems.

He knew it.

She knew it.

But still, like two magnets, their mouths crashed together again. A clash of teeth. Lips. Tongues.

A battle of wills.

Who would stop this before it went too far?

Which one of them would come to their senses first?

She tugged his shirt from his jeans with one hand and with the other began to fiddle with his belt.

There was her answer: definitely not her.

Definitely not him, either, she realized, when he gripped her face with both hands, deepening the kiss, almost to the point of pain. Like he wanted to swallow her whole.

His fingers gripped her hair, holding on tight, as she abandoned his shirt so she could use both hands to loosen his belt. When she worked the button free, but before she could grab the small tab to his zipper, his hand moved in a flash to snag her wrist, holding it firmly and stopping her intentions.

He broke his mouth free from hers. His intense dark eyes holding hers. His voice so deep it sounded like it had been forced to travel all the way up from his toes to his lips. "No. People like you have tried to control me almost my whole fuckin' life. You ain't doin' it now. Not ever."

She closed her eyes and wasn't sure if she was relieved or disappointed at him coming back to reality. Of seeing how wrong this was and being the one strong enough to stop it.

Just as the relief was seeping through her, he grabbed the back of her neck in a powerful grip, yanked her away from the door and over to stand in front of the full-length mirror on the coat closet door.

Why was she letting him do this? Manipulate her like this? No one else would ever get away with manhandling her.

But it got her blood boiling. Her juices flowing.

The raw, apparent need in his eyes stoked the flames inside her.

It was a look that didn't say, "I'm done with you." Oh no. It said, "I'm nowhere near done with you."

Heat bloomed from her center and her muscles quivered. She didn't want him to think she was afraid of him. Because she was anything but. However, she was afraid if she said anything, even to encourage him, he'd stop.

The truth was, she was nowhere near done with him, either.

Not even close.

Releasing her neck, he ripped her tank over her head, tossing it aside. His eyes took in her now bare breasts, the puckered nipples, the pointed tips, and they seemed to swell under his scrutiny.

Just him looking at her caused another trickle to slide from her clenching pussy.

A sigh slipped from her when he jerked forward, grabbing both breasts, not cupping them gently, but gripping them forcefully within his hands and squeezing, kneading, capturing the very tips between his thumb and forefinger and tugging.

Another trickle, another unrestrained groan.

Her hands gripped his head, the short hairs on the sides prickling her palms as he dropped his face, sucked one nipple deep enough within his mouth to scrape the throbbing tip against his molars.

A noise rolled up and surged from her throat as she slammed her head back and her short fingernails dug into his scalp.

A wet pop occurred as he moved to the other nipple, doing the same. Scraping, sucking, flicking. He squeezed them so hard the flesh turned white under his fingers and flushed everywhere else.

But it didn't hurt... *Hell no*, she wouldn't demand he stop, instead she'd beg him for more. She didn't bother to use words, but the pressure of her hands, holding him there. Hoping he'd pick up on her unspoken need.

He muttered against her damp flesh, "Eve's apple."

She breathed, "What?" Had he read her mind earlier?

His answer was taking that first bite. The one that couldn't be undone.

That ultimate sin. The mistake that changed everything.

His teeth sunk into her swollen, aching flesh, drawing a cry from her that turned into a long, drawn-out moan.

He was marking her. With his teeth. The sting both painful and delicious.

The bruise that would develop would remind her for days to come of this night. This moment.

Of allowing something she shouldn't.

She didn't care.

She didn't care.

She. Didn't. Care.

Her eyes rolled back and she forced his head to the as-yet unmarked breast. "Again," came out on a groan.

The sharpness of his teeth almost breaking her skin made her breath rush from her and her knees wobble. A wave of heat raced downward from his bite and pooled in her pussy, another warm trickle slipping from her. The bead of desire rolling down her inner thigh, past the cotton.

She no longer cared if he saw it. Or smelled how she burned for him.

Or if he discovered how her body had instinctively opened for him. Invited him inside.

A traitor opening the door to an enemy. Allowing an insurgent access to wreak havoc.

He pulled his head free from her hands, but continued to stare at her breasts. His rough fingertips skimmed over one bite, then the other.

"Fuck yeah," he whispered roughly.

He didn't look up, didn't look at her, instead flipped her

around so she faced the mirror. That was when he finally met her gaze.

His eyes were dark, filled with turmoil. But what they also held sent another drip of arousal down her inner thigh.

"I smell you," he growled softly. "Fuckin' smell how much you want my dick in your cunt. You want that, don't you?"

She couldn't push the *yes* from her throat, so instead she gave him a look in the mirror that said it all.

His eyes narrowed and the corners of his lips curled just barely. Not a smile, but the slightest smirk.

He knew he was in control, that at this moment, she'd allow him to do anything to her.

Anything.

And nothing he could do—not even his worst—would scare her. Nothing would make her demand he stop.

Not a fucking thing.

The second she lifted her chin and gave him that silent challenge, he moved like lightning.

With a hand to the back of her neck, he shoved her down, bending her over at the hips, then he grabbed her wrists and planted both of her palms on the mirror.

She tipped her head down, not watching it unfold, but instead listening.

His ragged breath, the rush of air, the swish of the boxers being dragged down her legs until they pooled around her feet.

He dragged his fingers back up her bare inner thighs, gathering the beads of wetness, then she heard him suck her arousal from his fingers.

Her own breath shuddered, her heart pounded, her blood rushed.

Her pussy thumped like it had its own heart.

He wasn't moving slowly but wasn't moving quickly enough, either.

"Fuckin' soaked," he murmured from behind her.

Her arms tremored, her fingers curled slightly as she pressed her palms more securely against the glass of the mirror.

Tomorrow those handprints, like the bites, would remind her of what happened tonight.

What she allowed to happen.

She unlocked her knees as he used his foot to spread hers farther apart. The same way an officer did to the subject they were arresting and was about to do a pat-down.

None of his movements were gentle and all of them calculated.

Her bed, even her couch, wasn't far away. But he didn't want to take her there. He didn't want to appear like he wanted this. That it was only sex between two people.

Because it was more than that.

This was a message to her. A reminder to himself. Both they were ignoring right now, but would reflect upon later.

When their minds were no longer muddled. When his cock was no longer straining against his zipper. When her pussy was no longer slick with wanting him. When her nipples no longer screamed to be twisted and plucked by his long, rough fingers. To be sucked deeply into his mouth.

Goosebumps swept over her skin as the jingle of his belt filled the pulsing space between them. The sound of his zipper being pulled down was deafening.

He did not rush. He took his time, drawing it out, stretching out that anticipation.

Maybe he wanted her to beg.

Maybe he wanted her to cry out for him. To him.

He wouldn't get that from her.

But she *would* get what she wanted. She only needed to be patient.

The rustle of denim and whatever he wore underneath came next.

Then what she was waiting for...

The heat and press of his flesh against hers.

The sigh as he dragged the fat crown from her anus downward.

To where she was open and waiting for him.

Ready to accept him.

Waiting for that initial satisfying stretch.

Once. Twice. He dragged the head of his cock through her folds, gathering her natural lube, pushing the head against her anus each time, not breaching, and not quite a promise, but more of a threat.

Like he'd take her there instead, when she *so* wanted him to fuck her pussy.

His arm crossed her hips, becoming an iron bar, holding her still, his hand cupping her mound, his thumb searched for her sensitive, swollen nub.

He circled, flicked, pressed it, making her body jerk.

Every cell in her body pulsed with the need for him to take her.

Take her hard. Take her fast.

To give her the orgasm she was dying for.

But if he kept rolling and pinching her clit the way he was, she wouldn't wait to come until he was—

He did it. He brought her there. That quickly. Without his cock inside her. With just his touch on her clit, with the burn of the bites on her breasts, with the anticipation.

She closed her eyes and let the waves sweep her away.

She had bitten back her whimper, her gasp, the rush of breath, so she had no idea if he knew she came.

But his hand was gone. It now controlled his cock again as he used the head of it to once again spread her wetness from her clit to her anus.

Then he smacked his slick, hard length against her ass cheek a couple of times, leaving stickiness behind on her skin, from her orgasm, from his precum. Using his other hand, he pulled one ass cheek away from the other, spreading her, opening her to his view.

Showing him all her vulnerability.

Right now, she wasn't a cop. He wasn't a felon.

She wasn't a Bryson. He wasn't a biker.

She was simply a woman. He a man.

Both wanting to satisfy the most basic need.

To forget everything but that very moment in time. That crack in the universe. Where on the other side, things were different.

Where it didn't matter who she was. Who he was.

Two beings giving and taking what they wanted.

"Head up," he growled. "Wanna see your face. Don't you fuckin' hide it."

She lifted her head and her hair fell away so she could meet his eyes in the mirror.

What she saw took her breath away.

She was totally naked. Her cheeks flushed, her eyelids heavy, her mouth parted, her breasts hanging heavily with the nipples still puckered and the beaded tips pointing toward the floor.

In contrast, he was still completely dressed. Still wearing his cut. Most likely on purpose. Like he would get a perverse satisfaction of fucking her with it on.

When she opened her mouth, to demand he get naked, too, he stopped her before the words could even escape.

Again, as if he could read her mind.

"No. Wanna make sure you know who's inside you, who's fuckin' you. Want you to watch me fuck you."

With one thumb pressing her anus, he used his other hand to slide his cock down again, this time pressing his hips forward just the slightest bit.

If she surged back, she'd impale herself. She'd get what she wanted faster than waiting for him to give it to her.

She forced herself to wait.

It was there. Right there.

And then he was inside her. Filling her. Giving her that delicious stretch.

With one hand on her hip and the other holding her shoulder, he drove into her hard, causing her whole body to jerk forward. Causing her to brace her arms so her face didn't smack the mirror.

But he held her eyes in the reflection, his nostrils flaring, his jaw set as he powered into her. He fisted her loose hair in his left hand, raised his right hand and she tensed with the realization of what he was about to do next.

His arm dropped, his hand a blur.

But she saw the motion, heard it land, experienced the sharp sting.

And the strike against her ass cheek caused her gasp at the initial shock of it to turn into a moan.

Holy shit, no one... *no one* had ever done that to her before.

She wasn't surprised he did it, but more shocked at her own reaction to it.

She was soaking him, her arousal sliding down her thighs as he continued to drive relentlessly into her. His cock pistoning in and out of her rim to root, their damp skin slapping almost as loudly as when he spanked her.

It was a risk to demand it, but she did anyway. "Again."

Like she expected, he hesitated, his teeth sinking into his bottom lip. He wanted to fight it, wanted to refuse to give in and give her what she asked for. Since it was no longer only what he wanted, but what she wanted, too.

It was one way he thought he could control her. Only taking what he wanted. Not giving her the same.

He was wrong.

Two could play at that game.

Whether he knew it or not, she had already come once. She would come again whether he spanked her again or not.

But to deprive her of that pleasure would be depriving himself of it, too.

His loss.

He yanked on her hair, pulling her head back until her neck arched, until the back of her head touched the plane of her back.

As her neck strained, she set her eyes on him, not through the mirror this time.

"Mirror, not me," he growled.

He was using the mirror as a barrier between them. A separation of sorts between reality and fantasy.

She struggled to lift her head enough so she could do just that. He wanted for her to strain against him, to feel the sting in her scalp as he tugged one direction and she fought to tip her head enough to look into the mirror.

But the second she did it, he gave her what she wanted. Harder this time. The stinging crack of his palm on her flesh, the violent ripple of her ass as he struck her.

Almost as if he was punishing her for making the demand.

"People like you have tried to control me almost my whole fuckin' life. You ain't doin' it now. Not ever."

But it backfired. Because what turned her on, turned him on even more.

His pace stuttered and his cock thickened even more inside her. That meant he was getting close. He'd have to work hard not to come.

The grip on her hair tightened and he used it to pull her back up to a stand. She was unable to stifle a gasp from the severe pull on her scalp.

That sharp gasp made his hips still, but for only a second. He jerked on her hair at the same time he thrust up.

His arm wrapped across her front like a steel bar, pinning her back to his chest. He squeezed one breast so tightly, it quickly became flush, the nipple peaked and aching. He rolled it between his fingers before pinching it hard, causing the air to flee her lungs.

The other buried between her legs. He grasped her mound like a claim, playing with her clit.

He slid his middle finger inside her, stretching her even further, as his cock speared her over and over.

The hand on her breast slid up her chest until it wrapped around the front of her throat again, squeezing. Reminding her how fragile her throat was, how it wouldn't take much for him to stop her from breathing.

That risk alone made every nerve tingle.

A flush worked its way from her chest up her neck. Her body quivered as he railed her hard, her breasts bouncing violently with each forceful thrust.

Her, not begging for mercy.

Him, not giving her any.

Even if she asked, he'd ignore her.

He was taking what he wanted, not giving a shit about what she wanted. She only had to hang on for the ride.

She grabbed his hair, yanking it hard. Taking pleasure at

watching his grimace of pain in the mirror. The same type of pain he had doled out to her.

"Bitch," he grunted.

When she jerked on it again, pulling it as hard as he had pulled hers, his hand squeezed her mound, his cock jamming hard up and in.

She snaked her other hand down, past his, to find his soaked balls. She could barely reach them, especially with his grip on her throat. But somehow, she managed. She got the soft, slick sac within her fingers and she squeezed. His hips jerked and he grunted against her neck.

Not hard enough to damage, only enough for him to notice. To give him the silent message that he was only in control because she had handed it to him.

Not because he took it from her.

Another bite. This time causing searing pain on the side of her neck.

Everything on her seized. Her heart, her breath, her muscles and then, like a fourth of July firework display, she exploded.

Her mouth opened and something tumbled out. She had no idea what.

Nor did she care.

Neither did he since he was too busy slamming against her, grunting loudly, his face hidden against her neck, sucking on the bite.

With one last thrust, a low and long grunt vibrated against her skin. She didn't need to see him having his climax in the mirror. She could feel it.

His jaw tightened. His muscles turned to stone. His root pulsed intensely, his cock throbbing deep inside her as he emptied himself.

Marking her inside.

Doing something forbidden.

Not only the sex between enemies, but unprotected sex.

Neither demanding any precautions.

Both of them turned on by how everything was wrong with what happened. How it happened.

If it was so wrong, why did it feel so right?

How was this the hottest and best sex in her life?

It was both nasty and brilliant.

Dirty and satisfying.

So wrong and so damn right.

With a last lick to the bite mark, he lifted his face.

His brown eyes locked with her light blue ones in the mirror. Neither willing to move just yet.

Neither looked surprised.

This wasn't any awakening. They didn't suddenly have an unbreakable connection.

This was just raw, animalistic sex.

For her. For him.

Neither would argue that.

It was what it was.

A morning-after mistake. An irrefutable regret.

And of course, a bad decision.

But it was done. It couldn't be erased.

The apple couldn't be uneaten. From here the exposed core would only rot.

"This was a fuckin' mistake." His voice was rough and scratchy.

"For once, we agree on something."

"We're just gonna forget this ever happened."

"I agree." She agreed even though she knew it was a lie. Neither of them would ever forget it.

"Nobody needs to know."

"Agreed."

"Like nobody, Jet." For once, he didn't sound so confident. Worry tinged his words. He was afraid someone would find out.

"Does it sound like I'm arguing? Do you think I want anyone to know I had sex with you?"

"You think I want anyone knowin' I fucked you?" he sneered.

No, she couldn't imagine he would. She was sure he wouldn't want any of his brothers to find out he fucked a cop. She could only imagine to those bikers it would be worse than fucking jailbait or maybe even being gay.

He slipped from her, stepping back, quickly yanking his jeans and boxer briefs back up and tucking himself away before fastening his jeans and securing his belt. Not even bothering to clean himself up first.

When he was done, she turned to face him, her hands on her hips. Not caring he was once again fully dressed while she stood still completely naked, the mix of his cum and her own dampening her thighs. The flesh damaged by his teeth throbbing with every pounding heartbeat. Her ass still stinging from his hand.

Both satisfied and empty from him no longer filling her.

Her eyes narrowed. So did his.

Her chin rose slightly. So did his.

Her mouth curled at the corners. His did not.

"Fuck you, Jet."

She continued to smile as she reached down and dragged her middle finger through her swollen folds, then lifted it, using the glistening digit to flip him the bird. "Fuck you, Rook."

His jaw shifted and his hands curled into fists.

For a second, she wondered if he'd haul off and belt her.

If he did, she would fight back. It was one thing to allow him to be rough when she wanted it. It was another to be abusive.

She had no idea if that was his intent but what they just did was pulling the anger from his very core. Bringing it bubbling to the surface.

He wasn't mad at her.

He was pissed at himself.

She knew exactly why.

He didn't hate her. And for that, he hated himself.

He spun on his boot, rushed out the door, slamming it behind him.

She stared at the door for a few seconds more to ensure he was gone.

And once she knew for certain he wouldn't return, she locked it and gathered her clothes. She needed to shower. To wash him off her. She didn't need his cum as a reminder of what they did. The marks on her breasts, neck and ass were plenty enough so she wouldn't forget for a while.

She smiled again once she realized he never told her what he came to say.

The whole reason he showed up at her apartment at midnight.

The whole reason he forced himself inside.

He left taking with him the perfect excuse to seek her out again.

She had no doubt he would use that excuse.

In fact, she looked forward to it.

Chapter Eleven

He was tired, but restless. He should go back to his room, but he doubted he'd be able to sleep yet. Why?

Because of that fucking bitch.

She was like a goddamn sickness. A virus attacking him from the inside out.

It had been weeks. Fucking *weeks!* And he still couldn't scrape Jet from his mind.

He'd tried. Too many times. With many different methods.

He failed every damn time. And it was all that bitch's fault.

If he didn't think of her, he couldn't get hard. Worse, he couldn't finish. Not until he pictured her in the mirror naked as he railed her hard while she ate it the fuck up.

Loving every fucking second of it.

Fucking *encouraging* him instead of resisting. Encouraging him to bite her, to spank her perfect, bitable ass.

To squeeze her neck, to fuck her roughly.

While the look in her eyes spurred him on to make her come.

I always like a challenge.

She wasn't the only one.

But now his challenge was to scrape her out of his fucking head. Out of his thoughts. Out of his dreams.

Out of his goddamn life.

For good.

No doubt, it had been a mistake.

He knew it the second he had pulled up to her place. The second he got out of the borrowed cage. The second he climbed down the back steps to the basement apartment of the house in town.

The second he pounded on the door.

The second she opened that door, wearing what she was wearing, looking how she looked. Tousled and sleepy-eyed, the outline of her hard nipples visible through the thin cotton. Her bare legs, her loose black hair begging to be pulled, those goddamn soul-sucking eyes.

Yeah, it had been a mistake.

Stupid fuck that he was, he'd done it anyway.

Every fucking time he'd been arrested, he knew he made a fucking mistake, too. But, of course, he'd done it anyway.

Because he couldn't not do it.

Just like he couldn't not fuck Jet.

So he did.

Look what all his bad decisions made him. An ex-con and a pig fucker.

He tilted the Jim Beam bottle to his lips and let the bite of the bourbon slide down his throat and the warmth pool in his gut.

He should take one of the sweet butts who remained back to his room and fuck her until he passed out.

That was what he should do.

The sweet butts had been busy ever since the club's Christmas party officially ended. Unofficially, it still wasn't over. Not until everyone had left or passed out.

He took another long swig, hoping the booze would at least dull the memory of Jet and the mistake he'd made. The mistake they'd done.

He glanced around The Barn. Music still loudly filled the large space and church was a fucking mess from when everyone partied earlier. The prospects would have their work cut out for them come Christmas morning when they had to clean everything the fuck up.

That was one reason why it was such a damn mess. His brothers knew they weren't the ones to have to do it. So, basically, the area was trashed. Typical after a really good party.

It started as a club-family get-together and, like normal, finished by turning into a night of depravity. Now only a few remained. The prospects, some of his brothers and the sweet butts who hadn't disappeared with anyone yet. Or had finished with their first conquest and were on the prowl for their next.

Trip had bought all of the sweet butts cuts for Christmas. Black leather vests with rockers on the back. The top one claiming "Property of," the bottom reading "Blood Fury MC," with the large Fury insignia patch in the center. They were similar to the ol' ladies' cuts but without a specific brother's name on the bottom rocker since the women belonged to the club as a whole. The sweet butts were available to anyone who wanted them. Whenever they wanted them. However they wanted them.

Their choice was either to be a sweet butt or not. After that their choices were limited.

Yeah.

Not long after the children left, those cuts were the only thing the sweet butts were wearing. It seemed once the clock struck a certain hour, all their damn clothes vanished.

Not that Rook was complaining. For the most part, their bodies rocked. Some were a little younger and thinner than he'd like, but still doable.

Now Jet's body...

Fuck.

Slender but not skinny. In shape and tight as fuck. Sculpted muscles but nowhere near overdone or manly, not with those tits and that fuckable ass and all that long, straight black, fistable hair falling around her face. Those fucking blue eyes, too...

Fuck. Just sitting at The Barn's bar thinking about her, his dick began to chub up. Fucking traitor.

He reached for the brass pipe sitting on the bar top in front of him, put it to his lips and lit it. He'd probably need to smoke a pound of pot and then drown himself in a barrel of whiskey to rid that woman from his system.

Of course, that pissed him the fuck off.

He'd never focused on any female for more than the time she was underneath him. That was it. A few minutes after he tucked away his dick, she was forgotten. Even if the sex was scorching hot. Even if the woman was into crazy shit.

No one stuck with him like that bitch Jet.

Fucking goddamn motherfucker.

He flicked the lighter again, lifted it to the bowl and took another long drag.

What did he need to do to get rid of her? Inject bleach into his veins to clean her out of his blood?

He needed to keep his mind busy on something else. Like the action that was happening at the end of the bar just a couple of feet away from him.

Ozzy had Lizzy's bare ass planted on the edge. He stood between her spread legs fucking her, while Angel, also on top of the bar, straddled Lizzy's face, both only wearing their new cuts. Ozzy's hand was squeezing Lizzy's tit, his other Angel's, and he wore a wide grin as he lazily pumped his hips and watched the two women do their thing.

The man loved his threesomes. He didn't give a shit if it was with two women or one where he double-teamed the female with one of their brothers. He also wasn't close to being shy.

None of them were.

Or at least his single brothers weren't. And the ones who had done time and learned quickly that privacy was a commodity. But once someone claimed their ol' lady, they tended to take it behind closed doors.

Except for Stella and Trip. While they didn't fuck out in the open, they also didn't hide it when they were about to jump each other's bones. Like tonight...

Trip and Stella were the last couple to remain. There was a reason for that. It wasn't the first time they'd hung around for a while afterward, once the kids were gone and things began to loosen up. Things like clothes and morals.

Trip was leaning back against the wall with Stella facing away from him but pulled to his chest. His one hand gripped the crotch of her jeans and his other arm was like a bar across her stomach holding her tightly against him. His mouth was to her ear as they watched. Rook could only imagine what the president said to his ol' lady.

What they were observing was Whip, sitting on one of the old green bus benches along the side wall, his jeans pushed halfway down his hairless thighs and his knees spread wide to make room for Crystal. He had one bent arm hooked behind his head and a fist in her hair. The young sweet butt was on her feet, leaning over with her bare ass in the air, her head bobbing up and down in his lap at a rapid pace. Rev stood behind Crystal, his jeans also halfway down his thighs, ramming her as hard as he could.

If he was Whip, Rook would be worried about getting his dick bitten off with as rough as Rev was slamming her.

This kind of open display of sex was one reason Sig and Red normally disappeared early. Avoiding it helped keep the demons at bay for both of them. Though, the deep-seated darkness that haunted them stemmed from two different reasons.

Reese and Deacon had stayed long enough to watch some of the adult action before Reese tugged the club treasurer upstairs to his apartment. Deke had left with a couple chin lifts to his fellow brothers, a big grin and eyes only for his woman. No doubt sporting a raging hard-on, too.

Cage and Jemma's house mouse, Tessa, had taken baby Dyna home hours ago. Once the sweet butts began shedding their clothes, Jemma also left, letting Cage decide for himself whether to stay or follow. Rook shook his head as his younger brother tagged after his ol' lady like a damn puppy. But then, Judge's younger sister was hot as fuck, so he really didn't blame Cage for going to get some of that.

The last time Rook saw Dutch was when his old man was banging some chick Rook didn't know—he assumed she was a hang-around someone invited tonight—in one of the empty bunkhouse rooms. With the door open, of course, and certainly not being quiet about it. Both Dutch's grunts and growled words, along with the *maybe* twenty-year-old's vocal responses, echoed down the hallway.

Rook's old man never had a problem snagging willing snatch. He had no idea how his father did it, but he did. Rook only hoped he'd be just as good at it when he was Dutch's age. Not that his father was ancient or anything, but he was certainly past his prime.

Rook also wouldn't be surprised if his old man crashed the rest of the night in that empty room since he was sure Dutch was trashed. The man loved to party until he passed out, usually using his naked companion as a blanket.

Rook shook his head.

Shade and Chelle had taken their kids home earlier, too, not allowing even the twenty-one-year-old Maddie to stay behind. Not when Shade couldn't keep an eye on her and not when he knew the direction most parties went later in the night. Maddie didn't look eager to leave when she was dragged out of there.

Shade would have fun keeping Chelle's oldest daughter from ending up riding a sweet butt's face as the sweet butt was getting fucked at the same time.

That actually caused a half-grin and made his dick twitch more than watching Ozzy nail Lizzy. Everyone was used to those two just getting it on whenever and wherever. Lizzy was a regular in Ozzy's bed, even though she wasn't his ol' lady and belonged to the whole club, like her new cut stated.

If Ozzy wanted the sweet butt to be unavailable to any of his brothers, he'd need to swap out that bottom rocker with one bearing his name. Until then, she was fair game.

To distract himself, Rook tried to picture Maddie in Angel's spot, riding Lizzy's face, but that fantasy turned quickly into Jet replacing Lizzy while Rook took Ozzy's place at the end of the bar.

Then he wondered if Jet would mind eating out another woman while he fucked her. Weren't most female pigs a lesbian or at least swung both ways?

Huh.

Now his half-chub began to grow.

Cassie and Judge, along with their daughter, Daisy, also left around the same time as Judge's sister, Jemma. Judge made sure their house mouse, the now nineteen-year-old Saylor, went along with them, since his son Ry was home from college for Christmas and had his own room in the bunkhouse. It was not only smart to keep a wild Saylor away from a hormonal Ry but to avoid seeing her older brother, Rev, banging Crystal right in front of anyone who wanted to watch.

Not that Saylor hadn't seen a lot of similar action since she came to live with Judge and Cassie. But still, it was one thing watching someone unrelated, it was another when it was your own brother.

Though, Rook had seen his own brother and father getting their rocks off plenty of times. It would be different if he had a sister...

When Rook glanced over toward that corner of church again, Trip and Stella were gone.

Yeah, they only stayed long enough to get worked up. If it wasn't blue ball weather right now, they probably wouldn't wait to get inside the farmhouse first.

It looked like Whip was done already since Crystal now had her hands planted on his shoulders to brace herself against Rev's harsh pounding. A few more thrusts and Rev's blond head was thrown back as he pulled out, yanked off the wrap and shot his load all over Crystal's ass.

Just then, Reilly came through the door that separated the bunkhouse from church. She took one glance at the bus bench, her chin snapped back, she frowned and her mouth got tight. After a few more seconds, her gaze hit the bar and landed on the Ozzy action and she shook her head. When she spotted Rook, she headed in his direction with her scowl now a big smile. That made him worry.

Fuck.

She settled on a stool next to him, grabbed the JB bottle and tipped it to her lips.

"Why you still here?" he demanded as he watched her throat roll. He wondered if she spat or swallowed.

"Why not?" she asked when she was done taking a long pull.

"Reese know you're still here?"

She rolled her green eyes at him. "Umm. First of all, she's not my mother. Second, even if she was, the last time I checked my driver's license, it indicated I'm twenty-five years old. Why do people forget that?"

"Maybe 'cause they don't want Reese rippin' off their balls with an evil smile and a cackle."

Reilly laughed in a way that said that long pull on the bourbon bottle wasn't her first. Or her second.

"You drunk?" he asked her with narrowed eyes.

Hers narrowed, too. "Didn't know I answered to you, either."

"You answer to all of us, Reilly. You wanna be a part of this club, then that's the fuck how it is. You walk around here like you belong, but you ain't a sweet butt, you ain't an ol' lady, you—"

"I'm nothing," she finished for him. "An unwelcome, untouchable tag-along. Right?"

"No one invited you, you forced your way in. Remember that. Trip tolerates it because of Deacon and Reese. That's it."

"Wow. Someone has a prickly burr up their ass tonight," she muttered and took another swallow of the Jim Beam, hissing when she was through.

"Just remindin' you that you bein' reckless and forgettin' who you are could really get someone fucked up. Nobody wants their colors stripped, no one wants to be taken out to the field and given a blanket party with that fuckin' club." He jerked his chin to where the wood club with the leather cord hung on the wall. The club used by the Originals and the same one Judge used on Cage not so long ago. The carved wood had dark stains from old blood on it.

It hung in The Barn as a reminder to follow the rules. But when his brothers were partying hard, sometimes they forgot those rules. Sometimes that shit slipped right from their muddled minds.

Sometimes temptations were stronger than consequences.

And Reilly was on the *do-not-touch* list along with Saylor and Tessa, Trip's younger sister.

However, Reilly tended to be a dick tease. Rook didn't think she did it on purpose, but it was more about how she lived life. To the fullest. Watching the blonde, green-eyed beauty tempted a lot of them. Drove a lot of them to touch themselves since they couldn't touch her.

Even Rook.

Well, before the black-haired, blue-eyed bitch stuck to his brain like a fucking leech sucking out his sense. *Damn it.*

"You ain't drivin' back to your place tonight if you've been drinkin'."

She cocked one blonde eyebrow in her very Reilly way. "So, where am I staying then?"

"In any of the empty rooms. Just don't pick the one Dutch is in."

She wrinkled her nose. "I saw and heard enough of that already."

Rook grimaced. "Didn't we all."

"Trip doesn't want women staying in the bunkhouse all night, though," she reminded him.

"Don't think Trip's gonna give a shit if you stay in one of the rooms. *Alone.* He just don't want it turnin' into a whorehouse."

She smiled and took another draw on the bottle. "That means I can't cuddle up with you?" she teased.

"I prefer to keep the colors inked into my skin right where they belong, fuck you very much."

She leaned closer and whispered, "We don't have to tell anyone."

"Reilly..."

She shoved his arm. "I'm just messing with you. I don't fuck assholes. Especially colossal ones like you. You know, wide and loose from all the fisting done to you in prison."

"Don't knock it 'til you try it." He ripped the bourbon from her fingers, finished it off and slammed the empty bottle on the shellacked bar top.

"I was drinking that!"

"I was drinkin' it first. So you know, you drank my back-wash. That's one way for you to take me down your throat."

"Eww. Gross!" she cried, but then laughed. Yeah, she was tipsy, for sure.

That meant she needed to stay away from any horny bastards including the new prospects who didn't know how dangerous it would be to put a finger on her, whether she encouraged it or not.

"You can't find an empty room, take mine."

Her eyebrows shot up. "You won't need it?"

"I'll crash elsewhere if I need to."

She grabbed his cheeks and squeezed them, giving him fish lips. "You can be the sweetest asshole sometimes."

"Just don't tell anyone."

She slipped from the stool. "I'm getting shirts printed, just so you know. In fluorescent colors, too."

He laughed, snagged her wrist and pulled her back to him. "You ain't so bad."

"Ooo. A compliment!" She wiggled her eyebrows. "Stop with all this sweetness. I can't take it. I might stop thinking you're an asshole."

He released her wrist and when she turned, he gave her a stinging smack on the ass. "Go. My room's unlocked. If you use it, lock the door behind you. You hear me?"

She shot him a smile over her shoulder. *Fuck,* she was tempting.

"And just ignore any dirty shirts or socks you find that are stiff," he called out.

She waved a hand over her shoulder and shook her head. His gaze remained glued to the swing of her hips and ass until she disappeared through the door she had come out of a few minutes earlier.

At least she had taken his mind off Jet for those few minutes.

Reilly certainly made working at the garage more entertaining. But recently he had noticed Rev's attention focused on her more often than not. Rook had warned him several times not to even think about it.

Rook's head swiveled back to the bus bench where the threesome had been earlier. Rev had disappeared and Crystal now straddled Whip's lap and rode him. From where he sat, Rook could barely hear the sweet butt's high-pitched cries over the loud rock playing through the speakers.

A movement from the back corner of The Barn caught Rook's attention. Where the steps led up to the second floor meeting room.

Some of his brothers occasionally disappeared up there for privacy with whoever they needed a moment alone with.

But it wasn't one of his brothers coming down those steps. The new prospect Rook sponsored wasn't alone, either.

Since Crazy Pete's had been shut down early so all the prospects, new and old, could attend the Christmas party, most were still lingering around The Barn and the bunkhouse. Possum was passed out in a corner half-hidden under the twinkling Christmas tree with a beer bottle still clutched within his fingers. Tater Tot sat on one of the benches in front of the roaring fireplace, a dumb, blank look on his face, like he was spaced out. Or brain dead. Or a little of both.

All night the prospects Rook sponsored had been trolling any female hang-arounds that had showed up earlier since they couldn't touch the sweet butts.

Since all three men hadn't been out of the joint for very long, Rook was sure they all were chasing as much tail as they could to make up for the time they hadn't had any. That was how Rook was every time he got sprung. He would take a week afterward, nailing anyone he could until his balls were so empty, his dick began shooting dust.

Unlike the thick cum that had filled Jet, then dribbled down her creamy thighs, the ones he wanted to take a bite out of. Leave his mark inside her and outside, too.

Fuck.

For once, he'd like to stop thinking about her. Maybe he should go hang with Reilly in his room since she seemed to be the only one to drag Jet from his brain, even if only temporarily.

But first he had to deal with Fitz, now known as Scar, as he hit The Barn's floor followed by a female who Rook recognized as Angel's friend. Rook didn't care enough to know her name yet, but the redhead was turning into a regular hang-around.

"Yo!" Rook shouted at Scar, who stopped in his tracks and so did the chick.

Rook jerked his chin up in an unspoken command for Scar to approach. The woman began to follow the prospect and Rook shook his head.

Scar stopped again and said something low to the woman, who pouted and planted a hand on her hip.

Rook sighed at the attitude. *What-fuckin-ever.* Hang-arounds were there by invite-only. An invitation that could easily be revoked.

So could a prospect's sponsorship.

When Scar reached him, Rook growled low, "What the fuck were you doin' up there?"

Scar tipped his head toward the woman who obediently remained standing where he'd left her. "Was doin' her."

"Not up there you ain't."

"Got the top of a fuckin' bunkbed, Rook. Sharin' a room with four other fuckin' guys. If I wanted to still do that shit, I'da stayed in prison."

"Nobody forced you to come here. Offered you a place to land. You don't wanna be here, then get the fuck out. You wanna stay, then don't be doin' shit that'll get you tossed. 'Specially since I brought you in. Don't fuckin' kick me in the balls 'cause you're emptyin' yours where you shouldn't be."

Scar's deep frown pulled at the thick scar that divided the whiskers on his jaw. "I ain't allowed to fuck her? She ain't a sweet butt."

"Don't give a fuck that you fucked her, it's *where* you fucked her." Rook jabbed a finger toward the ceiling. "Better not be one fuckin' drop of jizz on that table upstairs. The exec committee ain't gonna be happy if they go to have a meetin' and there's dried white shit on their precious table. You get me?"

"Yeah," Scar grunted.

"Our prez also told you to get that teardrop tat removed. You got that scheduled?"

A muscle popped in Scar's tight jaw. "Yeah."

With the time Rook spent with Scar on the inside, he was aware the man didn't like rules. He didn't like being told what to do. He was also aware that Scar might be an issue. But he figured if the man could make it through his first year being treated like dog shit, he'd be an asset to the brotherhood.

The man was a cold-blooded killer and wouldn't hesitate to do what he needed to do to save himself or anyone he was loyal to. His loyalty was his best trait. If you had his back, he had yours no matter what. No matter if that loyalty added more time onto his bid. Even so...

Rook hooked a thumb over his shoulder toward the front doors of The Barn. "Again, you don't wanna do what you need to do, then there's the fuckin' door. Warned you even before your ass got here, the first year's gonna be miserable as fuck. Still better than prison. You got pussy, better food, booze, a way to put scratch in your pocket and, even better, you ain't getting fucked with by the screws. Should feel like goddamn Heaven. So, decide this fuckin' second and tell me to my face right fuckin' now: you stayin' or you goin'?"

Scar glanced over Rook's shoulder toward the door, then back over his own shoulder toward the woman he just laid pipe with. When he turned back to Rook, he nodded.

"Good choice," Rook answered and offered Scar his hand. The prospect clasped it and they bumped shoulders.

Crisis averted. The club needed prospects, but only ones who wanted to be there. The second they didn't want to be there they needed to be cut out like cancer. Because cancer had the ability to spread, so that shit had to be dealt with a quickness.

Disease had spread through the Originals, causing their demise.

Trip wasn't the only one who wanted to avoid that mistake being repeated. All of them had been working hard to keep that from happening, to build a strong brotherhood. What started on shaky ground had settled and only became stronger each day.

No one wanted to see that get fucked up. So, the prospects needed to keep their asses in line or they were out. It wouldn't be a debate but a reckoning.

"You can fuck her anywhere but up there or in my bed."

"Got you," Scar grunted before turning on his boot heel, grabbing the woman by the arm and hauling her into the bunkhouse. As they were going out, the next possible problem walked in.

Billie.

He could do a round with the crazy-assed woman to try to purge Jet from his thoughts, but he knew it wouldn't do any good. He'd just end up on his knees, hurting and crying for nothing.

He wondered who she just got done working over because she appeared pleased with herself. He recognized that look. It meant she got off the way she liked getting off. The only two brothers unaccounted for right now were Easy and Dodge. Maybe he needed to start a rescue mission. Or a search party.

"Who's havin' second thoughts right now?" he asked her when the sadomasochist went behind the bar and poured herself a beer.

Billie looked up from filling the red plastic cup from the

keg tucked under the bar and gave him a smile that made Rook's balls contract in fear. "Who do you think?"

"Please don't fuckin' tell me Dutch moved on from that sweet young pussy to your abusive ass. Though, I might pay well if you force him to wear a red rubber ball gag while he's tied up and let me take pictures. Could use some blackmail material against my old man."

"Nope," answered the woman with the dark short hair, her signature leather collar and heavy goth makeup. "But I doubt Dutch would care if such proof was out there. He'd probably want a copy for his wallet so he could show it to everyone. Just like he shows Dyna's picture." She lowered her voice and made it gruff. "*Here's a photo of my Duchess and here's one of me naked, gagged and bound. Har har har.*"

Rook snorted. No truer words had ever been spoken. But it also made him stare at Billie wondering if she actually had worked his father over at one time or another.

He shuddered at that image now embedded in his head. Well, that was a good fucking way to evict Jet from his fucked-up brain.

Even so, no one understood what Whip had seen in the woman, now leaning on the other side of the bar, to make her his girlfriend, even for the hot minute it lasted. The woman didn't hide the fact she liked dick too much—and also took joy in making whoever was attached to it hurt—to stick with one man. Especially a quiet one like Whip. But it was smart to be suspicious of the quiet ones and Rook figured Whip might have some hidden kinks none of them knew about.

If he did, Rook didn't want to know the details, either.

It was bad enough when they all found out what shit Sig was into, what the man craved. What he needed to hold on to his sanity. But what he no longer got because of Red...

The VP made a huge sacrifice to be with his ol' lady. But

seeing their intense bond, everyone knew Sig didn't mind making it. Rook had never seen a couple live for each other like those two did.

If one stopped breathing, so would the other.

Rook came back to the present when Billie moved around the bar, beer in hand, and stepped in between his spread legs, running her hand from his knee to the top of his thigh. He froze, worried she'd grab his sac and squeeze it so hard it would drop him to his knees.

"You've been pretty cranky. You need a good fucking?" Between her hand and her commanding tone, she was clearly offering herself up, even though she'd just worked over someone else.

He still didn't know who the "victim" was. Not that it mattered. Because, in truth, he was not in the mood to go a round with Billie tonight.

The problem wasn't that he needed to get fucked, the problem was who he wanted to fuck.

That was what ate at him. What made him cranky.

The whole putting his dick inside Jet thing.

Just about every night he jerked off to the same memory over and over. It was on a continuous loop in his brain. He replayed everything he saw in that mirror.

He had used the mirror to distance himself from her. To separate himself from what they were doing. What they had done.

He tried to convince himself that watching it in the mirror was like watching porn instead. It wasn't him. It wasn't her. It was simply two strangers slapping skin together.

Only *he* had been the one behind Jet with his jeans only pulled down far enough to access his dick.

He had been the one to leave the marks on her tits and neck, a spot where he knew before he even did it, anyone would be able to see it. It gave him a sick sense of pleasure on how hard she'd have to work to hide it from others. And even better, every time she saw those bite marks, she'd be forced to think of him.

He also couldn't erase the sight of the red handprints on her ass. Whenever he saw them in his mind, he instantly got rock hard.

Like now.

Billie probably thought his reaction was because of her.

He wanted to rush over to her little dumpy basement apartment to repeat his mistake and slam Jet against that mirror again.

He wanted to force her to her knees, wrapping the strands of long, black hair around his fist, and making sure her ass faced the mirror so he could see her shiny pink pussy while he throat-fucked her.

So he could watch her reach between her legs and get herself off with her own fingers. Fingers that would easily slip inside herself because she was so fucking wet. Then he wanted to watch her fuck her own ass with one of those slick fingers.

He wanted all of that and more. He wanted that until his ears rang with her begging him to stop because she couldn't take anymore.

Or with her begging him to not stop.

A groan bubbled up Rook's throat and he grabbed Billie's wrist, preventing her from pulling out his dick. "Ain't for you."

Billie never took offense to being rejected, unlike some of the other sweet butts. She was thick-skinned, but then, she had to be to be into what she was. There was always someone wanting what she could dish out and also what she could take. She knew if one of the brothers didn't want her one night, they'd be searching for her another night when they were in the mood to have pain mixed in with their pleasure.

But tonight he couldn't look into Billie's face and come. Not without seeing Jet's.

The bitch ruined him.

Totally fucking destroyed him. He wanted no one but her.

That meant one thing.

He needed a different method to purge her from his thoughts. One he hadn't tried yet. One he'd been desperately avoiding.

Once that was done, he could simply walk away satisfied and move on. Get back to his life no longer haunted by her.

Dodge surprised Rook by wandering out from the bunkhouse wearing only boxers and scratching his balls as he walked a little bow-legged. He did a chin lift in greeting to Rook, who returned it, trying not to smirk at the thin, long welt marks crisscrossing his tattooed chest.

"Was wonderin' where you went," the bar manager muttered to Billie.

Well, there was Rook's answer. He didn't realize his former cellmate was into that kind of shit. Maybe he hadn't been scratching his nuts after all, maybe he'd been checking to make sure they were still attached.

"You ready for round two?" Billie asked him, tweaking one of his nipples that was swollen and red because it had been struck with whatever Billie used from her bag of torture devices she always had on hand. "I figured you had to recover."

"Ready for round two," Dodge answered with a smirk, rubbing at his injured nipple.

"Then, how about we head back to your apartment so I can take my time with you? You know Trip doesn't want any of us here come morning. And what I plan on doing to you next, I don't want to rush."

Dodge shot Rook a look. "Two fuckin' seconds, brother. That's all it took to get me rock fuckin' solid." He grabbed his hard-on through his boxers and grinned. "I'll get my fuckin' clothes. Time to jet."

Dodge headed back into the bunkhouse. That short trip gave Rook a good view of what the man's back looked like, which was worse than his chest, and with a last, lingering squeeze to Rook's thigh, Billie followed him, wearing a very pleased expression.

Time to jet.

Yeah, it was.

Time to get Jet out of his system once and for all.

He might not have her cell phone but that didn't mean he couldn't track her down. He knew what she drove, where she worked, and, even better, where she lived.

Finding Jet shouldn't be hard at all.

Unlike him.

Chapter Twelve

The borrowed cage he drove fish-tailed as he turned from Main Street into the unplowed lot at the garage, despite it being an all-wheel-drive. He jerked the wheel in the opposite direction and straightened out Jemma's XC40.

Him, driving a fucking Volvo. Could his life get any lower than that?

Cage had cursed Rook the fuck out when he pounded on the door to his brother's modular home at not even six this morning.

Not just any morning. Christmas fucking morning. It had snowed all fucking night, too. That meant he needed to borrow a vehicle that could get him where he needed to go. And today that was not his FXSB Breakout. Not if he wanted to keep himself and his treasured Harley in one piece.

He thought his younger brother was going to punch him when he opened the door in just his boxer briefs with his hair a mess and eyes squinty, curse words filling the air.

"Gonna wake up Dyna, asshole."

Rook had held out his palm. "Just need to borrow Jem's wheels."

Cage's eyebrows shot up his forehead. "For fuckin' what?"

"To check on the four-legged buttmunch."

Cage stared at him for the longest time while Rook stood waiting on the front deck, freezing his balls off.

He shook his outstretched hand again. "C'mon. I'll bring the little asshole back to the farm with me, so I don't have to borrow her cage again." Wouldn't have to borrow it again *today*, anyway.

"Don't think she likes you enough to let you borrow her cage."

"Don't ask her."

Cage huffed. "Yeah, right."

"Ain't you the king of your modular castle?"

Cage snorted, rubbing the sleep from his eyes. "Yeah, okay. I also like bein' inside that castle where it's warm, so I ain't stupid. I do somethin' she don't like, I'll be standin' outside lookin' in just like you are right now."

Rook sighed. "Forget it. Fuck that little bastard. He can starve."

That got Rook the reaction he hoped for. With a frown and another searing curse, Cage lifted a finger and disappeared deeper into the house, returning a moment later to toss him the keys.

"You fuck up her ride, I'll shoot you before she does."

Rook grinned. "She got your goddamn balls in a vise, baby brother."

"Yeah, well, she also sucks 'em like a pro, so fuck off."

"I heard that!" came a sleepy voice from deeper within the house.

Cage made a *told-you-so* face. "See? Now you're gonna have to suck 'em for me."

Rook gripped the keys tighter and blew him a kiss. "I'll let the little hairy prick with needle-sharp teeth lick 'em later. A smear of peanut butter will get him started."

Cage faked a loud gag and slammed the door in his face, causing snow to fall from the roof and onto his head. The cold white powder skittered down the back of his neck and slipped under his clothes, causing him to shiver. He swore his asshole brother did that on purpose.

Now, after parking Jemma's SUV—still in one piece—in front of the garage, he unlocked the front door and paused a step inside, waiting.

Like fucking clockwork. Furious high-pitched barking echoed through the empty garage.

"Just me, asshole." He needed to figure out a name for the little monster, though "asshole" fit perfectly.

Apparently, the dog didn't give a shit who it was since he continued to yap loudly.

"I feed your ass. Gave you a damn warm spot to sleep. Make sure you don't die of thirst, you motherfucker. Show me some respect!" he yelled out over the dog's barking.

That brought on another round of fresh, ear-piercing hell from wherever the asshole was hiding.

He sighed and headed over to his large two-tier rolling Snap-On toolbox along the far wall. He had pulled out the bottom drawer, removed the tools and filled it with clean rags and an old towel, making the fucker a comfy bed. A comfy *warm* bed out of the cold and snow.

He could see the depression where the mini-monster had made a nest to curl up and sleep.

The office was a lot warmer than the shop area, but he knew

better than to leave the creature locked in the office. Reilly wouldn't appreciate the smell, or the mess, if the dog pissed and shit where she worked. At least in the shop area, if the dog couldn't hold his piss or shit, Rook could hose down the concrete in the bays. He was tempted to pick up some of the tiny turds and scatter them inside Cage's toolbox which was lined up next to his.

A little token of his brotherly love and affection.

"Where you at?" Rook called out, looking around for the black-and-tan beast.

Since that day the dog had curled up in Rook's lap outside the garage bay, the little shit had only snapped at him twice. However, barking was a different story.

He refilled the water bowl, the food bowl and whistled for the dog to let him outside.

When he opened the rear door that led out to the storage yard, Rook heard tiny feet scrambling. He held the door open and waited. The dog sprinted toward freedom, then slammed on the brakes at the edge of the door frame, staring out at all that white bullshit covering the ground.

"Get out there and do your thing."

The shaking dog's front foot was held high in the air and he turned big brown eyes up toward Rook.

"Yeah, snow blows. I feel ya. But the shop ain't a toilet, so get your skinny ass out there and take a piss and a dump."

The dog glanced back outside, then took two steps backward and sneezed before once again turning his eyes up to Rook.

"You're shittin' me. You won't go out in snow? You that much of a pussy?"

Asshole yipped sharply at him.

"I get it. Your feet are the size of the tip of my finger. It's gotta be freezin' but that don't give you the right to shit and piss inside. A pit bull wouldn't be a pussy."

Three distinct yaps and a sneeze.

"Don't like me callin' you a pussy, do you?"

Yap. Yap. Yap. Sneeze.

"Then stop fuckin' bein' one!" Rook yelled impatiently, took his boot and scooted the three-pound rat out into the snow. "The faster you go, the faster you can come back in." Rook slammed the door shut before the dog could run back inside. "Hurry the fuck up," he yelled through the closed door.

Silence.

Thank fuck.

He pulled out his cell phone and double-checked the time. He needed to get out of there soon for his plan to work.

"You done yet?" Rook yelled.

Yap. Yap. Sneeze.

Rook cracked open the door and pressed his eye to the opening. The dog was out there shivering like crazy. But there was a yellow dot and a couple brown M&M's in the snow. Success.

He opened the door and Cujo ran back inside.

Cujo.

Yeah. He liked that. He reached down, scooped the dog up in one hand and only got a half-assed nip for his effort. He lifted the Chihuahua up in the air and turned him until they were eye to eye. "Cujo. You like that? Better than me callin' you Pussy. It's a tough name. A good name. Worthy of a little asshole like you."

Grr. Sneeze.

"Glad you're happy with it. But one more fuckin' bite and your name will be Mud."

Huff. Sneeze.

He pulled Cujo into his chest and the dog immediately

tried to burrow into his jacket where he had the zipper pulled down partway.

"Don't got time to hang right now, Cujo. Gotta go do somethin' important. Promise to come back for you later and take you back to the farm with me."

As long as his plan didn't get him arrested first.

JET INSERTED the key into the lock and turned it. Once the deadbolt clicked, she pushed open the door to her basement apartment.

She sighed, relieved to be home. First stop, shower. Second, her damn bed for some much needed sleep.

She had to work another midnight shift tonight but before that she needed to head over to her aunt and uncle's farm to hang with the fam for Christmas. And stuff her belly with good, homemade grub until she fell into a food coma.

While it would be more ideal if she didn't have to work tonight, as low woman on the seniority list she got stuck working the shitty shifts.

She shut the door and engaged the deadbolt again. After dropping her backpack on the floor at her feet, her fingers worked the large buttons free on her black wool coat.

Once it hung open, she reached for the light switch so she could put it away in the little closet. Her electric bill was high because it didn't matter what time of day it was, living in a converted basement, the place tended to remain dark. She needed to buy her own place, that was what she needed to do. With lots of windows and light. And space.

Buying a house was an investment, paying rent on a shitty apar—

Before her fingers could flip the switch, she froze as a

rush of air and a rustle, along with the heavy boot steps, was heard before a hand came out of the dark to grab her neck and fling her off balance.

The oxygen fled her lungs and her heart jumped into her throat as she bent over to grab for the .38 on her ankle. But before she could get to it, the big hand grabbed her neck again and pushed her against the mirrored closet door and squeezed.

Pot. Whiskey. Leather. Wet dog?

The smells wafting around her could belong to any of the men she'd arrested in the past. But they didn't belong to some random disgruntled arrestee out for vengeance.

No, they certainly did not.

She tried to slow her breathing so she could semi-calmly say, "With your expert skills of being a car thief, I shouldn't be surprised that you're a proficient burglar, too. But now, since the residence is occupied, your burglary turned to a robbery charge, a much more serious offense. And if you're packing a weapon, that increases the grade. I can stack on trespassing, B and E, and aggravated assault, too. Any and all of it breaks the conditions of your parole, anyway. Go directly to jail, do not pass go."

"Fuck you, Jet."

His deep growl made her pin her lips together so she wouldn't smile. But it also made a ribbon of heat swirl through her.

Cop-hating felon asshole biker needed to play on repeat in her head.

"I see your method of greeting fellow humans hasn't improved yet. For future reference, normally visitors give the person they're visiting a heads up that they're stopping by. After a polite knock on the door, they're usually invited inside. Your parents really sucked at teaching you manners."

"That wasn't the only thing they sucked at," he grumbled.

"Ah, now I see... You have Mommy issues."

When his fingertips dug deeper into the sides of her neck, she increased the pressure of the hand she had clamped around his wrist. She apparently touched a nerve.

She knew techniques where she could easily break free from his grip but if she tried them, they might end up in a physical struggle.

Not *might*, would.

While Rook was bigger than her, she'd taken down larger and heavier men than him. Most of them desperate to get free, which made them more dangerous than the man who currently pinned her to the mirror.

This morning, however, Jet was too weary for a physical challenge. It had been a long miserable night. She had dealt with one too many crashes due to the fallen snow, topped with endless domestic incidents due to the holiday and heavy drinking.

Luckily, Max had scheduled two other patrols in anticipation of the weather and the family spats, which happened whenever related people got together and they had a light-bulb moment discovering that they really didn't like each other. Those realizations usually were revealed once they were thoroughly pickled.

"Is there a reason why you're here? Other than the erection you're pushing into my stomach?"

"Yeah, to tell you you need to leave me the fuck alone."

Uh... what? "Are you drunk or just confused? You came here. I didn't seek you out." In fact, she hadn't seen him since the last time he was in her apartment.

She hadn't seen him parked at the bottom of the mountain, either. She assumed that meant he'd been keeping clear of the Shirleys after his last run-in with them. Smart on his part.

"Came here to get you outta my system."

She pursed her lips and stared at him. He seemed pretty pissed so maybe she should take that as a threat.

"And how were you planning on doing that? By strangling me?" She flexed the fingers encircling his wrist. Her other hand was pressed flat against his belly. It rose and fell with each ragged breath he took.

And it was certainly uneven. But then, so was hers.

"That's my second choice."

Dare she ask? "What's your first?"

"Fuckin' you."

She wasn't surprised by his answer, of course, because of the steel pipe pressing against his zipper. The evidence of his arousal couldn't be more obvious.

"Word of advice... Addicts don't get sober by feeding their habit."

The long, calloused fingers encircling her neck twitched, giving away more than he'd probably like. "Ain't addicted to you."

"Good. Because that could be a problem."

"Ain't a problem."

"A typical response from an addict." She was pushing him. She didn't know why. To get him to react? To get him to give up whatever his plans were? To bring him to his senses?

To bring herself to her senses?

The man broke into her apartment to get her "out of his system." That sounded as though he couldn't stop thinking about her.

Since the last time she stood naked in the exact same spot, she hadn't stopped thinking about him, either.

About what they did. And about how she wanted to do it again.

She just wished like hell it wasn't Rook.

She wished it wasn't a cop-hating felon asshole biker. But wishing it wasn't going to change it.

The man before her was who he was and nothing would change that. So, she either needed to make him leave or they needed to proceed in doing what he came there to do. That was one reason she hadn't taken his ass down, pulled her .38 and plugged a hole between his eyes.

She had every right to do just that. A parolee with a violent past broke into her place, got physical with her and also threatened her.

She had every damn right to protect herself from that threat.

But even though he'd gained access to her apartment in a way she needed to investigate and prevent in the future, even though he had grabbed for her in the dark and once again had her pinned to that mirror, it wasn't fear that rushed through her veins.

Not even close.

It was pure adrenaline.

It was the thought that he *couldn't* stop thinking about her.

And a little due to the fact that his lips were now only a hairsbreadth from hers. She could almost taste the pot and whiskey on her own. To her that would forever be the signature taste of her former—and soon to be repeated—bad decision.

Did she regret the first time? No.

But she thought it was once and done. That once he pulled up his pants, tucked his cock away and walked out her door, reality had clubbed him over the head. After that, she had hoped he'd steer clear, which would make it easier on her to do the same.

But...

Here he was...

Once again in her apartment. Uninvited.

Only, her body was rolling out the welcome mat.

A long breath hissed from between her lips and she curled her fingers tighter into the waffle-patterned cotton of his thermal shirt at his stomach.

She wanted to demand that he kiss her because the anticipation was killing her. But she knew if she did, he'd spout some bullshit about how he didn't kiss people he hated.

Or how he didn't take orders.

Or... whatever.

So, instead of waiting any longer, she released his wrist and his shirt to grab the back of his head with one hand, the back of his neck with the other and yank him down until the small gap between their mouths no longer existed.

In short, it was either kiss him or shoot him.

Shooting him would leave a damn mess and she'd lose her security deposit. It would also create a lot of paperwork.

Kissing him...

Well, that would be messy, too. But not in the same way that blood would stain the carpet.

No, it would just mess with her head. And, maybe leave a mess between her thighs like last time.

"Fuck you, Jet," he said against her lips during the fraction of a second he resisted.

Then it was like a floodgate opening...

He took the lead, controlling the kiss, controlling their mouths. Making the kiss his own, not giving her the opportunity to do anything but keep up with the intensity of his tongue and lips.

Plundering. That was what he was doing. Plundering her mouth like it was his to take, to do with what he wanted.

And, fool that she was, she let him.

A thrill skittered up her spine, leaving goosebumps in its wake. Making her breasts feel heavier than normal in her sports bra. Making her nipples want to poke holes right through it. Heat pooled between her legs and she couldn't believe how fast he made her wet.

He was a rude asshole and he turned her on. Somehow, he made her melt.

It was a sickness, she tried to tell herself.

Her own words came back to haunt her. *Addicts don't get sober by feeding their habit.*

He was quickly becoming an addiction.

She knew better.

She knew better.

She knew better than to mess with a man like him.

So wrong for her career, for the uniform she wore and for the oath she took.

So, so wrong.

They were no different than oil and water. Two liquids that could touch, but would never blend.

She didn't care.

He was here for one reason. To get her out of his system. He thought fucking her again would do that. Maybe it could do that for her, too.

Or it could backfire for them both.

Instead of smothering the fire, it could feed it, stoke it. Make it burn brighter and hotter than ever.

That was a real fear.

The first time hadn't been enough. Maybe Rook was wrong and the second time wouldn't be enough, either.

Then what? A third? A fourth?

Hand the ex-con a house key?

A sharp pull on her scalp brought her back to their kiss as he fisted her hair at the back of her head, as he ground his cock into her belly, and continued to kiss her like he hardly despised her.

If this went any further than a kiss, she would not be the only one naked. Not this time.

She found it interesting he didn't wear his cut tonight, but instead a heavy black leather jacket that had no patches on it at all. Nothing to identify him as a member of the local MC. Tonight, he was dressed like John Q. Public, even though he was anything but.

He broke the kiss and shoved his face into her neck, muffling his, "Fuck you, Jet," against her skin.

She could have laughed over how he tried his best to hate her. But the way his hips were rocking against her proved otherwise.

He hated himself. Not her.

He hated that he wanted her. The same way she wasn't happy with how she wanted him.

"Fuck you, too, Rook," she whispered. "Fuck you for not wanting to work with me. Fuck you for never thanking me for saving your ass from being raped. Fuck you for forcing your way into my apartment last time. Fuck you for breaking into it this time. Fuck you for making it impossible for me to shoot you right now when I have every right to. Fuck you for making me want you. Fuck you for making me wet. Just... fuck you, too."

He pulled his face from her neck and straightened to stare down into her face. "Damn, darlin'," he whispered, wearing a cocky grin.

She shoved his chest with both of her hands, forcing him to catch his balance by taking a step back. "Don't you dare smirk, you asshole. Just... don't." But it at least gave her a little breathing space.

"You want me."

"You wouldn't be breathing right now, otherwise, *darlin',*" she told him.

"How far could I push you before you'd stop me?"

"Do you want to try it?"

"Thinkin' I might."

"Why?"

He grabbed her wrist and pressed her hand to his erection. "Gotta admit, the thought of takin' it to the edge with you makes me hard as fuck."

"You were hard before that."

He tipped his head to the side and dragged her hand up and down his length. "Yeah, but not this hard."

"There's something wrong with you."

"There's a shitload wrong with me." His hand clamped around her throat again, but much looser this time and his thumb pressed to her pulse, which was pounding at a rapid pace. "Yeah, that shit might get you off."

"No."

He leaned in closer until his face was right above hers again and, "Liar," whispered over her lips.

"Get out of my apartment."

"Don't fuckin' take orders from people like you. Thought I made myself clear about that shit."

"Fine. Then don't get naked. I'm not going to order you to get the hell out, instead I'll strongly suggest it."

"Ain't leavin'."

"I didn't invite you."

"Don't give a fuck."

"You should."

He shrugged and smiled.

So damn cocky.

He slid his hand up her neck until it caught her jawline, pulled up her chin and stretched her throat. "Get naked."

Goosebumps exploded once again over every inch of her body.

Her breasts and pussy ached with need.

In her line of work, she had to take control and keep it. She had to be the one giving orders to control the scenario. She had to be firm with her commands.

He was trying to take that from her. He wanted to be the one to control the scenario, to give the orders, to make her comply.

It surprised her that she wanted that from him. "You need to leave."

He shook his head slowly. "No, darlin', that's not what you want."

"You don't know what I want."

"You told me and you're showin' me right now. The way you're breathin'. The shake in your voice. And..." He brushed the back of his fingers down her stomach to the elastic waistband of her nylon track pants and slipped his hand inside.

She sucked in her belly as, with excruciating slowness, he slid his hand lower, under her boy shorts and found how wet she was.

"Yeah," he breathed. "Wet and hot for me." He dragged his middle finger through her soaked folds. "Can't hide that."

He did it again, and then a third time, before dipping his middle finger inside her. Not rough, but gently. Not fucking her with her finger, but just teasing, testing.

A sigh slipped from her as he added a second finger. Still gentle, not pumping, but enough to drive her crazy.

"It gets you off to think about doin' what I tell you to, don't it? If I told you to drop to your knees and swallow my cock, you'd do it, wouldn't you? If I told you to bend over and spread your ass cheeks so I can fuck you there, you wouldn't say no, would you?"

Her answer was an unmistakable groan. She couldn't deny that she would do anything he'd demand right now.

And that was dangerous.

This spell he had on her was so damn dangerous. Reckless.

She needed to break that spell.

But maybe... later.

After.

Right now, the thought of doing everything and anything he demanded sounded like a good idea. Even though, she knew deep down it wasn't.

She had the devil on one shoulder, an angel on the other, and she was about to flick that angel off and tell her to go hide for a while. She needed to spend a little time with the devil.

A devil whose name was Rook.

"Get naked," she ordered him.

His eyes narrowed. "You first," he demanded.

"I was naked last time and you weren't."

"Yeah," he grunted, his fingers still gently probing her wetness, exploring her.

She bit back a groan.

"You're packin'."

"Not where you're searching me, I'm not."

He released her neck, and slipped his hand out of her pants and held it up between them. Even in the limited light, she could see the wet shine on his skin.

"Got that way for me."

She couldn't deny it, so she didn't.

"I tell you to clean off my fingers, would you?"

Good God, he was killing her right now. "I'd point you to the sink in my kitchen."

"Not what I meant."

"I know what you meant." She could hardly form those words when he lifted them to her lips.

"Do it."

Christ, why did his demands turn her on so much? She forced herself to keep from knocking him to the ground, yanking out his cock and riding him until she came. "No. You do it."

He cocked one eyebrow, then a slow grin spread over his face. For a moment, she thought he would force his fingers into her mouth, force her to suck them clean, force her to taste herself.

He didn't. Instead he took his time, sliding his slick fingers into his own mouth and sucking on them.

Her knees buckled as she watched his reaction. An average person might not have noticed, but being a cop, she was more in tune with slight motions and physical reactions.

A trickle of wetness slipped from her and was caught in her boy shorts.

When he pulled his fingers from his mouth, he said, "Ain't gettin' naked 'til that gun's off your ankle and outta reach. Survived way too long to be killed just tryin' to get more of what I just tasted."

"I'd be stupid to not have a way to protect myself. And how do I know you aren't packing?"

He grabbed his crotch and shook it. "I am."

She snorted and rolled her eyes. She then sighed in resignation. "Fine. Let's both drop our weapons first, then we can drop our clothes." That sounded like a fair compromise.

With a single nod, he stepped back, no longer crowding

her against the mirror. He smirked. "Wanna see me naked, huh?"

"It's only fair."

"Life ain't fair, darlin'."

That was for sure. If it was, it wouldn't be Rook making her wet right now, it wouldn't be Rook getting naked in front of her, it would be someone else. Someone she could invite over to the family's Christmas dinner later.

A table he'd never sit at.

A family he'd never have casual conversation with.

A home he'd never be welcomed in.

He shed his leather jacket, tossing it to the floor by the front door. She removed her wool coat, hanging it in the closet behind her.

When she turned back, he had his pant leg pulled up and was unstrapping a knife from his calf.

"You know you can't carry that shit, Rook."

He continued taking off his socks and boots, dropping them on the floor near his jacket. "Who's gonna know? You gonna snitch to my PO, Jet?"

She sighed and bent over to rip open the Velcro from her ankle holster and when she straightened, his eyes were not on her but the weapon.

She smiled. "You're worried I'm going to shoot you?"

"You haven't been tempted?"

She didn't bother to answer that since he already knew the answer. She slipped the holstered weapon into the pocket of her wool coat so she could put it back on before she left the apartment later. Then she shut the closet door, taking a slow, deep breath before turning.

When she did, she lost the breath that was supposed to be bolstering her.

It completely disintegrated.

She knew he'd have tattoos. She just didn't realize of what. Or how large.

She imagined he'd have his club colors tattooed onto his back. That was typical for most members of a real MC. Something not usually done in a casual riding club.

But it wasn't his back she was looking at. She started where his fingers were unbuckling his belt and ran her gaze up his stomach.

He was in much better shape than expected.

"I guess you worked out a lot in prison."

"Had time to fill," was his answer as he thumbed open the top button of his jeans.

His left arm was covered in a colorful sleeve that began at his wrist and ended on his muscular pec. In the dark, it was difficult to make out all the details, but the large tattoo which started at the bottom of his bicep and moved over his shoulder cap to cross his left pec was a snake. With wings? Maybe a mythical creature of some sort? Coming out of crashing waves. It made no sense and she had no idea what it was or what it meant, if anything.

No, not a snake, some sort of sea serpent, maybe.

His right bicep sported a wide tribal band, one that a white man would typically get. A tattoo they thought looked cool even though they didn't belong to any type of real tribe.

But, surprisingly, those tattoos were all she could see and seemed professionally done. She'd seen plenty of jailhouse and prison tattoos before and what he had were not those. These were not done while sitting in a cell while some hack using the end of a paperclip and the ink from a ball-point pen.

For some odd reason, she was relieved.

The tattoos he had didn't distract from his looks, which is

what originally drew her to him not even a year ago after starting at Manning Grove PD.

She wanted to tell him to turn around so she could see his back, to confirm her suspicion. To see the ink that represented the true "tribe" he belonged to, but she already knew how he'd react to that order.

Since he was getting undressed, she'd see it soon enough and she didn't want to distract him from what he was currently doing, which was shoving his jeans and whatever he wore underneath down his legs.

The man had no chest hair, so it didn't surprise her that his legs were only lightly furred and the hair hardly noticeable in the dim light because of the dark blond color. But the thick patch of short, wiry hair from where his erection protruded was darker than his beard.

She dug her fingernails into her palms. She wanted to touch him there. To feel the springiness, to explore the velvet-soft skin of his cock. To thumb the glistening bead of precum that had collected at the slit.

He stared at her while he stepped out of the gathered denim at his feet.

Now he was totally naked.

And she was not. At least not yet.

His hand fisting his cock snapped her out of her trance.

On just his body alone, he had every right to be cocky. While he was pretty to look at fully dressed, he was much more spectacular wearing nothing but his smirk while stroking his thick length.

He was no slouch there, either.

She kept all of those thoughts to herself.

Then his cocky grin died and his eyes narrowed. "What the fuck are you wearin'?"

Chapter Thirteen

Confused, she shook her head wondering what he was asking about and why whatever it was bothered him. "What?"

"That shiny shit clinging to your tits."

She glanced down at her shirt. "Under Armour. I wear that under my vest to keep me dry."

"Fuckin' skin tight."

This was an odd conversation to be happening when the man standing in front of her was buck naked. "It's supposed to be."

"You walk around just wearin' that?"

Why was he all bent out of shape about a shirt? Yes, it was snug but it needed to not be bulky. "I need to be careful with what I wear in the locker room since we only have one." That was why she wore her Under Armour home instead of peeling it off at work.

His brow dropped low. "What d'you mean?"

"We only have one locker room at the station. So, most of

the time Leah and I don't strip down all the way. And we certainly don't shower there. It's why I wear boy shorts, a sports bra and Under Armour when I work."

"You're in a fuckin' locker room with other men wearin' only a sports bra and your panties?"

This was a disturbing line of questioning. Especially from him. Especially now. "Well," she plucked at the dark blue skin-tight fabric at her stomach, "this over it and boy shorts."

"Fuckin' underwear, Jet. Struttin' around a bunch of horny pigs in just your fuckin' underwear."

"I wouldn't call it strutting."

His eyes narrowed.

"Why the hell do you care, anyway?"

Instantly his expression went blank. "I don't."

"Well then, good. What I do is none of your business."

His jaw shifted.

"*None* of your business."

It shifted again.

"You're only here to get me out of your system, remember?"

A muscle ticked in his cheek.

"So... can we get that process started and over with so I can go take a damn shower and get some sleep?"

"Waitin' on you."

"You wouldn't be waiting if we weren't having this ridiculous conversation," she reminded him. She hooked her fingers into her dark gray nylon track pants and shoved them down, toeing off her sneakers and stepping out of her pants like he had. "Unless you want to have another unnecessary conversation about my boy shorts, too?" She lifted a brow with her inquiry.

His chest rose slowly as he now focused on her powder

blue underwear. His stroking also slowed. "You wear that shit in front of those assholes?"

"Are you including yourself in that group?"

"Can see your pussy lips."

"You must have really good vision, then," she said as she grabbed the hem of her shirt and peeled it up her torso, tugging it over her head and dropping it on top of her other discarded clothing. Now she stood in only her sports bra and underwear. "Should I keep going or should I pause for your commentary on each article of clothing, since it's so enlightening?"

"Fuck you, Jet," he growled.

"You keep promising that, but right now you're only fucking your own fist. So, are you done bitching about what I wear in the locker room at work?"

He wasn't. She could see it on his face, but, amazingly enough, he kept his mouth shut.

"We wasted a lot of time with unneeded conversation. I didn't think you broke into my apartment to talk." No, he broke in to rid her from his system. That she damn well knew was only an excuse to get down her pants. Or boy shorts.

She yanked her sports bra over her head and flung it at him. It bounced off his face and dropped to his bare feet. He hadn't even flinched but his jaw was now popping.

And the tight grip he had on the root of his cock had made it turn even darker. She guessed, if the light was on, it would be a very dark purple.

She hooked her thumbs into the elastic waistband of her boy shorts and, with an exaggerated wiggle of her hips, shimmied them down.

Even in the dark, he had a gleam in his eyes as he followed the path of her underwear. He stared at her feet where the cotton landed for longer than she expected. When he slowly lifted his gaze, he took his time to take in every inch of her.

When he was done, his breath softly hissed from him, then he rushed her so quickly, she braced for impact.

He didn't grab her neck this time, but, instead, drove his fingers so deeply into her hair it loosened from the ponytail she had thrown it into after shedding her uniform at station.

His kiss was so damn intense, her toes curled into the carpet. His cock was so hard she feared it would leave a permanent imprint on her belly. The faint taste of pot and whiskey now blended with her own tang from when he sucked it from his fingers.

Driving his tongue deeper, he released her hair to hike her left thigh up to his hip and grabbed his cock with his other hand, putting it where it needed to be.

She expected it to be rough and raw like last time. His attempt to purge her from his thoughts.

To fuck her, come and then leave.

But that was not what it ended up being.

Instead, with a soft grunt, he slid inside her almost as gently as his fingers had been previously.

This time, they were face to face. Unlike last time, where she was turned away from him and they needed to use the mirror to see each other, to see what they were doing, using it as a separation of sorts.

Once he filled her completely, he hesitated deep inside her. She took that moment to savor the stretch and fullness, expecting him at any second to start ramming her recklessly. To try to quickly bring all of this to its desired end.

A sprint to the finish.

She trailed her fingertips down the indentation of his spine to the small of his back and then even lower until she gripped his ass, pulling another soft hiss from him. The muscles flexed under her touch and she tried to pull him deeper, even though that was impossible. With her being shorter, he had nowhere else to go but to pull out.

So, that was what he did. He shifted his hips until only the rim of his crown remained inside her and, again, he hesitated. He wasn't looking at her, but instead over her shoulder into the mirror, avoiding their direct connection.

Neither could deny something was there. Pulling at them both. Dragging them down to the point they couldn't avoid the truth because this time it wasn't staring back at them through a piece of mirrored glass.

While neither moved, the energy between them sizzled just like the first time, proving it hadn't been a fluke.

This was how it was between them. How it would be. Whenever they were close or touching.

The day he pinned her against her cruiser, the last time he pinned her against the mirror. And now...

This.

He drove up and into her again, watching himself in the mirror fuck her slowly and with care.

She dug her fingernails into the flesh of his ass, encouraging him to go faster, take her harder. To stop taking his time. To stop making this feel like something it wasn't.

Something it could never be.

Because of who she was.

Because of who he was.

What they had at this moment was all they'd ever have.

A simple physical connection.

Although, not exactly simple. If either of them dug beyond the surface, they would find something too complex.

Something troubling.

What else was troubling was the direction her thoughts had gone. Instead of taking what was happening at face value, she was the one overthinking it. Looking for something that might not even be there.

Something she was imagining.

She closed her eyes as his pace increased but still remained steady and unhurried. His hips rocked against her, driving his cock in and out of her. Grinding against her clit as he did so.

When she dragged her fingernails back up his spine, his flesh pebbled under her touch and he shuddered against her. In turn, that pulled a shudder from her.

No.

No, whatever he was doing was dangerous. Unneeded.

And shocking.

Especially from a man who declared he hated her, who told her to fuck off often. Who was only here to get her out of his system.

Or so he said.

But what he was doing was wedging himself deeper under her skin.

She couldn't allow that.

She couldn't.

Because it would end badly for both of them.

He turned his eyes from the mirror, from where he'd been watching himself fuck her, to her. When their gazes locked, his nostrils flared, and his jaw became set.

He didn't like whatever he was feeling. Not the sex part, but the rest.

She didn't blame him. She didn't like it, either.

Suddenly she was unexpectedly free, he was gone, and she had to catch herself so she wouldn't tumble to the floor at his feet. But before she could, he bent over, drove his shoulder into her stomach and lifted her into the air.

She gasped as all her weight pressed hard into his

shoulder and he only wobbled for a brief moment before digging his fingers into the backs of her thighs to secure her against him as he took long strides toward the back of the tiny apartment.

It had one bedroom, one bathroom and a small living space, so he didn't have to ask where to go, he found it within seconds.

He kicked her bedroom door wider so they would fit through it and then she was physically tossed into the air.

When she landed with hardly a bounce onto the memory foam mattress, she had to sweep her hair out of her face to see him standing at the end of the bed, staring at her.

His eyes were dark as he took her in. On her back, naked on her bed.

Since he had flipped the switch by the door when he plowed through it, she could now do the same to him. Starting at the top of his head, she rolled her gaze all the way down to the point she could no longer see him because of the mattress blocking her view. The dark blond hair, super short at the sides, longer at the top. The darker beard, not scraggly but well-maintained. The deep brown eyes that looked troubled. The strong set jaw, the corded neck and broad shoulders. The tattoos, his trim waist and stomach, his narrow hips, the trimmed bush of hair surrounding his protruding cock, the sparse dark blond hair covering his thighs and calves.

Holy shit, just seeing him naked made her want to touch herself. She'd been with some pretty good-looking guys before but none of them, not one, had done to her what Rook could and did.

Again, this disturbed her. It had to be because he was the tempting "forbidden fruit." Maybe she was the same for him. His brothers would never accept one of their own being involved, even if only sexually, with someone in law enforcement. They would consider that a threat to their club, their family and their way of life.

Her family, her fellow police officers and especially her chief and oldest cousin, would be shocked to know she currently had a Blood Fury member naked in her bedroom and was about to do more than just get an eyeful of him.

She was still on her first year of probation at MGPD and could be terminated for any valid reason. It wouldn't take much for Max to consider her involvement with Rook as a threat to her job, the force, to the Bryson family and, cousin or not, send her packing.

So, yes, today needed to be the day that they both got whatever it was out of their system and never looked back.

Unless, of course, he agreed to work with her in regard to the Shirleys, then they could keep things "professional." But right now, with both of them naked, what was happening was far, far, *far* from professional.

When her attention snapped back to the man standing at the end of the bed, she saw he was staring at the mirrors covering her double closet doors. The room might be small but the closet space wasn't lacking and those large mirrors would reflect everything that was about to occur on her bed.

"What the fuck is with this place and mirrors?" he growled.

"Mirrors give the illusion that the place is bigger than it actually is. Just like it gives you the disillusion that your dick is bigger."

His head twisted back to her. "You sayin' I'm small?"

She pursed her lips and pretended to inspect the hard-length he palmed. "Umm. It's... about average."

"Fills you up."

That it did. The length was perfect, the girth even better.

But she wasn't feeding into his arrogance. "With some room to spare."

"Maybe that has to do more with you than me."

Damn. She smothered her laugh at his witty comeback.

She liked men who had a sense of humor, had some common sense and street smarts, wasn't a wimp and didn't have the IQ of a rock. She wasn't sure how many of those attributes Rook embraced but it wouldn't matter if he had them all.

This was the last time they were having sex.

That meant they needed to make it count.

"At the rate we're going, I'm just going to lie here and watch you masturbate."

He continued to slowly stroke his cock. "That turn you on?"

She watched his fist slide back and forth for a few more seconds. Yes, it did. Knowing he was hard for her, knowing he wanted her even though she represented something he hated, knowing his being there with her risked his status with his brotherhood, turned her on. "Yes," she breathed.

He immediately dropped his hand, and she rolled her eyes.

"You're such a jerk."

His lips curved into a crooked grin.

As she opened her mouth to tell him to either get on her bed or get out of her apartment, he suddenly moved. He tackled her, shoving his hips between her thighs, grabbing her wrists, but before he could settle in, before he could slide inside her, she moved, flipping him over so she was on top.

As she tried to mount him, she quickly found herself on her back again. With a grunt, she used all her weight to roll him, so she was once again on top.

With a growl, she was flipped back to the bottom.

All they needed was some cherry Jell-O or warm baby oil and they could start their very own wrestling routine.

"Stay there," he growled, as he used his weight to pin her down.

"I thought men liked when women were on top," she stated, sounding a little out of breath. Okay, more like a bit. He might not be huge, but he was solid, strong and heavier than he looked.

"Like it when *I* want it. Right now, want this."

This man did not like giving up control that easily. Admittedly, she also liked that in a man. One who could be as demanding as she was. If a man tried to control her outside of the bedroom, it wouldn't fly with her, but inside...? She could make some concessions.

Especially, if they knew what they were doing.

Rook knew what he was doing and did it well.

Not that it would matter after this last time...

His murmured, "It's gone," drew her out of her own fairy tale.

His erection was pressed to the inside of her thigh, the precum at the end leaving a trail of silky fluid on her skin. His hands were planted in the mattress on either side of her head and his hips were pinning hers to the bed.

With his face only a few inches above hers, she blinked up at him. "What?"

"My bite on your neck."

Not *the* bite, but *my* bite.

Her fingers automatically went to that spot. Every day in the mirror she had watched *his* bite slowly disappear. Every day she'd had to cover the mark before leaving her apartment, going to work, to the grocery store or to spend time with her family.

Because a bruise like that would raise questions. Maybe even concerns.

Obviously, how she got it needed to remain a secret.

But throughout her shifts at work, she'd catch herself sliding a couple fingers under the high-necked shirt she was forced to wear to touch it. Remembering. Immediately, her nipples would peak, her breath would shudder and her pussy would clench.

Every damn time.

But, yes, it was now gone.

Shifting all his weight into one hand, he used the knuckles of the other to caress her skin where the bite had been.

He remembered *exactly* where it had been.

Exactly.

She hadn't forgotten, either. "So?"

His gaze lifted from where he touched her neck and it locked with hers. Then his hand continued on a path to her breasts where he squeezed each one and thumbed the tips of her nipples. "Gone there, too."

"They weren't tattoos. They don't last forever."

"Made you think of me."

Holy shit. He sounded so proud of himself! "Why would you care if I thought of you?"

"Wouldn't. Hope they pissed you off," he grumbled.

He was lying. She could read it in his face, so she lied, too. "They were a good reminder of that mistake and what— or who—to avoid in the future."

"Yeah, but here we are."

"Here you are. Uninvited, once again."

"Don't want me here," he said.

"It's not smart."

"No one ever said I was smart."

No, but he certainly wasn't unintelligent. Some of his actions in his past might be considered stupid, but he knew full well what he'd been doing when he did them and the consequences of those actions.

He simply did them anyway.

Being arrogant and stubborn wasn't being stupid. Though, some might classify it as such because it was easier to do so than try to figure out the real reasoning behind those questionable actions.

"Well, if you can refrain from marking me up again, I'd appreciate it." Another lie. Deep down, she wanted nothing more. "I'd also appreciate it if we could move this along at a much quicker pace, since I have to get some sleep before dealing with my family later."

He thrusted against her thigh. "Sounded like a demand."

"Again, more of a suggestion," she said lightly, reaching between them to grab his cock.

He smirked as she stroked him a couple of times. "Want my dick."

"You haven't heard me say no, have you?"

"Want my dick," he concluded, again sounding very pleased with himself.

Like the asshole was so damn irresistible.

Her sigh of impatience quickly turned to one of pleasure when, after she guided him to where he needed to be, he took her cue and drove inside her, hard enough to make her body jerk.

He slammed her again.

And again.

Yesss. Finally.

She didn't care about it being gentle, she just wanted it to be good. And unlike by the front door, he wasn't taking his time and being careful. He was giving it to her as hard as he could. Not kissing her. Not caressing her. Not making it sweet. But fucking her.

Arching his body, he pulled one of her nipples into his mouth, sucking it like he would die if he didn't.

Using the hand near her head to brace himself, he dug his knees deeper into the mattress, and began to power up and into her. She wrapped her thighs around his hips, dug her heels into the back of his legs to encourage his pace, gripped a handful of the hair at the top of his head and held him to her breast.

Yes. This.

This was what she wanted from him.

No talking. No thinking or overthinking. Just this.

She wanted this moment to simply connect.

Just these next few moments. That was all they needed.

And once it was over, it would be over. For good.

Shit. Once again, she knew that was a complete lie. At least, for her.

Whether this would help him move on, she didn't know. But she hoped it would, so she could move on, as well.

This hip movement was not like the gentle rocking and rolling earlier. This was him stabbing her with his cock, driving home the point that he was in charge. Both reminding himself and reminding her.

She wouldn't fight it. She had no reason to.

While she had wanted to be on top, to straddle him, it was only so she could watch him as she fucked him instead of the other way around. But what he insisted on—being on top—was fine with her, too.

He was ramming her hard, jolting her with each thrust, and the arm he was using to brace himself now also kept her in place so she wouldn't slide up the bed. His other hand squeezed and kneaded the breast he had his lips latched onto.

Her blood rushed not only from the motion of his hips, but from anticipation.

She expected to feel the biting sting of his teeth at any second. The mark that would announce, "Rook was here. I took this. This is mine." The marks she would stare at in the mirror for the next week and then want to dig out her vibrator and relive how those marks were made.

But he didn't, he kept up the punishing pace, probably waiting and wanting for her to beg for mercy... If so, he'd be waiting for a long time. She could take anything he threw at her and even more, if he wanted to push it further.

Truthfully, if he wanted her to think twice about allowing him into her bed, this was not the way to do it. That made her wonder if that was his purpose. If he could drive her to the point where she didn't want or accept him sexually, would it make it easier for him to walk away?

Interesting.

But at the pace he was going he would come well before she ever got a chance.

First of all, she needed to get out of her own head... And just appreciate—even though he was fucking like a horny caveman—he was still the best fuck she'd had in a long damn time.

Every time he drove his cock home, it nudged her closer to that edge. The grunts he made against the flesh of her breast were like a symphony to her ears and only made her wetter. The way he ground himself against her clit at the end of each stroke, only made her want more.

"Touch me," she begged. If she wanted it, she couldn't demand it. If she demanded it, he might not do it. Simply out of spite.

If he wanted to play games with her about who was in control, then, to get what she wanted, she could, too.

His teeth clamped down around her nipple, not deep enough to break the skin but enough to send a delicious shockwave through her, from her breast all the way down to where they were connected. That simple action made her sensitive nub swell even more.

When he didn't move fast enough, she reached between them to touch herself there, but he snagged her wrist and squeezed it tight, preventing her from doing just that. He pulled it from between them, replacing it with his own and did exactly what she hoped he would.

But that wasn't all. With a last light nip to the curve of her breast, he shoved his face into her neck and ran the tip of his tongue along the column of her windpipe. She tipped her head back to give him better access to her throat and so she could also feel the scratch of the wiry hairs along his chin and jawline along her skin.

Then she waited. For the bite, the claim, the mark that would once again remind her of her mistake, but also of how worthwhile making that mistake had been.

Because *yessss*, she wasn't feeling any regrets right now. None at all.

Who could regret sex as hot as this?

The sweep of his warm breath and the low, muffled grunts vibrated against her skin as he kept the wave-like motion. Driving her to the point those waves would break and crash along the shore. Loud. Fierce. With the power of the sea behind them.

But it wasn't the sea, it was Rook, and, with each powerful roll of his hips, he began to drown her in that dangerous ocean. Each push and pull dragged her under, tumbled her thoughts as she hung on tightly, using his hair she still gripped, and her fingers dug firmly into his ass.

She clung to him like she would a surfboard while riding

a wave as it swelled higher and higher. His thumb flicked roughly on her clit as that wave finally crested and when it broke, all the air hissed from her lungs.

The sharp pain of his teeth sinking into her neck at the same exact moment, turned her inhale into a moan instead and when it rushed back out, it became a cry she couldn't contain as she shattered around him.

Not only was her pussy clenching and unclenching around his thick length with each aftershock of the climax, but every muscle from head to toe convulsed along with it and then turned to liquid, just like the receding tide.

He still didn't stop. He continued on with his thumb on her clit, circling and pressing it faster and more frantically while, in contrast, he slowed the smooth roll of his hips once again to a gentle rocking. No longer stabbing her with his cock, he dragged it in and out of her more leisurely through the slickness he caused.

His lips stayed glued to her neck when his rhythm finally hitched, his muscles tightened, and his hips drove deep once more before he stilled, the groan that came deep from within his chest getting caught between his mouth and her skin.

Unexpectedly, she came again, the second climax not as strong as the first, but enough to make her gasp and attempt to pull him deeper to again ride out those ebbing waves. The base of his cock pulsed as he emptied inside her, absolutely nothing between them to stop him from marking her on the inside, too.

Once again, they hadn't used a condom, hadn't even discussed it. And Jet should know better but she didn't even care.

Reckless, for sure. But then this whole thing between them was.

One mistake after the other snowballed as they went.

Neither able to stop it from getting larger and picking up speed as it careened downhill. Eventually that momentum would be lost, the snowball would slow, even stop, and the sun would come out and melt it down to nothing.

Until the only thing left was a memory.

It was for the best.

Oh yes, it was for the best.

When she sighed, Rook lifted his face from her neck, stared down for a second at the bite he'd left behind, then braced his hands into the mattress again to lift his torso enough so he could look down into her face.

Jet had no idea what, if anything, would come out of his mouth next.

She shouldn't have been surprised when nothing did. Instead, his mouth got tight and he slipped out of her, rolled onto his back and right off the bed.

Well, that was that.

It was done. Over.

Though, she was nowhere near finished looking at him. The way his muscles bunched and flexed under the ink on his back representing his club, and in his ass and thighs as he walked right out of her bedroom without a damn word.

She blew a breath through her nose, stared up at the ceiling and laid a hand over her belly, feeling the result of what they had just done slip from her. She would need to get up soon or she'd have to change the sheets.

But instead of the front door closing, she heard her bathroom door close. Eventually the toilet flushed, the sink ran, and he rustled around in the tiny hallway bathroom.

She dropped her gaze from the ceiling to the doorway as he surprised her by striding back inside her room with something in his hand.

Her eyebrows pinned together when she recognized what

it was. He tossed the pill pack onto the bed near her but still said nothing.

She had no idea what the fuck was going on and why he'd carry her birth control from the bathroom to the bedroom. So, she had to guess.

"Bet you're relieved, right? You didn't ask, you assumed. That's what arrogant assholes do."

His lips flattened out.

She did not understand the man at all. And probably never would.

He hated her, but he left his mark on her. Not once but two times.

He hated her, but he had fucked her twice without even making sure birth control was covered.

He hated her, but seemed to be bothered that she was on birth control.

Or maybe she was imagining that, too, and it really was relief.

The man had the false notion that fucking her a second time would purge her from his system.

No.

That wasn't it at all. He *knew* it wouldn't. That was only the excuse he told himself so he could live with his decision, live with what he wanted when he hated wanting it.

Now, she saw it all clearly.

Because he could've walked out her bedroom door, got dressed and simply left. Not returned to the bedroom carrying what prevented her from getting pregnant.

Still...

For fuck's sake, her brain hurt. This man had broken her damn brain.

It also didn't help she was running on fumes, needed sleep and lots of it. Normally by now, she'd be in la-la land

and not staring at a naked biker in her bedroom. "This won't happen again, right? I don't need to change my locks or bar my windows?"

"Ain't gonna happen again," he grumbled, turned on the heel of his bare foot and she once again got to watch that spectacular ass waltz right back out of her room.

She would miss that view and the good sex that went along with it.

But *c'est la vie.*

And anyway, he still never thanked her for saving his ass on the mountain and hadn't even bothered to wish her a Merry Christmas.

His greetings sucked and so did his goodbyes.

"Merry Christmas, dickhead!" she yelled out. "Enjoy the lump of coal Santa left in your stocking!"

She snorted when a few seconds later the door slammed shut.

She hoped he bothered to put on his clothes before walking outside into the December weather. More importantly, so she didn't get evicted by Mr. Danson for a naked man leaving her apartment first thing Christmas morning.

She tossed an arm over her eyes and let out a frustrated scream.

Merry fucking Christmas.

Chapter Fourteen

Rook turned down the defroster so he could hear the engine better over the blowing fan. He slowed the truck on the snow-covered street so he could listen more carefully. The customer had been complaining about a noise in his engine and so far, Rook hadn't heard it. Since fresh fallen snow covered Main Street, and the township hadn't had a chance to plow it yet, he didn't want to gun the engine and possibly wreck.

Dutch would kick his ass if that happened.

Or try to.

Most likely Dutch wouldn't succeed unless he was whipping wrenches at Rook's head. That happened plenty of times in the past when Rook had enough of his father's shit and mouthed off to him.

Usually he'd hear a warning, "Boy!" or an even louder, "Ungrateful bastard!" before the alloy steel tool came flying in his direction. At least the shout gave him time enough to duck and avoid a permanent indentation in his melon.

He and his old man had gotten into plenty of brawls over

the years. Too many to count. Usually, at least one, if not both, ended up walking away with a bloody lip or nose or even a black eye.

Rook grinned.

His father was an asshole, so Rook got it honestly. But, even so, he wouldn't want any other father than Dutch. The grumpy old fuck was a better parent than Bebe ever was or could be.

Both Rook and Cage recognized the fact that Dutch had done his best. No matter how hard it was to raise two boys on his own and how imperfect his parenting was, the man never gave up trying.

Neither of them ever went to bed hungry or cold, either.

Even though it was still snowing, it had turned to light flurries and the wipers didn't have to work as hard. The customer needed to clean his damn windshield, though. It was smeared and made seeing the white-covered road in front of him difficult, especially when the center double-line was covered.

He continued to head toward the center of town away from the garage, hoping to find a route the plows had already cleared. Instead of finding a snow-free street, he spotted something else.

He blinked to clear his vision, then blinked again. Once that didn't change what he was seeing, he squinted and ducked his head to look through a cleaner spot on the dirty windshield.

What the actual fuck?

Standing on the snowy sidewalk, not fifteen feet from the front door of his salon was Manning Grove's one and only beloved gay hairdresser, Teddy Sullivan... Well, now Teddy Bryson, since he married one of those Bryson pigs.

Teddy was taller but not as bulky as the men surrounding him. Worse, he was outnumbered. Five to one.

And that right there wasn't fucking fair.

Nope, not fucking fair at all.

Rook growled as he witnessed one of the men rip the snow shovel out of Teddy's mittened hands and toss it out of his reach.

Oh no they fuckin' didn't. Son of a bitch.

Rook jerked the wheel, crossed the opposing lane of travel and ran the two left wheels of the pickup truck onto the sidewalk, almost striking one of the assholes who had begun to push Teddy, while laughing and shouting at him. He was being shoved from one man to the other like he was a goddamn ball bouncing off the bumpers in a pinball machine.

Rook shoved the shifter into Park with more force than necessary and kicked open the driver's side door in time to hear a shrieked, "I'll have you know, my husband's a police officer!"

"See? Told you he was a fucking fag!" one of them crowed, shoving Teddy so hard he stumbled and, with a painful cry, landed on one knee onto the snow-covered concrete.

"What the fuck's goin' on here?" Rook shouted, drawing their attention away from the man trying to get back onto his feet. Before he could, Teddy took a boot to the face, instead, and was knocked backward onto his ass.

The five men who weren't steady on their feet, either, turned toward him.

"You a fag, too?" one of them asked.

"Sure the fuck am, got a problem with it?" Rook answered, squaring off his shoulders and stepping closer.

"This town must be full of 'em," one of the drunks said.

Now that Rook was standing on the sidewalk at their level, he could see just how drunk those fuckers were.

They were not townsfolk, for sure. No citizen of the Grove would dare lay a finger on Teddy. Not one. They might say shit about him behind closed doors, but that was usually where it stayed.

No, these motherfuckers were tourists or in town to visit family for the holidays. These assholes were not local at all.

Because no one, *no one* dared touched Teddy.

"Asked you a fuckin' question," Rook growled, his fingers curled tightly into fists. "You got a problem with me bein' a fag?"

"Didn't know this town was a magnet for buttfuckers," one of them said, squaring off to face Rook.

"We got a thing for assholes around here, so you came to the right place," he told them.

One of the drunks chuckled. "The faggot's got a sense of humor."

Rook glanced past him to Teddy who was still down on the sidewalk, his face as white as the snow he sat in. "Adam comin'?"

The hairdresser shook his head, his mitten pressed to the corner of his eye where it was bleeding. "They took my phone and ripped the earbuds out of my ears. All I was trying to do was shovel the sidewalk."

Christ. "Which one of you motherfuckers got his phone?"

Another one squared off with him. "We didn't see a phone. He's a liar."

"Known this man almost my whole goddamn life. Never heard him lie once," Rook growled. "Unlike the lie that just came outta your fuckin' mouth."

"You think you're tough, but you're stupid. If you haven't noticed, you're outnumbered, dumbass."

Rook slipped his phone from the pocket of his leather jacket and tossed it to Teddy. "Call Adam now. You can't get him, call Dutch and have him send the rest of the guys."

Rook didn't watch to see if Teddy did as told. Instead, he kept his eyes on the men who now formed a wall between him and the fallen hairdresser.

"Go inside, Teddy," Rook ordered him.

"I'm not leaving you out here alone."

Rook's gaze quickly flicked back to him to see his phone to Teddy's ear and his lips moving. "Don't fuckin' worry about me. Go the fuck inside."

One of the assholes shouted, "Oh, tough guy here thinks he can take us all on."

"You don't think I can?" Rook asked him and grinned. That brought him a few amused chuckles. "Teddy, go inside."

"*I said* I'm not leaving you out here alone and Adam's on his way."

Somebody must not be hurt too badly if he was slapping Rook back with attitude.

But with Teddy's hubby on the way, it meant Rook needed to do what he needed to do before the pig got on scene and maybe brought the rest of the piglets along with him. He had no idea if Adam was working and would arrive in uniform or if he was off-duty.

It didn't matter either way. Adam Bryson was a pig through and through, just like the rest of them.

"Want to take on all of us at once or do you want to take us on one at a time?"

Cocky motherfucker. Rook shrugged casually. "Really don't got a preference. Whatever you pussies wanna do."

"Man, he sure talks a lot of shit," the biggest of the bunch hooted.

"He won't be when we're through with him," another one dared to say.

Rook now had no idea where Teddy was or what he was doing because he needed to keep his two eyes and two ears on five guys.

His anger might have made him a little more confident than he should be. But he'd been jumped a few times in prison and had survived, so what was five dumbfuck drunks who picked on men who couldn't defend themselves? Child's play.

Better yet, he was sober and pissed off, unlike the drunk stupid fucks in front of him.

He eyed each one up, trying to figure out who was the biggest threat. It wasn't necessarily the biggest man. Sometimes the smallest was the scrappiest and could be quick on his feet.

He never assumed bigger was badder. Big could mean clumsy and slow. He learned that lesson during his unneeded vacation in juvie.

He quickly figured out who the greatest threat was when the one on the left took a fighting stance.

Game on.

He fake punched the man straight in front of him and when that guy flinched and jerked back, Rook followed through with the right hook on the one who might know how to fight. The man wasn't expecting the strike to his jaw, thinking his friend was the recipient, which spun him off balance and took him down to one knee.

He shook off the shock to his hand—because bare-knuckle fighting wasn't like in the movies, it actually hurt like fuck—and used a boot to the temple to knock the mother-fucker out.

One down. Four to go.

With his mouth hanging open, the tallest guy stared at the man now K-O'd on the ground. Rook closed his gaping pie hole with a solid right undercut and sent him tumbling backward.

He spun on the other three, waiting to see who was next.

The heaviest one rushed him with a yell and his arms extended. As Rook braced, he heard a howl. A snow shovel came out of nowhere and whacked the fucker directly in the face. It was like the man hit a brick wall. The drunk's eyes went wide and his nose was now badly misshapen. Even better, gushing blood.

Since he was still standing, Rook gave him a shot to the knee with his boot, causing the blubbering asshole to crumple where he stood.

Two to go.

Neither of the men left standing looked enthused about taking on Rook. Or a gay man wielding a now bloody snow shovel.

"Which one of you pussies is next?" he goaded them, encouraging them to take a punch by wiggling his fingers in a *come-and-get-it* type of way.

With another frustrated scream, Teddy didn't bother to wait to see who volunteered and once again used the shovel, this time to crack the closest one on the back of the head.

"Damn, dude," Rook muttered, but grinned as he watched that man fall to the ground in a heap.

"*I said* I wasn't leaving you out here alone to defend my honor," Teddy huffed and began to wildly swing at the only one who remained not bleeding and on his two feet.

That man scooted out of the shovel's reach but right into Rook's. Rook slugged the man square in the face, made impact with his nose, and ground out a curse at the pain shooting through his hand and up his wrist.

He shook it out again and glanced around at the fallen drunks and growled, "Now, get the fuck out of my town."

As one tried to rise, Rook planted his boot in the center of the drunk's back and forced him back down to eat the snowy concrete.

"Yeah, take that, asshole," Teddy yelled as he leaned over the fallen drunk.

"I see any of you again, the last thing you're gonna be worried about is the pigs arresting your ass. My brotherhood's a lot worse than theirs. And nobody, *nobody*, touches Teddy."

"Fag," he heard muttered. Rook wasn't sure from which one.

"Honey, you keep throwing that word around like it's an insult," Teddy said. He did his signature two snaps and a clap along with an ass wiggle. "I wear that badge with pride."

That he did.

Teddy skirted the men getting to their feet and wrapped an arm around Rook's waist, leaned into him and said, "Now, as this handsome fella said, get the fuck out of our town." He then smiled up at Rook and winked.

Teddy's brave face was only a mask since Rook could feel the man trembling against him.

But having Teddy glued to his side wasn't smart if the men tried to rush him. Luckily, they didn't and got to their feet grumbling, helping the one who was still a bit groggy from his temporary nap.

In the distance, Rook heard sirens and that sound alone shot automatic panic up his spine.

"Get the fuck outta here before his husband plugs a hole between your eyes," Rook growled, watching the five grumbling men stumble away in the direction Rook had come.

The west end of town.

"Gonna give Oz a call to see if they're stayin' at our

motel. If so, they're gonna find their shit out in the parkin' lot." Teddy still had his phone. "You find your phone?"

He pouted. "They tossed it in the snow and then smashed it."

Rook glanced at the hairdresser's face to see a trickle of blood coming from the corner of his green eye. A small cut was right below his dark eyebrow and would turn into an ugly bruise.

Bryson would be pissed that anyone put their hands on his husband.

"You okay?" Rook asked Teddy.

He shook his head, still trembling and hanging onto Rook. Rook put an arm around his shoulders and Teddy turned into him and gave him a bear hug, instead.

Fucking assholes.

If he hadn't been outnumbered, he would've taught those motherfuckers a better lesson.

With his face buried in Rook's open jacket, Teddy asked, "Why do you gorillas smell so damned good? Manly."

"It's transmission fluid and gas."

"No, it's leather and testosterone. A gay man's fantasy." He pulled away with a sigh.

The sirens were getting closer. With the snow covering the street, Bryson probably wasn't driving as fast as he'd like.

"Do you have a cigarette I can bum?" Teddy asked, the shake had now reached his voice.

"Thought you quit a long time ago."

"I did. But I could really use one right now."

"Got something better than a cigarette for your nerves," Rook told him with a half-smile.

Teddy glanced toward the direction of the oncoming cruiser. "He'll be mad about the cigarette, but if he catches me smoking something else..." The dark-haired man shook his head.

Rook gave him a chin lift in understanding, pulled his tin from his inner pocket of his jacket and plucked out a hand-rolled. He put it to his lips, snagged his lighter from the same pocket and lit it. Once it was burning even, he filled his lungs with the smooth smoke and then handed it to Teddy.

The hairdresser's fingers still held a tremor as he accepted it and took a long drag on it himself. Just as Teddy was blowing the smoke out, the cruiser pulled up in front of the truck Rook had parked illegally.

If Bryson gave him a ticket for that, he'd shove it up the pig's ass.

Teddy turned his gaze from the cop, who was quickly climbing out of the black-and-white, back to Rook, reaching out and touching the sides of his hair. "You need to get your hiney in my chair soon before you look all raggedy like Cage. Only one of you can pull off the disheveled look."

"And it ain't me, I guess," Rook murmured, his spine stiffening as Bryson rushed over to where they stood.

"What happened?" Teddy's husband looked worried and his eyes immediately landed on the still bleeding cut.

"Bunch of drunk fuckers jumped him," Rook answered taking the hand-rolled cigarette back from Teddy.

Bryson frowned at it but kept his mouth shut. Smart. "You see them?" he asked Rook.

"He took care of them, lover. He was like a white knight driving up in a four-wheel-drive black steed. Very hot and sexy."

"They local?"

"No, I've never seen them before," Teddy answered, eyeing up the cigarette Rook was now smoking.

Rook offered it to him again but Adam stepped between them, blocking the hand-off.

"Ain't fuckin' pot," Rook grumbled.

Adam ignored that. "What did they do? What did they say?"

"I was outside shoveling and had my earbuds in, listening to some of my '70s disco playlist. You know, the one I listen to when I'm in a mood to dance. I was wiggling my tush and singing along while I cleared the sidewalk. I never saw them coming until it was too late."

"Gay bashers," Rook mumbled.

Adam's crystal blue eyes turned toward him and ice slithered down Rook's spine. It was exactly like staring into his sister's eyes. Same dark hair, same blue eyes, same fucking uniform.

Everything about them was the same. Just different equipment where it counted.

All of those damn Brysons had those ice blue eyes that could see things they shouldn't.

"Lover, they called me a fag like it was an insult."

Bryson's jaw got hard and he tipped Teddy's face to inspect the cut better. "Doesn't look too bad. It just needs to be cleaned up and maybe a butterfly bandage. Do you want me to get you an ambulance?"

Teddy shook his head, breaking free of Bryson's grip, then flapped his hand around, acting as if what just happened was no big deal. "No. I have clients scheduled most of the day since it's New Year's Eve. I can't go gallivanting off to the ER. I'm not losing business because of those assholes."

"But—"

Teddy cut Bryson off. "I'm fine, lover. I'm just a bit shaken up, that's all. They were just a bunch of drunk bullies."

"Get him inside," Rook told Bryson as he went to pick up the shovel. "Do what you need to do with him." He noticed the blood splatter on the blade of the snow shovel. He turned it away from Bryson, so the pig wouldn't notice.

The less Bryson knew, the better. Also, the less Rook could be accused of.

"I need to go find these guys and charge them with harassment and assault," Bryson insisted.

"They're leavin' town and know better than to come back."

Adam turned toward Rook with an arm wrapped around Teddy's back. "That isn't good enough."

"They were bein' drunk and stupid. They learned their lesson." Bryson needed to go inside so Rook could call Ozzy. "If they're stayin' at The Grove Inn, we'll make sure they know they're no longer welcome there. Or here in town."

Bryson's blue eyes narrowed. "How will you do that?"

"Ask 'em politely to leave," Rook answered matter-of-factly.

Teddy tugged on Bryson's patrol jacket. "C'mon, husband, I need to go inside and warm up, and you need to take care of the cut on the love of your life's eye." He pressed a kiss to the pig's cheek. "I'm in need of some TLC."

Bryson stared at Rook for a couple more heartbeats, then, with a slight nod and his arm still around Teddy, he turned and took the hairdresser inside.

Rook sighed, relieved that he wasn't sending the cavalry to go looking for those douchebags. It was their word against Rook and Teddy's. Just because they were in the wrong didn't mean Rook wouldn't pay for protecting Bryson's husband. He'd been fucked like that before for helping someone out of a jam.

Those drunks had been handled and if they weren't,

Rook would make sure the situation was finished and those assholes would never even think about returning to Manning Grove.

He removed his phone from the pocket Teddy had slipped it back into and called Oz.

"Yo," was the brother's gruff greeting.

"Hey, you got a bunch of drunk, loudmouth assholes stayin' there?"

"Need to be more specific. Always got assholes stayin' here. Just 'cause they can pay more don't mean they ain't fuckin' assholes."

"There's five of 'em. Might be headed back there now."

"Hang on." A pause filled the other end of the phone. "Think I see who you're talkin' about." He snorted. "You give them those fuckin' bloody noses?"

"Me and Teddy."

Ozzy hooted loudly into Rook's ear. "Teddy?"

"Yeah, with a damn snow shovel. They jumped him, was pushin' him around, callin' him a fag."

The man on the other end got really quiet.

"Oz?"

"Yeah." That response was soft and flat.

"They ain't fuckin' stayin' there a minute more."

"Hear you, brother. Want me to send them packin'." That wasn't even a question from the older biker. It was a confirmation.

Rook glanced back over his shoulder to the large picture window at the front of Manes on Main. Inside, Teddy was sitting in one of his salon chairs and Bryson was standing between the hairdresser's thighs and doing a bit of first aid to the injured eye.

Even from where Rook stood, he could see Bryson wore a

worried expression, while Teddy stared up at him with nothing but love.

Nostrils flaring, Rook spun away and pursed his lips as he considered the options. "Nah. Not yet. Gonna send Scar, Castle and Bones to do the eviction. Just want you to keep an eye on those fuckers 'til the new prospects get there. Gonna text them now."

"Got it."

"When they get there, make sure all three of them do the job. Good test for these recruits."

"Agreed."

"Lemme know when it's done."

"Will do, brother."

He hung up with Ozzy, texted the three prospects and then considered the still snow-covered sidewalk while he waited for their response. A few seconds later, he received confirmation that they were all headed toward The Grove Inn.

With a sigh, he then put his back into clearing the concrete, watching the blood get cleaned off the metal blade, now sporting a head-shaped dent, with each pass. When he was almost done, he heard the jingle of the salon's door and Bryson stepped outside, taking in the work Rook did.

Bryson stepped into the path of the shovel as Rook pushed it. He only had a couple more passes to finish the job, but Rook stopped and straightened, doing his best to not let his lip curl into a snarl.

"Owe you, man."

Rook only stared at the pig's outstretched hand. After a few more seconds, Bryson's fingers curled and he dropped it to his side.

"Only a bit of snow."

"Not talking about the snow, but I appreciate that, too.

You could've kept driving but you didn't. You stepped in and didn't let it get worse than it was."

Rook jerked his chin slightly but said nothing. This conversation was unneeded. He didn't do it for the pig, he did it for Teddy. He couldn't give a fuck about Bryson and his badge-wearing family.

He wanted nothing to do with any of them. He was only civil with them all because he had to be due to the business they gave the garage. That was it.

Rook spat into the nearby pile of snow. "Didn't do it for you. Did it for him."

"Right. Well, thanks," Bryson muttered before going back inside.

After clearing the remaining snow, Rook propped the shovel against the building and stared through the window at the two men who didn't hide how much they meant to each other. Neither cared about what society thought about their marriage. They both loved each other enough to risk being bullied, insulted and even jumped for who they were as men and who they were to each other.

Watching the two of them interact inside the salon, he could see why they'd take that risk.

It was too damn clear.

With a last look at the couple, Rook jumped into the truck and headed back to the garage to wait for word from Ozzy that the eviction from both the motel and town had been successful.

If not, he would go down there himself. Even if what he had to do violated his parole.

Because the next time he wouldn't be alone in teaching the unforgettable lesson those men needed to learn.

He wouldn't be alone at all.

Chapter Fifteen

JET PARKED her Toyota in one of the diagonal empty parking spots in the lot at Dutch's garage.

After putting her Highlander in Park, she shut off the engine and stared at the building. During the summer all the bay doors would be open, the front door would be propped wide, and she'd be able see the men working inside. Being the beginning of January when the weather was as cold as a witch's tit, it was all closed up to keep the heat contained.

They'd had six inches of snow overnight while she worked, but it had tapered off by the time she left station at the end of her shift and now the roads were cleared and so was the garage lot.

Of course, not one Harley was lined up outside like they normally were during the warmer months. The club had some hardcore riders, but she rarely saw anyone in the Fury riding when it was this bitter cold or snowy.

She had no idea what Rook drove in the winter and she shouldn't care. She just knew she hadn't spotted Dutch's loaner car, the Honda, or any car at the bottom of the mountain. But then, it wouldn't be smart to sneak up there and do whatever they were doing when the ground was covered in snow and the trees were barren, making them easier to spot.

Yes, going up there to mess with the Shirleys at this time of year would be stupid. But stupid and stubborn sometimes went hand in hand. And those bikers were certainly stubborn. She pursed her lips.

But then, so were cops.

And maybe a few Brysons...

Actually, all of them. By blood or by marriage.

Including her, obviously, because here she was, taking time out of her next two nights off to stop by the garage to talk to Rook.

But at least she had a valid reason.

She told herself it was that reason why she opened her car door, pulled her scarf tighter around her once again unmarked throat, and tugged her knitted wool cap more securely over her head.

Instead of pulling on just any warm beanie, she had picked the cutest winter hat she owned. The cream-colored cable-knit cap with the brim emphasized her light blue eyes and long black hair. While she wasn't into lipstick, she had swiped on some pink-tinted lip gloss, so her lips wouldn't chap in the dry air.

Uh huh. Right.

She sighed, slammed shut her driver's door and strode across the lot before she allowed herself to change her mind.

Yanking open the door, she stepped into the darker interior and paused a second for her vision to adjust. Air guns and a car lift being powered into the air filled the building, along with a stereo blasting some classic rock.

She heard a couple of voices coming from the garage's

office to the right. One she easily recognized as Reilly, the other sounded like it could be Rev.

She spotted Dutch in the corner standing in front of a bench with his back to her, while he worked on something. Whip stood under the car that he'd just raised on the lift with his face tipped up, examining whatever he needed to work on. Cage was leaning into the engine compartment under the hood of a Ford in the bay nearest to where Jet stood. And Rook...

She took a deep inhale, the smell of fuel, motor oil and burnt brake pads filling her nostrils.

Rook was at the far end of the garage with a woman. She was standing close and holding his right hand in both of hers. With her head tipped down, her long dark blonde hair covered her profile. Rook's head was also tipped down and his lips were moving not far from the top of her hair. He was saying something but nothing Jet could hear.

It appeared very cozy. Maybe even intimate.

Maybe he hadn't lied and fucking her twice to get her out of his system actually worked.

Once the whine of the air guns went quiet, Jet tried to hear what they were saying to each other but failed.

She moved in between the rear of the vehicles and the closed bay doors. The only one noticing her was Whip, who watched her walk past his work bay with a curious look and a slight chin jerk.

She returned it and kept going, waiting for him to shout a warning that "a pig was in the house." Surprisingly, he didn't. Maybe because she was in civvies instead of her uniform. Or maybe because the young mechanic and biker didn't see her as any kind of threat.

Some men didn't see women cops as real police officers.

She wouldn't be surprised if any of the men in that garage thought the same.

But that wasn't why she was here, wasn't why she had decided to seek out Rook.

It didn't matter what any of them thought of her. She had something to say to the man who still didn't have any clue she was moving closer since he was concentrating on the blonde who looked a few years older than Jet, now that her hair was no longer covering her profile.

She was frowning at the hand she held. A hand that was swollen and bruised. "You just need a little ice on it, baby. I don't think it's broken or anything." She shook her head. "Why do you guys always have to get physical when words would work just as well?" Her tone wasn't harsh but more of a soft scolding.

"Words weren't gonna matter in this case, Lizzy," came Rook's answer, just loud enough for Jet to hear.

"Now, let me see you, sweetie," she cooed using baby talk, releasing his hand and reaching for his chest. "Let me give you a little loving."

At those words, Jet screeched to a halt behind a car where she was just out of their view, not wanting to watch the two of them embrace. She needed to leave and just come back another time.

Or not at all. This visit had been a bad idea.

A high-pitched bark pierced the air and the woman not only quickly yanked her hand away, but took a step back.

Jet noticed she wore skin tight jeans and high-heeled boots. Unlike the dirty non-sexy Uggs Jet wore. The blonde's make-up was also flawless. Unlike Jet's lack of makeup and thin swipe of lip gloss that was probably chewed off by now.

"Now I know why you call him Cujo," the woman laughed, not at all bent out of shape that the Chihuahua, which must be the bulge in his coveralls at his chest, almost chomped off her fingers.

"Told you," Rook said with a chuckle.

A damn *chuckle*.

Bastard.

Lizzy smiled up at him with a soft look in her eyes and ran the backs of the same fingers she almost lost down his cheek.

"Why's the dog always gotta be a dick, like you?" Cage called out on the opposite side of the garage, not even bothering to lift his head from the engine compartment.

"That's why the little terror fits right in," Whip called out.

Rook shook his head, dug into his coveralls and pulled out the little black-and-tan short-haired Chihuahua, putting him onto the floor. The dog, which Jet was shocked to find was wearing some tiny hooded Harley-Davidson sweatshirt, scrambled away from the woman and beelined right toward Jet where her feet had frozen in place. The complete trek to her accompanied by yapping.

"Christ, that bastard's gonna make me deaf!" Dutch bellowed from the far corner.

"What?" Cage asked in a shout, teasing him.

Cujo began to circle her and continue to bark.

Damn snitch.

All eyes landed on her. Including Lizzy and Rook's.

The only set of eyes not holding any kind of surprise was Whip, who now grinned.

Rook's formerly easy expression had become a scowl and his eyes had narrowed.

Jet squatted down and put out her hand. The dog yipped, sneezed and stared at it confused.

"Normally, I carry dog bones in my duty bag, but I don't have any on me right now, buddy. Sorry."

"Cujo."

Jet glanced up at Rook, who had moved closer, his arm thrown casually around Lizzy's waist.

When she didn't say anything, Rook said, "Name's Cujo, not Buddy."

Her gaze dropped from Rook's hard face to the arm around the blonde's waist. She rose to her feet and jutted out her hand. "I'm Jet Bryson."

Lizzy took it with a smile. Not catty, not fake, but actually genuine. "I know who you are. I've seen you around. I'm Elizabeth but the guys call me Lizzy."

"The guys," Jet repeated. "What do you prefer?"

She shrugged one shoulder and Rook nuzzled her ear with his nose which made the woman giggle. "Liz or Lizzy is fine. I'm used to it. Stop, Rook!" She slapped him away and rubbed her ear.

Cujo did another round of barking at Lizzy's feet.

"Why you here?" Rook asked Jet.

"I just needed a word."

He frowned. "With who?"

Jet rolled her eyes.

"That's okay. He's all yours. Oz will be here in a few to pick me up." Lizzy leaned in and kissed Rook's cheek. "Thanks for squeezing my car in. Just text me when it's done."

"I'll catch up with you later," Rook said with a cocked eyebrow, making it sound like they had a date or he was getting payment for the work in something other than currency.

"You know where to find me," the blonde teased, pinched his cheek and slipped past Jet where she stood sandwiched between the bay door and the rear bumper of a black pickup truck. "Nice to finally meet you, Jet."

"Same," Jet answered, making room for her to get by. The whole time Cujo barked at Lizzy's heels.

"Cujo, quit it!" Rook yelled.

The dog didn't quit it, he only barked louder.

"Gonna eat that damn dog for dinner if he don't shut the fuck up," Dutch bellowed over the music.

Rook snapped his fingers at the Chihuahua. "Shut it, asshole, before my old man fries you up and dips you in ketchup."

Nearby, Whip made a gagging sound.

Once Lizzy left the garage, the dog came trotting back like he was proud of himself for ridding the garage of some perceived threat.

"Got five seconds to say whatcha need to say."

Jet glanced down and saw Cujo sniffing at her boot. She slowly squatted down again, not making any sudden moves. When he didn't scurry away in a frenzy of barking, she moved her hand closer, tucking her fingers so she didn't lose the tips.

The dog's tiny cold nose bounced off her skin. Then again.

"Aren't you sweet?" Jet cooed.

"He ain't sweet. Say whatcha gotta say, Jet, and get out."

"Nice way to treat your customers."

"You here for a problem with your Toyota?"

"No."

"You here to drop off one of the pig mobiles?" he asked.

"No."

"Then right now you ain't a customer."

She could feel the dog tremble as he allowed Jet to slide

her fingers over the apple-shape of his head. Carefully, she scooped him up and stood, holding Cujo to her chest.

The dog didn't freak, he didn't look pissed. He seemed content to be held. Even nuzzled her hand a little just like Rook did with Lizzy.

Huh.

"Aren't you the sweetest?" she said again, ignoring the shocked look on Rook's face.

"Holy shit," came from Whip.

"Is she holdin' that little fucker?" Cage asked. "Without bein' ripped up?"

Dutch was now standing next to his youngest son, also staring at Jet holding Cujo. Both looked dumbfounded.

"What?" Jet asked, wondering what the big deal was.

"What?" Reilly exclaimed from behind her. "No one but Rook's been able to handle that dog. Not one of us, no matter how much we try. He growls and barks and snaps at us like he's possessed. You walk in and within minutes you're cuddling him against your chest."

"Maybe he's not possessed, maybe he's just picky."

"Can't be that picky if he picked Rook," Reilly said with a snort.

"Maybe he's just misunderstood," Jet said softly, petting Cujo's little snout and ears. He released a little groan and nudged her hand to pet him some more.

Dutch barked out a laugh, shook his head and went back to whatever he'd been working on.

Cage disappeared back under the hood of the Ford. Whip, Rev and Reilly now were the only ones within earshot.

"By the way, stud muffin, better not let Ozzy catch you pawing his woman," Reilly warned.

"She ain't his woman," Rook growled.

"Close enough," Reilly chirped and walked back to the office with a sly grin.

"She belongs to all of us," Rook shouted at her back. "Unlike you, who somehow gets a free ride without puttin' out at all."

Reilly shot him the bird over her shoulder and disappeared.

"Real fuckin' nice, asshole," Rev growled, shaking his head and heading over to a Nissan on a lift in the second bay.

Jet continued to stroke the dogs head as she turned her attention back to Rook. "What does that mean?"

"What?"

"The whole 'she belongs to all of us' thing."

"Couldn't stay away?" he asked, avoiding an explanation.

"I could. Believe it or not, you're not that irresistible."

Whip snorted nearby.

Rook's jaw shifted and he shot a scowl at the younger mechanic, grabbed Jet's arm and propelled her toward the office. All eyes followed their path.

When they reached the office, he pushed her inside and ordered, "Out, Reilly."

"It's my office!"

"The fuck it is. Out!"

"You're such an asshole," she grumbled, pushing past them both.

Cujo gave a single bark at the younger woman as she did and Jet gave the dog a reassuring squeeze.

Rook slammed the office door shut and spun on her. "Why the fuck are you here? You tryin' to cause shit for me?"

"No, if you would've given me a chance to talk out there," she tilted her head toward the garage bays, "they all would've known why I was here and it wouldn't have been a big deal. Now you made it seem like a big deal."

He scrubbed his hands down his face and took an audible breath. When he was done probably silently cursing himself out for his knee-jerk reaction, he dropped his hands and muttered a, "Fuck."

"Now they're all out there wondering what needs to stay private between us. Good job, Captain Obvious."

He growled out another, "Fuck."

"Anyway, the whole reason I stopped by was to thank you for what you did for Teddy."

"Your brother already thanked me."

"I'm not my brother and Teddy is a big part of our family. I appreciate whatever you did to stop whatever was happening. Teddy hasn't shared many of the details and my only thought about why is that he's trying to protect you for whatever reason."

Probably because Rook had gotten physical with the men who had harassed Teddy. He probably wouldn't have gotten in any trouble for it, but Rook wasn't one to trust law enforcement. And he was on parole.

"He don't need to protect me."

"No, but you protected him. And unlike you, I like to thank the people who help me or my family get out of harm's way." She gave him a look that reminded him of how she saved his ass without a simple thank you in return. His mouth tightened. "One thing he did say was you told those assholes you were gay, too."

Rook didn't bother to confirm or deny it.

"You had mentioned that you and Dodge were close and made it sound like you two kept each other company during those long and lonely nights when you did time together."

"Yeah. And?"

"Did you and Dodge..."

"Prison's a lot like Vegas. What happens in prison, stays in prison. Only difference, the slots don't pay out the same."

She rolled her lips under for a second before asking, "Does that mean you're bi?"

She was asking a question she had no right to know but she was curious and he didn't have to answer. He could simply tell her to "fuck off" like he normally did. He wasn't shy about telling her where to go or how much he hated her. She also couldn't deny she enjoyed busting his balls, the direction this conversation was currently taking.

"Ain't bi. Love pussy. Love stickin' my dick in cunt that's soft and wet and has tits attached. Ain't into a hairy shit canal with a dick attached."

Jet shut her gaping jaw and rolled her lips under again, trying not to show her amusement of how bent out of shape he got over her question. She did her best to school that amusement from her voice. "So, just to be clear, you weren't *gay for the stay* while in prison?"

He snorted. "Didn't say that."

She grinned and shoved his shoulder. "Really?"

He grimaced. "Didn't give or take dick while inside."

"There are other ways for two people to get off. Do you need a list?" she teased.

"Got my own list, fuck you very much."

"Anyway, nothing wrong with being bi. Or even gay. And since both Teddy and Adam are gay, I'm glad you don't have a problem with it."

"Got a problem with the badge your brother wears, not who he fucks."

"Good."

His brow dropped low. "Why the fuck do you care if I did, anyway? Shouldn't matter to you if I'm a huge homophobe."

She shrugged one shoulder. "Nobody likes a homophobe."

His eyebrows rose. "Other homophobes do." He sighed. "That all you stopped by for?"

"Yes. That was the only reason."

"Said your piece."

"I did."

"Then, you have a good fuckin' day, *Officer Bryson*. Make sure to leave the dog on your way out." He barreled out of the office, leaving her where she stood.

Jet lifted the dog until they were eye to eye. "Your daddy's a complete asshole, do you know that?"

Cujo gave a little woof and a sneeze.

Yes, that was why the dog had picked Rook.

Birds of a feather...

ROOK WAS FUCKING PISSED.

So fucking pissed.

Not at Jet. At himself.

For fuck's sake, at her, too.

For showing up today at the garage, just when he thought he was finally getting her out of his thoughts. But fuck no, she had to waltz right into his place of work to thank him for saving Teddy's ass.

It almost made him regret doing it.

He grimaced. *Christ*, he would've done it no matter what. Teddy didn't deserve the treatment those drunks gave him, and Rook would save his ass whether he was married to a pig or not.

He'd managed to avoid her since the last time he broke into her apartment and fucked her in her bed. In front of those large mirrors.

He closed his eyes and pictured it all over again.

Why the fuck couldn't he quit her?

But no, her standing there in her jeans and tan leather jacket that emphasized her slender curves, with her black hair loose around her shoulders and those fucking big blue eyes. And that knit cap she was wearing that made her look...

Fuck.

He scrubbed his palm over his aching erection that was trying to split his zipper.

For the rest of the fucking day, he couldn't concentrate on shit because the only thing he could see was Jet on her knees at his feet, his dick, rock hard and shiny from her spit, sliding in and out of her glossy pink lips.

He'd even tried to piss her off by using Lizzy. But Jet didn't seem to give a fuck about the sweet butt.

Maybe she no longer wanted him and he was alone in still wanting her.

Obsessing about her.

It was a fucking sickness with only one cure.

His thirst for her made his skin itch. Made his fingers twitch. Made him want to bend her over the hood of a car, leave his handprint on her ass and fuck her so hard he left bruises. Made him not even care who the fuck watched.

That was how far he'd fallen into that sickness.

All the mistakes he'd made in life, he knew better than to make them, but did it anyway.

Just like now as he moved quietly through her dark apartment.

A goddamn sickness. That was all it was. One he couldn't shake.

He paused in the tiny living space that included her couch, TV and galley-sized kitchen and shrugged off his heavy leather jacket. He tucked his socks into his boots once he'd removed them.

He began to remove his belt but thought better of it. It could come in handy. He tugged his long-sleeved tee over his head, pulling off the thermal shirt he wore underneath it at the same time, leaving him bare-chested and barefooted.

He stared down the short dark hallway to the partially closed door of her bedroom. Then his feet began to move in that direction on their own. The apartment was quiet except for the heat kicking on, so he needed to walk just as quietly.

He pushed the bedroom door open farther and he let his gaze slide through the room, relieved to find her alone. Because if she hadn't been, that would've been awkward as fuck and he would've been backtracking out of her place as fast as he could.

But thank fuck no one else was in her bed. His jaw shifted even at the possibility.

Of seeing her in bed with another man.

Of another man coming inside her. A place where he'd been and already staked his claim. Of that man's mouth touching her neck where he'd already left his mark.

Of some other man's ears filling with her whimpers and the cries of a name other than Rook's as her pussy pulsated around another man's dick.

Yeah, it was a sickness all right. Because he knew they had no ties. Nothing prevented her from inviting another man into her bed.

And that was what she would do. Invite him into her apartment, into her bed, into her. Unlike Rook who just took what he wanted and didn't ask first.

Her breathing was heavy, but steady, as she sprawled diagonally across the bed on her belly. All the bed coverings had been pushed down to the bottom of the mattress like she'd been restless and kicked them off.

She wore nothing but a pair of boy shorts—he couldn't tell the color—that clung to her round, shapely ass and her thick hair spread across her pillow and along her bare back like a silky midnight waterfall.

Her right cheek was pressed into the pillow, so she faced away from where he stood, but he had no doubt she was knocked the fuck out. Sleeping like the dead.

He paused, took a breath and closed his eyes.

Why the fuck was he here?

Why was he driven to break into her apartment again?

Why couldn't he resist whatever she had that pulled at him?

What was it about her?

It wasn't only her looks or her body.

It wasn't only her *give-as-good-as-she-gets* attitude.

It wasn't only her damn stubborn confidence.

But it was the way she had looked at him long before they ever fucked for the first time. Like he was just as much a piece of that forbidden fruit to her as she was to him.

Knowing he shouldn't eat that fruit made him want to do it even more.

Knowing that it was risky made him want to do nothing but take that chance.

Fuck the consequences.

Then he took her that first time and the sex with her was just like her attitude. Brazen and brave. Yeah, she could give as good as she got.

Rook could give as good as he got, too.

Seeing her sleeping and vulnerable on her large bed made the blood in his veins run scalding hot, made his dick flex in his briefs, made his mouth water with the memory of her tangy feminine taste on his tongue. Arousal he caused.

He caused it.

He made her wet with wanting.

He wished to fuck she didn't want him. It would make it so much easier to walk away and not keep getting sucked back in.

But not once had she said no. Not fucking once. No matter how rough he'd been, how rough he could be.

Any other female seeing him touching and nuzzling another one would've stomped away in a fit.

Not Jet.

Hell no, she asked if he was bi, instead. He wanted to laugh at that but it wasn't even funny.

When he opened his eyes again, he spotted her .38 in a leather holster on the nightstand. Sneaking up on a cop in the dark in her own bedroom when she wasn't expecting him was dangerous. But having a gun nearby made it deadly.

He went over to the nightstand, snagged her revolver and placed it on the dresser on the other side of the room and out of her reach. Mostly to ensure she didn't plug him with a bullet before he got a chance to plug her with his dick.

Keeping a hand on his belt buckle so it didn't jingle and doing the same with the chain on his wallet, he shucked his jeans and boxer briefs, leaving them where he dropped them in the middle of her bedroom floor.

He switched on the small lamp by her bed, one that had a red filmy fabric square thrown over it and the muted light gave the room a soft glow. He glanced toward the bed to make sure it hadn't woken her.

It hadn't.

She had to be exhausted as fuck.

He carefully sat on the edge of her bed, thankful that her

mattress was one that didn't shift and jiggle, most likely made from some sort of memory foam. But she was so knocked out he could probably jump up and down on her bed like a trampoline and not wake her.

He started at the top of her head and touched every inch of her he could see. He didn't touch her with his fingers—not yet, because he wanted to take his time before she awoke—but used his gaze instead. The silky flow of her loose hair. The curve of her shoulders and biceps, her fingers with the short nails and not a speck of color on them. The gentle arch of her spine, the hollow created where the small of her back met her ass. The firm, muscular globes of that ass.

He wanted to bite her there. Taste that firm flesh. Lick the crease that separated them. Explore her where she was very possibly untouched.

Where he'd be the first. Maybe even the only.

That thought pulled his balls tight. But he ignored the urge to take her right that second and continued his visual exploration down her very fit thighs, the tender skin behind her knees—one with a freckle he wanted to lick—her shapely calves, and ending at her feet.

With the way she laid, he couldn't see her toenails but assumed they were as bare as her fingernails.

She was far from high-maintenance. He'd never seen her dressed any way but casual. Even so, her kind of casual was hot as fuck.

He couldn't imagine her having the patience to sit her ass in a chair long enough for a manicure or pedicure. Her apartment was full of mismatched furniture because she wasn't out to impress anyone. She only needed a comfortable couch to relax on and a good mattress to get some sleep.

Simple.

No games.

Not complex at all.

The biggest issue he had with her was the reason she carried that gun.

If it wasn't for that...

She'd be fucking perfect.

Even with that hanging over his head, he couldn't just stare at her, he needed to touch her. To feel the softness of her smooth skin under the rough pads of his fingers. To run his nose along the indentation of her spine. To follow it with his tongue.

Then his lips. Maybe even his teeth.

To mark her flesh, to make her his again, even if it was just for the time those marks remained. So every time she looked in the mirror, she was reminded of him.

With excruciating slowness, he moved over her onto his hands and knees and even more carefully slid her hair away from the back of her neck. And when he could see that delicate line, he pressed his mouth to the very top.

Not to sink his teeth in, no.

But he kissed her at her hairline and pressed his lips along every inch of her neck and down that steel spine of hers, shifting down the bed until his mouth was at the top of her underwear.

At mid-back she had jerked awake, but didn't move even an inch until he finished. She didn't need to make him aware that she was no longer sleeping. Goosebumps had broken out along her flesh and told him what he needed to know.

She knew it was him. She accepted his presence even though she probably hated that he had no problem breaking in again. She probably hated the fact that he'd managed to climb on the bed with her without her waking up until he touched her.

She probably hated the fact she'd been so tired, she'd been vulnerable.

She should be glad it was only him breaking in and not some other sick fuck. One who wanted to hurt her and not simply fuck her.

He dragged his tongue from the small of her back along the valley and prowled up her body again, only stopping once he reached the base of her neck.

Her fingers now clenched the sheet beneath her. Her mouth had parted, and she panted softly, but her eyes remained closed.

Her reaction only due to his mouth on her skin.

And maybe the anticipation.

He pressed his lips to her ear and growled, "You taste so goddamn good, darlin'. So fuckin' good. Your pussy's gonna taste even better. Want it soaked first. Want you drippin' for me."

A soft breath hissed from her and her eyes squeezed shut even tighter.

"Your nipples hard? Wantin' my fingers and mouth on them? Your sweet cunt weepin' for my dick?"

The hiss turned into a sharp inhale.

He took tiny nips along the line of her back, watching her flesh quiver as he went. She might be the forbidden apple but her ass was a goddamn perfectly ripe peach and he needed to take a bite of it.

On his hands and knees, he prowled his way back down her body until he caged in her legs. He tugged the wide elastic waistband of her boy shorts halfway down her ass, exposing some of that edible flesh.

"This how you normally sleep? Just wearin' your panties? Nothin' else?"

Her voice was rusty and still held a tinge of weariness

when she answered, "Was too tired to pull anything else on after my shower. These long stretches of midnights are killing me. Especially during the holidays and snowstorms."

When he glanced up, he could see the evidence of her exhaustion in the shadows under her thick, black lashes.

That was okay. She didn't have to do shit except come all over his tongue and then down his dick. He'd do the work and also enjoy the results.

"I'd ask you for a massage with those strong fingers of yours, but us women know you think the word massage means sex." Her words came out thick, like they were coated in cold molasses.

"Only know how to give an internal massage," he confirmed against the skin of her ass.

A soft snort escaped her. "Of course."

"Want me to leave, darlin'?" He traced the tip of his tongue over her creamy round flesh, drawing it closer and closer to the tempting crease. He dipped his tongue between her cheeks for only a split second, said, "Didn't hear your answer," then latched his lips on the curve of one cheek.

His tongue swirled over her pebbled flesh, her muscles quivered beneath his mouth. She was anticipating the sharp sting. Her skin was so damn smooth, almost perfect. He slowly bit down, causing her to arch off the bed and into him, driving his teeth deeper. The noise she made at the back of her throat caused his dick to throb painfully.

If he wasn't careful, he'd come all over the sheet instead of inside her.

He released her flesh and pulled away to see the mark he left behind. *Now* her ass was perfect.

He worked her boy shorts down her legs and off her feet, tossing them over his shoulder.

Fuck yeah.

All her curves and lines, all her creamy skin, were now exposed, now available to him.

She watched him with her bottom lip tucked within her teeth.

"You didn't answer, darlin'. Want me to leave?" he asked as his fingers slid along her leg from her ankle to her hip. When he got there, he rolled her onto her back. "Yes or no, Jet."

She stared at him on his knees between her legs, one hand stroking his dick. He collected the beaded precum and smeared it around the swollen, sensitive head with his thumb.

"If you don't say no now, gonna take it as a fuckin' yes," he warned her. "Can see how slick your pussy is for me already and I wanna bury my face in it. So, that's what I'm gonna do."

He could wait no longer and dropped to the bed, planting her feet on his shoulders and burrowing his hands under her ass to lift her up. This way he could take a closer look at the pink, shiny flesh that caused a hunger deep inside him.

A hunger, a thirst, a need only she could satisfy.

He licked his lips, took one last glance at her face, then dove in, first sucking on the hard nub at the top, then dragging his tongue down her plump folds and collecting the sweet tang.

She squirmed and her fingers dug into his hair, her short nails into his scalp. Not to pull him away, but to drive her pussy harder into his face, to grind against his mouth, to spear herself with his tongue.

Her juices were being smeared on his lips, his face, into his beard, onto his tongue and he fucking couldn't get enough of it. He thrust against her mattress once, twice, then forced himself to stop because it wouldn't take much more for him to shoot his load.

And there was only one place where it needed to be.

He sucked harder, licked faster, nibbled her clit and her lips. Touching the tip of his tongue to her tight, puckered hole, wetting the rim, making it glisten. He replaced his tongue with his finger, pressing, testing, stroking.

He had to block out the sounds she made because they were driving him mad, driving him to the brink he was trying to avoid because it was too soon.

He teased her more, feeling the tight ring loosen, encouraging him. He took the invitation and slipped the tip of his finger inside while continuing to devour her cunt.

As soon as he drove his finger in to the second knuckle, she stiffened, bowed off the bed, smashed her pussy into his face and a wail filled the small bedroom. He couldn't miss the way even her anus pulsed around his finger.

Jesus fuck, he was going to blow soon. He couldn't take much more.

With one more lap of his tongue, to collect any and all of her sweet juices, he surged up and over her, wrapping her legs around him and settling in between her thighs.

She was boneless and every muscle now loose as she stared up at him, her face showing not only the satisfaction the orgasm brought her, but also the exhaustion. Something she couldn't hide, even if she wanted to.

"Don't gotta do shit, darlin'. I'm gonna do everythin'."

"I want to be on top."

He shook his head. "Not this time."

Not this time. Yeah, that came out of his fucking mouth.

Not this time. Next time.

When she was more rested, he could lose his mind while watching her ride his dick. Because he wanted that as much as her. He wanted to see her naked on top of him, see how shiny his dick became with each rise and fall on his length. So he could see himself stretching her before he filled her with his cum. Then he'd want her to keep going so she drove it deeper inside her, so she coated both her own insides and his own dick with it. Then he'd flip her around and pound her until he came inside her again.

But, yeah, next time.

Next fucking time.

He had no doubt there would be a next time. And a time after that.

Because at that very moment, he'd stopped lying to himself. That very moment proved he wouldn't be able to walk away.

He couldn't give this up. Couldn't give her up.

No matter who she was. No matter what she did.

He knew it the first time he fucked her against the mirror by the front door. The first time he marked her neck and tits. He knew he'd never just be able to walk away. He'd ignored it.

But he couldn't now.

He could no longer deny the truth.

Jet was his.

Only, he didn't know what to do about it.

Chapter Sixteen

His weight was crushing because after coming deep inside her, he'd simply collapsed with his face pressed into her neck. His tongue lazily stroked over the bite he'd given her when she'd orgasmed the third and most recent time. His cock still twitched occasionally, and his chest still pumped, each heavy breath beating a pattern against her damp skin.

He hadn't been lying when he said that she wouldn't have to do a damn thing. He'd done it all. He'd given her one orgasm with his mouth, with a little help from that intrusive finger, and two more while he plowed into her like he might die if he didn't.

Even as exhausted as she was, every second of it was...

So bone-melting, muscle-shaking, heart-pounding awesome.

Too bad he was a dick.

At least he had a great dick—and tongue—to go along with his alpha asshole attitude.

In truth, she should be more disturbed about him forcing his way into her place for a third time. He was damn lucky he was good in bed. He was also lucky he had moved her .38 out of reach so if she had jerked awake thinking she had an intruder, she didn't accidentally shoot his cocky ass.

Or shoot him not so accidentally.

"You want to tell me how the hell you got in here? I secured the window you jimmied open last time." She had one hand resting right above his ass, the other one loosely gripping his bicep. She wasn't holding him there, but she also wasn't pushing him off her.

She kind of liked the weight of him, especially since they were still intimately connected.

"Bein' a pig, would think you know deadbolts are useless."

She was learning to ignore the "pig" insult, but it still made her want to roll her eyes every time he used it.

"You picked my deadbolt?" she asked, surprised. Though, she shouldn't be, the man had done time for hot-wiring cars and going for joy rides.

"Ain't tellin' my secret," he murmured against her cooling skin, sending a shiver along every inch of her exhausted body. His cock began to soften and he'd soon have no choice but to move.

If he hadn't picked her deadbolt, the only other way he could've gotten in was by using the tried-and-true method called lock bumping. After he had entered her apartment the first time, he must have made it look like he jimmied the window to throw her off on purpose.

Unfortunately, it had worked. *Clever son of a bitch.*

"Did you ever think of simply knocking instead of committing a crime every time you feel the need to fuck me?"

He lifted his head. "Didn't know that was an option."

"Well, since I know getting my locks changed won't stop

you from entering my place whenever you damn well please, I'd rather know you're coming."

"So you can shoot me first?" His cock finally finished deflating and slipped from her, leaving a slick path in its wake. With a groan, he rolled to her side, apparently not in a rush to clean up, get dressed and get the hell out of her apartment.

"Tempting. Very tempting," she murmured.

No, he was definitely not in a rush to escape since he remained glued to her side, a hand cupping her breast and his thumb strumming back and forth over her still taut nipple. The one with another shallow bite mark surrounding the areola. That one wasn't deep enough to likely leave a bruise, but it still had been hot as hell when he did it.

"You won't. You like my dick too much."

"But the problem is you come attached to it."

His body jerked sharply against hers. "Didn't hear you complainin' while I ate your pussy."

"Well.... No," she reluctantly admitted.

"Didn't hear you complainin' while I fucked you."

He certainly hadn't heard one peep of complaint from her about that. "You're right."

"Also didn't hear you complainin' when you came like a geyser, soaking my dick, my balls and the damn sheet."

Yes, the wet spot she still laid in. "Of course not."

"So, does it matter how the fuck I got in here?"

It should. "I guess not," she said on an exaggerated sigh.

"Didn't think so."

"But it bugs me that you broke in and the noise didn't wake me."

"You were out, darlin', dead to the fuckin' world."

She had to have been for him to bump her damn lock,

and have time to get naked and climb into bed with her. "That's not good."

She either needed to get an alarm system or move to a more secure apartment with one already installed. Not necessarily to keep Rook out, but others. And maybe make him actually knock instead of entering her place without warning whenever he damn well felt like it.

"It's good if you need the sleep. Apparently, you fuckin' need it."

"Should I remind you that you disturbed that sleep?"

"Didn't hear you complainin' when I ate—"

"We already went through that list, *fuck you very much*."

She blinked when he chuckled. Actually freaking chuckled. Like he had with Lizzy earlier in the day at the garage.

She grabbed the hand that was squeezing her breast and stopped the mindless movement of his thumb. It was distracting her. It also disturbed her that it was an intimate action one lover would do to another while they recuperated from some really awesome, mind-blowing sex.

Hell, it disturbed her that he had provided that awesome, mind-blowing sex.

That really awesome *unprotected* sex.

She dropped her eyes from the ceiling to study his face. His gaze didn't meet hers, instead he stared at where her hand laid on top of his on her breast. He had tucked a pillow under his head like he actually belonged in her bed and left his hand on her breast like it belonged there, too.

"Do you wear a condom when you fuck her?" *For chrissake, Jet, do you really want to know?*

"Her?"

Yes, unfortunately, she did. She really wanted to know. She told herself it was because he hadn't worn one once with her, when really, she wanted to know if Rook slept with her. For some odd reason. *Sure, Jet.*

"Lizzy," she answered.

She also never had sex with anyone before without wearing one even though she was on birth control pills and had been since she began having sex in her late teens. If a boyfriend lasted a few months, then she would have considered eventually going without a condom. But none of them had lasted long enough.

But then, none of them had been as arrogant or cocky as Rook.

None of them had been as good in bed, either. A couple had come close, but not close enough.

"Wear a wrap when I fuck any of 'em."

While his answer gave her some relief, she didn't like the turn of the conversation and repeated, "Any of them?" because she was so tired maybe she misunderstood.

"The sweet butts."

She pushed up onto one elbow and shoved his hand off her breast. "What the hell is a sweet butt?"

"A woman who belongs to the club."

"Belongs?" Her eyes narrowed and she watched his expression carefully. "Like property?"

"Somethin' like that."

"And that's it? She just *belongs*? Because you shouted at Reilly about her *belonging* to the club without putting out."

"Reilly's untouchable. Just like you. Can't fuck her. Shouldn't be fuckin' you."

"But you keep coming back for more."

"And you keep lettin' me."

This whole scenario was messed up.

What happened to him hating her for being a cop? Had he forgotten he hated her because he'd been drinking or was stoned? Did he forget she was a cop only when she was naked?

Or had he thrown in the towel when it came to him getting her out of his system?

Maybe he expected this to become a regular hook-up instead of the occasional angry hate fuck she thought it was.

"I think you're confused on the difference between breaking and entering and an invitation."

"You haven't shot me yet."

Well, listen to him all proud of himself. "Not yet."

"For not wantin' me to *enter* you, you sure get wet and loud."

"Like you, I sometimes make bad decisions."

"Wouldn't call what we did bad. It was pretty damn good."

"I wouldn't call what we've done," she waved a hand over their naked bodies now covered in dried sweat, "smart, either."

"Gonna agree with you on that point."

"Well, miracle of all miracles. You agree with me for once."

He grinned.

That damn cocky grin.

His head flopped to the mattress when she yanked the pillow from under his head and whacked him in the face with it.

"Hey!"

"Why are you still in my bed?" she demanded.

"'Cause I wanna be."

"Why?"

"Why fuckin' not?"

"You hate me, remember?"

"Don't hate your pussy."

"Are you freaking serious?" She whacked him again, harder this time, as he attempted to protect his face with his arms.

"Yeah, no joke."

"Fuck you," she shouted.

"Already did."

"You're such an asshole."

"That ain't an insult, darlin'."

"It should be."

"But it ain't."

"I hate you."

"You don't hate me," he scoffed.

"Don't act like your cock is one of a kind. It isn't. I can get dick just as good elsewhere."

"But you don't."

"How do you know I don't?"

When he rolled over her so unexpectedly, she froze. He yanked the pillow from her hands and tossed it to the side, and used his weight to pin her to the bed, his face barely inches from hers.

That handsome face now wore a hard, serious mask. "I'm fuckin' you without a goddamn wrap, Jet. You better not be gettin' dick elsewhere."

She wiggled her finger in her ear. "I'm sorry, what? You want to repeat that?"

He dropped his face another inch and growled, "You better not be gettin' dick elsewhere."

"Uh... Have I been sucked into some alternative world? Did my orgasm teleport me to some other planet? Because I can't be on Earth right now."

"It wasn't just one fuckin' orgasm, tonight it was three and I'm totally fuckin' serious."

"You keep telling me you hate me," she spouted in his

face. "Since when does that make the sex we're having—no," she shook her head, "not *having* because that would mean it would continue—*had* become exclusive? How much pot did you smoke before coming here? A half pound since your brain is that baked?"

"Now you're the asshole," he muttered.

"And you'd be correct on that. We've had sex three times, Rook." She held up three fingers and shoved them into his face. "Three. And each time you've forced yourself into my apartment to have it. That does not warrant any kind of exclusivity. And anyway, you were all over Lizzy earlier. So, where do you even get off telling me I'd better not be having sex with anyone else?" She shoved her palms into his chest but he didn't even budge. She growled in frustration. "You can get the fuck off me any time now. You know where the door is. Make sure you lock it behind you."

"Fuck you, Jet—"

"See? There you go."

"I didn't finish... Fuck you, darlin', I'm not leavin'."

"Why would you even want to stay?"

"I'll admit, fuckin' you the first time was a mistake. The second time, too. I'll even throw in this third time. But the fourth time—"

"There won't be a fourth time," she said, cutting him off.

"The fourth time won't be a mistake," he finished.

"There won't be a fourth time," she repeated, "because you're leaving and if you do break in here again, I *will* shoot your ass."

"No, you won't."

"You want to bet?"

"Yeah. I wanna bet."

She narrowed her eyes and growled at him. "I'm

assuming Lizzy isn't the only sweet butt," she air-quoted the insulting term, "you boys have available. Am I correct?"

He jerked up one shoulder. "Yeah."

She rolled her eyes. "Why does the club have them?"

"'Cause we can."

"That's such a non-answer. By what you said to Reilly, I assume they cater to your every need." She lifted one eyebrow to make her point. "Am I right?"

"Somethin' like that." His face gave away nothing.

He didn't like this line of questioning, but she didn't care. She found it appalling that women were used like that. "Please tell me they aren't being paid." Because that would make a bad situation actually illegal.

"Ain't bein' paid."

"So, they do it because you all are just so great in bed."

"Ain't just about sex, Jet."

"But sex is a big part of it."

He avoided meeting her eyes. That was her answer. They were like badge bunnies. Women—and sometimes men—who chased cops and, for some reason, wanted one—or many—of their very own. However, a lot of them ended up being passed around like candy because no one wanted to settle down with someone who had also done half the force.

These sweet butts had to be similar. In this instance, they chased bikers instead.

"If your club has sweet butts why do you want me? Why do you keep breaking into my apartment? You have available and willing women at your disposal. Women who aren't tempted to plug a .38 hollow point into you center mass."

His nostrils flared. It was only a slight movement, but she caught it. She wasn't sure if it was due to the fact that she mentioned shooting him or because of what he said next.

But what he said next made her heart tumble within her

chest and slapped her upside the head with the realization that something had changed somewhere when she least expected it.

"You ain't them," he said simply.

"Well, no shit—"

"They ain't you."

She closed her mouth and swallowed any words that had been on the tip of her tongue. In fact, she totally forgot what they had been.

They ain't you.

"I don't understand," she whispered. But, *holy shit*, she understood.

She understood all right.

Those orgasms really did transport her to some alternate universe. Because the two of them were barreling down a track they could not, should not, travel, especially in the boxcars life had assigned each of them.

While the sex had been great, it couldn't be anything more than that. And it really shouldn't happen again since it never should've happened in the first place.

The threat of the train derailing was very real. They came from two completely different worlds. Between work and her family, she lived and breathed the police culture.

He lived his life the exact opposite. His whole life he couldn't give a shit about the law. He'd proven that time and time again. He probably committed a crime daily, even by simply smoking pot, and didn't give a shit he did so. All it would take was one misstep for his parole officer to throw him back in prison to finish off his current sentence.

And would he learn from that time spent behind bars? Hell no. Because he hadn't learned any of the other multitude of times he'd been arrested and had his freedom ripped away for doing something stupid.

Rook did what he wanted and didn't give a flying fuck. That's how he lived his life. That wasn't how she lived hers.

Even the simple act of being in bed with him risked her career. Risked her livelihood. Risked her relationship with her family.

All of it could go up in a cloud of pot smoke, leather and Harleys.

Her life did not revolve around good sex, it was simply a perk. And, yes, he was great at it but that was all.

What had happened in her apartment with Rook could never go any farther than physical attraction and similar sexual tastes. It couldn't, even if they wanted it to.

Not one of his brothers would accept a cop within their midst and she doubted anyone except Teddy would accept a man like Rook within the Brysons' world.

It just wouldn't work. It could never work.

They didn't even like each other, *for shit's sake.*

This was all too much for her over-tired brain to process. The middle of the night was not a time to break down and analyze what was currently happening or those three words he said.

Without bothering to give her an explanation to what he meant by those three powerful words, he rolled out of bed. She was relieved he was finally leaving and she could go back to sleep and think about this at another time. Or never.

Yes, never sounded better.

But he walked right past his discarded jeans and under-wear, out her bedroom and within seconds, she heard her bathroom door shut across the hallway.

Maybe if she ignored him he'd go away.

But it was hard to do that when he sauntered back into the room like he belonged there. She shouldn't be so damn shallow but his body alone was enough for her to invite him back into her bed.

However, like normal, he didn't wait for any invite. He came back with a clean cock and a tin in his fingers. Without a word, he settled on the bed next to her and leaned back against her headboard, opened the tin in his naked lap and pulled out a joint.

"Uh..."

He tucked it in between his lips, pulled a Bic lighter from the same tin and lit it.

"Are you fucking serious?" He couldn't be serious.

"Whataya gonna do? Arrest me? Whataya gonna put in that little box where you fill in the location for the arrest? Jet's bed? Bet your pig brethren would love that shit. Bet they would love to know whose cum's fillin' your pussy right now."

She pulled herself up to a seat next to him and watched in disbelief as the smoke he'd pulled into his lungs escaped his lips and drifted toward her ceiling.

"First of all, my lease doesn't allow smoking. And that's the legal shit. Second of all, unless the law changed since the time I went to sleep earlier, what you're doing is not only illegal but breaking your parole."

"You sure like to remind me about my parole, darlin'."

"It's probably something you should keep in mind every time you do something to break it. Unless you don't mind finishing your sentence behind bars."

"I do."

"Then that's a good reason to be aware of not only what you're doing, but who you're doing it in front of."

Without even the slightest concern, he took another long drag from the joint, held it for a few seconds and this time when he let the smoke roll out of his mouth, he sucked it back up into his nostrils.

What a useful skill that was.

After one more long hit, he pinched out the end and tucked the lighter and joint back in his little tin, setting it on her nightstand like he did it every night.

"Shit should be legal," he finally said.

"I'm not going to argue that, but until it is, it isn't."

"When's the last time you popped someone for smoking a little weed?"

"Never."

"You just look the other way?"

"No, for personal use, I just issue a citation and let them pay the fine. If it's enough for distribution, then I'd have cause for an arrest."

He jerked his chin toward the tin. "Issue me a citation then."

"You'd just rip it up and throw it away. Or smoke it."

He twisted his head toward her and smirked.

God, that damn smirk! She couldn't decide whether she should punch him in the mouth or kiss him.

"Doesn't your PO drug test you?"

He shrugged. "Sure."

"And you've never pissed hot?"

"Nope."

"He hasn't taken hair samples?"

Rook pursed his very skilled lips and considered her. "Keep my hair really fuckin' short."

He certainly did. It was much shorter than most of the guys in his MC. Shaved on the side and short on the top. "That's why?"

"One reason."

"They could pull any hair. Even pubic."

"My PO wants to get on his knees and stick his face in my

dick, he's welcome to. But, if you haven't noticed, I trim my shit down there, too."

She'd noticed. It wasn't shaved clean but it was short. "You shave your pubes before you have an appointment with your PO," she concluded.

"Yeah." Another damn cocky grin.

She grabbed his arm and lifted it. His pits were bare. So was his chest. But he had a light fuzz on his legs. She tugged at a few strands of his leg hairs and shook her head. "Doesn't mean he won't show up at the garage at any time for a surprise test."

"Doubt he will. He's pretty fuckin' overworked."

She sighed.

"Why'd you wanna become a pig?"

What now? "Why do you want to know that?"

"Wanna know why you'd do somethin' so dumb."

She snorted. "Dumb? Like going to prison?" She took a deep breath. "Are you serious with that question?"

"Yeah."

Was he trying to get to know her better? Like actually get to know *her* instead of only her body?

Why she became a cop wasn't a secret so, in truth, no reason existed not to tell him. "Why not? It's in the blood. My dad was a Marine and a *cop*. I saw how proud he was of his career. Saw how proud he was when Adam enlisted and then went on to earn his badge. I wanted to make my dad proud, too, by serving my country and then serving my community."

"You were a Marine?"

She was surprised he didn't know that. Maybe he'd forgotten or when he had learned that fact he hadn't cared at the time.

"Still am. Once a Marine, always a Marine. *Oorah.*" The

last was whispered and not shouted like normal. "Both my father and uncle followed in my grandfather's footsteps. They encouraged their sons to do the same."

He stared at her. "But not you." He grabbed her left hand, which had been fisted on her thigh, used his fingers to spread out hers and planted her hand onto his chest, keeping it pinned there with his own.

"Not me," she whispered.

What the hell was he doing? Trying to be intimate?

What the hell was going on with him?

"You did anyway."

He was confusing the hell out of her. This type of touching. These types of questions. "Yes."

"You make your pop proud?"

She tried to pull her hand away from the heat of his chest, from the smooth skin beneath her palm, but he forced her to keep it there. Where she could feel his steady and strong heartbeat.

"If you expect me to tell you a story where I start crying because I was chasing my father's love, you won't get that from me."

She didn't follow her path to achieve her father's love, she always had it. She could be serving ice cream at a Baskin-Robbins for minimum wage and, as long as she was still a contributing member of society, he wouldn't care. He'd love her just the same. So would her mother.

She knew she was damn lucky. Luckier than most. She had definitely won the great parents lottery.

"He was proud," Rook answered for her.

"Yes. More than proud of my decisions. But he didn't want to pressure me. He wanted it to be my choice. Honestly, he's the best dad ever. Right next to my uncle. My grandparents were awesome and passed that gene down to their sons, who passed it down to my brother and my cousins."

She knew Rook's gruff and rough-around-the-edges father was also an original member of the Blood Fury MC back in the day when it was an outlaw club. She had heard that Dutch had raised his sons practically on his own, but she wondered about his mother.

Was the lack of a mother in his life the reason he ended up in jail or prison all those times? Had it been some sort of acting out?

It didn't matter. They hadn't met on eHarmony. This wasn't a date. They also weren't planning on dating. She didn't need to know the intimate details of his life and he didn't need to know hers.

Getting more deeply involved with him would make an already complicated situation that much worse.

Anyway, it was time for him to leave. "Okay, I need sleep."

"Soon. Ain't done with you yet."

"Rook, I really need sleep."

"Gonna get some, when I'm done with you."

"Why do you get to decide when you're done with me?"

"Didn't hear you complainin' while I ate your pussy."

She slapped a hand to her forehead. "Oh God. Here we go again."

"Didn't hear you complainin' while I fucked you."

She moved to quickly straddle his lap, "Shut up," and crushed her mouth to his.

That kept him quiet for quite a while.

And, of course, the lack of sleep ended up being worth it.

Chapter Seventeen

For the last seven weeks they'd fallen into a pattern.

He'd show up around seven a.m., slide naked into her bed, and wait for her to drag her ass through the door after finishing her shift.

They'd fuck, shower, then he went to work while she went to sleep. On her nights off he would show up in the middle of the night and leave early in the morning, usually by five, to head back to the bunkhouse and crawl into his bed to make it seem like he'd slept there all night. This way no one would question his whereabouts.

Luckily, he'd only been busted a couple of times sneaking in through the rear door of the bunkhouse, thinking everyone was crashed in their bunks.

One time by Scar restlessly prowling the corridor. Another time by Easy.

Easy caught him because he'd been shuttling some chick out the back door while Rook was coming in. After two wordless chin lifts, each found their own beds and never brought it up in conversation.

Their activity, besides sex, for the last few weeks basically came down to Jet and him hiding and keeping secrets.

Rook had to hide where he went and who he was with from his brotherhood.

Jet had to hide who was sleeping in her bed and sliding between her thighs from her fellow pigs and family.

What she didn't hide was the fact she was paranoid. Truthfully, so was he. But not enough to stop using the key she had hidden for him in one of those fake fucking rocks by the door.

But it sucked.

They couldn't go anywhere. They couldn't be seen together. He had to sneak into her apartment before light or after dark and leave the same way.

He couldn't park the old Honda, or whatever car he could get his hands on, next to hers. He had to park it down the street in front of a neighbor's house no matter how cold, wet or snowy it was. He had trekked through it all like the goddamn mailman with an important package to deliver. Of course, that package was in his pants.

He'd gotten to the point he'd wear a hoodie so he could hide his head. Sometimes he'd even wrap a scarf he'd pilfered from Reilly around the bottom half of his face. And he never wore his colors.

He could get away not being recognized now because it was winter. Once the weather changed, he had no idea what he'd do. *If* this thing they were doing even lasted that long.

He knew he should quit her, quit coming to her place, quit sinking his dick into her, quit leaving his mark on her skin.

But he couldn't.

He fucking couldn't.

It ate at him when he showed up like an addict for his next fix. It ate at him when he left her because he didn't want to go.

Not once had she asked when he'd show up next.

Not once had she begged him to stay.

That ate at him, too.

The more time he spent with her, the more time he wanted to spend with her. But she acted like she could quit him at any time. That if he just stopped showing up, it wouldn't wreck her one bit.

He figured she'd simply shrug it off and say, "Hey, the sex was great while it lasted."

Whether that was true or not, he wasn't sure since they hadn't talked about it. When they did actually have a conversation, it was about stupid or mundane shit.

The garage.

Cujo.

Her cousins' kids.

Teddy and Adam.

Her time in the Marines.

His time in prison.

Never about the Shirleys.

Never about the club.

Never about her job.

When they were naked and in her bed, neither of those last two things existed. It was simply easier that way.

Their time together was spent in a bubble. Unfortunately, he was waiting for that bubble to fucking burst.

Because it would.

When it did, he worried about the fallout it would cause. Who would get fucked the hardest.

But until she removed that hidden key, changed her

locks, installed an alarm system, he kept following that pattern.

And, bonus, she hadn't shot at him once.

One night he'd even caught her tracing the club colors on his back when she thought he was sleeping.

Another night she'd caught him staring at his latest bite mark when he thought she was sleeping. The same as he was doing right now. Staring at the one he gave her two mornings ago, which was beginning to fade.

Tonight was her night off and he'd slipped away from the bunkhouse to use that damn key, to climb into her damn bed, to slide into her.

Maybe slide wasn't the best way to describe what had happened.

When he had walked through her open bedroom door, she had been waiting for him wearing nothing but a wicked smile. That alone would've gotten him instantly hard if the anticipation already hadn't driven him to that point.

Her hair was a black cloud nesting her head, her knees were bent and wide, and she was touching herself.

"You're late," she said breathlessly, giving him an indication on how long she'd been waiting and getting herself warmed up.

"Apparently."

"I started without you."

That she did.

He couldn't strip off his clothes fast enough. He'd kept his eyes on her the whole time as he did so and when he was finally naked, his dick had its own heartbeat and his balls were pulled high and tight.

But tonight had been more than wanting to fuck her.

He had to keep stopping to take a breath because the urge to push her past the point of pain had been very real.

Not because he hated her.

But because he didn't.

And that fucking scared the shit out of him. It also made him a bit ragey.

That hate he now felt was directed at himself. He hated the fact he no longer hated her.

He had been teetering on that fine line. The one separating what he felt for her. Before the night she saved him up on the mountain, both of his feet had been firmly planted on one side of that line. In January, he began straddling it, and now...

Now, he was about to step over and stand on the side that was foreign to him. The line he never thought he would cross.

Not with anyone.

Especially her. A fucking cop.

He was sleeping with the enemy.

For fuck's sakes, it was more than that. Way more than it ever should've been. He never should've allowed himself to get that far. To bring that second foot over.

But here he fucking was, his feet now cemented on the other side of that damn line.

Everything he believed in and followed in his life now seemed upside down. Even himself. He didn't know which way was up.

Worse, he had no idea where she stood. Not even the slightest fucking clue besides being willing to have him in her bed. Not once had she said no to what he'd done or whatever he wanted to do.

Without her being aware of it or even wanting to, Jet might have shoved him over that line.

Right now, he had no idea what time it was, he just knew it was the dead of night. He had set the alarm on his cell phone to wake him up at four-thirty so he could get back to the farm before his brothers found him missing.

He was currently wrapped around Jet's back, possessively cupping one tit with one hand and her cunt with the other, his middle finger sliding back and forth between her slick pussy lips, still swollen from the brutal and welcomed pounding he'd given her. He lazily dragged his finger through the cum he had planted deep inside her. Her ass was red, the skin still hot against his where he'd spanked her without mercy. Not that she asked for any.

In fact, she had begged for each and every palm-stinging strike.

She had also shocked the shit out of him when she asked him to use her own cuffs to restrain her hands behind her back.

To allow that, she had to trust him.

It blew his mind that she trusted him enough to be restrained.

She trusted *him*.

He had never been so fucking hard in his life than when he had her on her knees on the bed with those silver cuffs pressing into the pale skin of her back. With his fingers wrapped around her throat, controlling each breath she took.

Holding her life within his hand was another sign of her trust.

Each slap of her ass was hard enough to leave a handprint to go along with every drive of his dick to get deeper inside her. In his desperate, crazy need to somehow become a single soul with her. To possess her fully.

So no one could have her but him.

With every pause he was forced to take so he wouldn't shatter, so the pleasurable pain she begged for didn't turn into an abuse neither of them wanted, he denied her orgasm, denied his own.

Each pause that pulled them back from that dangerous edge turned their desire into a frenzy of searing white flames that could scar them both.

An undeniable burning desire neither could douse.

One he never experienced before. And he'd done some crazy, over-the-top shit with Billie.

But this wasn't Billie. It was Jet.

Billie he could only take in small doses. Jet he couldn't get enough of.

Billie was shared with his brothers. As long as he fucking breathed, he would never willingly share Jet.

When his middle finger slipped inside her cum-filled cunt and he began to work her more thoroughly, a little moan slipped from her lips. Her hips moved the slightest bit as she rode his finger and rocked the crease of her ass against his once again hard dick.

Yeah, he couldn't get enough of her.

She released a soft sigh and rolled to her back, careful not to dislodge the finger gliding smoothly in and out of her, which he would soon replace with his dick.

Even in the dark he could see her eyes were now open and the welcoming smile now directed at him. Puffs of air escaped her parted lips.

A sharp pain shot through his chest as he stared down at her. She reached up and gripped his face, pulling him down to kiss her, to groan encouragement into his mouth.

He squeezed his eyes shut and let the words swirl through his head, but would never allow them to slip over his lips for the universe, or even Jet, to hear.

Can't get enough of you, Jet.

Can't fuckin' get nearly enough of you.

Can't have you, either.

Wanna make you mine, but you can never belong to me.

I can never fuckin' belong to you.

He didn't know what to fucking do about their situation. Maybe Jet didn't even see it as a "situation." She was likely content with keeping it simple and getting his dick when he was available to give it to her.

She was likely content with what they already had.

He should be, too, but he wasn't.

He wasn't sure what he wanted and how to get it, but he knew what they had right now wasn't enough.

But the enough he wanted would be impossible.

When their kiss ended, he didn't pull back right away. His mouth hovered over hers and he simply breathed her in.

When she whispered his name, he realized he hadn't masked his expression.

His heart began to thump heavily. "Yeah."

He didn't want to talk about it, he didn't want to "explore" what he was feeling. He didn't do that shit.

Thank fuck she quickly snapped him out of his despair by asking, "Why do you have to have the same name as my father? It's a bit disturbing."

That was not what he was expecting her to say next. But then almost everything with Jet was unexpected. If she had something to say, she said it. If she wanted something in particular during sex, she demanded it or had no problem begging for it. If he went too far, she wasn't afraid to tell him.

But he had no idea that her father's name was the same as his. That had to be fucking strange. He'd be weirded out to fuck a woman named Bebe. To him, his mother's name alone would be a big turn-off.

"It's a common name," he answered.

"I know, but why do you both have to have that one?"

"You call him Randall?"

"No. Dad."

Yeah, she was working on getting him out of that dark head space. The space where he couldn't stop hating himself for what—and who—he wanted. He wondered if she felt the same. Did she hate herself for wanting him? A pig-hating ex-con biker and grease-monkey?

If not, maybe she should.

"Nobody calls me by my real name. Everyone's called me Rook since I was... Fuck... fifteen, I guess."

"Truthfully, I'm glad you don't use it. You'll never hear me calling you by your real name."

"Ain't gonna get bent about that."

Even his own family probably forgot what his real name was. None of them had ever called him Randy once he adopted his nickname. Jemma had used it a couple of times to piss him off when she'd first come back to town because he was being a dick. Other than that, the name on his birth certificate was gathering dust. It only occasionally had the dirt kicked off it whenever he was processed during an arrest.

"Since you were fifteen," she repeated. "I guess that isn't a road name, then. That was after the original Fury imploded, right?"

"Yeah. A few years after. Some Fury kids were given nicknames but not all of them." He had wanted one, but none ever stuck.

"How did you get it?"

In the last seven weeks, they hadn't talked about anything too personal. She hadn't asked about his mother, he hadn't dug deep when it came to her family. So this line of conversation was curious. Not to mention, strange timing.

So once again, that confirmed she had seen something in his face that he hadn't wanted to reveal.

Even so, his erection was now screaming, his fingers were coated in their combined juices and he was ready to fill her once again. Fuck having conversation.

"In juvie," he reluctantly answered.

"How?"

"Cheated at cards. Made a bit of scratch doin' it. Got accused of being a rook one night after winnin' a game. Name stuck. I liked it."

"You don't mind being called a cheater?"

"It fuckin' fit since it was true. It's also a chess piece," he reminded her.

"You play chess?"

"Fuck no." He'd played checkers plenty of times in juvie and while in prison, but never the more complicated game of chess. He never had the patience to learn the rules. He also couldn't make scratch or cheat at it as easily as he could with cards. "Rook's another name for a crow, too. Crows are fuckin' smart."

"Are you smart?" she teased.

"Already know the answer to that. If I was, wouldn't be lyin' naked in your bed right now."

Her body shook as she laughed quietly.

Her laughter swept away any remaining dark thoughts in his head. His mouth twitched and he brushed his thumb over her lips which were curled with amusement.

Those lips that were really fucking good at giving head. *Christ,* his dick was quickly turning to steel thinking about having her mouth on him with her long silky black hair spread over his lap.

"Tell me... What's the worst thing you've ever done?"

He rolled over until she was under him and he stared directly down into her eyes. "Fucked a cop."

Even in the dark, her blue eyes sparkled. "What's the second worst thing?"

"Fucked her more than once." That was when the slope had become dangerously slippery.

"But here you are," she whispered.

"Here I fuckin' am."

He grabbed two pillows and tucked them under her head, tilting it perfectly for what he wanted to do next. When he did that, Cujo, who was curled up on his own damn pillow on Jet's side of the bed, lifted his head and gave Rook an annoyed look for disturbing his little rat bastard dreams.

Rook ignored the Chihuahua and shifted up to straddle Jet's chest, his erection now jutting out hard and thick toward her mouth. He caught the drop of precum clinging precariously to the tip with the pad of his thumb and held it to her lips.

His dick flexed when she took his thumb into her mouth and licked it clean while continuing to stare into his eyes. He grabbed the beaded tips of her nipples and rolled them roughly between his fingers.

Fuck. Yeah.

While he came for the sex, he stayed for her. While she most likely assumed he stayed only for more of the scorching hot sex.

He plucked both nipples, stretching them as far as he could, and her husky moan filled his ears.

Leaning over, he gave her a long, crushing kiss, tasting himself during a fierce war of their tongues. After a few breath-stealing moments, he pulled away enough to whisper against her mouth, "You need a tattoo of my name."

Suddenly he couldn't swallow, a lump wedging itself tightly in his throat.

Why the fuck would he say that out loud?

That one stupid slip just handed her power over him. That revelation gave her the knowledge of how he felt, which he had been keeping buried deep. She could use it to destroy him, whether she'd do it on purpose or even by accident.

He squeezed his eyes shut, hoping like fuck she would just ignore what he said.

But, of course, she fucking didn't.

"Why would I want something so permanent for something so temporary?" she asked, sounding confused.

That lump in his throat turned into a crushing weight on his chest. He could no longer hear over the rush of blood in his ears.

He had fucked up and shown his hand. He'd laid his cards on the table face-side up.

The bite marks he left behind were temporary, in time easily forgotten. Him wanting his name permanently on her body went far beyond that. It fed into that sickness.

"I gotta go."

Her expression held a mix of both annoyance and surprise. "What?"

"Gotta go," he muttered again, climbing off both her and the bed before heading over to his pile of discarded clothes. He tugged them on with more force than necessary, yanked on his socks and boots, not even bothering to take the time to lace them up. Once he was fully dressed, he returned to the bed to scoop up Cujo, who did a half-assed cranky snap at him. His typical "I'm an asshole" warning.

He ignored the tiny bared teeth and also the woman, who was now up on her elbows, still temptingly naked, but quiet as she watched him, not bothering to hide her confusion.

He was a goddamn dumbass. No doubt about it.

A stupid, weak dumbass who had jumped over that

fucking line and right down a deep, dark hole he knew was there. He'd done it anyway.

He tucked Cujo into his leather jacket, zipped it up, and got the fuck out of there before his disappointment turned to fury and he did something neither of them would be able to recover from.

Especially him.

But he was afraid it was already too fucking late.

Chapter Eighteen

As his brothers gathered in The Barn for a church meeting, Rook pushed toward the front of the group to be closer to Trip, Sig and Judge. The prez, VP and sergeant at arms faced the rest of the Fury members. Everyone who could be there was required to have their ass there, including the three new prospects. Only Tater and Possum weren't in attendance since they needed to assist Stella at Crazy Pete's. With his presence required at the farm, Dodge couldn't be with her to help manage the bar.

They all knew what the meeting was about because word had already spread. The Shirleys, of fucking course. The only sharp thorn in their fucking sides.

Rook and the rest of them would be happy when they no longer had to utter the name belonging to that fucking hill-billy clan ever again. When the last one was gone, they needed to be forgotten forever.

Only, he had no idea when, and if, that would actually happen since even after getting rid of all the men, the women and children would still exist. But tonight's meeting wasn't about the Shirley breeders and spawn.

Fuck no.

It was about the remaining inbred goat fuckers. And about the recent and disturbing, but not unexpected, event Castle and Bones had only reported this morning to the three men standing at the front of the group. That event was the arrival of two vans on the mountain. This time not filled with more breeders, but men, instead.

The prospects reported seeing at least fifteen but they couldn't get close enough to get a good count due to the lack of cover. If that number was correct, that gave the Shirleys a total of twenty-two men with the seven Rook and Easy had left breathing before winter set in.

Whether it was ten, fifteen or even twenty-two, it was one too many. It also meant the clan was increasing their numbers since the Fury had been thinning out their herd.

One van was reported to have an Ohio license plate, the other from Alabama. Knowing the Shirleys, those plates were stolen, since being a self-proclaimed sovereign nation, they didn't register or license any of their vehicles.

Even so, Rook wondered how many more pockets of the Guardians of Freedumb existed in the world. Did they have an endless supply in which the fucked-up Pennsylvania clan could draw upon? And if they did, was getting in a war with them futile and might end up being never-ending?

In truth, hundreds—maybe even thousands—of their sovereign nation could exist, whether they were Shirleys or not. There were only thirteen patched Fury members. Thirteen. That was it. Not including the prospects, which gave them another measly five.

Rook's stomach churned at the thought of them getting involved in an endless war. A war that would only end once the Fury was completely annihilated from being outnumbered.

He could see the stress in Trip's and Judge's faces. The club enforcer continually tugged at his long, bushy beard with his girl sitting at his feet. Jury was glancing up at the big man and whining softly like she knew shit was bugging her daddy.

Cujo was tucked in Rook's cut with his little head poked out as he surveyed the activity. Any time Justice or Jury even remotely came near, the dog bared his teeth and released a ferocious, but ridiculous, growl. Rook would remind the little shit that those two American Bulldogs could eat him like a damn snack, then use his tiny-ass bones to pick their teeth.

Cujo didn't give a fuck and still wanted to kick the bigger dogs' asses. His attitude normally made Rook grin but not tonight. Because tonight, nothing was a grinning matter.

"We need to keep vigilant as fuck." Trip had his voice raised so everyone could clearly hear him even though he stood a head above everyone else on an upside-down plastic milk crate. "We figured they might pull in some more men and that's exactly what they fuckin' did."

A grumble rose around Rook causing Cujo to yap a few times before sneezing twice and groaning as he nudged his little nose against Rook's neck.

It was one thing if they only had to worry about their fellow brothers, but they had to worry about the women and children, too. Like Rook's niece Dyna.

The only one currently safe, since he was back at college, was Ry.

But Rook was pretty fucking sure most of the worry Judge couldn't hide had to do with Cassie and Daisy. Maybe even with his house mouse Saylor since she was now an important part of Judge's household.

Hell, the enforcer most likely worried about all of them, since it landed on his shoulders to help keep everyone who lived and breathed the Fury colors safe and all in one piece.

At first, Judge didn't want the position his father had held back when the Originals existed. Rook didn't doubt the man now regretted reluctantly accepting it. But Judge was the type of man who would keep his word, stick to what he committed to and do what he had to do. No matter what.

"From what Castle could tell, two vans arrived carrying fifteen additional Shirleys with dicks," Trip continued. "With the number they still have, we're estimatin' that gives them twenty-two now. *If* they don't bring in more. We can't assume those two vans are the only ones comin'. However, the more men they bring in, the more women they're gonna need to produce their spawn. For fuck's sake, let's hope this is it."

"You think they're only bringin' in the men for their women? To produce more snot monkeys?" Rev asked from where he perched on the edge of one of the pool tables near Rook.

Trip shook his head. "Fuck no. While the ultimate goal might be to increase their numbers and, most likely, bring in fresh blood, none of us standin' up here believe that's the only reason."

"What are we gonna do about it?" Ozzy asked, leaning against the other pool table, a beer bottle hanging between two fingers and a hand-rolled tucked into the corner of his turned down mouth. "The Originals would've just gone up there and massacred them all in one shot. Cleaned up that fuckin' mess and that would've been that. Right, Dutch?"

Sprawled on one of the green bus benches, Rook's old man only grunted in answer.

Dutch and Ozzy were the only Originals in their midst. At least as of now. Whether more existed out there somewhere, those survivors either didn't have any interest in coming back to Manning Grove or hadn't gotten word that the Fury had been resurrected and was actively recruiting more members.

"We ain't goin' up that mountain anymore," Sig announced, taking a step forward and raising his voice. The VP hated the Shirleys more than anyone. If it was up to him, he'd hire one of those fire-fighting tanker planes to drop a load of gas on that mountain and then he'd light the damn match himself. He didn't give a fuck if women and children were up there when it happened. He'd turn that whole mountain into a charred wasteland. "We're done doin' this shit piecemeal. We gotta draw them out. Bring them to us. Draw them into our territory where we have the advantage. Not go into theirs anymore where they have it, which is on Hillbilly Hill."

Dutch shook his head and muttered, "Ain't a good idea. Not only dangerous, but I got a grandbaby now. We clash with them in a big fuckin' way, it's gonna catch not only the local and state's attention, but the fuckin' feds, too. Too fuckin' old to do any more time or even catch a bullet. And this old fuckin' man wants to see his Duchess grow up. Don't want my baby girl visitin' her grandpappy with a bullet-proof partition separatin' us."

"You got a better idea, old man?" Sig asked Rook's father.

"Dutch is right." Smoke rolled out of Ozzy's mouth as he spoke. "If it's an all-out blood bath, it's gonna catch the pigs' attention. Not just the local five-o but the state and possibly the feds, too."

"Risk we might have to take," Trip grumbled.

"Not likin' that risk," Shade spoke up. "That could mean some of us catchin' bids. Maybe long ones. Possibly even life." He now had Chelle's two daughters and a twelve-year-old son to protect. He used to go up the mountain not caring if he lived or died. That all changed after claiming his ol' lady and making a new family.

"And it's the middle of fuckin' winter," Ozzy complained.

Trip shrugged. "Best time. No cover for their asses to hide behind."

"No cover for our asses, either," Judge reminded their prez. "I'm all for gettin' this shit done and over with so I can sleep easier, but do we really wanna draw them here? To our fuckin' home?" He shook his head and combed his fingers through his thick beard. "Too fuckin' risky. Be better to finish this once and for all elsewhere. Not sure it's smart to spill that amount of blood in our own backyard."

"What are we gonna do? Just sit and wait? Let them decide when to strike, or is it smarter to force their hand?" Trip added, "It's better if we control the fuckin' narrative. When it happens and where."

"You're talkin' about an actual fuckin' war, Trip. It was one thing to go up there and start thinnin' the herd. It was quiet and didn't draw attention. The only people knowin' about it was us and them. Drawin' them off that fuckin' mountain and down here to this farm..."

"We'll be ready for them," Trip assured Judge.

"Not likin' this," Cage muttered next to Rook. He could understand why it would bother his younger brother. Not because they wanted everything with the Shirleys done and over with, but because of doing it on the farm where his baby and his ol' lady lived, too. Those motherfuckers took Dyna once. Cage didn't want those armed rednecks anywhere near his daughter again.

Trip nodded. "I hear you all. But I'm not fuckin' likin' the fact they're bringin' in reinforcements. We knew they'd eventually strike back, they got no choice if they wanna survive. But us bein' taken by surprise is riskier than anythin'. Ain't you all tired of wonderin' who the next victim will be? Which fuckin' child? Which ol' lady? I want this shit cleaned up before I have my own goddamn sons."

Every man standing in that building could understand Trip's need for peace before bringing kids into the world. They could also understand the worry of their brothers who already had kids.

"Gotta say I've been wantin' this for a while," Sig spoke up. "They can't pay enough for what they did to Red."

"Yeah, well, I fuckin' worry about Dyna every fuckin' minute of every fuckin' day. What's to stop them from just killin' my daughter instead of only usin' her for bait like last time? I'm with Trip, this shit's gotta end. Just don't like the idea of doin' it here," Cage said.

"And now there's twenty-two of them, not countin' their male teens. They get them involved, they outnumber us big time. We not only need boots on the ground for this, we need men to protect our women and children while it happens," Judge said. "Not even sure how to address this shit with our women. Don't want them to know, also don't want them not to know. Need to be upfront but don't want them to worry. Not only for themselves and the kids, but for us."

"That's why we need to control the situation. The where and when," Trip said. "If we do that, we can move our women and kids out before it happens."

"And take them where?" Sig asked.

"Reese's house in Mansfield," Deacon volunteered. "Perfect spot. We can get them there quickly. They'll still be close but far enough to keep them safe. Not one of those dumb hicks knows about that location. It's perfect."

"Reese gonna be okay with that?" Judge asked his cousin.

Deacon nodded. "She wants this shit with the Shirleys over with as much as the rest of us. She worries about Reilly.

Anythin' happens to her sister, she will lose her fuckin' mind."

Rook twisted his head toward Rev when he made a strangled sound at that. He narrowed his eyes on the younger brother, but Rev's face gave nothing away.

"Okay, so say we do this. Say we draw them here, so we have the upper hand. How we doin' that? How the fuck are we drawin' them here without takin' one of their kids?" Easy asked.

"Think they'll care if we take a few of their women?" Rev asked no one in particular.

Trip was the one that answered. "Not sure. Not sure what their women are worth to them. They might have the attitude that they can make more. The other problem is that they start 'em young. Soon as they start bleedin', they start breedin'. So, will they care if a few of the older ones go missin'? Not sure."

"But breedin' still takes a certain age," Rook said. "And I ain't sure if they have any kind of feelings for these women or if they're just considered livestock." From what he'd seen the times he'd been up there, none of those men acted like they gave two shits about their women. They seemed to be disposable. Walking wombs who did the men's dirty work.

"Like Red," Sig muttered loud enough for Rook to hear.

"If they ain't valuin' their women like we do our ol' ladies, then takin' some of their breeders ain't gonna do us any good," Shade said in his slow and careful way of speaking. "Kids gotta be worth more to them."

"Don't like the idea of takin' any of their kids. That's a hard line for me to cross. Most likely for any of us to cross," Judge said, getting a few murmurs of agreement. "Bad enough we had to use a few as shields when we rescued

Dyna, but we didn't take 'em off the mountain and we had no plans to hurt them."

"We might not fuckin' like it but we gotta consider it," Trip said next. "Not sure what else we can take of theirs to get them down the mountain."

"You could go try to repo one of their damn cages, prez," Deacon yelled out, causing a few chuckles.

"Yeah, they sure didn't like that," Trip said with a grin. That grin quickly faded away. "Another option is we could just wait on them to make the first move. Wait for them to do whatever they're currently plannin'. Since we're aware it's comin', all we gotta do is prepare for it and get the prospects to continue to watch the mountain in the meantime. When those assholes start to move, we put our counter move into play."

Trip was talking like the Marine he was. No doubt that experience helped him be a good leader.

"Will that give us enough time to get our women and kids to Mansfield? To get all of us set up and ready? To actually be prepared so we ain't caught with our fuckin' dicks spinnin' in the wind?" Cage asked.

Trip flipped his ball cap up and off his head. He raked his fingers through the longer hair on the top, then yanked the hat back on. "It could if we get that gun stash here on the property. Make sure we got more than enough ammo. Make sure we got a solid plan in place first. We'd all have assigned positions for when it goes down. Figure out how, once they put their filthy feet on the farm, we can draw them farther onto the property and maybe even funnel them to a location where we're all waitin'.'"

Judge mindlessly stroked Jury's ears. His dog now leaned against the man's leg with her eyes closed in what looked like ecstasy at the attention. "Maybe. Couldn't hurt for the executive committee to strategize, create that solid plan. Get the guns here. Maybe have our positions set ahead of time. But that also means we gotta give our women the heads up. They can't balk when we give the order for them to gather themselves and the kids and move. That means no arguin' from any of them. We don't got time for that shit. Could be life or death."

"No argument? Have you met them? That even possible with our women?"

Judge glanced at Deacon, not bothering to answer his rhetorical questions. Instead, he told his cousin, "Probably best if you stay in your place for now, while Reese stays at hers. This way she's there and ready since she's the most argumentative. And also, you're here and ready instead of twenty minutes away in Mansfield."

Deacon's lips pressed thin.

"You can live without pussy for a coupla weeks," Judge barked at him. "'Specially if you wanna keep that pussy safe."

"Could you live without pussy for a coupla weeks?" Deke shot back at his much larger cousin. "And we don't even know how long it'll be before they make their move. What if it's months?"

"Doubt it's gonna be months," Shade said softly. "Knew it was gonna happen. They just needed to bring in their reinforcements. Now they're here, why would they wait and risk losin' any more of their men?"

"I agree," Trip said. "Shade, you, Rook and E retrieve whatever guns you snagged from up the mountain and move them here to the farm into an easily accessible location. But not where Daisy or Jude, or even the sweet butts, are gonna come across them. Want that done tonight, you got me?"

"Yeah," came from the three of them.

Trip continued, "Once we're done with them, they need

to be destroyed. Don't want that shit on this property. Don't need the ATF up our fuckin' asses. But for now? We need them close. We need to be prepared. And like I said earlier, we need to stay vigilant. You see somethin', you report back to one of us. Don't care how fuckin' unimportant you might think it is. Let us worry about whether or not it's a threat."

"Need everyone to stick close," Judge added. "And that means every-fuckin-one. Includin' you, Deke. Probably best if Reilly stays with Reese right now, too."

Another sound came from the back of Rev's throat. Rook narrowed his eyes on his club brother and fellow mechanic. He sidled up closer to the pool table, where Rev still perched, and muttered under his breath, "You got a problem with Reilly stayin' with Reese?"

Rev kept his eyes on Trip to avoid Rook's. "No."

"Good. The only one who should have a problem with it is Reese or Deacon. You ain't on that short list."

Rev's mouth pulled tight. "Safer for her to stick close."

"Safer for her to be with Reese when she ain't with us at the garage. 'Specially if Deke leaves Justice with them."

Rev's only response was a flare of his nostrils. Seeing that meant Rook would be keeping a closer eye on Rev and Reilly. He'd also mention something to Cage, too.

He wouldn't bother mentioning that possible problem with Dutch because his old man wouldn't give a shit if anybody and everybody was boning Reilly. *Hell*, if he could bone Reilly without Reese stun-gunning him in the nuts, he'd probably try.

"All right. The club's officers are gonna go upstairs and put together a plan. Once we got that done, we'll share it with the rest of you. Shade, E and Rook, you got your orders. Everyone else, keep your eyes and ears open. Let's not overdo the beer, whiskey or weed right now. Need everyone alert.

Also want the three new recruits to continue takin' turns watchin' the mountain and reportin' back with anythin' worth reportin'. Let's keep communication lines open and be ready to move quickly when necessary."

"Keep a close eye on the women and children, too," Judge added. "We *all* need to do that. Don't just keep an eye on the kids that came from your nuts. My kids are your kids. Your kids are mine. The Fury kids belong to all of us. Let's remember that."

Another murmur of agreement moved through the group of men.

Trip clapped his hands together once and said, "All right, that's it for now."

As everyone started to disperse, he stopped them by yelling out, "Hang on." Trip waited until everyone was looking his way to say, "Know the motto the Originals used was utter shit, but it was what they had. We took the spilled blood and those broken bones, rose from the ashes and built a new and stronger brotherhood. Our brotherhood keeps rising, getting tighter and stronger to the point where it'll soon be unbreakable." He glanced toward Cage. "When those motherfuckers took Dyna, I heard Cage mutter somethin' on the mountain, and it's stuck with me ever since. I want it to be ours. Something new like us. Yes, we live and die for our brothers and will continue to do so, but right now, Cage's words are a fuck of a lot more fittin'..."

Rook glanced at his brother as he gave Trip a chin lift. The prez returned it.

Trip then yelled, "Hell hath no fury like..." He raised both of his arms over his shoulders in encouragement.

"The Blood Fury!" came the deafening shout from everyone in church.

"Hell's about to rain down on those hillbilly goat fuckers!" Sig yelled.

"Fittin' as fuck," Rook muttered.

The executive committee went upstairs for their meeting, everyone else wandered off to do what they needed to do, and Shade and Easy came up to him. They headed out to the hiding spot where they'd stored the Shirley guns and ammo.

Hopefully, between the three of them, by the time they returned they'd figure out a secure spot on the farm where to store them.

Rook had a feeling they would need that stash. And soon.

* * *

AFTER DROPPING both him and Easy back at The Barn, Rook watched Shade pull away in the black van to return to town and his family.

"Let's go, asshole," he called to Cujo, who had just marked fifteen spots in the beaten-down snow. Rook didn't think there was any more piss left in the dog's three-pound body to make it worth lifting his leg a sixteenth time.

Even so, if the Chihuahua thought either Justice or Jury had pissed anywhere close by, he needed to show his over-inflated dominance by marking over top of it.

Cujo gave a high-pitched yap and a sneeze that almost launched his whole tiny body into the air before tearing past Rook through the door and into church.

While the little shit was getting better around the guys, he still wouldn't let anyone pick him up except for...

Fuck. Except for Jet.

The person he'd steered clear of since he abruptly left her bed a couple of weeks ago. He hadn't seen her in town. She hadn't shown up at the garage. He hadn't used the key.

What he had used was his fist—a lot—along with a latex pocket pussy he kept hidden at the bottom of his sock drawer. They both got way more of a workout than they should've when he had sweet butts available to take care of his needs. All he had to do was text one, if they already weren't on the property.

He sighed, pissed at himself that he hadn't. Actually, more like he couldn't.

But what he needed right now was to smoke a fatty and down a few shots of whiskey.

Luckily, a fire still burned strong in the center fireplace since he needed to thaw his bones, too. Being the middle of the night at the end of February, it didn't take long for his nuts to go into hibernation.

A warm, skilled mouth could easily coax them back down.

Unfortunately, he wouldn't find that tonight since church was quiet. Sweet butts weren't allowed in The Barn or the bunkhouse during a church meeting and, if any had shown up afterward, they were already warming someone else's bed.

The only one who would be keeping Rook warm tonight was Cujo. And he wasn't big enough to even keep his fucking foot warm. Worse, the little shit preferred to sleep on his very own pillow by Rook's head. Just like when they'd been at Jet's.

Jet hadn't minded Cujo in her bed but then, she hadn't minded Rook in her bed, either. And the asshole dog was probably a better choice for a companion.

He went behind the bar and grabbed an already half-kicked bottle of Jack. After patting his pockets to make sure he had his tin and lighter, he went over to the fire and settled on one of the bus benches. He kicked his feet up onto the ledge of the stone hearth and zoned out for a few seconds as he stared into the flickering flames.

Cujo began to do his typical frenzy of barking and circling Easy's ankles as the man approached.

"Shut the fuck up, asshole," Rook yelled.

"If that fucker latches onto my ankle, he's gonna find himself launched to the moon by my boot," Easy said in warning.

"Won't be the first time. But just an FYI, he don't forgive and forget. You might find a few chocolate-covered raisins hidden in your boots when you least expect them. Motherfucker loves gettin' revenge."

Easy grinned and settled next to Rook, propping his boots up on the ledge, too. He gripped a full bottle of tequila in one hand and lifted his chin at the tin Rook now had balanced on his thigh. "Gonna burn one?"

"One. Two. Maybe even three."

Easy did his typical soft, easy laugh. "Gonna be comatose if you burn three by yourself."

"Ain't by myself, now am I?"

Easy grinned and shook his head, his long, light brown hair falling loose around his shoulders. "Fuck no. Break it out."

E tipped the tequila bottle to his lips as Rook pulled some Kush out of his tin and filled a rolling paper with the beautiful bud to prepare a fatty. After rolling it, he licked the edge of the paper to seal it shut, tucked it between his lips and lit it. Once it was burning smoothly and he'd taken a couple of hits, he passed it over to Easy, who sighed, leaned back and stretched out. "This is the fuckin' life, ain't it?"

"Would be if we didn't have those *Deliverance* wannabes creating havoc."

"Yeah," E breathed before taking a long hit on the joint.

He blew the smoke out toward Cujo, who tucked his tail and went scurrying away from the stream of smoke like it was a ghost chasing him. "Yeah, other than those fuckers, this goddamn life is fuckin' perfect. Don't need anythin' else."

A deep aching need for something else had been eating at Rook. For *someone* else, more like it. Someone he needed to forget. He was proud of himself that he'd resisted her for the last two weeks.

She was a headache that aspirin wouldn't cure.

He twisted the cap off the Jack and lifted the bottle to his lips, taking a long swallow. He let the whiskey warm his insides and after a few moments, his nuts began to peek out from their hiding spot deep within his body cavity.

"So goddamn lucky to have found this fuckin' paradise," Easy murmured. After taking one more hit and passing the joint back to Rook, he dropped his head back and closed his eyes.

Everyone knew where Rook came from. He was the son of an Original. He and Cage had been born and raised in this town. But Rook had no idea where Easy came from or why he ended up in Manning Grove prospecting for the club.

Everyone had their own reason for wanting to be a part of the Fury and if the man wanted to share that reason with Rook, he'd listen. If he didn't, Rook wouldn't get bent about it.

Everyone in that club had their secrets, too.

Right now, Rook's was the black-haired, blue-eyed, badge-wearing, frustrating, hot as fuck, dick-hardening woman.

As he stared into the fire, the image of Jet on her knees with her hands cuffed behind her back, taking his dick doggy-style with his thumb fucking her tight ass showed up in the flames.

He closed his eyes in an attempt to wipe that image away.

It didn't work.

He preferred not to pop a boner sitting next to Easy. In his desperate attempt to avoid that, he blew out a breath and took another long draw of the Jack. He glanced down when Cujo appeared next to him and put his two tiny front feet up on the bench. He wanted up in Rook's lap.

Spoiled motherfucker.

Easy eyed up Cujo. "He likes you."

"You think?" Rook asked, the sarcasm thick.

E laughed and took another swig of tequila. "Not sure why he does since you're such a dick."

"'Cause he's a dick, too. Us dicks gotta stick together."

"Like a bag of dicks," Easy joked.

Rook reached down, scooped up the damn dog and peeled off the tiny sweater Reilly insisted he buy for the tiny rat bastard.

Easy held out his hand for the joint and almost lost a finger when Cujo lunged for it. He shook his head. "Never pictured you with a dog you gotta dress up. Gonna buy it a damn tutu?"

"Dog don't have enough hair to keep it warm. Reilly said it'll freeze to death without a coat or sweater." Jet had also mentioned it but he couldn't tell Easy that.

"You always listen to Reilly?"

Rook shrugged one shoulder. "Only sometimes when I want her to shut the fuck up."

Easy grinned and turned back to stare into the fire. "Woman knows how to run her damn mouth."

"Have you seen her around the bunkhouse lately?"

Easy pursed his lips and tilted his head. After a few seconds, he said, "Only when shit's goin' on and she needs to be here. Or wants to get in the middle of shit she don't belong in."

"Notice if she's been hangin' with anyone in particular?"

Easy glanced at him, his brown eyes narrowing. "What d'ya mean? Like with one of the ol' ladies?"

"No."

His brow shot up. "Oh, shit. Someone doin' her?"

"Don't know. She's hard to read since she flirts with just about anyone with a functionin' dick." Rook snorted. "Well, except for Dutch."

"Why d'you care?"

"Just tryin' to avoid drama. We don't need another blanket party."

"Yeah, your brother was fucked up for a bit after his."

Rook stroked the short black-and-tan hair and Cujo circled a few times on his lap before curling up with a groan. "Yeah, well... Figurin' Reese will be the one wieldin' the club, instead of Judge, on whoever touches her."

Easy grinned. "I'd be more scared of Reese clubbin' me than the big man."

"Yeah," Rook breathed. "She'd probably go for the nut sac."

Easy's grin turned into a grimace and his hand automatically covered his crotch.

Rook had considered breaking the no-touch rule with Reilly a few times in the beginning. She touched everyone near her as much as she talked, and while it might be innocent on her part, having a hot, young blonde doing a lot of handsy shit tended to send a man's thoughts into the damn gutter. With a hard-on.

But now, having worked with her as long as he had and dealing with her smart-ass attitude, getting involved with her might've driven him crazy enough for him to kill her instead of fuck her.

What he liked about Jet was the fact she was a tough bitch when she had to be, especially when it came to her job, but she dropped that masquerade in the bedroom when she gave him control.

Just how he liked it.

His blood began to rush and his dick twitched.

Yep, in bed that power was handed over without hesitation. And that was hot as fuck.

Strong but bendable, that was what she was. And definitely fucking flexible.

He groaned, forcing himself to keep from rubbing his dick.

He took another hit off the joint, offered it to Easy, who waved it away, and he put the roach back into the tin. He dislodged a comfortable Cujo from his lap and, as he was getting to his feet, he heard the front door of The Barn bang open behind them followed by a rush of cold air.

He turned his head and just about shit his fucking pants.

Chapter Nineteen

THE BITTER WINTER air wasn't the only thing that rushed through the open doorway.

Rook's heart completely seized when he saw Scar shoving someone inside. Someone who didn't belong in The Barn, even on a good day.

The slam of the door behind the prospect restarted Rook's heart with a bang.

Jesus H. Christ.

Someone just might die tonight. And it wouldn't be him or Jet.

Rook forced himself not to rush over and rip the hands Scar had on Jet off of her. Especially the hand that was tightly gripping the back of her neck.

Nobody... *Nobody* put their hand on her neck. That neck belonged to him.

She belonged to him.

Every muscle on his body went as tight as a guitar string and his short fingernails dug into his palms. As difficult as it was to do, he managed to remain where he stood.

Steady, brother. Think with your head 'stead of your fuckin' fists. Figure a way outta this without blowin' your damn secret.

That wouldn't be good for her or you.

Breathe. Just fuckin' breathe.

Cujo had beelined to where the tall man kept a secure grip on Jet, forcing her farther into The Barn. Rook's nostrils flared when Scar used his snow-covered boot to sweep the dog out of his way. Cujo growled and latched onto the bottom of his pant leg as the prospect shoved Jet so hard, she fell forward and landed with a grunt onto her knees.

Rook quickly inspected her from head to toe to make sure he didn't need to plug a bullet into Scar that very second. He spotted the empty holsters for both her gun and taser along with her damn cuffs hooked to Scar's belt loop. The same ones they used in bed a couple of weeks ago.

Fuckin' son of bitch.

Cujo continued to growl and snap at Scar as he jammed Jet's taser into the back of her head. "You don't fuckin' move. Not even a fuckin' inch."

Her hair had been partially pulled free from one side of the knot she kept it up in when she worked.

"What's goin' on?" Rook said, trying to keep his voice level, even as Jet's crystal blue eyes met his.

"Found this pig bitch outside."

Why the fuck would she come to the farm? Especially in the middle of the night?

Thank fuck she didn't appear panicked and seemed to be more than patient with the man who could kill her and not even blink when he did.

She was biding her time.

Even so, he couldn't let her do whatever she might be

thinking about doing. Knowing Scar like he did, it wouldn't end badly for him, but it would for her.

Rook would not allow that to happen.

Her right hand was pressed flat to the side of her calf and his eyes automatically landed on her ankle where she kept her backup weapon. Her .38.

Fuck.

He shook his head the slightest bit, hoping she'd pick up on it. "What'd you do with her gun?"

"The fuckin' bitch tried to pull it on me."

"Where's it at?" Rook asked, keeping his tone as level as possible and taking a step closer.

"I got it."

"Where?"

Scar's face went dark and he frowned. "Why you care?"

"'Cause she's well-known in this town, Scar. This ain't the big city where the cops outnumber the cockroaches. They're all known and loved here. And most of them are related. The club's already got enough shit goin' down with one family, we don't need another one who wears badges breathin' down our fuckin' necks, too."

"She was outside bein' nosy."

"Pigs tend to be nosy, brother, you know that. Always lookin' for a way to trap us and throw us back behind bars."

"Yeah. That's why she's here. Lookin' for a fuckin' excuse to throw us back into concrete boxes."

"Doubt she's here for you. Are you, Bryson?" Rook gave Jet a look he hoped she could read.

Thank fuck she could. She shook her head. "No. I didn't come here looking to make trouble."

"Pigs are always trouble," Scar growled, shoving her head forward again with the end of the taser.

Rook saw Jet's jaw tighten. "Sure we can work out whatever the fuck this is about."

"You want me to get Trip?" Easy asked softly, right behind him.

Fuck, he'd been concentrating so hard on Scar and Jet, he'd forgotten about Easy.

"No, no reason to pull the prez from his warm bed and away from his even warmer ol' lady. I got this shit."

The less others were involved in this matter, the better.

Rook held a palm up toward Scar. "Look, brother, I know her. The PD and her family are our customers at the garage. Wanna keep it that way. Dutch will be pissed if you fuck up that lucrative source of income. Lemme handle this. I'll find out why the fuck she's here and send her on her way. Nobody's gotta get hauled in tonight. Includin' you if you don't do anythin' stupid." Which he already did and Rook only hoped Jet would let it slide.

"Don't like that pigs are sniffin' around here, Rook. You didn't say shit about that before I came."

"No, 'cause they normally ain't a problem. They usually leave us the fuck alone. She probably got a good reason to be here? Don't you, Bryson?"

Jesus fuck, come up with a good fuckin' reason, Jet.

"In the middle of the fuckin' night? She shoulda arranged a meet with our prez."

That would be true if what Rook said was also true. But it wasn't. What he said was a big, fat lie.

"Let her up, give her her shit back and go hit your rack. I got this handled."

"I have some info for you about the Shirleys," Jet finally said, playing along.

"Why the fuck would you give us info on our enemy?" Scar barked, jamming the taser into the back of her head again, even harder this time, making Jet set her jaw and narrow her eyes. Her fingers twitched against her uniformed leg. Probably itching to grab her .38.

Holy fuck. She needed to keep her shit together and so did he. If they didn't, it could all go sideways quickly.

The last thing he needed right now was to get into a brawl with the prospect. Doing so might out what him and Jet were doing... *had done.*

That shit was over. Tonight was a good reminder on why that had to be.

He never figured saving a pig's ass would end up on his life's to-do list.

"Hit your rack, Scar. Now. And I'm gonna smooth out the shit you just caused."

Scar's frown deepened into scary territory. "She fuckin' caused it by comin' here."

"Remember you're a goddamn prospect, brother. That's it. If you can't take orders, then pack your shit and get the fuck out. Tonight. And here I am, once again, havin' to warn you not to make me regret sponsorin' you."

Scar's head jerked up and his nostrils flared as his almost-black eyes hit Rook's.

Rook wouldn't want to meet the fucker in some dark alley. But right now, he had no choice but to go head-to-head with the man to diffuse the situation and, normally, Rook really sucked at diffusing shit. He usually leapt in feet first and figured out the rest later.

Another reason he'd spent a bit of time inside.

"Put her shit on the bar and go to your fuckin' rack," he growled, squaring off his shoulders.

Several thumping heartbeats later Scar finally moved, causing Cujo to break into a fresh chorus of yapping. It also allowed Rook to finally breathe again.

The prospect lumbered over to the bar, set down the taser and pulled the Glock from the back of his waistband to place it on the bar top, then slipped what looked like a cuff key from his boot. He unlocked the cuff, freed it from his belt loop and set the metal restraints with a clatter next to the taser and gun.

For a moment Scar stood there and stared at Jet's stuff. A little too long for Rook's liking. Then he heard a low, "Better not make me fuckin' regret this, either." The prospect's body jolted sharply and then, with Cujo snapping at his heels, he strode toward the steel door separating church and the bunkhouse.

After it slammed shut, Rook's gaze slid from the closed door back to Jet, who was getting to her feet and tucking her fallen hair back where it belonged.

"Think she's lyin'? You didn't break parole, did you?" E asked him quietly.

"Every goddamn day," Rook answered distractedly as he watched her go over to the bar and put her weapons and cuffs back where they belonged on her duty belt.

Easy kept his voice low when he asked, "Why the fuck would she come by herself? She shoulda brought a damn army since she was comin' into enemy territory."

"She ain't here to arrest anyone," Rook assured him, hoping that was true. Though, Scar was probably on the top of her shit list after he manhandled her.

Shaking her head, Jet turned from the bar. "You know, I can hear you."

"You here for Easy?" Rook asked her, knowing she wasn't but wanting to ease his club brother's mind.

"No."

Without looking at him, Rook said, "Go, E. I got this. I'm used to dealin' with her ass at the garage."

"I'm out. That fuckin' uniform ruins how smokin' hot she is."

Yeah, it did. There was nothing hot when it came to the uniform of their enemy.

Cujo pranced over with his tail up—and actually wagging—to the woman who should not be anywhere near the farm or The Barn. Jet squatted down and scooped up the dog, who decided to give her a few licks on her chin.

Easy made a sharp noise beside him.

For fuck's sake, that fucking dog just might've given away their damn secret.

"Go," he muttered to Easy. "Make sure that surly motherfucker stays back there. Trip will be pissed if we get on the local five-o's bad side. He don't want a repeat of how hated the Originals were in town or with the PD."

Easy nodded. "Got it."

"Thanks, brother."

Easy nudged his shoulder. "You sure you okay out here on your own? I can check on the prospect and then come back out here if you need me."

"Will text you if I do. Don't think I will. I'll get whatever info she came to share—long as she wasn't usin' that as an excuse to cover her nosy ass—and send her back out into the cold."

He kept his eyes on Jet, but the air moved around him, and he heard Easy make himself scarce.

As soon as the door to the bunkhouse securely closed behind the younger brother, Rook beelined right to where Jet stood by the bar, holding his fucking dog. "What the fuck are you doin' here? You can't be here wearin' that shit."

Seeing her standing in The Barn, especially wearing her pig skin, was like seeing the devil walk into a real church. He expected lightning to strike her down at any moment.

Jet plucked at the uniform shirt under her open cruiser jacket. "This? But I can be here without it?" She shrugged. "Okay, then."

Her fingers began working on the snaps of her belt keepers.

"What the fuck are you doin?"

"Removing my uniform since I can't wear it in here."

Rook snagged her wrist and stopped her. "This ain't a game, Jet. You know you can't be here at all."

Her lips thinned out. "I had no way to get a hold of you, Rook."

"There's a reason for that. But, if necessary, you coulda found an excuse to come to the garage instead."

"This couldn't wait."

He glanced over his shoulder to make sure the door was still securely closed and no one was eavesdropping. "You fuckin' know better than to show up here, Jet. You showin' up here like this threatens my way of life. Threatens all of us."

She didn't bother to hide her frustration. "Well, you left and never came back. No word. Nothing. It was either hunt you down at the garage or here."

"Why the fuck are you huntin' me down at all? You had somethin' important to say, you coulda fuckin' called."

"I don't have your damn number," she reminded him.

No, they never exchanged numbers because what they'd been doing wasn't supposed to be a regular thing between them. But it had turned into a regular thing for weeks before that last time two weeks ago. "Gonna ask again, Jet. Why you here? Want the truth."

"The info on the Shirleys is the truth."

He frowned. "What info?"

"Two vans full of men were spotted heading up the

mountain. Whatever you guys are doing up there, I wanted to make you aware."

He wanted to sigh in relief since that was info they were already aware of, but he had no idea why she would warn him. "Why?"

"So you don't step into anything you can't scrape off."

"Why the fuck do you care if we do?"

She didn't answer.

So, he rephrased it. "Why the fuck do you care if *I* do?"

She still didn't answer.

Goddamn it. "Jet."

She was way too quiet.

"Fuckin' answer me, Jet. You risked comin' here to tell me info I already knew for a reason. Need to know that reason."

She lifted her chin and met his eyes. "I'm invested in you, you asshole."

He tried not to grin and barely succeeded. "Yeah? Well, you kicked me in the goddamn nuts, darlin'."

"By coming here?"

"That, too, but that's not what I'm talkin' about."

Her lips pulled down into a frown and he remembered the taste of them on his own. He was tempted to take her mouth again, but he was hyper-aware of who all was in the bunkhouse. Nothing stopped any of his brothers from walking into The Barn and seeing them with their lips locked together and his hand on her neck where Scar's had been.

That fuckin' motherfucker.

"Wait. Are you referring to when I said that we were temporary? Aren't we? Weren't we? I mean..." Her brow pulled low. "How could it be anything more?"

She was right. They couldn't be anything more. He knew that, but it had still been a kick in the balls when she actually said it. It had burst the fucking bubble they had been hiding in and ignoring reality.

Even so... "You just said you're invested."

She chewed on her bottom lip, suddenly not looking so confident.

Christ. What a fucking mess.

He thumbed it free, keeping a sharp ear open for anyone coming into church. He squeezed his eyes shut for a moment, took a deep breath, then opened them. "You ain't the only one," he admitted on a sigh.

Goddamn it.

"Shit," she whispered and cupped his face. "We're supposed to hate each other. It's easier."

He stared down into hers. That motherfucker touched her. He fucking touched her. He couldn't wipe seeing that out of his damn mind. He couldn't wipe out how he felt when he saw it. "Darlin', nothin' about this is easy. Not a goddamn thing."

She nodded and dropped her hand. Her lips pressed thin again as she turned and headed toward the door. He followed her.

She stopped in front of the door and handed him Cujo. He glanced down at the little shit and then back up to her. She was no longer looking at him, instead she faced the door and said, "It never will be, either."

He could hear the disappointment in her voice. She had tried to hide it but he heard it. Loud and clear.

He didn't bother hiding his because their disappointment was minor in the whole scheme of things. "Nope."

She stood there for what felt like hours when it was probably seconds, then her head jerked up, she took a sharp audible breath and turned back toward him, the disappointed woman gone and the confident cop in her place. "So, you already knew what I came to tell you."

"Yeah."

"Tell me you aren't going back up there."

"We ain't going back up there." At least that wasn't a lie.

"You never told me why you were going up there in the first place."

"Yep."

She took a deep inhale, probably to tamp down her frustration. "You won't, either."

He shook his head. "Not willingly."

Her mouth pinched tight. "I'm going to warn you now... I need to know, Rook, and I'm not going to stop until I do."

She was like Cujo with a damn Milk Bone. The little shit would never give it up until he was finished with it.

"Soon there will be nothin' to know."

Her dark eyebrows knitted together. "What does that mean?"

"It means that we didn't start this shit with them, but we're gonna end it. It also means you need to get off this property while you still can and you need to forget what I just said. Which was more than I shoulda." She turned to go but, *damn him*, he reached out and snagged her arm to stop her. "You're also gonna forget what Scar did."

"Not sure I can."

"Gonna let it go, darlin'. Do it for me. I'll make him pay in other ways, yeah?" Prospects were normally treated like dog shit, but he'd make sure Scar got every shitty job possible and he'd even make up some.

"The man has some major issues, Rook."

"Darlin', we all got issues."

"Everyone in your club or everyone in general?"

He snorted. "Both."

"My biggest issue with you is you keeping me in the dark

about what's going on up there. There's something brewing and I need to know what it is. My PD protects this town and we need to be prepared."

"Not with this."

"You should let me determine that. For my safety and the safety of my fellow officers."

"Don't give a fuck about those other pigs."

She stepped closer, fisted his shirt and turned her face up to his. "And what about me?"

"You're okay. Sometimes."

She smiled and released his shirt. "There's the asshole I know and—" Her smile disappeared and so did his grin.

Fucking fuck.

He sucked on his teeth and stared at her for way too long, trying to read everything behind those almost transparent eyes. But she had quickly hidden whatever had been there. "When's your stretch done?"

"After tonight, I'm off for the next four."

He nodded. "Key still there?"

"Yes," she whispered.

"Go finish your fuckin' shift, darlin'."

Without another word, she turned and walked back out into the cold night.

He stood in the doorway and waited until she climbed into the cruiser and remained until he could no longer see its taillights.

For fuck's sake. Now what?

Chapter Twenty

"Gonna tell you this shit but it don't go any farther than you," Rook warned her.

She expected him to demand that she promise, but he didn't. She assumed it was because he trusted her.

He saw law enforcement as his enemy but he trusted *her*. That sent a swirl of warmth spiraling from her chest into her belly.

They were naked in her bed. No uniform, no cut. Just them. She laid on her side facing him with him flat on his back. Cujo was curled up and snoring softly on his own pillow next to hers.

How the dog fell asleep and stayed that way through what she and Rook did as soon as he walked in the door and for the hour afterward, she'd never know.

Rook was mindlessly brushing his fingertips back and forth over a spot on his neck. She smothered her smile into her arm to hide it. She had marked his neck tonight and he let her, which surprised the hell out of her.

She had been teasing him by nipping at his throat, kissing

and licking his skin along his neck when he'd encouraged her to do it. It was the hottest thing ever and now she understood why he loved to do it to her.

He had been marking his claim. And now she marked hers.

Ever since he asked if the key was still in its hiding spot, she had been anxiously excited while waiting for him to show up. She had even caught herself pacing twice.

In the two weeks they hadn't seen each other, she realized how much she wished what they had didn't have to be a secret or temporary. But she had no idea how to get around that problem and not cause issues for either one of them.

If they continued on the way they were, they would get caught. Eventually, someone would see them. Someone would spot Rook sneaking in or out of her apartment.

She guessed she could find a place out of town to solve that issue. Though, she doubted anywhere within sixty miles would truly be safe. And for her job, it was required to live close to Manning Grove, preferably within town limits. Even if that wasn't a requirement, she didn't want to be far from her family, anyway.

Even so, no matter where she lived, she was sure questions would eventually be raised by his club brothers about why Rook simply disappeared some nights. Or why he snuck into the bunkhouse in the early mornings.

Questions might also be asked why he wasn't taking advantage of their accommodating sweet butts the same as he had in the past.

Or at least, she sure as hell hoped he wasn't taking advantage of their generosity while at the same time he spent time in her bed and inside her. Especially since he hadn't used a condom with her once.

He twisted his head toward her and misread her frown. "You got a problem with that?"

Yes, she damn well did. *Oh wait.* "With?"

"With keepin' what I tell you to yourself."

"Depends on what it is." She wasn't giving him some blanket assurance without even knowing what info he was about to share.

"It'll effect your family, too, if you don't," he warned.

"What will?"

The way his chest expanded slowly made ghost-like fingers crawl down her spine.

"Darlin', Levi's sperm donor was the clan's former leader."

She rose up on her elbow and propped her head on her hand. "What?"

"Yeah. How Levi came to be was how all this shit with the Shirleys started. Well, if you don't count them shootin' at Trip and pluggin' a bunch of holes in his wrecker when he tried to repo one of their fuckin' hoopties."

She wasn't sure what to address first. The fact that Levi came from Shirley blood or that the Shirleys were shooting at people and getting away with it. "They shot at Trip? Why didn't he file a report?"

Rook raised one eyebrow in answer and she rolled her eyes.

He ignored her gesture and began to talk...

She wasn't sure if she blinked once, or even breathed, as Rook told her about Sig finding Autumn, Levi's birth mother, running down the mountain naked and pregnant.

She also wasn't sure if she believed the story because it was so freaking crazy.

He told her about the clan taking Dyna in revenge for the club taking Vernon Shirley's unborn son.

What she *was* sure about was huge chunks of those stories were missing. But the little he revealed was horrifying. That meant the complete story had to be even crazier.

And damning. For both the Shirleys *and* the MC.

No wonder the club wanted to keep law enforcement out of it.

But after what happened to Autumn, and then Dyna, the beef between the Shirleys and the club had grown to epic proportions.

He wouldn't explain why he'd been up that mountain those times she caught him or the time she rescued his ass before being raped by those crazy mountain women.

She shuddered at the memory.

She finally asked, "What aren't you telling me?" when he simply stopped talking and left some really important details unsaid.

When he didn't answer, she prodded, "There's a war going on in our town under our very fucking noses and I'm assuming Max is clueless about it. If he is and he finds out, he'll blow a damn gasket. But Matt and Carly have to have an idea of how their son was conceived, right? I mean, they agreed to adopt Levi, they have to know some of the details?"

"Not much. The bare minimum. To keep your cousin from goin' up there himself, doin' somethin' stupid and leavin' Levi fatherless."

For chrissakes, that sweet, innocent baby boy had come from really tumultuous beginnings.

"I can't believe Matt agreed to that." She sighed. "God, Carly wanted a baby so badly that my cousin would do anything to give her what she wanted. Even keep his mouth shut when he shouldn't."

Just like Jet would keep her mouth shut when she shouldn't, either. She mentally groaned.

"Levi's their son now, no one else's. So, don't say a fuckin' word to him and stir shit up. Don't fuckin' say a word to your chief, either, Jet. We're handlin' this."

She rolled until she was straddling his waist and staring down into his face. "That's a huge ask, Rook."

He had to know that keeping what he just told her to herself went against the very fiber of her being. Being a cop was in the Bryson blood, that meant she had a hard time not being loyal to the blue. By keeping the secret of what may be going down between the clan and the club, she felt like she was a terrible cop. Even a traitor. To her PD, to her own family.

"Wouldn't have told you shit if I thought you couldn't keep your fuckin' mouth shut."

His words were once again proof he trusted her and was placing his own freedom in her hands.

Christ, that was a dilemma she really didn't need.

Rook was only her lover but the PD—no matter whether an officer had the last name of Bryson or not—was her family.

Even so, whatever the club was doing on the mountain was for *their* family. *Their* brotherhood. While she understood it, she didn't like how they were going about it.

She also didn't like that the Shirleys weren't legally being held accountable for the heinous crimes they'd committed. Law enforcement should be dealing with that clan, not civilians. Not a bunch of bikers.

She planted both palms on his smooth, warm chest and leaned forward. Her eyes held his serious dark brown ones. "I mean... kidnapping, rape, assault, child abuse, underage brides, drugs, illegal stills, guns and who knows what else... And you just want me to ignore all of that? If I went to Max with the little you told me, but kept your name out of it, he'd have to do something about it and your club's problem would be solved. Did you ever consider that?"

"Solved by Manning Grove PD? Doubt it," he scoffed. "You would need to call in the big guns to clean up that mountain."

"Well, yes, it could be a joint task force. Our department and the state. Maybe even the feds, if needed. We could charge the key players—"

"Right. I know the game, Jet. They'd get arrested, then they'd all get out on bail while waitin' for their hearings or trials. While they're out, they'd continue to be a threat to the Fury. No fuckin' thanks. We're doin' what we gotta do so they're never a threat again. To us or anyone else."

Her blood turned to frozen sludge. "And that means...?" She knew what that meant. She wished she didn't.

"Means we're doin' what we gotta do to keep our family safe."

She stared down at him. "I don't like what you're inferring." In fact, it was causing a searing burn to radiate through her chest.

"Don't gotta like it, darlin'. You'd protect your family no matter what you had to do, right?"

"You already know that answer."

"Right. We're doin' the same thing."

"You're talking about murder, Rook."

"Talkin' about what we gotta do to protect our own. You think they haven't tried to kill any of us?"

"Have they? Besides shooting at Trip?"

"Yes, darlin', they have. If you haven't figured it out, they were gonna kill me after those... *females* were done with me. After they got what they wanted."

"Your sperm."

What he gave to Jet willingly. Even though the result

wouldn't be the same in the end. The Shirley women wanted babies. At this point in her life, Jet did not.

He grimaced. "And what they did to Red..."

"Red?"

"Autumn."

"You guys call her Red because of her hair?"

"Yeah. In the beginnin', Sig didn't know her name. She didn't say much. Red was fucked up for a long time 'cause of those redneck motherfuckers. Still is."

"Is she getting any help?"

He huffed a shot of air out of his nose. "No."

"She should."

"She's got Sig."

"Who's also messed up in the head from what I've heard. How is that helping Autumn?"

"That's between them, darlin'."

She sighed, recognizing when the man was done talking about a certain subject. "Okay, let's take out the possible manslaughter or murder charges, even if they're done in self-defense. How many of you are on probation or parole? It won't take as much for you to get thrown back into custody as it would someone catching a fresh charge."

"Nobody's gonna catch a charge."

He said that with too much confidence. He was fooling himself. "You can't guarantee that."

"Long as the pigs keep their snouts outta it, nobody's gonna catch any charges."

"You can't be that naive. In fact, I know you're not." She traced his lips with her fingertips and he nipped playfully at them. She wasn't feeling so playful right now. Not with the risk the man in her bed was about to take. "You have six months left on your parole, Rook. Do you really want to go back inside? Possibly for life?"

When she had stripped him of his clothes earlier, only feet inside her door, she had noticed he'd recently shaved everything on his body. The dark blond hair on his head was shaved clean on the sides and trimmed super short on the top, his pits were totally bare, the little path of hair that ran from his navel down to his cock was gone. So was the wiry nest around his crotch. Even his legs were smooth. She had to assume he had a PO appointment recently or one coming up soon. Maybe he didn't realize that if they wanted to, they'd find a hair follicle somewhere on his body that would still give him a positive drug test. She doubted he shaved around his asshole.

With as regularly as he smoked marijuana, even his urine could test hot for thirty days. She was sure he'd smoked more than once in the last month. The more he smoked, the longer it stayed in his system.

Did she agree with weed being illegal? No. But Rook had to follow the conditions of his parole with no exceptions. That meant no drugs, no weapons and definitely not killing a bunch of hillbillies. Even to protect his club and family.

She sighed.

Being involved with him felt like she was about to put her foot in a bear trap. And once it snapped shut, she'd have no way to free herself.

In the beginning, she figured once she ate the sweet flesh of that forbidden apple, she'd toss the rotten core. However, her hunger had gotten the best of her and she couldn't stop taking more bites.

Surprisingly, the core also didn't end up being as rotten as she'd thought. It was only slightly browned and bruised. Even then, she couldn't toss it. She had the urge to plant the seeds found in that core and grow something better.

This whole thing between them and what was going on

with his club seemed hopeless. Totally damn hopeless. And that made her heart hurt. It also made her worry for him.

"What are we going to do, Rook?" She knew he didn't have the answer, either, but she wished like hell he did.

He cupped both of her breasts and squeezed them gently, his thumbs lightly brushing over the tips. "Wish I fuckin' knew," he murmured. He released a loud, resigned sigh. "Shouldn't have come here tonight."

That was the hard truth. "No, you shouldn't have. And I should've removed that key."

"Yeah."

"But you did and I didn't. And here we are."

"Here we fuckin' are," he echoed softly.

Here they were, *again*, unsure what to do. Not only with what was within their bubble but with everything outside of it, too.

"Gonna tell you somethin'... Was close to killin' that motherfucker when he put his hands on you."

Last night, she had seen it in his eyes when it happened. It was one reason she had restrained herself. She stayed as calm as possible to keep him calm. The situation would have become way worse if he had lost his shit.

"I was fine. I was just waiting for the right moment to grab my backup weapon."

"Glad you didn't."

She was glad she didn't have to. Even without Rook getting involved, going against Scar would've ended up being a fight for her life. The prospect was more than twice her size and acted like he had nothing to lose. That attitude alone made someone more dangerous. And she knew exactly what his teardrop tattoo meant. Quite simply, nothing good. "He's trouble."

"Yeah. But Trip's big into givin' second chances."

"It probably isn't his second. It probably isn't even his twentieth. I hope you don't regret bringing him into your club. Cancer tends to spread quickly if it's not caught early and dealt with aggressively."

"I hear you, darlin'. He's got the next year to prove himself."

"If he doesn't get thrown back in prison first."

"That, too. If he becomes a headache, we'll deal with him but, right now, we need him."

They were circling back to the Shirley business. And that gave her heartburn.

"Why are the Shirleys bringing in men, Rook? Can you tell me that much?"

"Probably just bringin' in fresh blood since everyone up there's related."

It was more than that. They brought in two van loads. They were upping their numbers for whatever was going on between them and the club. They were preparing for something.

She dropped her head low enough so her lips were right above his. She whispered, "Don't get yourself killed," against them.

"Would you miss me?" he whispered back. "Or just my dick."

"Unfortunately, I need you attached to that dick since it won't function properly without you."

He threw his head back and laughed, then she squealed as he used all of his weight to spin her over and pin her to the bed. "You're right. I'm attached to this dick. So, to get it, you get me. Sorry, darlin'."

"A damn hardship," she teased.

"Somethin's hard," he murmured, thrusting his hips enough to push his erection along her inner thigh.

"You always seem to rise to the occasion."

"That I do, darlin'."

She assumed he'd be landing in her bed for the next four nights.

She couldn't argue that, even though that niggling voice at the back of her head said she should. She ignored it since she actually looked forward to spending that time with him.

Because of that, the key would remain right where it was currently and so would Cujo's pillow.

Rook crushed his mouth to hers, twisting one of her nipples, and edged the crown of his cock closer to its final destination. The slick, hot, mind-blowing fist of Jet's pussy.

His pussy. For the time he was with her, it was his. No one else's. Not even hers. His.

He couldn't get enough of it.

He couldn't get enough of her.

Was that a fucking problem? Fuck yeah.

Was that a problem he'd solve tonight when she was waiting and willing? Fuck no.

Was it a problem he'd solve in the next four nights during her stretch of days off? Not unless he was crazy.

He needed to solve the problem, he just wasn't ready to do it yet. He thought he was two weeks ago when he walked out her door. But seeing another man's hands on her, then seeing her tonight, made him realize he couldn't quit her just yet.

Not yet.

But he'd have to find the strength to do it soon. Because being discovered could create a problem he'd never be able to solve.

As their tongues tangled, she spread her legs even wider,

giving him plenty of room to sink deep inside her. Just as her hips were surging up to encourage him to do just that, ZZ Top's *Tube Snake Boogie* ringtone on his phone blared, making him freeze.

"What the fuck?" he muttered.

They both twisted their heads to look at the time. It was almost two in the fucking morning.

She lifted up on both elbows. "Who's calling you this late... or early?"

"No fuckin' clue," he groaned as he kept his hips cushioned between her thighs but stretched his arm out far enough to snag his phone off her nightstand.

By the time he grabbed it, the ringing had stopped. He scrolled through his missed call list and saw it was Rev.

Why the fuck would Rev be calling him in the middle of the night?

Unless...

ZZ Top filled the room again and he quickly swiped the screen to answer it.

Before he could even grunt a greeting, Rev was already talking. "Trip ordered me to find your ass since no one knows where the fuck you are, brother." Rook could hear the edge in his voice, which instantly put Rook on edge.

"Fuck," he groaned, scrubbing a hand down his face since reality just smacked him in it.

"Where the fuck are you?"

"Found a hot piece at Pete's. Landed in her bed."

Jet's body jerked sharply beneath him and he glanced down at her. What the fuck else was he going to say? He was just about to fuck Jet Bryson for the hundredth time?

Right.

"He's pissed 'cause he told everyone to stick close and you didn't stick close."

"What's goin' on?"

"Castle spotted the Shirleys gatherin' their men, along with their weapons, and loadin' up a coupla vans."

"Shit."

"Yeah, shit. They're probably on the move now. Gotta get your ass back here."

"Who's watchin' the lane?" Though, Rook doubted the Shirleys would just drive up the damn farm lane like they were invited. However, they did only share two working brain cells among their whole clan so if they did, no one should be surprised.

"Bones."

"Who's watchin' the perimeter?"

"The rest of the prospects."

He nodded even though Rev couldn't see it. "Women and kids?"

"Already on their way to Mansfield."

He nodded again, more to reassure himself than anything. "Good." With the women and children safe, they had less to worry about and could concentrate on whatever shit was going down.

"Just a warnin', Trip's blowin' a fuckin' gasket."

Rook ignored that. Like Jet, Trip was a problem he'd have to deal with later, but not now. "Dodge and Ozzy?"

"Already here," Rev answered.

"Shade?"

"On his way."

"What about my old man?"

Rev hesitated just long enough for Rook to catch it. "Not sure about him. Was told to find you, not Dutch."

"All right." He rolled off Jet with his phone still pressed to his ear. "On my way."

"Better be quick."

Fucking motherfucker.

His screen went dark and he threw the phone on the end of the bed as he yanked on his clothes.

He spared a glance for the warm, naked woman in the warm bed. She was now sitting up, wearing nothing but a huge frown.

He was sure he didn't look happy, either. He expected the Shirleys to move soon but not this soon.

"Where are you going? What's going on?"

He shook his head as he finished dressing and sat on the edge of the bed to pull on his socks and lace up his boots. "Gotta go. Club business."

"Rook, don't shut me out."

He had no choice. He got to his feet, shrugged on his jacket and tucked his phone into his back pocket. "Gotta go. Keep Cujo for me, yeah?"

"Why? What's going on?" she shouted, beginning to climb out of bed.

"Stay in bed," he ordered. He softened his voice a tad to say, "I'll call you later."

"You don't have my damn number!" she shouted as he rushed from her bedroom, out into the late February night, back to the farm...

And, worse, the unknown.

Chapter Twenty-One

"WE'RE FINISHIN' this once and for all. Tonight." Trip had slipped into military mode as they gathered around the spot where Easy, Shade and Rook had stored the stolen Shirley weapons.

They had confiscated long guns and a few handguns or whatever was on or nearby a Shirley when they got culled from the hillbilly herd. It couldn't be more fitting that their own guns would be used against them.

"Gotta keep our eyes and ears open and our mouths shut," Trip continued as he handed out rifles and shotguns to everyone standing in a half-circle in front of the tiny, abandoned hunting shack. Shade had discovered it in the woods months ago. They assumed Trip's grandfather had used it during deer season. Or squirrel or what-the-fuck-ever season hunters killed animals.

The area around it was overgrown, and the shelter was leaning dangerously. The wood rotting and well on its way back to the Earth from where it originally came.

It had been the perfect spot to store the guns. The only

problem was that the night was dark, the temps down to nutsicle weather and the location wasn't very close to The Barn and the farmhouse.

Trip considered the distance as a good thing. He wanted to draw the Shirleys as far from the club's home base as possible. He figured if everyone set up in the woods, they might be able to draw the inbred goat fuckers into the open field. Then they'd have no problem picking off those motherfuckers, even in the dark with only the light of the moon and glow of the fresh fallen snow.

Of course, nothing ever went that smoothly. Even so, they'd still do their best to stick to that plan.

"Everyone make sure your AR, shotgun or whatever I handed you is loaded and ready to fire. Safeties off. Fill your pockets with extra ammo. This needs to be over and the casualties cleaned up before daylight. Shade brought the van so we can load up any bodies and take them immediately to the crematorium to get rid of any evidence of their existence."

"Hey," Sig called out. "Castle just texted me. He saw some other vans he didn't recognize. Didn't look like Shirley vans. They didn't come off the mountain, either, but were hoverin' nearby."

"More black vans?" Judge asked.

"He couldn't tell what color but they were dark and windowless."

Trip and Judge exchanged looks.

"Could be feds," Judge guessed, tugging at his beard with one hand while holding a sawed-off shotgun with the other.

"Who the fuck would call in the fuckin' feds?" Sig growled. He glanced around the half-circle. "None of us."

Oh shit.

Trip tugged his baseball cap lower. "They never cared about those uncle-daddy fuckers before, why would they care about them now?" He glanced at Judge. "Think someone tipped them off?"

The club enforcer shrugged.

What. The. Fuck.

Besides the Fury, who else knew what was going on up the mountain? According to Jet, Max Bryson had given his piglets the order to stay away from the Shirleys. They hadn't seen any state oinkers sniffing around, either.

"What reason would the feds come 'round unless they were given a heads up?" Sig asked, a sharp edge to his voice.

"I don't know," Trip answered, "but after tonight, after this is over, we need to dump these guns. We don't need a fuckin' raid."

Judge jerked his chin up at Deacon. "Did the women and kids get to Mansfield okay?"

"Yeah," Deacon answered his cousin. "Checked with Reese. They're all there and they're all good."

Trip raised his voice. "Like I said when we went over the plan the other night, we don't shoot first. Let's try to draw them into the field, if possible. If they take cover, this fight will last longer than necessary. Let's also try to take out as many as possible using stealth. You all should have your knives on you. Shade, do what you do best. The rest? If you can get close enough without dyin' or gettin' injured, take 'em out as quietly as you can. Once the gunfire starts, expect shit to hit the fan. Keep to cover. Stay low. Be careful of crossfire. You ain't gonna be able to live with yourself if you shoot one of our own."

"Think more of us need military backgrounds," Cage whispered to Rook.

"Yeah. Thank fuck for Trip," Rook answered under his breath, trying to picture Jet in a Marine uniform and being stationed in the middle east or somewhere in an active combat zone.

He wondered if she ever killed anyone. He'd have to ask her. But right now, he needed to concentrate on the shit going down in their own combat zone.

"Phones on silent," Judge ordered. "Communicate by text. If any of the prospects spot the vans or Shirleys on foot, they're to send out a group text with the number of bodies and the direction they're headed."

"Thinkin' they'll park off the farm somewhere and sneak in," Shade murmured.

Trip continued, "Right, which means they'll hit the farmhouse and bunkhouse first, assumin' we're sleepin'."

This type of situation was the exact reason windows weren't installed on the first level of The Barn or the bunkhouse. It had been a tip Trip had received from Zak, the president of the Dirty Angels, during one of their meets. That club had a lot of experience dealing with people who'd wanted to steal their women and kill their members. Even take over their territory.

"Shade, Ozzy and I will head back up there. Got my four-wheeler parked near The Barn. It's loud, so it'll catch their attention. Will head this direction and hope they give chase. Shade and Ozzy will take out as many as they can before they get to the field." Trip held up his hand and took a breath. "Look, this sounds more organized than what it'll be. Once they arrive, things will go sideways quickly. This ain't a military maneuver, but we fuckin' got this. Our brotherhood survived goin' into their territory twice to save our own, so I'm figurin' we got 'em by the balls by havin' them where they don't know the terrain as well. They'll be in our backyard now, not their own."

"Just do your best," Judge said.

"Do your best to keep breathin', too. Don't wanna lose even one of you motherfuckers," Trip said. "We worked too goddamn long and hard to get where we're at now. Can't let some fuckin' hillbilly clan fuck that up. But we also can't breathe easier 'til they're dealt with. So..." He clapped his gloved hands together once. "Let's fuckin' do this... For one! For all!"

"For our brothers we live and die!" The rest of them finished the Originals' motto. It wasn't a favorite with any of them but it was what they had. For now.

"Hell hath no fury like the Blood Fury!" Sig added on a yell. "Shirleys about to find out what the fuck that means."

Everyone grunted loudly and stomped their boots on the frozen ground, then went to the location they were previously assigned.

This was it. What they'd been waiting for.

The beginning of the end.

THEIR PHONES WERE BLOWING up with all the group texts. One text rolled in after another as Rook hunkered down behind a tree, hoping his balls wouldn't crack off, roll down his pant leg and out onto the ground like a frozen meatball.

They'd been waiting for over an hour outside in the dark and in the late February weather. He was no longer worried about dying by a Shirley, he was more worried about being found frozen stiff like a damn human Popsicle.

He tried to use thoughts of Jet to warm him up, but if she was the one who tipped off the feds, the heat he applied to her ass with his hand would be more than warm.

Getting fucked by the feds was not something on his damn wish list.

His phone lit up again in another flurry of texts.

Trip: *Every 1 stay steady. Sumthn definitely up.*

Judge: *Nobody move from ur spot.*

Shade: *2 clan vans cut off by 4 more unknown. All black.*

Bones: *Possibly feds.*

Bones: *Fuckn feds. ATF. FBI.*

Bones: *DEA 2.*

Sig: *THIS IS SOME GODDAMN BULLSHIT!*

There was a long pause. Rook hated not knowing what the hell was going down. Where their positions were, they couldn't hear anything except the winter wind in the leafless tree branches above them. And their nut sacs cracking like a frozen pond.

Trip's next text got his heart restarted and his blood flowing again. *Every 1 move now. Stay silent. No lights. Huntn shack. Unload all weapons. Both Shirleys & ur own. Want nothn on ur person. Not even a butter knife.*

The next one came from Judge. *Once u dump ur shit, get back to church if u can w/o being seen. Meet there.*

What the fuck is going on? was what he wanted to scream into the woods, but instead swallowed it back down.

From where he crouched, he could see his brother in the shadows about a dozen trees away, also shivering and freezing his nads off. Rook forced his numb feet to move in his direction.

"You get those?" Rook whispered when he got there.

"Yeah. Fuckin' feds. Those motherfuckers just fucked us up the ass without lube."

"Gotta dump these weapons and get our asses back. I can hardly bend my fuckin' fingers. Maybe it's better we didn't get into any kind of shootout. Might not have been able to pull the fuckin' trigger. Or aim without shakin'."

"Yeah, nighttime in February ain't the best time to try to be accurate with guns," his brother agreed with his teeth chattering.

"Let's go," Rook urged, whacking his younger brother on the shoulder.

"You see Dad?" Cage asked as they followed their own footsteps in the snow back to the hunting shack.

Rook shook his head. "Nope. You?"

"No. It's too fuckin' cold for an old man like him to be hangin' out in the woods."

Rook was surprised his brother was worried. "He's a tough old shit. He'll be fine."

"Yeah," Cage laughed. "He'll probably find some young, hot piece of ass to warm him up later."

Right. Their father had some magical talent with getting hot, young pussy to climb into his bed and onto him. *Hell*, half the time they didn't even make it to the old man's bed. Dutch had never been shy about who, what or where when it came to snatch. Unfortunately, that was how both Cage and Rook learned about the birds and the bees, by witnessing it firsthand. In stereo and 3D living color.

It surprised Rook that Dutch only ended up with two kids. Two planned kids, anyway. He wondered if there were any out there unplanned who Dutch didn't know about.

Or maybe some he did know.

Speaking of unplanned snot monkeys... "Least you know Dyna and Jem are safe."

"Yeah, for now. We don't know what the fuck's goin' on, though. Why the feds got involved and what that means to that damn clan. Maybe even to us."

"We'll figure it out," Rook reassured him.

"Worry every fuckin' day, brother. *Every* fuckin' day

since the day Dyna was found outside the garage as if she was a goddamn stray kitten."

"Or stray dog," Rook added, thinking of the little beast most likely warm and snoring in Jet's bed.

Where Rook should be right now, too.

"Bein' a fuckin' father is nerve-wrackin'," his younger brother admitted, scraping fingers through his disheveled hair.

"I know."

"No, you don't. You think you fuckin' know 'til you have one of your own. Then... You. Will. Know," Cage emphasized each word. "No wonder men go bald or gray early. The pressure of not fuckin' up is overwhelmin'. Definitely got more respect for Dutch bein' able to keep us breathin' and with all our limbs."

Rook could hear the stress and strain in Cage's voice. "Look. I worry about Dyna, too. Maybe not like you, but I still worry. We all do. This is why we needed to finish this shit with the Shirleys tonight. Now..." Rook growled in frustration. "Now we don't know what the fuck's goin' on."

"Think someone tipped off the feds?" Cage asked, sounding just as frustrated.

"Had to."

"One of us?"

"No fuckin' way." Rook shook his head as they reached the shack where a couple of the others were already unloading their guns and knives into the run-down building.

"Local pigs?"

Rook lifted a shoulder and dropped it. "Maybe."

"You'd think if the local five-o knew what the fuck was goin' on up there, they'd be crawlin' all over our asses, too."

"Yeah, don't make sense. Figurin' it wasn't any of them." He sure as fuck hoped not.

Within twenty minutes, they had made their way back to the rear of the bunkhouse without seeing any feds—or getting shot at—made their way inside and directly to The Barn where almost everyone else was already waiting near the fireplace, warming themselves up.

Rook was relieved to see the fire burning strong and headed in that direction himself. The cold had even penetrated to the very center of his bones. He needed several shots of whiskey to warm his insides while the fire warmed his outside.

He snagged a bottle of Jack from Whip's fingers and guzzled down enough to make a fire light in his gut. He shoved the whiskey bottle back at Whip and glanced around to see who was still missing.

Just two of the new prospects. Castle and Bones. All thirteen patched members, along with Scar, Tater and Possum, were now gathered in The Barn with ruddy cheeks, frozen crystals accumulated in their beards and their hands rubbing together to bring back some feeling. Some even were rocking from boot to boot to get their blood flowing.

With relief, he spotted Dutch doing the same on the other side of the hearth, a cigarette hanging precariously from his lips. "Boy," Rook's old man called out to Whip. "Bring that fuckin' whiskey over here. My old bones need that shit more than you."

Whip jerked his chin up and headed around the fireplace to his club brother and boss.

"So?" Sig started, clearly agitated. His fingers were twitching and every muscle in his body appeared locked solid. Clearly, not from the cold.

The VP's patience was slim on a good day. Right now, it was nonexistent. He looked about to beat someone to death before spitting on their body and pissing on it, too.

"Someone better start talkin' soon," Sig growled, now pacing stiffly. "Tonight was supposed to be the end of this bullshit. The end of them. Did those motherfuckin' feds fuck that up?"

"Seems so." Trip sighed as his eyes tracked his *about-to-blow* half-brother. "Here's the thing... We got no choice but let the Feds do some of our dirty work at this point. The only good thing is it'll keep our hands clean for now and whatever they don't clean up for us, we'll handle once they're through."

"Our hands are hardly clean, prez," Shade murmured nearby.

Trip's nostrils flared as he glanced at Shade. "Yeah, got that. But those rednecks ain't gonna share shit with a government the clan don't recognize as their own. Not even to cut a damn deal. They'd rather die first before givin' any badge-wearing pigs even the slightest help."

Judge grumbled, "Let's hope they stick like hot tar to their hatred of anyone with a shiny shield."

"Or to anyone who announces that they're from the federal government," Trip added. "Look, we can't do shit about it right now. Come light of day, and once the dust settles, we'll see what we can find out and regroup. Figure out who's still up the mountain, who ain't. Who's still a threat. It sucks, but it's all we can do for now. In the meantime, we continue to stay vigilant, keep close and keep communication open."

"Should I tell the women it's safe to come home?" Deacon asked.

Trip shook his head. "Not yet. The women need to stay with Reese 'til this all shakes out. 'Til we got better details and see who all the feds scooped up in their net. Still could be some stray dingleberries hangin' off the hillbilly goat's ass."

"Dingleberries I'll deal with," Sig growled.

"Ones we'll all handle when the time's right," Trip corrected Sig. "If they grabbed them down here, don't mean there ain't more feds up there. We don't have any clue who tipped them off or why. Or even what the feds were lookin' for."

"We don't know shit," Sig growled. "Least we had a finger on their fuckin' pulse before. Now we're clueless."

"Only for now," Trip reminded him.

The undercurrent in church became tense the instant the front door banged open and a cold blast rushed in.

You gotta be shittin' me.

It was goddamn déjà fucking vu.

Once again, it took everything in his damn power not to rush forward to the spot where Jet was being hauled into church by a prospect. Not by Scar this time, but by Castle. Not in uniform, but normal clothes and her black wool coat, winter hat and thick gloves.

Fuckin' fuck.

Her blue eyes met his briefly before sliding through The Barn and taking in all of the Fury members and assessing the situation she now found herself in. Again.

The woman must not have learned her damn lesson the first time.

With two large hands restraining Jet's arms behind her back, Castle announced, "Found this outside. Got no clue who she is or why she was out there. Don't think she's a fed. All the feds were wearin' jackets clearly claimin' who they were. They also cleared out."

Everyone in that room, except for the newest prospects, already knew who Jet Bryson was. What she was.

They also all knew she had no reason to be on the farm. Especially tonight.

Unless...

"What the fuck," Rook muttered under his breath.

Unless she had been involved with the tip off.

"She's a local pig," Scar called out. "Caught her here before."

"Before?" Trip asked, his eyes sliding from Scar to Jet, his forehead wrinkling under his baseball cap.

Oh, fuck.

"Yeah, late the other night. Rook said he'd handle it."

Motherfuckin' Scar.

That motherfucker was done. Totally fucking done.

And so was Rook if Scar didn't keep his fucking mouth shut.

Trip's dark gaze landed on him. "Handle what?"

"Did handlin' it include gettin' that mark on your fuckin' neck?" Scar asked with his eyes narrowed and focused on Jet's claim. His hand went halfway up to it automatically but he caught it and forced it back down. Now that he shucked his coat, it was visible. He'd forgotten about the damn bite with all the other shit going on.

"Cujo," he muttered lamely.

"Ain't no dog bite, that's a bitch's bite," Scar said, now sitting firmly at the top spot on Rook's shit list. "Bet if we force her mouth open, her teeth will match the mark on Rook's neck."

Rook locked gazes with Scar. He was done sponsoring any future prospects. Done.

"Fuck, son, you doin' her?" Rook heard behind him. He already knew from the tone of Dutch's voice, if he turned around, his father would be wearing a wide, impressed grin. Horny bastard.

Rook started when a hand came out of nowhere to touch his neck and stretch the skin around the bite. "Christ," Trip muttered, then turned toward Jet, tipping his head toward Rook. "That your mark?"

"No." The lie slipped from her without even the slightest hesitation.

Trip turned and locked gazes with Rook. "That her mark? You sleepin' with the enemy?" Trip leaned in closer and whispered, "You fuckin' lie to me, your colors will be stripped and it'll be done in a way you'll wish you never fuckin' lied."

Rook opened his mouth and nothing but air hissed out.

Trip stepped back, closed his eyes, took a deep inhale through flared nostrils and opened his brown eyes again. "Upstairs," he growled, then shouted, "Up-fuckin-stairs!" He glared at Rook. "You." He pointed at Judge. "You." He turned and pointed at Jet. "And you. Upstairs now."

Jet's mouth opened to argue but Rook shot her a look. Her mouth snapped shut and she yanked herself free from Castle's grip. When she approached Trip, she said in a low, steely voice, "I don't answer to you."

"I know who the fuck you answer to, Jet. And I can tell you he's gonna be more pissed than me."

"You don't know that."

Trip got into her face and growled, "The fuck I don't." He turned on his boot, then paused, and his jaw shifted sharply. "That's it for tonight. Go hit your racks, warm pussy or a bottle. I don't give a fuck. Just go do it elsewhere."

Rook heard a murmur from his brothers as he followed his prez and sergeant at arms across the floor. After latching a hand around Jet's forearm, he dragged her along with him.

"I don't answer to him or any of you," Jet grumbled only loud enough for Rook to hear.

He jerked on her arm in warning, but said nothing

because he was ready to lose his shit on her for showing back up on the farm once again, stupidly putting them both at risk.

Once they were upstairs, both Judge and Trip took their normal spots at the table with Trip at the end and Judge to his left.

"Somebody better do some fuckin' explainin' and better do it right fuckin' now." Trip's voice held a razor edge sharp enough he could use his words to slice Rook's throat.

At that very minute, Rook would welcome that.

Judge leaned back in his chair, crossed his big arms over his even bigger chest and stared at them, not saying a word. With his expression, he didn't need to.

Trip slammed his hand on the table. "Someone fuckin' talk!"

"I..." Jet started, then petered out.

At least she tried, Rook couldn't even get one word past his tight throat and clenched teeth.

"You two fuckin'?" Judge asked bluntly in his deep grumbly voice.

"Remember what I told you downstairs about lyin'," Trip warned.

Rook guessed answering Judge's question would be as good a place as any to start. He ignored Jet's eyes burning a hole into the side of his head and cleared his throat to loosen it. "Yeah."

"How long?" his prez asked.

Rook grimaced.

Trip leaned forward and shouted, "How fuckin' long?"

"Uh... since... a while."

"How long is a while?" Judge asked calmly. Though, Rook figured the enforcer wasn't so calm on the inside. Judge was much better at hiding his anger than Trip. But he could also be a lot more fucking scarier when that switch finally flipped.

"It started as a hate fuck," Rook admitted reluctantly, wishing the floor would just open and drop him all the way to the Earth's molten core.

Jet made a little noise next to him.

"And now?" Trip asked, sitting back and tilting his head, his eyes now focused on Jet. Almost as if he was seeing her in a new light.

Rook snuck a glance at her. She was staring at him, also waiting for his answer. He was surprised she wasn't tapping her foot impatiently.

Fuck...

"And now?" she echoed Trip.

Judge barked out a short laugh. "Oh fuck. This is goddamn priceless."

"This ain't funny," Trip grumbled but half-smirked anyway.

Rook agreed. None of this was funny, it was painful.

"Yeah, it is," Judge said. "'Cause dependin' on how he answers, his ass is gonna get kicked either comin' or goin'. Maybe even both."

His balls were already going into hiding and he no longer had the winter temps as an excuse. He blew out a breath. "Ain't a hate fuck anymore."

Judge cocked an eyebrow. "So, she's just a fuck now?"

Rook snuck another glance at Jet, who now had her arms crossed over her chest and an eyebrow cocked just like Judge.

His Adam's apple was now lodged at the top of his throat. "No."

Judge put a finger behind his ear and bent it forward. "Sorry. What?"

"No, she ain't just a fuck."

"Jesus Christ, we already dealt with enough shit tonight, now this," Trip muttered and shook his head. "Why you here, Jet? Did you tip off the feds?"

"No. It wasn't me. After he left..."

Rook's head snapped in her direction and he saw her grimace at her slip-up. He grimaced, too.

"That's where you were when we couldn't find you," Trip concluded.

Shit. Rook breathed out a, "Yeah."

"She know what's goin' on?" Judge asked, his expression now serious.

"No," Jet lied. "He doesn't talk about club business. But he got a call and rushed out, leaving Cujo behind and I got worried. So, I got dressed and followed. I saw the task force out on the road blocking in the two Shirley vans and taking them into custody."

"And then decided to stop on in for a fuckin' shot of whiskey and to shoot the shit a little bit?" Trip's question was dripping with sarcasm.

Jet snapped her head up and gave Trip a solid stare. "I badged one of the agents and got some info. I wanted to make Rook... all of you aware of what was going on."

Judge's eyes narrowed on her. "Why? Why the fuck would you wanna make us aware of what the feds were doin'?"

"As a thank you for Levi."

Once again, Rook's head spun toward Jet. She was making up shit now. To cover her ass and his.

"We owe your club big time for allowing my cousin to adopt their son. You made their family—our family—complete."

She was spinning some bullshit like a damn pro. Rook was impressed.

Both the prez and the enforcer stared quietly at Jet. Finally, Trip asked, "What else they tell you?"

Rook hoped Trip's boiling anger being reduced to a bubbling simmer was a good sign.

"While they were picking up the men down here, they had a team up on the mountain doing a raid. They're pulling the women and children clear of the compound until they can figure out who to charge and who to let go. Apparently, they have a stash of explosives up there along with everything else. They're planning on having a meeting with Max in the morning to catch him up to speed, but the agent I spoke with didn't say how they knew what was going down tonight, or even if they did know. It could've been coincidence."

"How much info can you get from your cousin?" Trip asked.

She frowned. "You want me to get info from my chief and report it back to you?"

"How much do you value his dick?" Trip asked, jerking his chin toward Rook.

Jet blinked. So did Rook, wondering where Trip was going with this.

"Figure you like his dick, what about the rest of him?"

"He's okay," Jet answered Trip slowly.

Judge barked out another laugh and slammed the table with his big paw.

Trip kept a straight face. "Just okay?"

She shrugged. "Yes. That's about right."

Rook shot her a frown, but she kept her eyes pinned on Trip, who asked, "So, you don't care whether he lives or dies, then?"

She waited a shitload too long before she admitted, "I'd kind of care. He's kind of good in bed."

Damn.

"Just kinda?" Trip asked, tipping his head back and looking down his nose at her.

"Yes. I mean, I do have some really good vibrators..."

Trip snorted. Judge dropped his head, and his big body shook.

The Fury president sobered quickly. "Thinkin' you'd care a whole fuck of a lot. So, if you wanna help Rook, you'll get whatever info you can and report back."

"To you?" she asked, not hiding her surprise.

"You can tell stud muffin there. He'll pass along any info."

"You're not mad?" Jet asked.

"Fuckin' furious," Trip answered.

"We tried to hate each other," Jet admitted casually with a shrug.

"How'd that fuckin' work out?"

"Not well," she answered Trip honestly.

"Yeah, love's like that. It gets you when you least expect it. It also makes you fuckin' stupid."

Chapter Twenty-Two

Rook opened his mouth to deny that they loved each other but Trip shot him a look daring him to deny it.

He snapped his mouth shut instead and pressed his lips into a thin line. He'd fix that misconception when his ass wasn't sitting in the hot seat.

Now was not a time to defy his president. Now was the time to smooth things over so he didn't get his colors stripped. And if he got to keep them, so a blanket party wasn't thrown specially in his honor instead.

His little brother getting one was difficult to watch. Being on the receiving end would suck even more.

"Now," Trip began, "need to have a little convo with lover boy here. So, Jet, you're gonna have to excuse us while we conduct club business. I look forward to hearin' whatever you find out from your chief."

"Rook," Jet whispered, drawing his attention from the two men sitting at the table. She didn't mask the worry in her eyes.

"Go," Rook assured her. "Will pick up Cujo when I'm done here."

"I don't want to—"

"Go. It'll be all right." He didn't want to do this with her in front of Trip and Judge.

"But—"

"Jet," he said a little too sharply. He gave her a look that said, "Not now."

After a slight hesitation, she gave him a small nod and without another look at him or the men at the table, she turned and left the second-floor meeting room.

Once her footsteps became faint, he turned back to the table and waited.

And waited.

He wasn't liking the silence.

Trip finally dragged his hands down his face, groaned and shook his head. "Can't believe this shit. You of all fuckin' people."

"You and me both, brother. Fought it. Hard as I could." And that was damn true.

"Not hard enough, apparently. How the fuck did this even start? From you dealin' with her at the garage?"

He could lie but the truth might prove to them how Jet wasn't like the rest of the PD. At least, in his eyes, she wasn't. Whether Trip and Judge would see her that way, he wasn't sure. "She caught me and Easy on the mountain one night."

"So, you fucked her to keep her quiet?" Judge asked, his eyebrows pinned to the bottom of the black knit cap covering his hair.

Rook shook his head. "Fucked her to get her outta my system."

Trip snorted. "Yeah, could've asked any of us, that don't usually work."

He grimaced and reluctantly admitted, "She also saved my ass."

Both men sat up straighter and their eyes became more intense.

"Wanna explain that?" Judge asked.

"Not really," he answered truthfully. "Not somethin' I really wanna relive."

"Thinkin' we now need to hear it," Trip insisted.

"Fuck," Rook whispered, then lifted his head high and met their gazes head on. "Got caught up there by some of the Shirley women. Stepped into a trap they'd set up on our trail. Didn't see it 'til it was too late." He went on to explain the rest of what happened that night, telling them most of it but not all. "Truthfully, her bein' nosy about the clan and our involvement with them saved my ass. She got me free. By her-fuckin-self, too. Otherwise, I wouldn't be breathin' right now. Worse, some Shirley babies might've ended up lookin' like me."

"Poor fuckin' kids," was the only thing Judge said, which surprised Rook. He expected one or both of them to ream him out for not telling them about that close call sooner.

"Christ," Trip whispered, sitting back and scraping a hand along his bearded chin. He shot a quick glance at Judge whose face was back to being unreadable.

Once again neither of them said anything for what seemed like forever, though it might have been only a few short moments.

"This is gonna have to go to the table," Trip finally said. "Need to figure out where we go from here. Where you go from here, if you ain't willin' to let her go. Assumin' you're not, right?"

"If I could, I would," was the best answer he could give. "This whole thing between us was a goddamn surprise for me, also, prez. I could lie and say I'll untangle myself from her, but that's what it would be. A damn lie."

"We already went over what'll happen if you lie when it comes to any of this." Trip paused and frowned. "Guessin' you wanna keep your colors?"

"Fuck yeah," Rook breathed. "But get it if I can't. Don't wanna do shit to fuck up this club, this brotherhood. Earlier you talked about how long and hard we've worked to get this far, to build somethin' solid. If keepin' her means I gotta step out, I gotta step out."

But, *fuck*, he didn't want to do that. Just the thought of that made his chest tight. He was an important part of this club and the club was now an important piece of him. It also gave him a reason to keep himself out of jail and roll his ass out of bed every morning.

He also wanted to stand strong next to his baby brother and Dutch.

For once in his life, he wanted to do his old man proud. Sticking to something for more than a few months, like the club and his job at the shop, might do that.

"But you wanna keep her 'cause you love her, right?" Judge asked quietly. "Not just 'cause she's a good lay. Wanna make her your ol' lady."

Jesus fuck. Judge's words hit him like a solid kick to the gut.

He *did* love her.

Of course he hadn't told her, because he hadn't even realized it himself until it had been mentioned in this very room. But if he thought about it—*really* thought about it—it had to be what he was feeling, even as foreign as it was to him. "Truth? Don't think I can live without her. Like I said, I'd be lyin' if I said I could quit her. Hate that I can't, but I can't."

Trip rolled his lips inward for a second. "Yeah, you got it

bad. I fuckin' have no clue how we're gonna handle this or if this thing between you two is even gonna fly. If the exec committee votes for acceptin' her, then we're gonna have to take it to a church meetin' for a vote. Needs to be unanimous from every fuckin' patched member, Rook, every goddamn one. And you know why. This brotherhood's our fuckin' life. She gets a guilty conscience, regrets her actions, or you piss her off, that life could be flipped upside down lickety-fuckin-split. None of us wants to catch another bid. Not one of us wants to spend another fuckin' second behind bars. She could be a real fuckin' threat to that."

"For me, too."

"Yeah, all that shit that's happened up on that mountain…" The Fury president sighed. "You ain't the only one who could do a life-long bid if any of that surfaces. She worth that risk?"

He wanted to say yes, but he knew the risk involved more than him. It involved every Fury member.

"She's a Bryson by blood, Rook," Judge reminded him. "That blood's thicker than anythin' you could ever fuckin' give her. If she puts her family first, you're fucked. We all could be fucked."

"Christ," Trip said on a sigh. He stared at the club's insignia carved into the center of the table. "If we allow this, we'd need to make rules. For her, for you. Rules that can't be fuckin' broken. My job as prez, Sig's as VP, Judge's as sergeant at arms… the first priority for us is to protect what we've been workin' so hard to build. Hell, to rebuild." Trip sighed again, ripped his baseball cap off his head and tossed it onto the center of the table. "I had a goddamn dream, Rook."

Rook released a slow breath. "Hear ya."

"That fuckin' dream came to life. I was buildin' a life I could be proud of. Stel and I got plans. A weddin', kids…

Makin' Jet your woman might even put my future kids at risk. You think of that?"

Rook got what they were getting at. He did. "Yeah. Like I said, I fought it, but she got under my skin. If it comes down to it and I got no choice but to flay off that skin, I will. But, truth? I really don't wanna."

"Yeah, you want it all," Judge said, "but at whose expense? Who's gonna pay in the end havin' five-o among us? It's just fuckin' crazy and dangerous as all fuck. Not anythin' the Originals would've allowed."

Trip agreed. "Yeah, she would've been dead and buried before even makin' it inside their church. Your pop wasn't playin' and neither was mine. Their hatred of the local pigs ran deep."

"Yeah, it did." Judge blew out a breath. "Trip wants to protect his future family, but I got one now. Got two kids who need me. Wanna have another..."

"I get it," Rook answered.

"You sure?" Trip asked. "You know this could cause shit between us and the chief, right? Between us and all those Brysons. Don't matter that Levi's now a Bryson. You're fuckin' Adam's damn sister. Not sure he's gonna take that well. Neither will her cousins. Wanted to keep a good relationship with the PD so they don't fuck with us. But, hell, this could fuck that up. Don't need all those fuckers breathin' down our necks.

"Can tell you this, though, if everybody—and I mean everybody—votes okay with you claimin' her at the table, then she can't be wearin' any of that shit here. She's gotta leave her job behind before she steps even a toe on this property. Every fuckin' time. 'Cause the minute she's in pig mode and sees somethin' she feels the need to report? It's over for her. It's over for you. Gonna need to keep her on a very short fuckin' leash."

Christ. Claiming her at the table? Keeping her on a short leash? Did they have any idea who they were talking about?

"First of all, ain't sure she's willin' to be claimed. She ain't that type of woman. Second, don't think she'll let me snap on any kind of leash. Without me goin' into detail... She don't mind me bein' bossy in the bedroom, but the second we're out of it?" Rook finished with a shake of his head.

Trip's lips thinned out. "Yeah, don't need details on that shit, but if she ain't gonna let you keep a short leash on her, that could be a problem."

"Would Stella?" Rook asked Trip. His gaze slid to Judge. "How 'bout Cassie?"

"Here's the problem, brother," Judge began. "A pig without its skin is still a pig. That stink starts at their very fuckin' center. Our women don't have that stink clingin' to them. That's the difference 'tween our women and yours."

Trip grabbed his ball cap from the center of the table and slapped it back on his head, tucking his longer hair under it like he normally did. "Fuck. So done talkin' about this shit right now. Let's see what she brings back to us from the pig pen. Let her prove herself and prove how loyal she's gonna be to you. That right there may determine the direction we need to take with her." Trip tipped his head. "And with you." He shoved the president's chair back from the end of the table and stood. "Well, this whole fuckin' night turned into a damn shit show."

"Yeah," Judge agreed. "Woulda rather have had those fuckers die than be snared by the feds. Every breath they still take freely means they remain a threat."

Rook, relieved they were done talking about his damn sex life and how it might fuck up his non-sex life, asked, "What's stoppin' them from comin' back if they make bail, or the charges are dropped or reduced?"

"Nothing," Judge answered.

Trip tapped his index finger on the table. "Unless the feds seize their property."

"Expectin' they will. Don't mean they won't try to reclaim it. They don't give a fuck about what the government says. They only recognize their own sovereign nation. You know they're gonna blame us for siccin' the feds on them. Still gonna wanna make us pay," Judge warned.

"Then we got no choice how to handle them. We'll just finish out our plan," Trip said.

"Guess who ain't bailin' their asses out?" Judge grumbled as he got to his feet. "Gonna put the word out to all the local bondsman, too. Those inbred hillbillies are gonna have a tough time buyin' their freedom."

Trip came around the table and stopped in front of Rook. "Report back as soon as she's got somethin' to report. If she don't, then we're gonna assume she's hidin' shit from us. And, I'm tellin' you now, that ain't gonna work. For me," he pointed at Judge, "for him. Or for you. Now, get the fuck outta here. Had enough of this never-endin' fuckin' night."

"I COULD LOSE my job because of this, Rook." Jet was sitting on the edge of her bed with Cujo in her lap, gnawing on her bottom lip.

Normally that would make his dick pay attention. Tonight it didn't. He was fucking exhausted and drained. He wanted to climb into bed—whether here or back at the bunkhouse—and forget tonight ever happened.

He understood her concern over the possibility of losing

her job, but he could lose his fucking brotherhood. The colors on his back could end up being meaningless and a waste of ink.

"Ain't gonna lose your job. Your fuckin' cousin's the damn chief. And your brother and cousins are also on the force. They might as well rename the damn department Bryson PD," Rook told her, pulling Cujo out of her lap and putting him on the floor. The Chihuahua sat at his feet and stared up at him with his big brown eyes like he was an innocent motherfucker.

Yeah, he was just as innocent as Rook.

"I swore an oath and I'm breaking it by not only being with you, but by me looking the other way. Or, worse, gleaning intel from my chief to hand over to you and your club."

"What do you wanna do, Jet? What? Just fuckin' tell me. You hid a key for me. You didn't stop me from comin' here. You coulda locked me out, installed an alarm, turned over and went back to fuckin' sleep. You didn't. You wanted this as much as me. We knew it was risky. We knew we might get caught. We did. So, now what? What the fuck do you wanna do? Got no fuckin' clue. So tell me, you wanna end this right here and now? Want me to take my dog, get the fuck out of your place and just walk away? I could do that. My life would be a lot easier without you in it. So would yours. It's the simple fuckin' solution."

She blinked and her face paled even more than it already was. "You could just walk away?"

Standing in the middle of her bedroom with his hands on his hips, he closed his eyes and just breathed for a moment. When he finally opened them, he asked, "Can you?"

Her expression became hard. "Do you think I would've put up with any of that bullshit with Trip and Judge if I could? Don't you think I wanted to tell them where to fucking go? I didn't. You know why? Because of you."

"So, now what?" Rook asked. He was so fucking tired. Between the adrenaline rush waiting for the Shirleys to attack, from waiting out in the freezing cold weather, to the shit with Trip and Judge... And now this.

Honestly, going back to prison would be less complicated. Less stressful.

He knew what to expect inside. He knew what was expected of him.

Real fucking life was much harder.

He ground the heels of his palms into his eyes and groaned. When he was done, he asked softly, "What do you wanna do, Jet? If you ain't gonna be good about keepin' your mouth shut about the club or willin' to gather info from your cousin on the Shirleys, then say it right fuckin' now. I gotta know where we stand."

"If I'm not?"

"Then I know where we stand." His chest was cracking wide open and he rubbed at the pain radiating through it. He reached down and scooped up Cujo.

When he turned for the bedroom door, she called out, "Wait."

He glanced over his shoulder and saw her on her feet and on the move. He put Cujo back on the floor and turned.

"I don't want you to go," she said when she was toe to toe with him.

Her light blue eyes were troubled and he could see the conflict on her face. He was pretty fucking sure his held the same.

"Don't wanna go, darlin'," he whispered. "Why don't you talk to Max in the mornin' and see what you can find out.

Let's get past that hurdle first. Give Trip and Judge some info that will appease them."

"You don't want to give up your club." It wasn't a question because she already knew the answer.

"Just like you don't wanna give up your badge."

"Of course I don't. But, Rook, I don't want to give you up, either."

"Why? Why, darlin'? Why the fuck do you want me? This would be so much fuckin' easier if you didn't."

"Because I love you." She lifted her palm to stop him from speaking. "I love you but I hate who you are. I straddle that thin line between those two emotions, just like you do. I hate that things between us can't be easy, just like you do. I hate that you can't walk away from your brothers, but I also respect that. I hate your past, but I recognize that it *is* your past. I worry about your future. I worry about *our* future. This will never be easy. Never. Maybe it'll get to the point where it becomes so hard, so impossible, that we hate each other again."

"You never hated me, darlin'." No, he never saw hate in her eyes once. Not all the times he caught her staring at him at the garage. It wasn't hate but regret that she was interested in him but knew she couldn't have him.

"Okay, fine, but you hated me," she said.

"Hated who you were."

"Not *were*. Am. Being a cop is a big part of who I am. So, you hating that piece of me means you also hate me."

"Don't hate you."

"But do you love me?"

He forced himself to swallow the lump in his throat, unsure if those words could even pass his lips.

"And if so, is our love even strong enough to make it worth all this trouble?"

"Don't know, darlin'."

"Do you want to find out?"

Did he?

Yeah, he fucking did.

"Tell me you love me and that you're willing to do your damnedest to make this work. I need to hear that, Rook."

No one ever told him they loved him. Not once.

Not his mother, not his father, not even his brother.

Did his father and brother love him? Probably, but they'd never say it to each other.

Jet was the first person to actually say it in all of his thirty-four years.

Of course, the first time he heard it, it had to come from a damn cop. How fucked was that?

But Jet was more than her job. A whole hell of a lot more.

He was now pretty fucking sure what he felt for her was love. It had to be because if he walked away from her, or she kicked his ass to the curb, he was afraid it would tear him open, rip out his heart and crush it.

No, he was wrong. He wasn't *pretty* fucking sure, he was *damn* sure.

Now, he just needed to tell her.

To give back what she just gave him.

To reassure her.

Judge had once said that dogs were a good judge of character. And if Jury didn't like someone, there was a good reason.

He glanced down at Cujo and then back up at Jet, the only other person his little asshole dog would let handle him.

He grabbed her around the back of the neck and yanked her toward him, slamming her chest into his. He dropped his head and saw her mouth pull into a knowing smile as she stared back up at him.

"I'm still going to make you say it," she warned.

"The bite on my neck ain't enough proof?"

"Nope."

"How about me eatin' you out 'til you scream?"

"No."

"How about me fuckin' you 'til you soak the bed?"

"Nice try."

"You don't want any of that?"

"Oh, I'm going to get all that. But not yet."

His lips hovered over hers. "Love you, darlin'. Hate your uniform but love you."

She rolled her eyes but her smile widened. "And?"

"And we're gonna do whatever we need to do to make this work."

"It won't be easy," she warned.

No, it wouldn't be easy. But they'd make sure it was worth it.

Chapter Twenty-Three

Using one knuckle, Jet rapped on the door frame to her cousin and chief's office since the door was wide open. Max had an open-door policy unless he was having a "discussion" with one of his officers or was on a phone call he needed to keep private.

He was a great chief and leader. Jet had been relieved when he extended an invitation to her to come work for Manning Grove PD. She had been miserable at her former PD, a smaller force with the officers also being very close-minded.

She had been the only female officer and, while they didn't insult her to her face, they did it a lot behind her back, thinking she didn't know. She did.

Max had been her savior and for that, she'd be forever grateful.

That made this upcoming conversation even more difficult.

Her stomach churned as the dark-haired man, with the

same-colored eyes that mirrored hers, glanced up and waved her in.

He didn't smile. He didn't joke.

He seemed way too serious.

Most likely it had to do with his meeting with the head of the federal task force not even an hour earlier.

When she spotted a plain, dark gray sedan in the PD's lot, she knew exactly who it belonged to. So, she made herself scarce until the meeting was over. Instead of returning to her apartment, she had taken a drive through town, stopped at Coffee and Cream for a caffeine fix and then took a little detour out to Copperhead Road, checking for any visible activity up on the mountain.

The lane to the clan's compound was blocked off with another plain, dark gray sedan and an agent, keeping out anyone who didn't belong.

Like Jet.

On her way back to station, she buzzed past Dutch's Garage but didn't stop in. Things were too raw from last night and she didn't want to push herself on the club right now. Things needed to settle a little bit first, then she'd see how everything eventually shook out.

She figured it would be bumpy for a while.

However, she would share whatever info she could that might ease Trip and Judge's mind about the safety of their brotherhood and family. That meant they wouldn't get any confidential info and definitely nothing that would risk her PD or the task force.

"Hey," she greeted Max, trying not to chew nervously on her bottom lip. After closing his office door, she took the seat that he indicated with a tilt of his head in front of his over-flowing, but organized, desk.

He narrowed his blue eyes on her. "What's up? Not sure why you're here on your day off."

"I heard about the raid last night."

One dark eyebrow lifted, and he sat back in his seat. "How about that. I heard something interesting, too. It went something like this... One of my off-duty officers badged one of the agents so she could ask questions. I only have two 'shes' on my force and I know Leah wasn't on County Line Road in the middle of the night. Not when she has her hands full with two boys, a baby girl and a man-baby. That rules her out from being the one running around sticking her nose in the feds' business."

Normally, they would get a good laugh at Max poking fun at his brother, Marc. Today, neither laughed.

"I'm actually surprised to see you this morning, but also glad you're here so I didn't have to call your ass in to explain yourself." He leaned forward slightly. "Why were you there and how did you know what the hell was happening?"

Jet grimaced and her ass cheeks clenched slightly. "Hear me out before you flip out, okay, Chief?"

"Glad you remember who the hell I am, *Officer*."

"First, I just want to say that I respect—"

"Don't lube me up first, just give it to me quick and dry. How did you know what was going down?"

"I didn't." Truth.

"Then why were you on County Line Road in the middle of the night, especially on your night off?"

"I..."

Max lifted an eyebrow again. "You...?"

She blew out a breath. She wasn't sure if she should reveal what was going on between her and Rook. But she *was* sure they wouldn't be able to keep it a secret for long since the club now knew.

Or all of the members of the club *would* know soon if they didn't already. News traveled fast in a town like Manning Grove. She was sure it traveled even faster in a close-knit brotherhood.

"A while back I caught some of the Fury members going up the mountain." More truth. So far, so good.

He pressed his palms to his desk blotter and spread his fingers, staring at them for a second. "After I told you to stay away from there?"

"I was doing my normal patrol." That truth had a bit of a bend in it.

Max lifted his head and gave her a dubious look. "On Copperhead Road."

"Yes. I occasionally drive past there to keep an eye on things but stay off the mountain like you said."

"I have a feeling I'm not going to like this story."

Jet couldn't argue that. "One night I stopped two Fury members coming down the mountain and tried to get some info from them. If they were going up there..."

"Why were they going up there?"

"The why they wouldn't share, but I at least hoped they'd share what they saw."

"Who asked you to do that?" The question was asked way too calmly and made her more anxious than if he had yelled it.

"No one. I decided to take the initiative on my own."

"I told you to stay away from that clan and you didn't."

"I did."

"Semantics. You tried to back door your way up there by using the MC."

"I figured it was another way to find out what was going on up there."

He laughed but it didn't sound humorous. Not even

close. "You expected bikers to share with you, a law enforcement officer, details of any illegal activity."

Put that way... Yes, it had been a lame attempt, but at least it had been an attempt.

"Who?" Max asked.

"Who?" she echoed, delaying the inevitable.

"Who were you planning on partnering with in this little endeavor of yours?"

She frowned. "Does it matter?"

Max's angular jaw shifted hard. "Most of those guys are ex-convicts, Jet. Not the best people to partner with."

"I'm aware of that."

"Tell me, how much intel did you get from these Fury members?"

"I didn't."

"Of course you didn't. And do you know why? It wasn't your place to know. It was mine. You think the feds don't keep their finger on the pulse of these sovereign nations? They're threats to our national security. When van loads of them start shifting around and crossing state lines, the feds sit up and take notice. They're going to sniff out what these crazies are up to and that's what they did."

"So, no one tipped them off?" The club would be relieved to hear that.

"Nobody had to. The local clan was small compared to some of the other factions in other states. The FBI was watching the larger groups and, of course, the main players. Clans that could do a lot more damage than the Shirleys. Well, until now. The Shirleys landed heavily on their radar once they brought in those vans of men from the other factions the feds were watching.

"That's another reason I didn't want you up that mountain. Not only for your safety, but I didn't want you interfering with any possible federal investigations. The FBI had been in contact with me in the past, but only gave me minimal details. Info they could share, but info I had to keep close to my vest. Certainly not info I could share with my most junior officer. Who, if you've forgotten, is you."

"Chief—"

Max cut her off. "They told me to keep my people clear, Jet. That's why I told you to keep your ass off that mountain. Though, I shouldn't have had to tell you why. You should've obeyed my order without question. They have a Joint Task Force up on the mountain right now comprised of ATF, FBI, DEA agents and others. Once they gather evidence, they plan to destroy the stills, confiscate the guns and ammo, dismantle the meth labs and remove any children they find. So, there you go. Now you know what you could've screwed up. All without discussing it with me first. If you thought taking the 'initiative' would get you ahead, you were wrong." Max planted his knuckles onto his blotter, rose from his seat, leaned over his desk and barked, "You disobeyed a direct order from your chief."

The blood drained from Jet's face.

"What else are you keeping from me, Jet?"

She needed to tell him. He'd only be more pissed if he found out about her and Rook from someone other than her. He'd be furious if he stumbled upon her connection with a member of the Fury.

"Um..."

Max plunked back down in his seat. "I'm assuming I need to be sitting down for what you're about to tell me next. Especially with the way you look right now."

"How do I look?"

"Sick and a bit worried. If you're hiding something else from me, something that might affect this PD or your position on my force, and you don't spill it right now, I will fire you the second I find out. You might not be on probation any longer, but that doesn't mean I can't can your ass. I *will not* have you undermining me or risking the safety of my officers."

"It's not like that."

"No? Then how is it?"

"I've been," she squeezed her eyes shut for a pounding heartbeat and swallowed, "seeing someone."

His brow scrunched low. "Why do I feel this doesn't warrant a congratulations?"

"You might not feel that it does."

Max drew a hand down his mouth and chin. But he said nothing, only waited, which made it worse for Jet.

"I've... um... been seeing Rook Dietrich."

"Rook Dietrich," Max echoed flatly.

Jet didn't know if he forgot who Rook was or was just in shock. "You know... Rook. Dutch's son. Cage's older brother."

Max sat back in his chair, a dumbfounded look on his face. "Didn't he just get out of prison not long ago?"

"Yes, he—"

"Wasn't his last charge and some of his prior charges of aggravated assault on law enforcement officers?" His questions were getting louder.

"Yes, he—"

Max growled, "Isn't he still on parole?"

"Yes, he—"

"Are you out of your fucking mind?" Max roared.

She opened her mouth, but the only thing that escaped was, "Didn't you tell me on Thanksgiving something along the lines of how I should learn to separate work and my personal life?"

Lame!

"He's a fucking felon, Jet!" Max slapped a hand on his

forehead. "Holy shit. Do I need to schedule you for a psychological evaluation?"

"No, I—"

"In what reality are you living in?"

She couldn't answer that, so she didn't. She figured she'd let her cousin get out whatever he needed to get out of his system, then once he did, she'd try to explain.

Hopefully by then she could actually think up a good explanation because sitting in this office in front of her chief, she realized how reckless being in a relationship with Rook was.

She could easily ignore reality when her and Rook were in their bubble. But last night that bubble had popped and there was no patching it up. The contents were revealed when it burst open. Their relationship had been exposed. They couldn't go back, they couldn't fix it, they couldn't erase it.

They had to deal with it like two adults, especially if they wanted their oddball relationship to work.

Rook wanted that. She wanted that, too.

Everyone else in their lives might not want that.

Especially the man sitting on the other side of the desk.

"Did you ever consider what would happen the minute you had to arrest one of his club brothers? Or even him? He's no angel, Jet. It hasn't been long since his last stint in County. I'm assuming you ran him and saw everything on his sheet."

"Yes."

"Then, I just can't wrap my head around this."

"The heart wants what the heart wants." She grimaced at the lame cliché. This was not the explanation she had wanted to come up with. Even though it was true.

"The heart," he repeated incredulously. "Are you sure it's your heart and not something else?"

"Max..."

Max eyes went wide when he realized she assumed he meant sex. "I wasn't talking about... I meant..." He winced and shook his dark head. "Jet, for your whole life you've done exactly what *you thought* was expected of you. The Marines, the police academy, even coming here to work with the rest of the family. You've been on the straight and narrow your whole damn life. We all have. We've all done what we as Brysons thought we needed to do. We followed in our fathers' footsteps, our fathers had followed in theirs. Did you ever think that maybe you'd want something different? Maybe you'd need to step off that straight and narrow path? That the path the rest of us took wasn't for you and you just assumed it was one you needed to take? Maybe you'll find you'll never be happy or content following it and will need to create your own way. Or... could it be you just want a taste of a bad boy? Maybe what's between you two will get old quickly and you'll move on. But," he lifted his finger into the air, "do you want to throw away your career just for that taste?"

"I never expected this to happen." Again, more painful truth.

"Of course not. Relationships sometimes form when you least expect it. Sometimes with the person you least expect. And you know I'm speaking from experience. Even so, I don't know what the hell you were thinking to get involved with an ex-con biker. I really don't. And that doesn't come from your chief, that comes from a family member who loves you, Jet."

She remained quiet when he dropped his head and stared at his desk blotter for a few heartbeats.

When he lifted it, his voice was calm but commanding. He was back into chief-mode. "This isn't good for the town, the department and certainly not good for me, the chief, to allow this to continue, Jet. You need to decide whose side you're on. Ours or theirs. I know they're trying to keep their noses clean, which I appreciate, but I also know," he leaned forward and locked his gaze with hers, "that it's not sparkling clean. Their shit's a bit murky. I've been tolerant up to now. But whatever the reason was that you caught them up that mountain should be suspect. They had no reason to get involved with the Shirleys. None. And if it has something to do with Levi, then I need to know what."

Oh no. She wasn't getting into Levi's background with him. It wasn't her place to reveal Levi's bloodline or how he came to be. If Matt hadn't told his own brother, then Jet wouldn't be the one to do it, either.

When she didn't answer, he continued, "I can't and won't give the members of the Fury special treatment because you have a... a... *connection* with them." He sighed and raked fingers through his short, dark hair. "Unfortunately, you're binding my hands, Jet. While I want it to be your decision on where your career goes from here, *your* choice with who you're involved with does not give *me* any choice but to give you an ultimatum." He paused and took an audible breath. "You break it off, or you turn in your badge."

The little blood she had left in her face drained away and her mouth gaped. Her heart began to thump even harder in her chest. She wouldn't be surprised if Max could actually see it beating through her sweatshirt.

Was she going to let falling in love with Rook destroy her career? Had it really come down to this? Him or her badge? Could she even choose? Was there one she wanted more than the other?

She couldn't answer those questions because her head was spinning, and her thoughts were colliding into each other.

It should be an easy answer. She was a Bryson, she should choose her badge over a man any day.

Any damn day.

"Don't look so shocked. You really didn't think you'd be able to walk in here, tell me you're hooking up with a Fury member—one who has a long record that includes being violent with cops, I'll remind you again in case you've forgotten—and expect me to wish you two the best and then invite him to dinner with our family? A family of cops who he hates because of the uniform we wear and the job we do?" Max shook his head. "I'm waiting for your answer. The answer shouldn't be difficult."

But it was. "Max, I... I need some time."

His mouth became a slash as he stared at her, his ice-blue eyes holding a little bit of disbelief and a whole lot of disappointment. "Not a problem. I'll give you the time you need. As of immediately, you have ten days on the street. Unpaid. Maybe those ten days will give you time to figure out how important your career is to you and whether this fling is worth risking it."

"It's not a fling," she forced up her throat. She wished it was. She wished it had been quick and dirty, then over with. In the end, it had been anything but.

"That's unfortunate. Now, go to your locker. I want you to turn in your service weapon and badge. You've got five. Not a minute more."

Her knees wobbled as she stood. Her breathing strained when she left his office, ran out the back door to the parking lot and grabbed her badge from her purse. She rushed back inside and into the thankfully empty locker room. She opened her locker and pulled her holstered service weapon from her locked gun box.

She caught herself staring blindly at one of her uniforms

hanging inside. The one she planned on wearing when she returned from her regular days off. Now she wouldn't be allowed to wear it for the next two weeks.

Her sight began to blur as she dragged her fingers over the smooth black leather of her duty belt that hung on a hook next to her uniform, then she glanced down at her duty bag on the bottom of the locker.

Her locker was all business. It was only used to store what she needed to do her job. That was it. She had no pictures, notes or drawings taped to the inside, unlike everyone else she worked with. Why? Because she never had anyone special in her life before besides her family.

She had no children and for the longest time, no love interest.

Now she finally had one, it was someone she couldn't hang his picture up inside the gray metal door.

She didn't even have a picture of him, anyway. Though, ironically, she had access to plenty of his mugshots.

Once she closed her locker, she pressed her palm and her forehead against the cool steel. She didn't have time to feel sorry for herself right now. He'd given her a time limit for a reason. He didn't want to drag this out.

It was painful for both of them.

In the next minute, she found herself back in his office and standing in front of his desk. Her brain numb and unable to find the right words. Most likely because they didn't exist.

Max tilted his head toward his desk. "Leave your badge and service weapon."

She placed the leather badge holder that held her MGPD shield and ID on a stack of files. After unsnapping her holster, she pulled her Glock free, dropped the magazine and racked the slide, locking it open. A .45 round flew from the chamber and made a defining ping on the tiled floor in the achingly silent office. She picked it up, placed her gun on the desk with the single round, the full mag and her badge.

With a sting in her eyes, she stared at those items on his desk. It felt like someone had punched a hole in her chest where her heart used to be.

"If you have an answer before your suspension is over, I'll hear it, but you will still serve that suspension before putting one foot back in this station. And just in case you think I'm being harder on you because of who you are, I would do the same with any of my officers and not only because you're family. Now... Get out of my office."

She nodded, avoiding his gaze, turned and stiffly moved toward the open door.

"Jet," he called out.

When she glanced back over her shoulder, his fingers were steepled in front of his mouth. "Whether you believe this or not, I'm looking out for your best interest. As your chief *and* your cousin."

Jet paused, swallowed hard and looked at the cousin she loved like a brother and the chief she respected. "Are you?"

She could see clearly on his face, as he didn't hide it, he hated doing this to her, but he felt he had no choice.

She understood his quandary. He needed to do what he thought was best for his PD. Unfortunately, he shouldered that responsibility alone.

Without another word between them, she nodded and walked out of his office, then went straight home to her empty apartment.

Even though it was not even noon yet, she stripped off her clothes and crawled into bed, pulling the covers over her head.

That was when she finally allowed the hot tears to fall and burn their way down her cheeks.

She had no idea when they finally ran out.

She also had no idea when and if the deep ache in her heart would ever dull.

WHEN HER SWOLLEN EYES OPENED, her bedroom was dark. She found herself on her side with Cujo curled into a ball against her stomach and a warm, naked Rook wrapped around her back, holding her tight.

She had cried herself to sleep earlier and never heard the boys come into the apartment or join her in bed.

She'd already been tired from the shit that went down with the club late last night and from the time spent with Rook after that, but her conversation with Max had drained her past the point of physical and mental exhaustion.

She reached back and curled her fingers around the side of Rook's freshly shaved head. He covered her hand with his and squeezed.

"You hungry?" he murmured in her ear.

"No." She wasn't sure how she could eat with a concrete block lodged in her stomach.

"Brought you loaded fries from Dino's."

Her stomach growled at that news. "Maybe I could eat."

Even so, neither of them moved.

"Guessin' your meetin' with your cousin didn't go well."

"Ten days on the street. Unpaid."

At her answer, his muscles tightened against her back. "You told him about us."

"Yes. He gave me an ultimatum."

"Fuck," Rook cursed softly.

He flipped her onto her back and he propped his head in his hand, looking down into her face. Because of the lack of light, his eyes were only dark shadows but she could see how tense his now clean-shaven jawline had become.

"You or my job," she finished softly, hoping it didn't start a fresh round of tears.

He stared at her for what had to be the longest minute ever. Other than his tense jaw, his expression remained unreadable. No shock. No disappointment. Nothing. Whatever his reaction was to that news, he hid it well.

Too well.

"I told him I needed time."

"So, he gave you ten days." He combed his fingers through the tangled tresses of her hair and breathed, "Sorry, darlin'."

"Me, too," she said on a sigh.

"You don't need time. I ain't worth losin' your career over. The choice is easy."

She pulled herself up onto her elbows. "Don't say that."

He tilted his head. "Gotta hear the truth. Hate to say it, *really* hate to say it, but your cousin's doin' the right thing."

"Giving me an ultimatum?" she asked in surprise.

"He's doin' what he think's best for you."

"He doesn't understand."

"Sure he does. He's just not blinded by it, darlin'. You are." He buried his fingers into her hair and made her meet his eyes. "Listen, you can't throw away your future 'cause of me."

"My career isn't my whole life. I need a life outside of it. A life where I'm allowed to love and be loved."

"Bein' a pig's a big fuckin' part of it."

"It doesn't have to be." She swore he'd call cops "pigs" to his last dying breath.

"I'm thinkin' it's an all or nothin' thing, Jet. Not soundin' like he's gonna let you have one foot in his world and one foot in mine."

"How is it that Trip is being more reasonable than Max?"

"Not sure if Trip is. Think he's tryin' to compromise but maybe that's not smart on his part. Or... Hell, maybe it is. Maybe he knew you bein' with me would never fly with your cousin. Maybe he counted on your chief to take care of the problem for him."

"You're saying he let Max be the bad cop while he was the good cop? How fucking ironic."

"Think about it, darlin', you could be thrown into some really sticky moral shit. There might be days where you gotta pick a side. Ain't fair to you. And when you're forced to choose a side, then what? You risk fuckin' me over or you risk fuckin' over Max. Max is family, I'm just a fuck."

Her breath caught. "You're not just a fuck."

"Maybe this ultimatum's the slap upside the head we both needed."

"You're not just a fuck!" she insisted loudly. "Stop saying that! Do you think I would've ripped myself open to Max today if you were just a fuck?"

"I don't want you makin' the wrong decision and regret-tin' it. Don't ever want you regrettin' bein' with me. Thinkin' if you make the wrong decision you'll get to the point you do regret it. Maybe not today, but down the road. It won't hurt as bad now to go our separate ways as it would later. 'Specially if we have babies."

Babies? Where did that come from? She couldn't wrap her head around that idea right now. At the moment, it wasn't the most dire issue they were currently dealing with.

"What are you saying?" she whispered. She didn't need him to answer that, she knew exactly what he was saying. "No." Going their separate ways wasn't even an option. "No.

For once I have something of my own. I have what *I* want. Not something I did or achieved because I thought it was expected of me. I can't help who I fell in love with. Should I have to pay a penalty for that?"

"We're always payin' in one way or another, darlin'."

Her heart squeezed painfully. "I'm not giving you up."

"Jet, I'm the worst fuckin' person you coulda fallen in love with."

"No, Charles Manson or Jeffrey Dahmer would've been worse. And that's just two out of a long list."

"Damn." He didn't hide his fleeting smirk.

"Tell me something…" she began.

"Anything," he answered.

"Would it be easy for you to walk away from this? From us?"

"If it was, I woulda done it already. But do you even got a choice at this point?"

"We always have a choice, Rook."

"Don't want you to regret the one you make."

She swallowed past the tightness of her throat. The one he loved to possess with his hand, with his mouth, with his teeth. She sighed. "I know you're not perfect and, of course, neither am I, but can you at least promise me you'll do your best to keep your ass out of prison? I draw the line with visiting you behind bullet-proof glass."

"Can't promise that, darlin'. Gonna protect myself, my family, includin' my niece, my brotherhood," he brushed his lips softly over hers, "and you. If that means I gotta get my hands dirty, then that's what's gonna fuckin' happen. And this is where I go back and mention that moral conflict again."

"I'd do whatever I need to do to protect my family—all of them—and you, too, Rook. I wouldn't expect anything less."

"How I'd do it and how you'd do it are two different things," he reminded her.

"Not necessarily."

"Your badge protects you. Let's you do shit I'd never be able to do without gettin' tossed behind bars. You know that, right?"

"Yes," she whispered. "But I'm not giving you up, Rook."

Not now. Not ever.

He turned his face away from her and she stared at his shadowed profile. Even in the dark she could see his eyes were closed.

He didn't want her to give him up, either, but he wouldn't say it out loud. He wouldn't put that pressure on her.

When he turned back to her again, he said, "Darlin', take the two weeks. Think long and hard about it. If you want me to make myself scarce durin' that time to make it easier on you, I will. You wanna fuck me into a coma durin' those two weeks, ain't gonna say no. But the final decision's yours and yours alone. Just want you to make the right one. The one that's best for you. You. Not me. Not Max. Not your family. The one you'll be able to live with. That's all I'm askin'."

"Okay," she whispered. She could give him that. She could give herself that.

"And don't let my awesome fuckin' dick be your decidin' factor."

Jet rolled her eyes. "Okay, then. That makes the decision easy."

"Know it's hard to resist."

"It's not hard right now," she said, trying to relieve some of the heaviness between them.

"It can be."

"How about after we share those loaded fries," she suggested.

"You prefer Dino's fries over my dick? Damn."

"Well, they are famous. You're just infamous."

He snorted and dropped his head to nuzzle her ear. "If you don't kick me out right after, gonna mark you inside and out tonight."

She wrapped her hand around the back of his neck and yanked him down to her. "We can reheat the fries later."

"Yeah, they'll taste better after I smoke a big fatty anyway."

She shoved at his shoulders. "Not funny."

"You hear me laughin'?"

"I'd rather hear you grunting as you fuck me." And chase away the stress of the last twenty-four hours.

"Anythin' you want, darlin'."

"Anything?"

"For you? Yeah."

Her heart swelled at his answer. They became quiet for a few moments and she simply enjoyed the solid weight of him on her.

In truth, Rook was the biggest asshole she knew. But he was her asshole and she planned on keeping him.

She didn't need two weeks to figure out her choice. It had been made weeks ago. She just wasn't aware at the time how that choice would change her life.

Maybe Max was right. To be happy, this Bryson might need to branch off and follow her own path.

Wherever it led.

As long as Rook was traveling it with her. Along with a little ankle-biter named Cujo.

Epilogue

When life grabs you by the balls and never lets you go...

Rook heard Jet's Toyota pull up to their tiny modular home. The small ranch-style house had been placed near his brother's on the other side of the tree line from The Barn. It might be small, but it was still bigger than his room in the bunkhouse and Jet's former shit-hole basement apartment.

What it did have was an oversized walk-in shower that they made use of. A lot.

That meant they wasted a lot of hot water.

Even lukewarm water.

Sometimes even bone-chilling cold water.

But this morning using that shower would have to wait. They needed to get good and dirty first.

"Honey, I'm home," Jet called out in a teasing manner as she opened the front door and stepped inside. Cujo tore past him and danced around her feet with his tail wagging and him whining for her attention.

Get in line, asshole.

From where he hid, he watched as she stripped off her light windbreaker and shoulder holster, then slipped the chain holding her badge over her head. A badge that no longer said Manning Grove PD, but instead, Fugitive Recovery Agent.

Thank fuck for Judge and Deacon. Rook would owe them for life.

She fucking loved her job, kicked motherfucking ass while doing it and, hard to believe, loved working with those two dickheads, too.

He grinned. His ol' lady was a badass bounty hunter.

It was sexy as fuck and he swore it gave him a permanent boner.

Most men would probably worry about their woman chasing after and taking down fugitives. Not him. Some of her stories were like foreplay. Especially when she had to get rough with the skip.

Then she'd come home and let him be rough with her.

It was goddamn perfect.

Even better, she rarely had to work nights. That meant she was in his bed almost every night, ready and willing.

With as much as they fucked, he was surprised she hadn't gotten knocked up yet. Even with her on birth control.

But maybe it was better that way, since she was still getting her feet wet with her new job. She also enjoyed going out in the field and would prefer it even if that wasn't expected of her since Judge wanted to stick closer to home. If she was carrying his kid, Rook would insist she stay safe in the office.

He seriously never even thought he'd ever want his own snot monkey until he saw his brother with Dyna. But he was leaving it up to her to decide when she stopped taking her birth control. She could surprise him or give him a heads up first, but either way he'd be okay with her decision.

Her body. Her choice.

He'd simply go along for that wild ride.

With her equipment now set aside, she squatted down and scooped up Cujo, letting the little shithead bathe her face with his disgusting tongue. Did she forget what he licked with that?

Rook grimaced.

Ah, fuck it, what was a little red-rocket flavored dog spit?

"Where's your daddy?" she murmured to the dick-licker.

As she came around the corner from the living room into the kitchen, he shot his hand out and grabbed her neck. He swung her around and pinned her to the wall using his body.

Slightly tilting his hips, he showed her how hard he was.

After sliding his hand around to the front of her throat, and without a word, he plucked Cujo from her hands and dropped him carefully to the floor. Once he straightened, he crushed his mouth to hers.

A proper welcome home.

Especially since he'd slept in their bed alone last night.

The furry asshole didn't count.

She tightly gripped the wrist of his hand on her throat and, with her other hand, grabbed a fistful of the longer hair at the top of his head and pulled.

Fuck yeah, that made his dick throb and press painfully against the zipper on his jeans. She was in the mood to tussle this morning.

He sometimes let her win, but not often.

He lifted his mouth away from hers only enough to growl, "Where's *your* daddy?"

She scrunched up her nose. "Gross, don't say that. Especially since you two have the same name."

Rook snorted. "Bet he never spanked you as good as I do."

"Rook! Stop it." She shuddered and ripped on his hair harder, causing his scalp to burn. Between the pain and the thought of leaving her ass red and burning made his dick thicken even more. "I'll never want to have sex again. Now I need to bleach my brain."

"You know you can't resist my dick. Don't even fuckin' try."

"Yes, but like I've told you before, you, unfortunately, come attached to it."

"You love me," he murmured, their mouths so close, their breaths mingled.

"You should be glad I do. Anyone else manhandling me like that would've been pepper-sprayed and received a hard shot to the balls with my knee by now."

"Good," he whispered. "Anyone tries to fuckin' touch you, you kick their ass. And when you're done, I'll kick their ass next."

"Judge and Deke have me covered."

"No, you're mine. I got you covered."

"No, *you* are going to stay out of prison. Remember?"

Right. He promised to do his best to do just that.

Speaking of... "You catch your man?" The last time he talked to her, she'd been running an overnight surveillance on a skip with Deke.

She dropped the hand from his wrist, grabbed his balls. "Sure did."

He smirked when she squeezed gently. "Meant your skip."

"Yes."

"Any problems?"

She never told him about the bad shit, only the fun stuff. Most likely to keep him from getting involved and to keep his promise of avoiding more time in the joint.

Which, if anyone hurt her, just might happen. Promise or not, she was smart enough to avoid telling him some details that might send him off the rails. The only time she couldn't hide a physical altercation was when she came home with a bruise that he knew he didn't give her during sex.

Seeing those made him struggle with losing his shit. But she was an expert at distracting him. And by the time she was done wearing his ass out, he had no energy left to track down whoever it was and give that person an ass-beating.

"I'm still breathing," she answered.

"Ain't funny."

"But true."

"You'll be breathin' hard soon enough," he assured her.

"You sound pretty damn confident of that," she teased.

"I'm a cocky asshole, remember? Of fuckin' course, I'm confident of my skills."

She snorted and massaged his aching balls. He might be the one breathing hard if they didn't move this elsewhere soon.

He pulled her away from the wall and smacked her ass hard. "Want you in bed, naked, legs spread apart, fingering yourself. Like five minutes ago."

Her breath stuttered and heat filled her face and eyes.

Her, "I need to put my weapon and badge in the safe first," came out breathless.

Fuck. Yeah.

She was probably already wet, too.

He jerked his head to where she'd placed them by the front door. "Then go. We only got a coupla hours before we all meet for the club run."

"I had hoped to get in a catnap beforehand, too. So, how about we compromise and do a quickie, then I take a nap."

"How many orgasms you want?"

She pursed her lips in thought. "Three."

"Three with a quickie? Damn, woman, then we gotta

hurry. Get your shit taken care of and get in bed like I told you."

She gave him a huge smile and hurried back into the living room.

As she carried her stuff to the closet in the hallway where she secured her guns and badge, he muttered, "If we ever have fuckin' kids they ain't becomin' pigs like the rest of your family. Tellin' you that right now."

With her head tucked inside the closet as she opened the safe, he heard, "They'll be whoever they want to be. We'll let them decide who they are."

"Sure. Except for pigs. And thank fuck they won't have that Bryson name."

"There's nothing wrong with my last name. I have a great family."

Now was not the time to get into that argument. Not if he wanted to get laid this morning.

And then fuck her in the shower.

Then fuck her again after the club run and pig roast later.

Then maybe in the middle of the night, too.

The rough and tumble fucks they had were the best. But the slow and sleepy fucks were almost just as good.

Hell, just being inside her anytime was good. Hearing his name on her lips while she soaked his balls was even better.

She pulled her head from the closet and straightened. "Shit. That reminds me... My parents invited us over for dinner next weekend."

Well, that was enough to make his hard-on die a quick death. "Us?"

She closed the closet door and turned to him. "I'm pretty sure I said *us*."

"Since I don't got time to spank your ass durin' our quickie, was plannin' on it later. Now I'm rethinkin' that."

She laughed and shoved his arm. "Yes, *us*. You. Me. Them. My mom's cooking."

He frowned and drew his thumbnail across his forehead. "Just them?"

"Well... and Teddy."

Rook cocked an eyebrow and waited. He knew her only too well by now.

"And Adam," she added softly with hope in her eyes.

He didn't want to fucking disappoint her. He never wanted to disappoint her. Even if he had to swallow some of his hatred for the men in blue. He might have to make an exception for some of the Brysons. Maybe.

He'd see.

"Your brother know I'm gonna be there?"

Her eyes went wide. "You're going to come with me?"

He frowned. "Ain't that why you fuckin' mentioned it?"

She planted her hand on his chest. "I want you to do whatever you're comfortable with. They'll understand if you don't come to dinner and I don't want to force you into it. I also don't want it to cause tension between the people I love."

"Can't promise there won't be tension, darlin'." The only good thing about her family was none of them had ever fucked him over. At least not yet. He could do his best to be civil with them if they returned the favor. However, he'd do it for her and only her.

But the second they disrespected him? All bets were off.

He wouldn't be treated as less of a person than Jet. Not by anyone.

He also wouldn't let Jet be treated less than him. Again, not by anyone.

Including a fuckwad prospect who was skating on thin ice with him and a couple of other Fury members.

Even though he'd had a serious sit-down with Scar after

that night at The Barn, Rook continued to keep a sharp eye on him. The man still had a long way to go for Rook to ever trust him again. Or for him to prove himself.

Time would tell whether Scar would pass a vote to become a fully-patched Fury member. In the meantime...

"Your pop gonna ride my ass about your decision?" If so, that would ruin any good food her mother made. And he'd tasted some of her leftovers Jet had brought home. The woman could cook.

"He just wants me to be happy. My mom feels the same way."

So did Rook. "You happy?"

"I'm still wearing a badge. It's just a different type of badge."

"A better kind."

"Sure," she murmured. Her face became animated. "Hey! You know what I'm not happy about?"

"What?"

"Us still standing in this hallway instead of us getting naked and sweaty." She tugged on his hand and he followed her down the short hallway to their bedroom.

He smothered his smile when her fingers twitched in his hand as soon as she spotted it.

What he'd left for her on the bed.

Giving it to her today was perfect timing since she was joining them on a run for the first time.

"Rook," she whispered.

"Yeah?"

She released his hand and approached the bed to run her fingers over the smooth black leather and the rockers that claimed she was "Property of Rook."

He wasn't sure if she'd wear it, but he at least wanted to give it to her. Whether she wore it on the run was her decision. Just like she wanted him to do whatever was comfortable for him when it came to her family, he wanted the same for her with his.

She turned wide light blue eyes to him. "Are you kidding me?"

He stepped up behind her, wrapped his arms around her belly and pulled her against him. "You belong to me?"

"Of course."

"I belong to you?"

"Yes."

"Then no, I ain't kiddin'."

"The ol' ladies only wear them on the runs."

He shook his head. "Ain't true."

She turned in his arms and frowned. "When else do they wear them?" Her expression quickly changed from confused to just the opposite. "Oh," she breathed.

"Yeah. Oh."

She smiled.

He grinned.

It ended up not being a quickie.

Not a quickie at all.

His time with her actually took longer than he'd ever dreamed.

In the end, it lasted forever.

There's a thin line between love and hate.
What side you stand on may be left to fate.
© Jeanne St. James

Sign up for Jeanne's newsletter to learn about her upcoming releases, sales and more! https:// www.authorjeannestjames.com/

From a past of righteousness to a future of anything but...

Rev rarely does what's expected of him.

The Blood Fury member's rebellious nature tends to lead him on the road less traveled.

In his youth, he fought the chains meant to restrain him, meant to force him on a righteous path. A path he never chose. A path he never planned to follow.

He prefers to pave his own road, taking detours to forge his own future.

Even if it's one full of sin.

But an unexpected call drags him back to the painful past he's left far behind. One he's tried to forget.

No good reason exists for him to return. Except to witness the final moments of the person who made him and his sister suffer.

Maybe even get a taste of revenge.

However, he's not sure he can deal with it alone. He wants someone to stand by him and help give him strength.

A woman who also carves her own path and spits in the face of restrictive rules.

The problem is, she's off limits. No matter how tempting she is, no matter how satisfying the sin would be, touching her is one rule he can't break.

Ultimately, mistakes are made.

Secrets are forced to be kept.

Because he's a sinner.

He was born one.

He will die one.

And in between, he plans to enjoy the life he chose.

Sins and all.

**Turn the page to read the prologue of
Blood & Bones: Rev**

Blood & Bones: Rev
Blood Fury MC, book 8

Prologue
For I have sinned

HE HATED IT.

Hated her.

Hated them.

All of them. Every last one.

He hated kneeling.

He hated praying.

He hated the endless drone of their voices.

He even hated the ten wooden chairs that formed a circle around him.

In those chairs sat his mother and nine other women from their church. When the women had entered the room, they refused to look at him and his mother demanded he keep his eyes lowered to the open book in his hand.

Why?

Because Michael was a sinner.

His spine, from his tailbone to the top of his neck, felt ready to splinter.

The skin on his bare knees was about to split open from kneeling on the stack of wooden rulers.

His muscles cramped from keeping perfectly still so the Bible balanced on his head wouldn't tumble to the floor.

His arms trembled from holding the "good book" open in his hands.

He wasn't allowed to move except to turn the wafer-thin pages.

His mouth moved as he followed along with the passage but not one word escaped. His eyes didn't need to focus on the tiny print on the well-worn pages because he had been forced to read the Bible so many times he knew the passage by heart.

Not that this particular scripture meant anything to him. It didn't.

Because he was a sinner.

He was born one.

He would die one.

And in between, he planned on living a life full of sin.

Keeping his head tipped down to hide it, one corner of his upper lip pulled up into a sneer.

He would remain in the center of that circle surrounded by these women and their monotone voices until the elder, the one who looked like a walking corpse, decided he had atoned for his latest transgression.

In the meantime, if he dropped the Bible, he'd get ten lashes. If he stood without permission, he'd get twenty. If he told them all to fuck off, he had no idea how many lashes he'd be *blessed* with, but a bar of soap would be forced into his mouth, and he'd be locked in his room without supper. To think about his inexcusable actions, he would have to sit in a wooden chair with his hands in his lap, his feet flat on the floor while he continued to pray and ask for forgiveness until his father came home.

His father would be the one to decide whether the prayer circle was enough punishment for his latest offense. If it wasn't, he'd dole out whatever punishment he deemed worthy and wouldn't stop until the man was satisfied Michael had learned his lesson. And, of course, Michael vowed to never do it again.

The thought of dealing with his father made him lock his joints and make sure his head didn't wobble even the slightest bit.

He no longer believed in God. Because if there was one? He or she wouldn't allow his parents to hurt him or Sarah the way they did.

In the churches his friends attended, they were told God was full of love and forgiveness. That Jesus died for their sins.

In his parents' church, they were taught to fear God. That he was always watching. He would judge them and how they lived their lives before he decided if they were worthy to take that final walk through those pearly gates.

Michael knew if anyone was denied entrance to Heaven, it should be his parents. Not him. Not Sarah.

If his parents were welcomed into God's embrace, then he wanted nothing to do with it.

Nothing at all.

But if he continued on his current path, he was told he wouldn't be welcomed, anyway. That he would be locked out.

Because he was a sinner.

Last night he had committed what his mother told him was an egregious sin.

Today's prayer circle had been formed because she caught him this morning in his sister Sarah's bed.

This was a sin his father would never allow to go unpunished. The prayer circle would be a start, but it certainly wouldn't be the end.

The gasps of his mother and then her screams had woken both him and Sarah from a deep sleep. He only saw a blur as she rushed over to the bed and grabbed handfuls of his hair, using it to yank him out of the bed and onto the floor.

Her face had been a mottled red, a mask of fury, when she tried to continue dragging him across the floor. He'd been too heavy and she hadn't been strong enough. He'd also resisted by pressing his weight and his fingernails into the worn wood planks to prevent her from hauling him out of the room.

He'd only gotten a quick glance at his sister to see her sitting up in her bed, once again crying. Her shocked, pale face had become almost translucent. Her mouth gaped open and the words she screamed to stop their mother went ignored.

He had climbed into Sarah's bed last night when he'd heard her crying through their shared wall. His only motive was to comfort her because no one else would. Eventually, she cried herself out and fell asleep. Unfortunately, so did he.

His first mistake was trying to comfort his sister. To chase away her pain and tears.

His second was holding her in her own bed.

The third was him falling asleep once she stopped crying and her steady breathing also lulled him into sleep.

The fourth was never waking up so he could return to his own bed before morning, like he normally did.

The fifth was him remaining asleep until his mother walked in to wake his sister.

His sixth was getting caught.

His mother automatically thought the worst. It hurt that his own mother didn't trust him. She believed him guilty when his motives were completely innocent.

She refused to hear his excuses because she saw evidence she would not dismiss.

She noticed something a teen boy hadn't been able to control.

Something he could never control.

His erection wasn't from holding his five-year-old sister. It was because he was fourteen and didn't know how to control it. It happened often when he least expected it. It also happened at the oddest times.

It happened enough to be embarrassing.

It happened in school. At the bus stop. While playing baseball. In the middle of the night. In the middle of the day.

Even during a long, boring sermon in church.

He wished it didn't happen, but it did.

And his mother wouldn't hear that it meant nothing.

All he'd wanted to do was comfort his sister from whatever their father had done to her last night. For whatever sin their father perceived his daughter had committed. Whatever reason he came up with to punish her. A made-up excuse to lock the door of her room with him inside.

The more he fought his mother to keep her from dragging him from Sarah's room, the angrier and crazier she got. Spittle flew from her mouth and clung to her lips. Her hands curled into claws. Her words got harsher, louder and more hurtful.

All she was doing was upsetting Sarah. Michael didn't want to upset his sister any more than she already was. So, he reluctantly climbed to his feet and allowed his mother to yank him from her room. He never once looked back.

He was forced into a tub of searing hot water and the brush she gave him to scrub his sins clean didn't have soft bristles. They weren't even firm. They were like a Brillo pad against his skin.

She stood over the tub and supervised him as he scrubbed every inch of his body until it was red and raw. She made him scrub his penis until the tender skin bled and the bristles left visible scratches behind.

"You scrub that filth off your skin. You scrub those sins free of your soul. You wash away those ugly, ugly, forbidden thoughts."

When the water was pink and cold, when his mother's anger had turned to exhaustion, she forced him to stand in the tub and turn in a circle to make sure he got every spot. Once she pulled the drain plug, she left him standing there shivering with his hands over his raw, burning privates.

He hadn't cried. Not once.

Instead, he had taken himself elsewhere to a far-away place. Anywhere other than that bathroom. Because he couldn't cry.

His father told him over and over real men don't cry.

If he cried, it only made things worse.

But he wanted to cry. Not because of the burn of his skin but because his parents only saw what they wanted to see, they never listened to the truth.

They saw him as a wayward child who needed more discipline.

The same as Sarah.

Their goal was to teach her how to be a good and obedient wife for her future husband. How to be a good mother to her unborn children.

For Michael, it wasn't the prayer circle, it wasn't the scrub of the brush, it wasn't his mother's harsh words that he feared. It was what his father would do when he came home later.

Last night, their father had made Sarah cry.

Tonight, it would be Michael's turn. Only, he would have to hide every single tear.

**Continue Rev's story here:
https://books2read.com/BFMC-Rev**

If You Enjoyed This Book

Thank you for reading Blood & Bones: Rook. If you enjoyed Rook and Jet's story, please consider leaving a review at your favorite retailer and/or Goodreads to let other readers know. Reviews are always appreciated and just a few words can help an independent author like me tremendously!

Want to read a sample of my work? Download a sampler book here: BookHip.com/MTQQKK

Sign up for Jeanne's newsletter: https://www. authorjeannestjames.com/
Join her FB readers' group for the inside scoop: https://www.facebook.com/groups/ JeannesReviewCrew/

Also by Jeanne St. James

Find my complete reading order here:
https://www.jeannestjames.com/reading-order

Standalone Books:

Made Maleen: A Modern Twist on a Fairy Tale

Damaged

Rip Cord: The Complete Trilogy

Everything About You (A Second Chance Gay Romance)

Reigniting Chase (An M/M Standalone)

Brothers in Blue Series

A four-book series based around three brothers who are small-town
cops and former Marines

The Dare Ménage Series

A six-book MMF, interracial ménage series

The Obsessed Novellas

A collection of five standalone BDSM novellas

Down & Dirty: Dirty Angels MC®

A ten-book motorcycle club series

Guts & Glory: In the Shadows Security

A six-book former special forces series
(A spin-off of the Dirty Angels MC)

About the Author

JEANNE ST. JAMES is a USA Today, Amazon and international bestselling romance author who loves writing about strong women and alpha males. She was only thirteen when she first started writing and her first published piece was an erotic short story in Playgirl magazine. She then went on to publish her first romance novel in 2009. She is now an author of almost 70 contemporary romances. She writes M/F, M/M, and M/M/F ménages, including interracial romance. She also writes M/M paranormal romance under the name: J.J. Masters.

Want to read a sample of her work? Download a sampler book here: BookHip.com/MTQQKK

To keep up with her busy release schedule check her website at www.jeannestjames.com or sign up for her newsletter: https://www.authorjeannestjames.com/

www.jeannestjames.com

Newsletter: https://www.authorjeannestjames.com/
Jeanne's Down & Dirty Book Crew: https://www.facebook.com/groups/JeannesReviewCrew/

facebook.com/JeanneStJamesAuthor

instagram.com/JeanneStJames

bookbub.com/authors/jeanne-st-james

goodreads.com/JeanneStJames

<u>Get a FREE Sampler Book</u>

This book contains the first chapter of a variety of my books. This will give you a taste of the type of books I write and if you enjoy the first chapter, I hope you'll be interested in reading the rest of the book.

Each book I list in the sampler will include the description of the book, the genre, and the first chapter, along with links to find out more. I hope you find a book you will enjoy curling up with!

Get it here: BookHip.com/MTQQKK